Soulstream

Volume 1

creator/writer/artist/letterer

Saida Woolf

Scout Editor
WAYNE HALL

Production Director
DC HOPKINS

Brendan Deneen, *CEO*
James Pruett, *CCO*
Tennessee Edwards, *CSO*
James Haick III, *President*
Joel Rodriguez, *Head Of Design*

Don Handfield, *CMO*
David Byrne, *Co-Publisher*
Charlie Stickney, *Co-Publisher*
Richard Rivera, *Associate Publisher*

FB/TW/IG:
@Scoutcomics

LEARN MORE AT:
www.scoutcomics.com

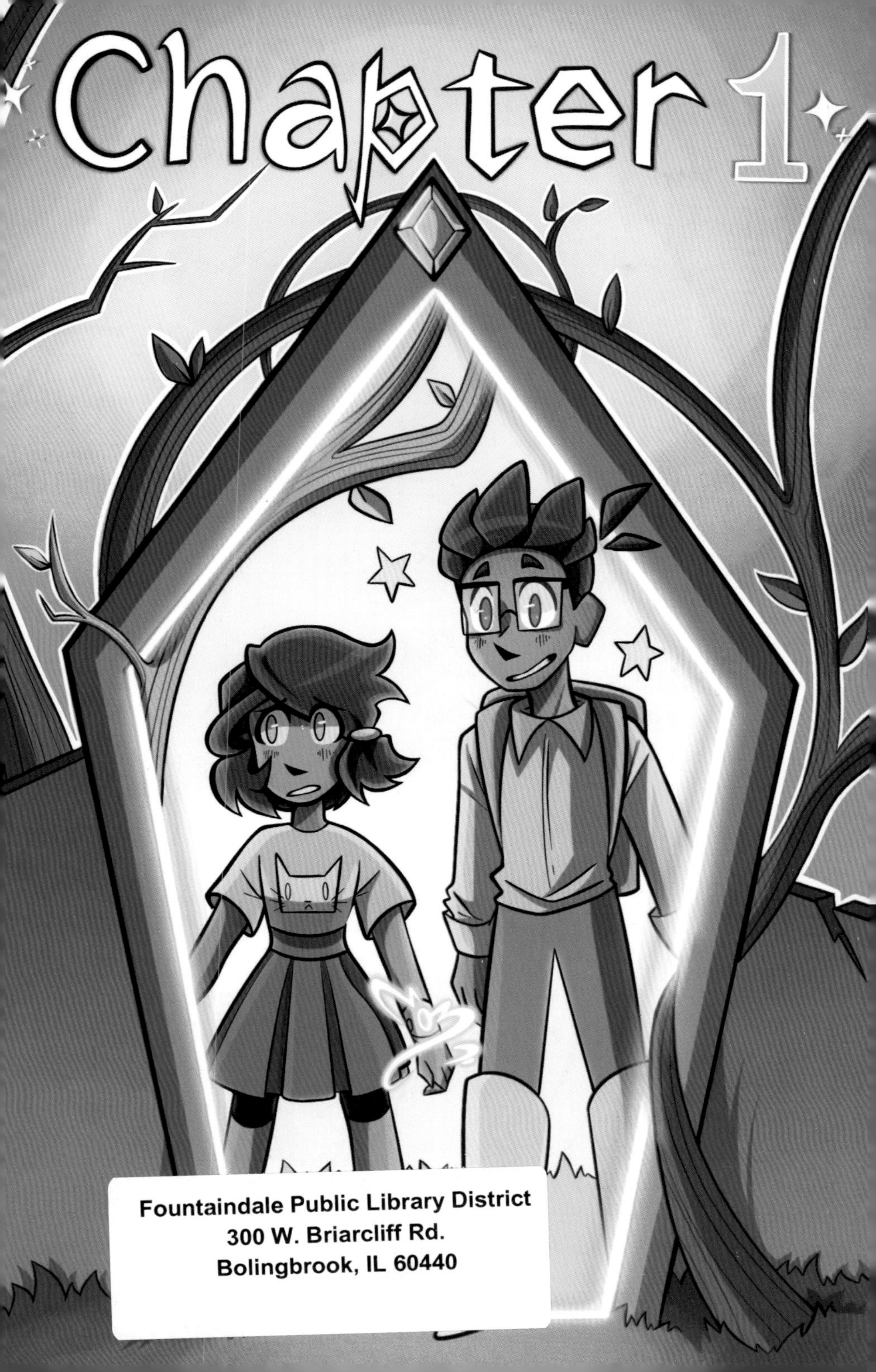
Chapter 1

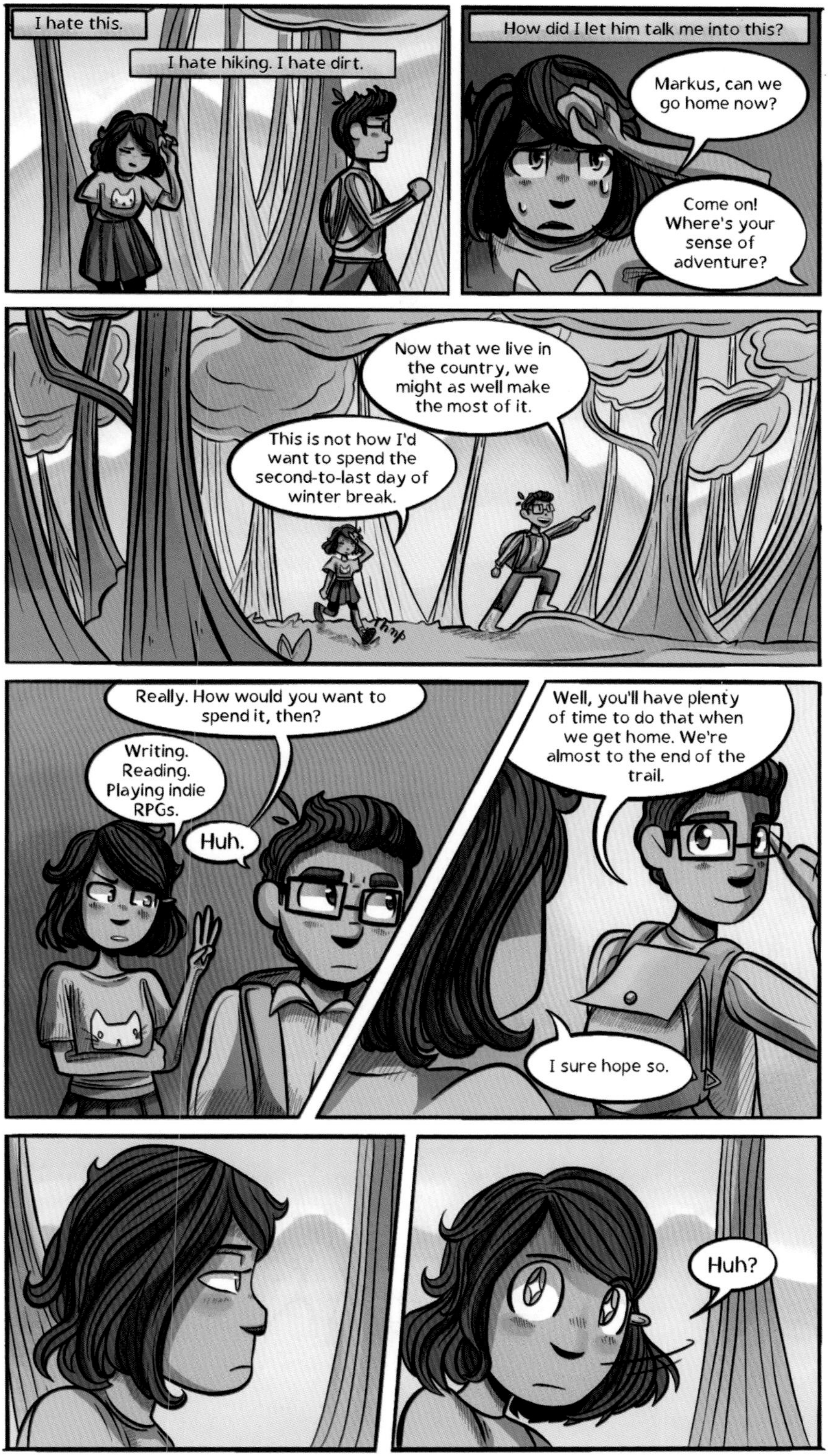
I hate this.
I hate hiking. I hate dirt.
How did I let him talk me into this?
Markus, can we go home now?
Come on! Where's your sense of adventure?
Now that we live in the country, we might as well make the most of it.
This is not how I'd want to spend the second-to-last day of winter break.
thmp
Really. How would you want to spend it, then?
Writing. Reading. Playing indie RPGs.
Huh.
Well, you'll have plenty of time to do that when we get home. We're almost to the end of the trail.
I sure hope so.
Huh?

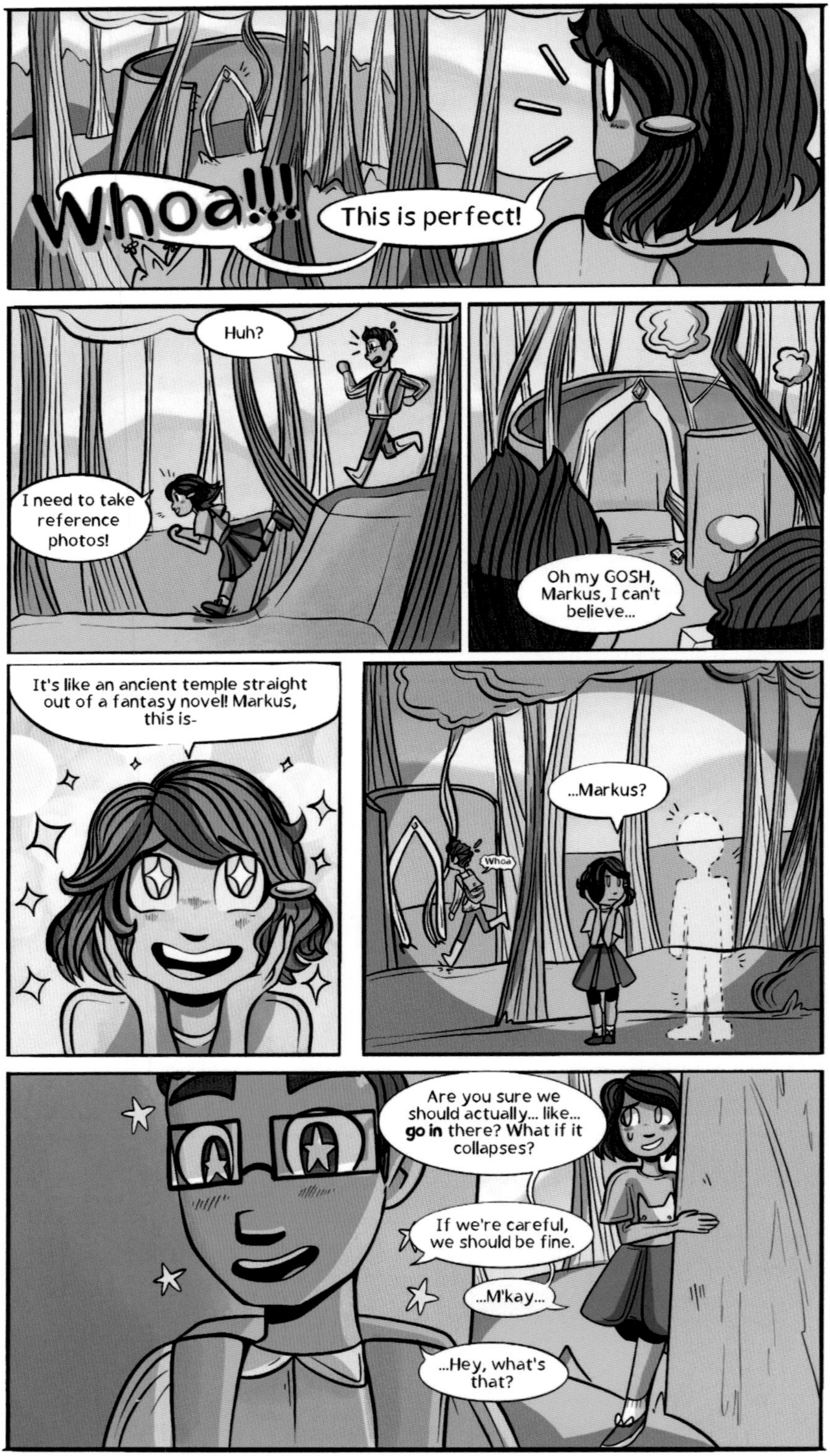
Whoa!!!
This is perfect!
Huh?
I need to take reference photos!
Oh my GOSH, Markus, I can't believe...
It's like an ancient temple straight out of a fantasy novel! Markus, this is-
...Markus?
Whoa
Are you sure we should actually... like... **go in** there? What if it collapses?
If we're careful, we should be fine.
...M'kay...
...Hey, what's that?

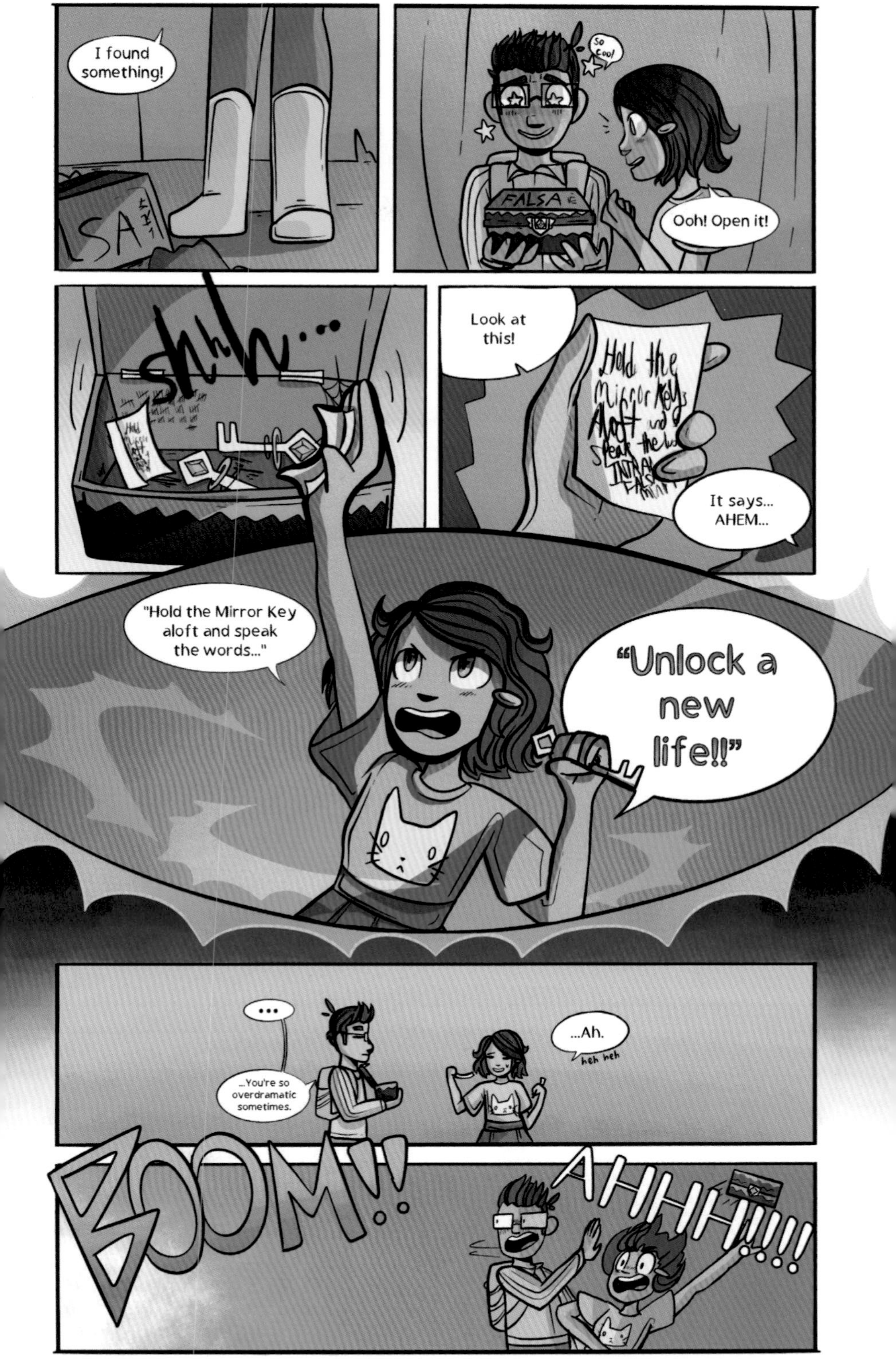
I found something!
FALSA
So Cool!
Ooh! Open it!
shhhn...
Look at this!
Hold the Mirror Key aloft and speak the words
It says... AHEM...
"Hold the Mirror Key aloft and speak the words..."
"Unlock a new life!!"
...
...You're so overdramatic sometimes.
...Ah.
heh heh
BOOM!!
AHHHH!!!!!

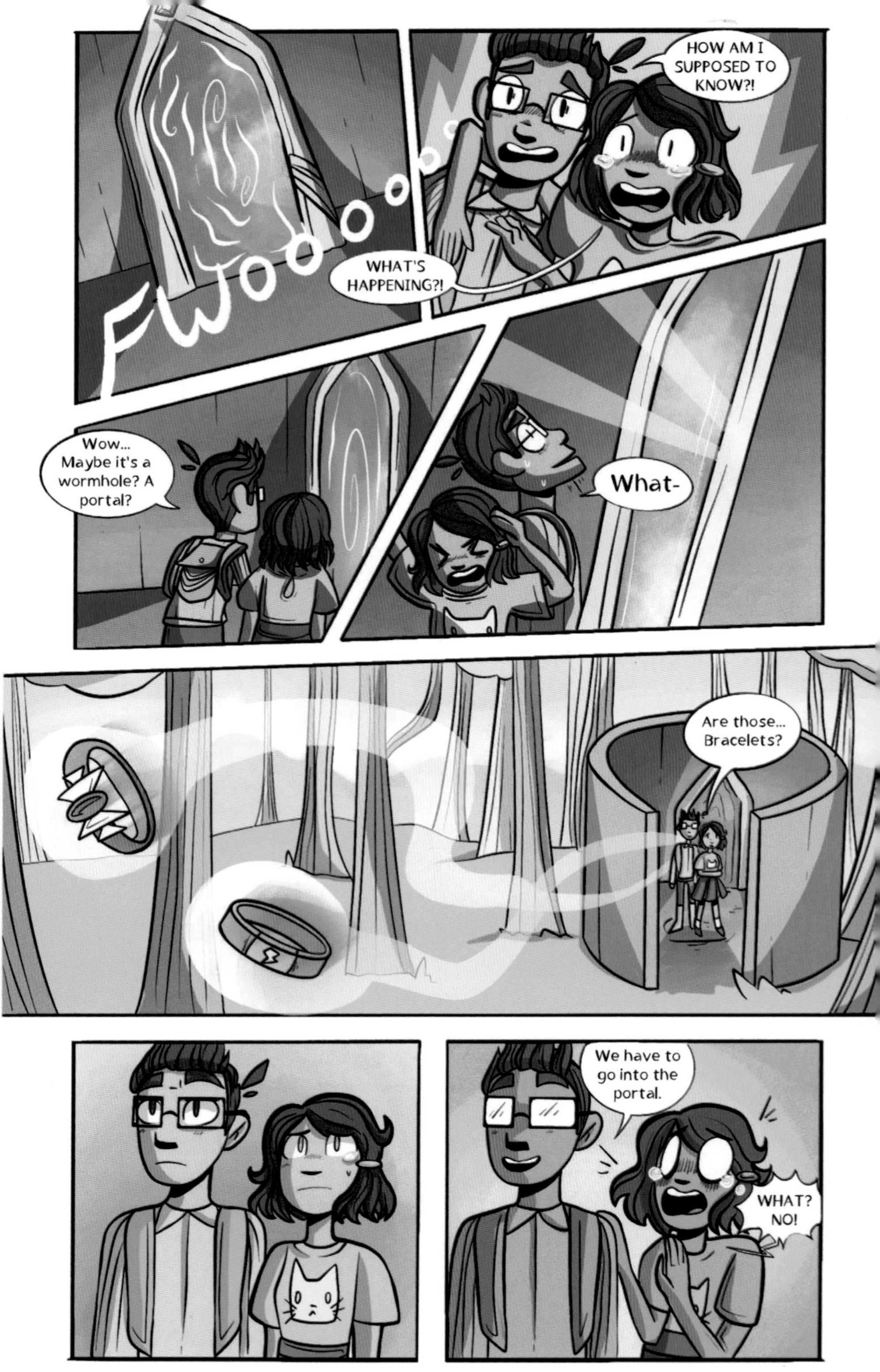
FWOOOOOO
HOW AM I SUPPOSED TO KNOW?!
WHAT'S HAPPENING?!
Wow... Maybe it's a wormhole? A portal?
What-
Are those... Bracelets?
We have to go into the portal.
WHAT? NO!

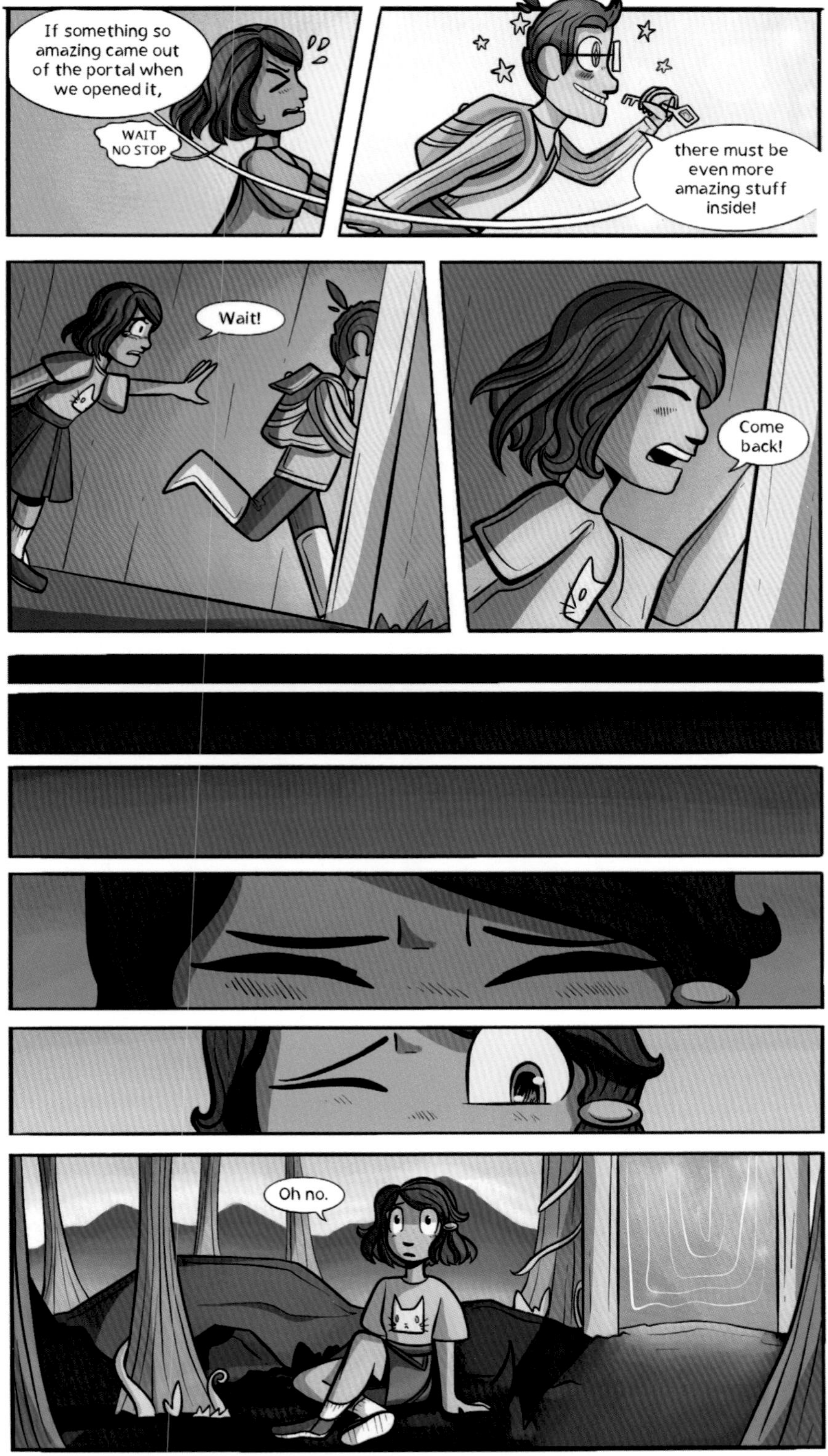
If something so amazing came out of the portal when we opened it,
WAIT NO STOP
there must be even more amazing stuff inside!
Wait!
Come back!
Oh no.

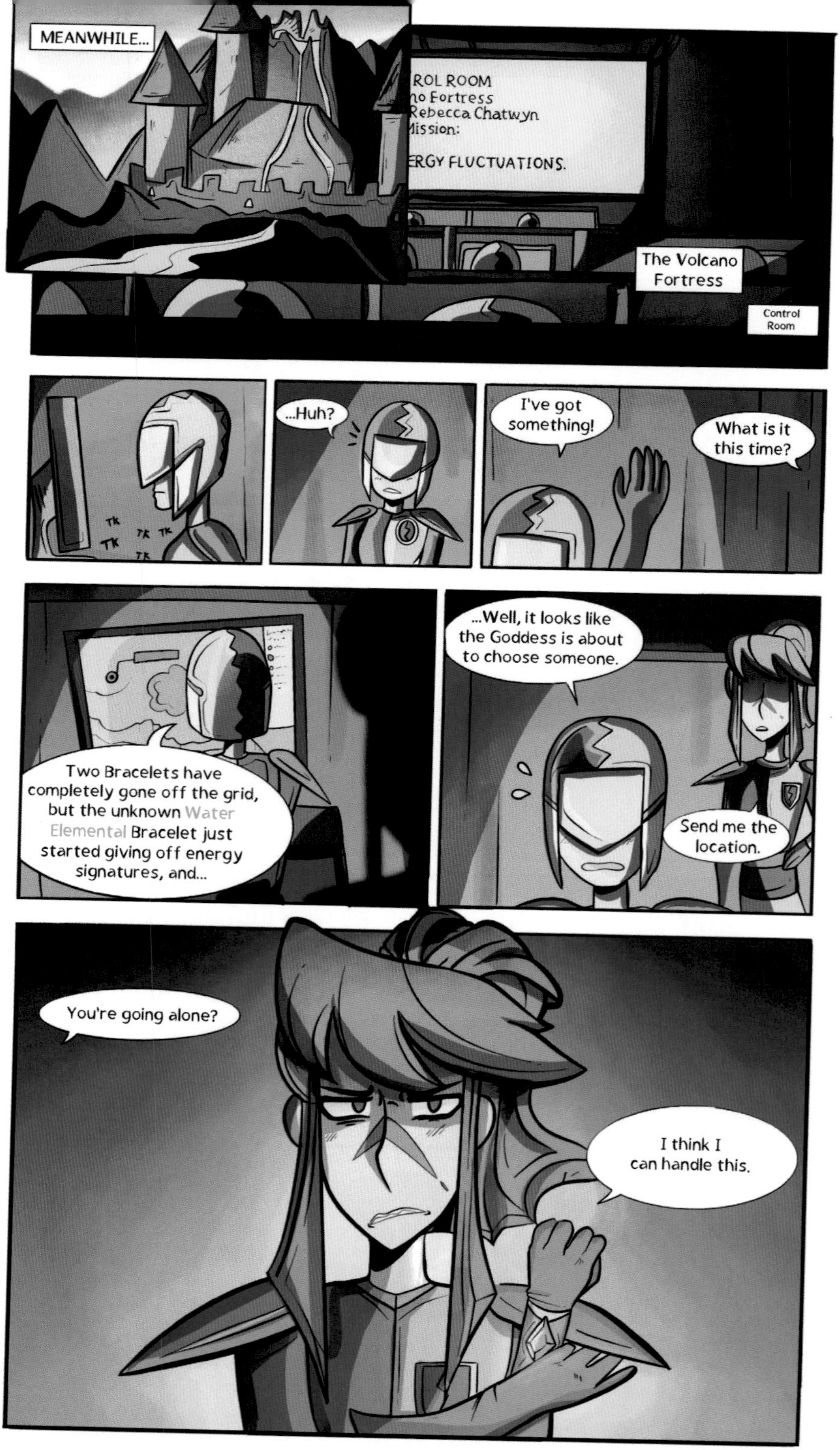
MEANWHILE...
ROL ROOM
no Fortress
Rebecca Chatwyn
Mission:
ERGY FLUCTUATIONS.
The Volcano Fortress
Control Room
TK TK TK TK TK
...Huh?
I've got something!
What is it this time?
Two Bracelets have completely gone off the grid, but the unknown Water Elemental Bracelet just started giving off energy signatures, and...
...Well, it looks like the Goddess is about to choose someone.
Send me the location.
You're going alone?
I think I can handle this.

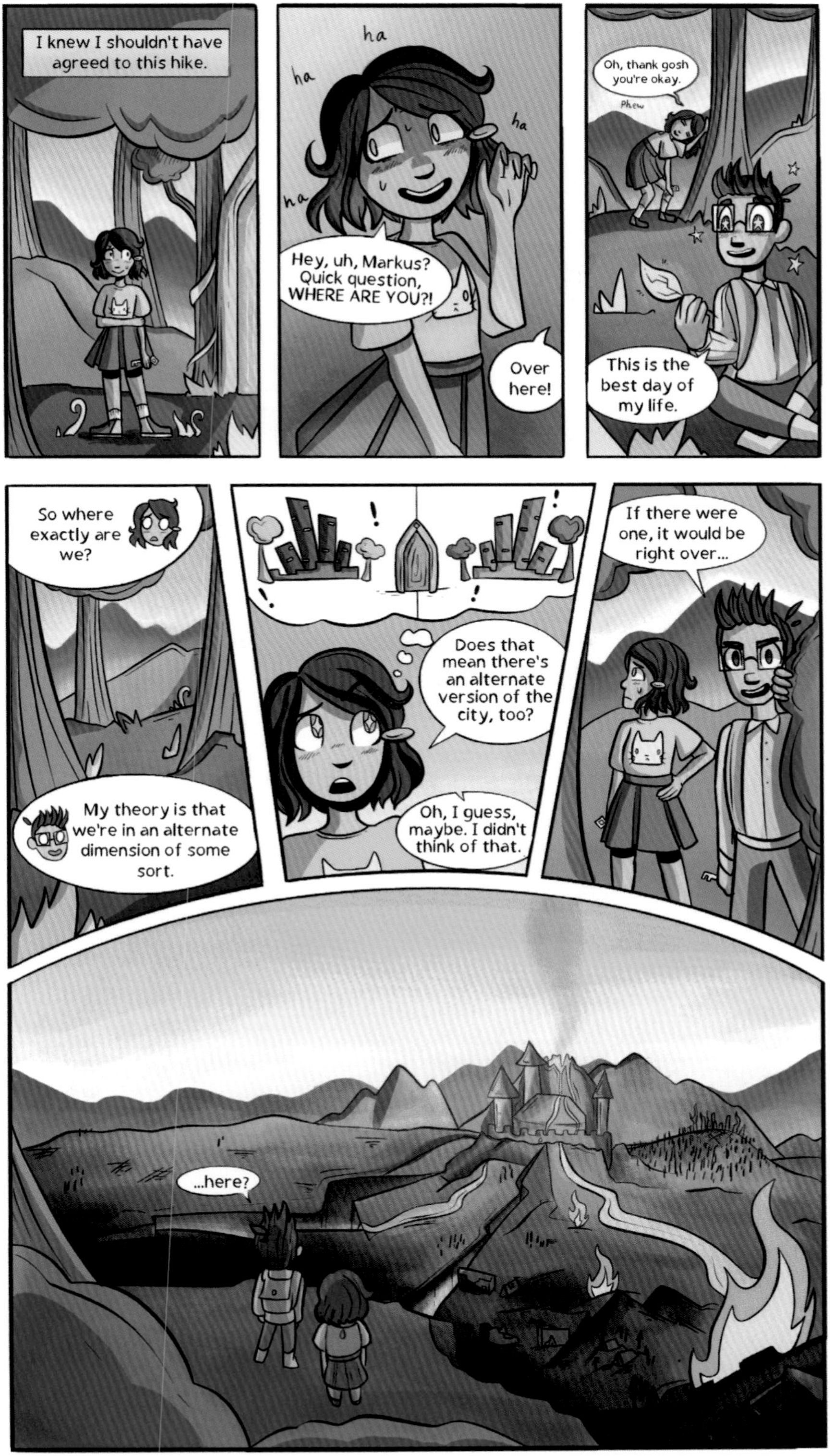
I knew I shouldn't have agreed to this hike.
ha
ha
ha
ha
Hey, uh, Markus? Quick question, WHERE ARE YOU?!
Over here!
Oh, thank gosh you're okay.
Phew
This is the best day of my life.
So where exactly are we?
My theory is that we're in an alternate dimension of some sort.
Does that mean there's an alternate version of the city, too?
Oh, I guess, maybe. I didn't think of that.
If there were one, it would be right over...
...here?

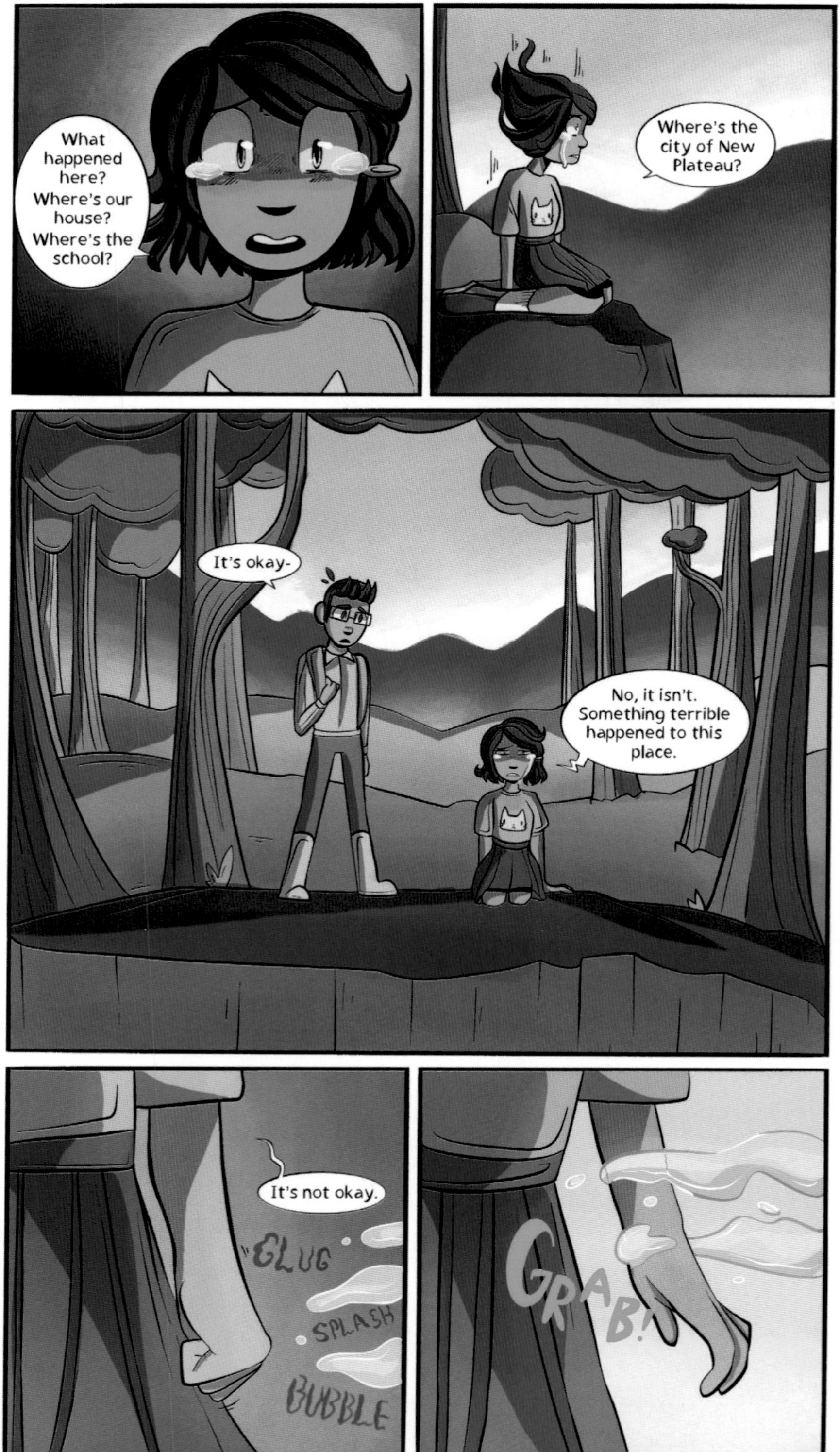
What happened here? Where's our house? Where's the school?
Where's the city of New Plateau?
It's okay-
No, it isn't. Something terrible happened to this place.
It's not okay.
GLUG
SPLASH
BUBBLE
GRAB!

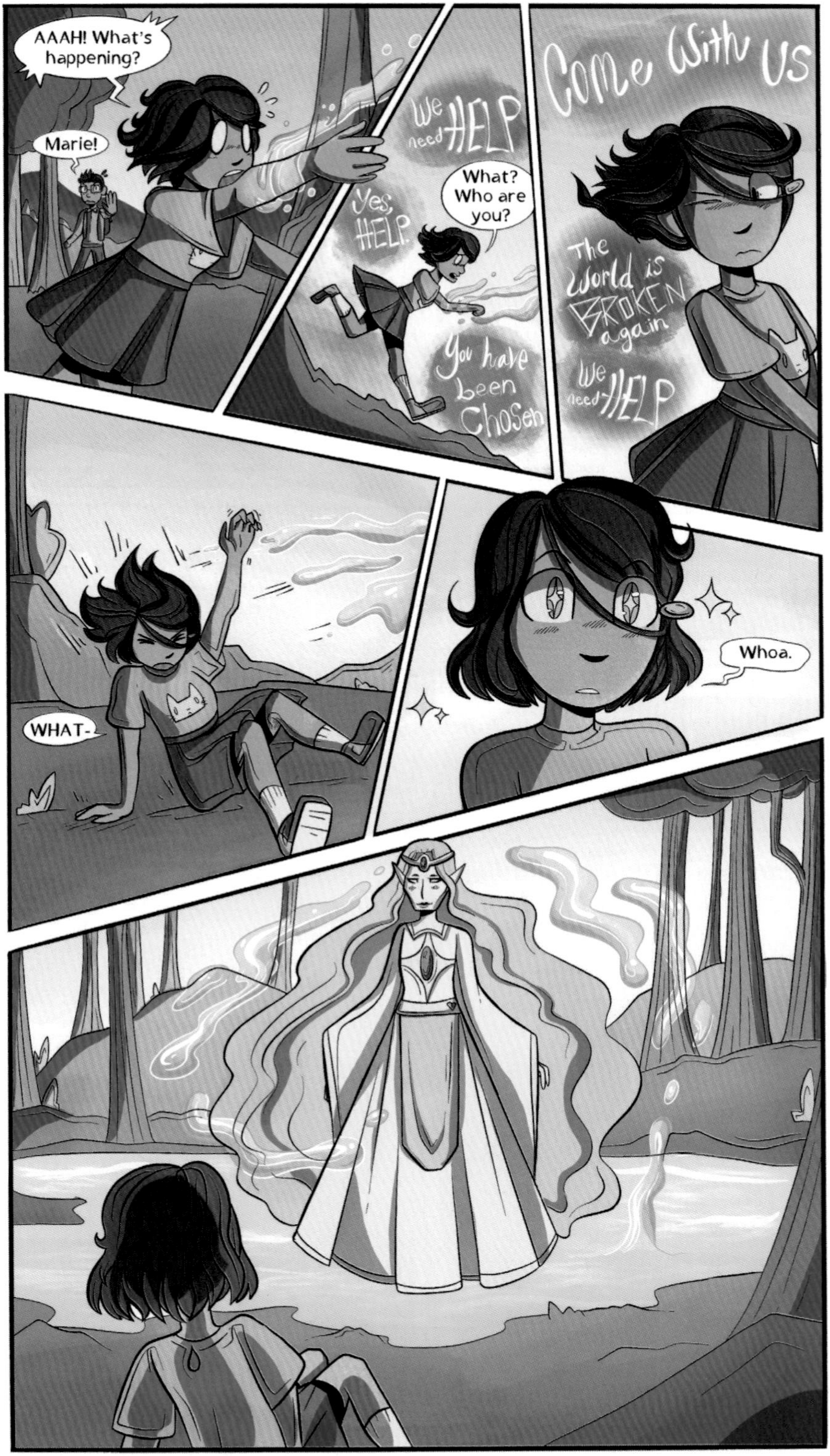

AAAH! What's happening?
Marie!
We need HELP
Yes, HELP.
What? Who are you?
You have been Chosen
Come With Us
The World is BROKEN again
We need HELP
WHAT-
Whoa.

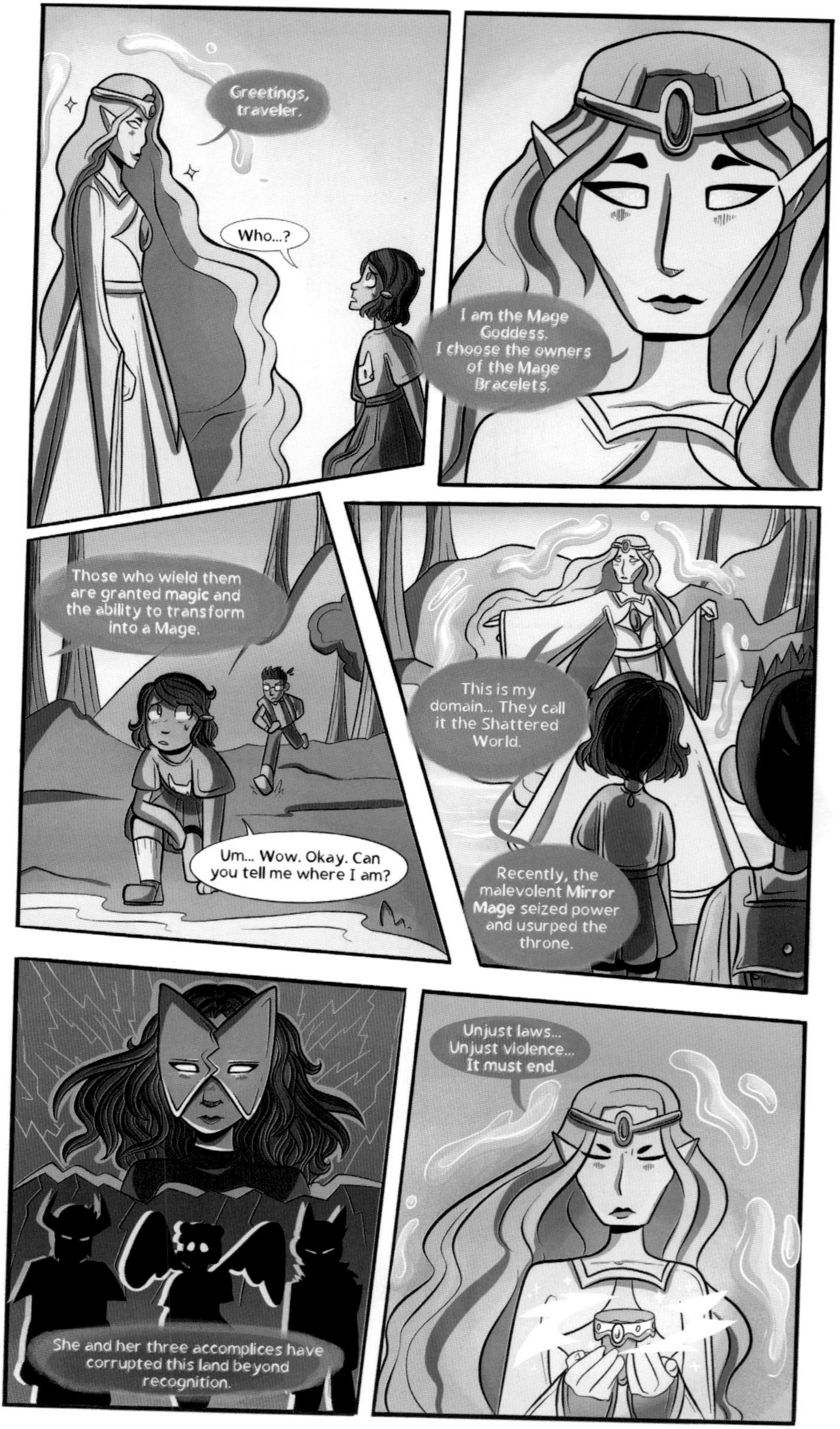
Greetings, traveler.
Who...?
I am the Mage Goddess. I choose the owners of the Mage Bracelets.
Those who wield them are granted magic and the ability to transform into a Mage.
Um... Wow. Okay. Can you tell me where I am?
This is my domain... They call it the Shattered World.
Recently, the malevolent Mirror Mage seized power and usurped the throne.
She and her three accomplices have corrupted this land beyond recognition.
Unjust laws... Unjust violence... It must end.

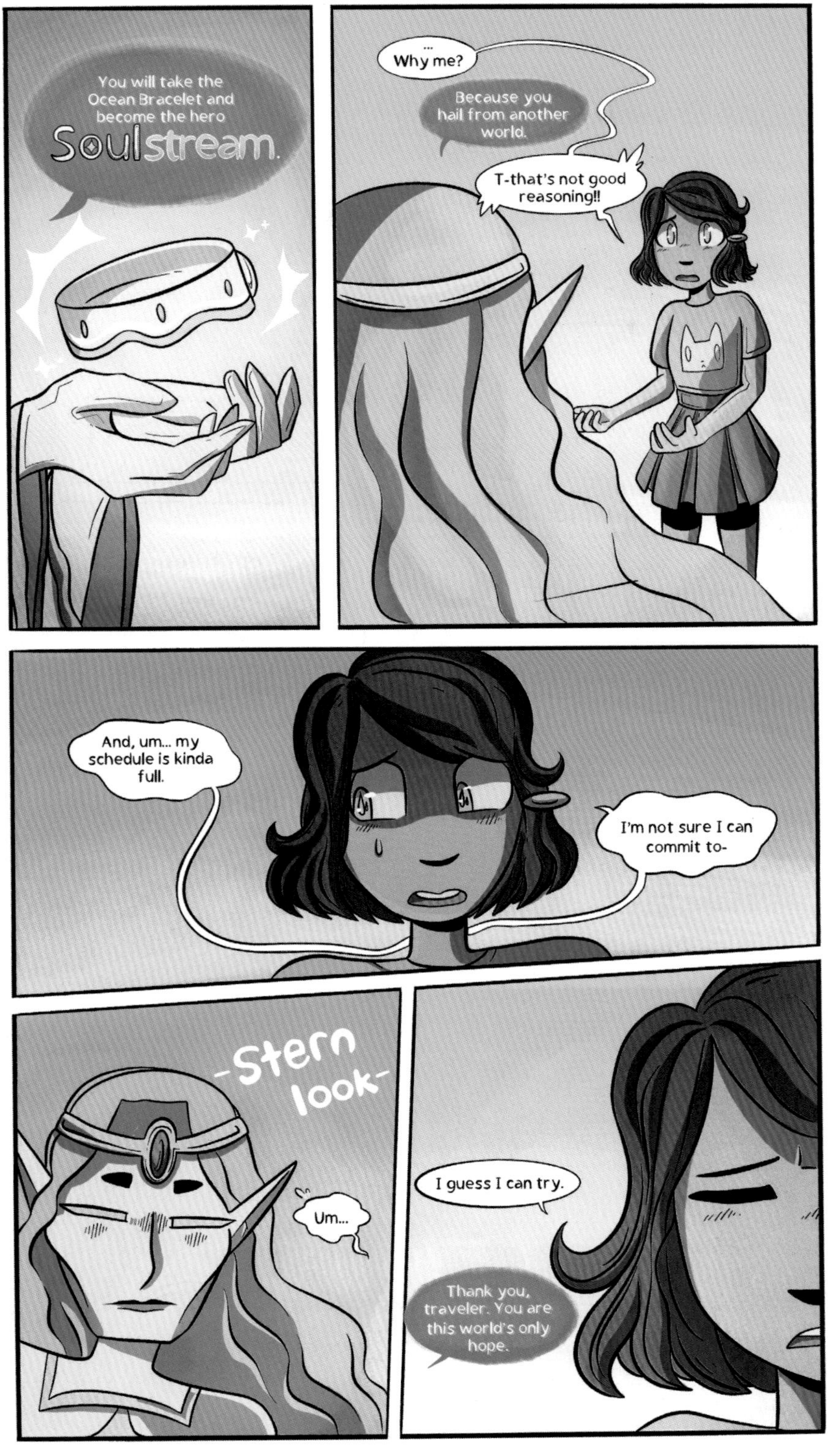
You will take the Ocean Bracelet and become the hero Soulstream.
... Why me?
Because you hail from another world.
T-that's not good reasoning!!
And, um... my schedule is kinda full.
I'm not sure I can commit to-
-Stern look-
Um...
I guess I can try.
Thank you, traveler. You are this world's only hope.

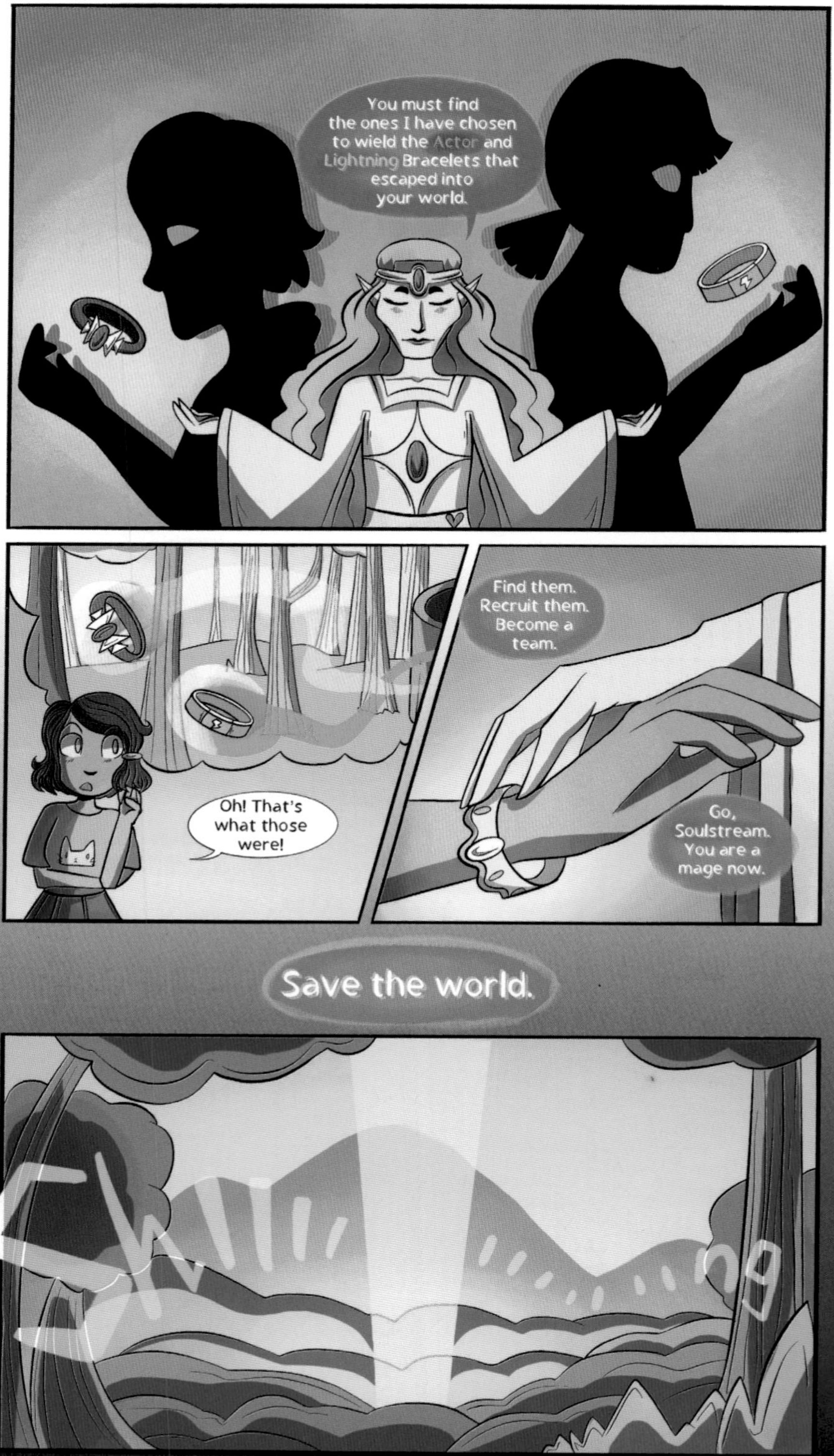
You must find the ones I have chosen to wield the Actor and Lightning Bracelets that escaped into your world.
Oh! That's what those were!
Find them. Recruit them. Become a team.
Go, Soulstream. You are a mage now.
Save the world.

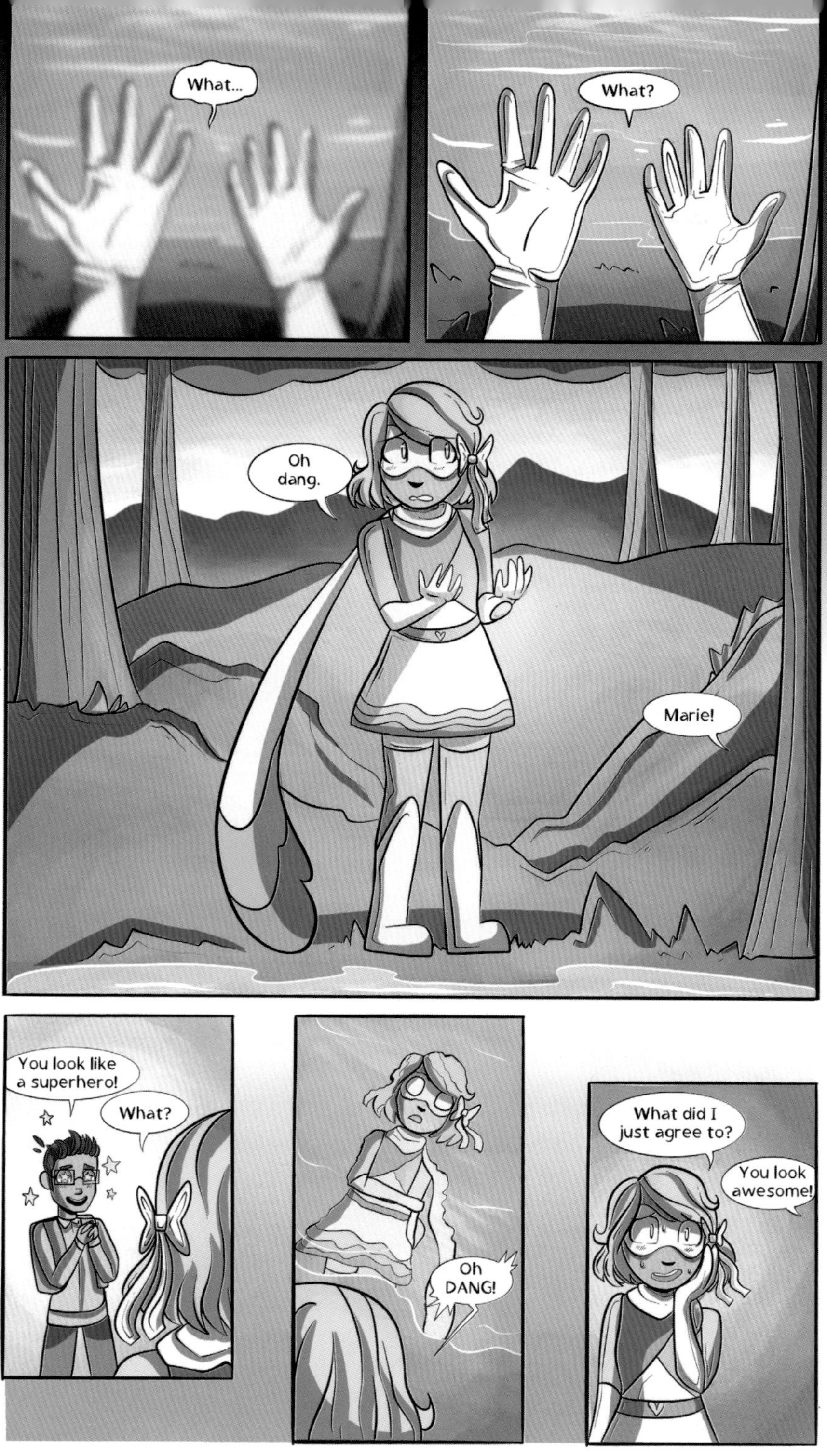
What...
What?
Oh dang.
Marie!
You look like a superhero!
What?
Oh DANG!
What did I just agree to?
You look awesome!

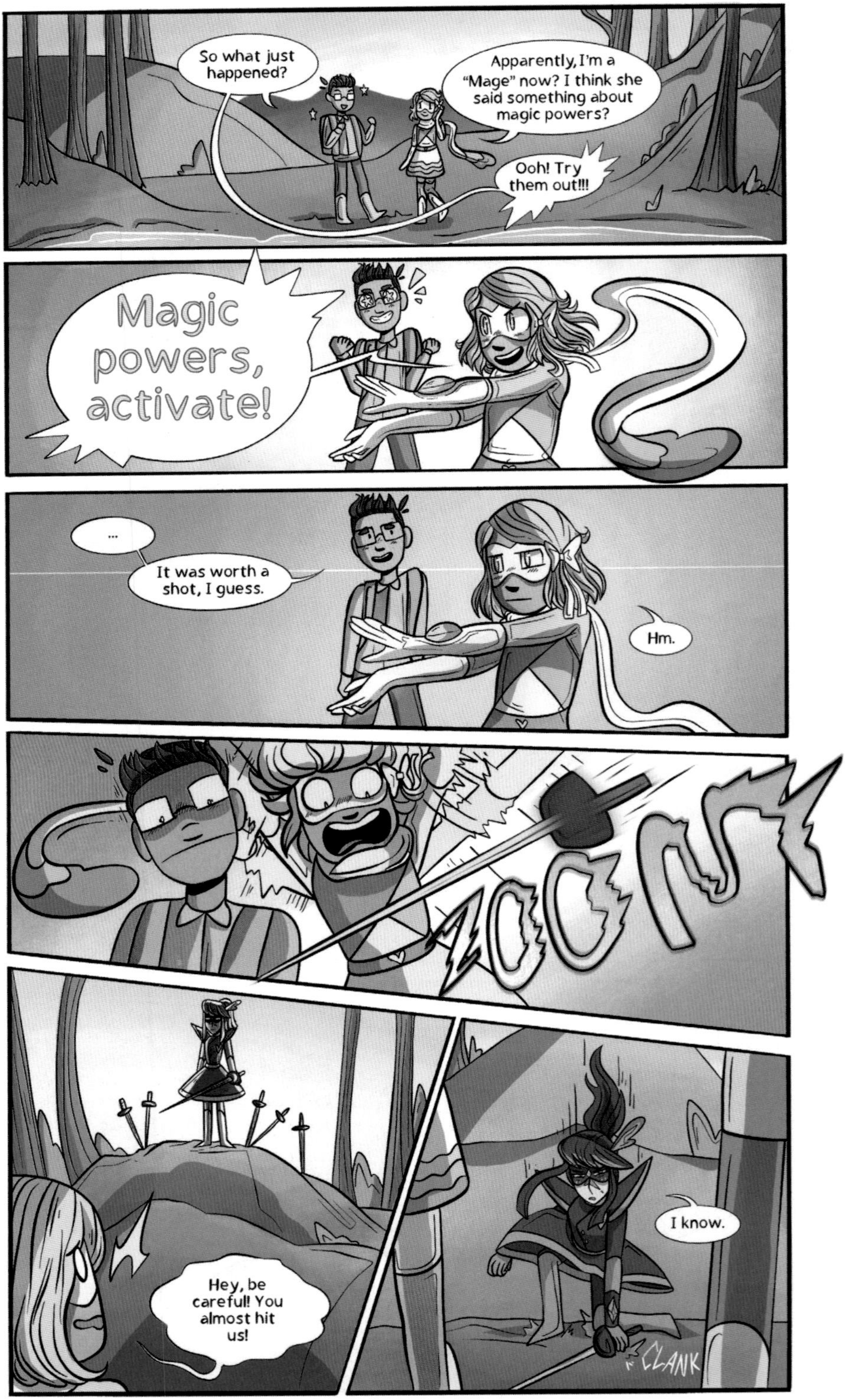
So what just happened?
Apparently, I'm a "Mage" now? I think she said something about magic powers?
Ooh! Try them out!!!
Magic powers, activate!
...
It was worth a shot, I guess.
Hm.
ZOOM
Hey, be careful! You almost hit us!
I know.
CLANK

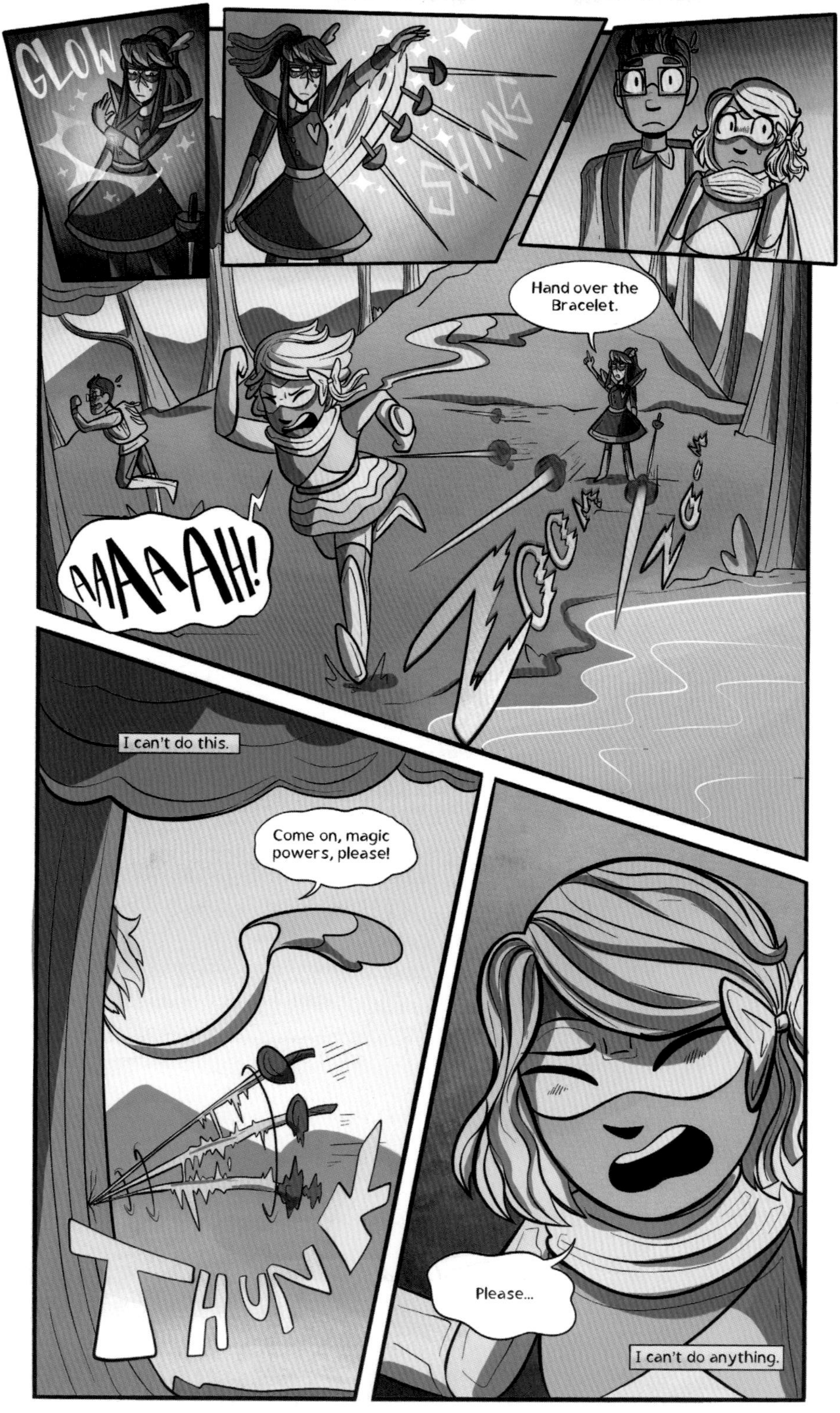
GLOW
SHING
Hand over the Bracelet.
AAAAAH!
ZOOM
ZOOM
I can't do this.
Come on, magic powers, please!
THUNK
Please...
I can't do anything.

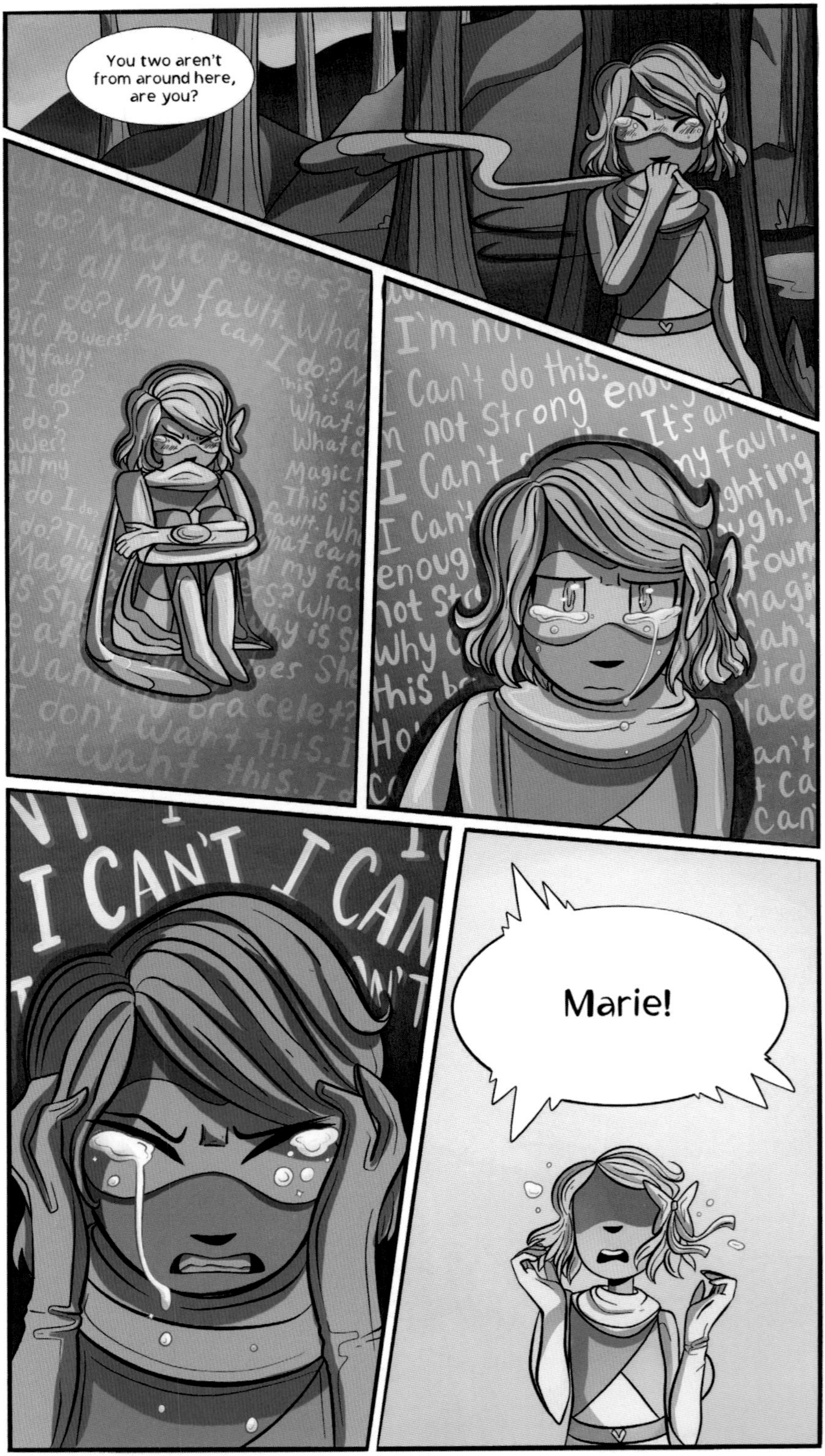
You two aren't from around here, are you?
Marie!

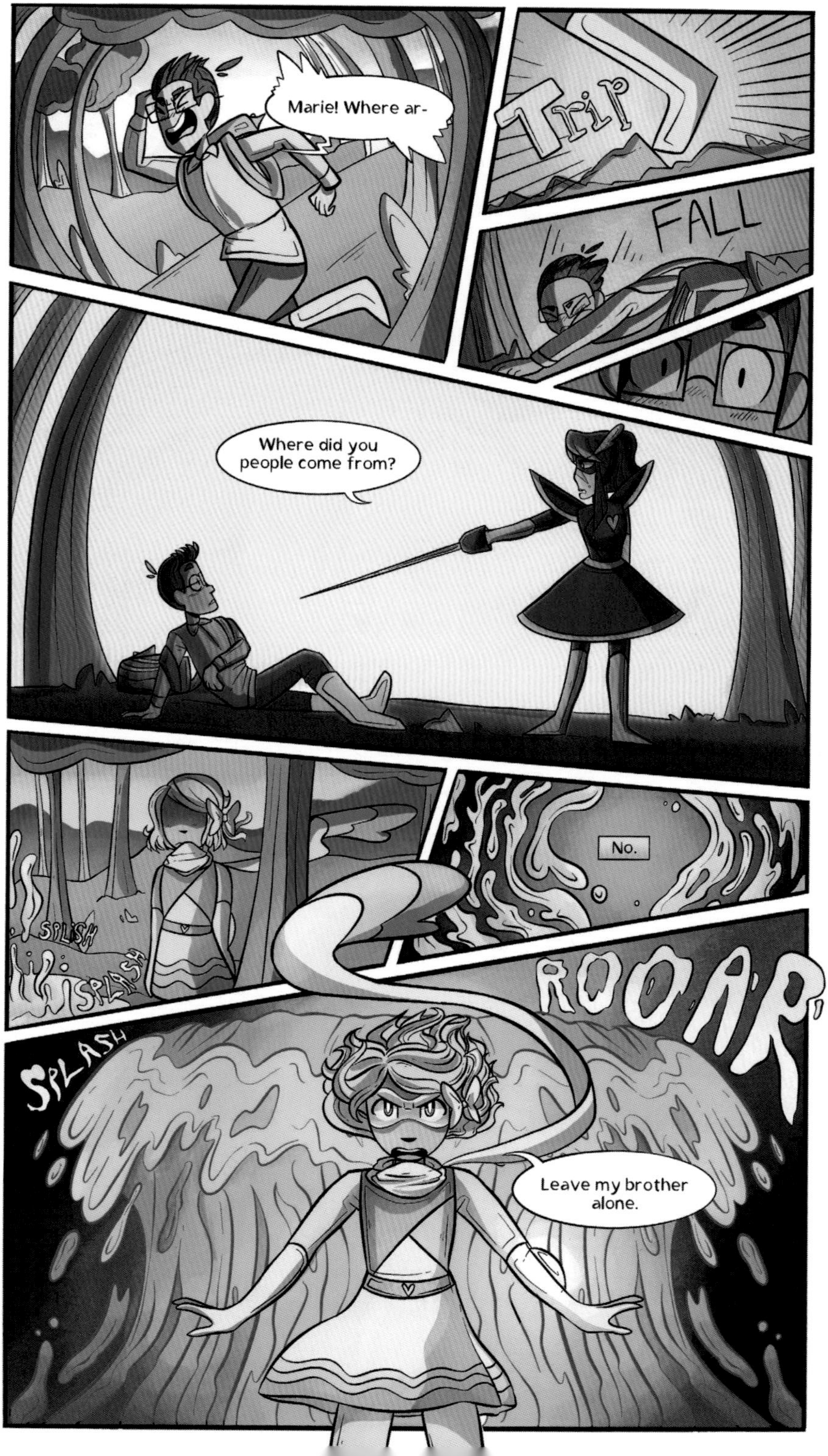
Marie! Where ar-
Trip
FALL
Where did you people come from?
SPLISH
SPLASH
No.
ROOAR
SPLASH
Leave my brother alone.

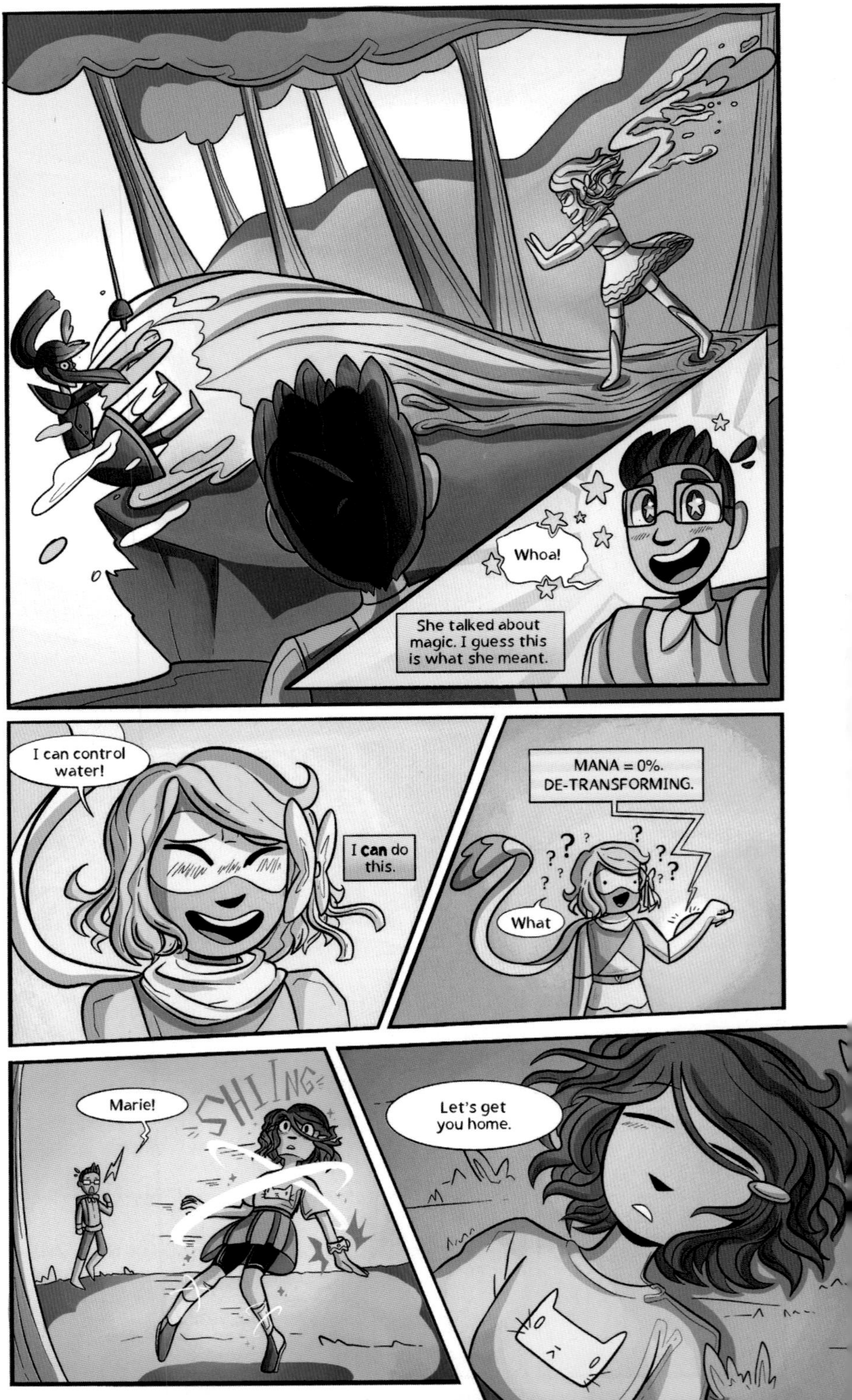
Whoa!
She talked about magic. I guess this is what she meant.
I can control water!
I **can** do this.
MANA = 0%. DE-TRANSFORMING.
What
Marie!
SHIING
Let's get you home.

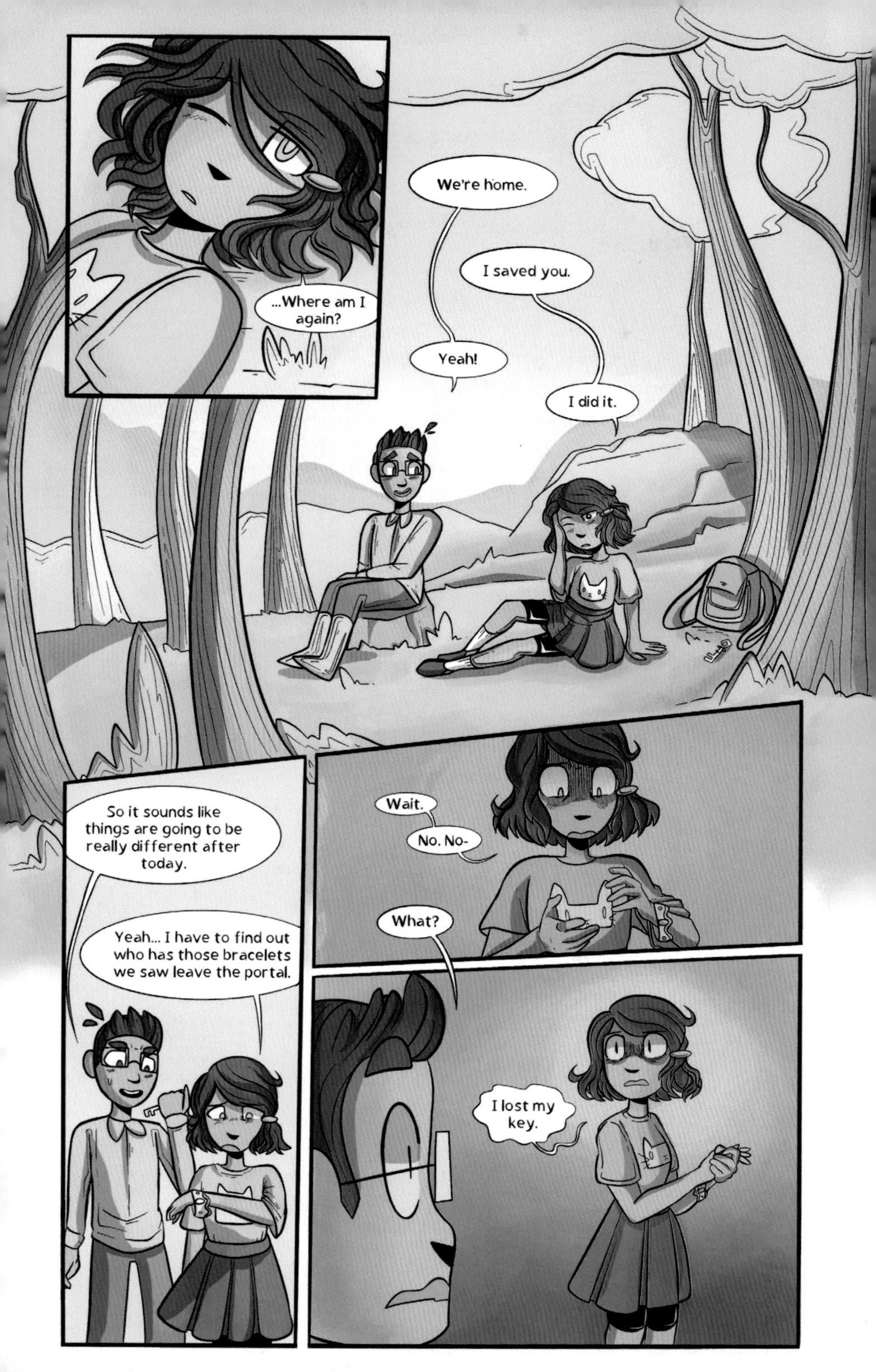
...Where am I again?
We're home.
Yeah!
I saved you.
I did it.
So it sounds like things are going to be really different after today.
Yeah... I have to find out who has those bracelets we saw leave the portal.
Wait.
No. No-
What?
I lost my key.

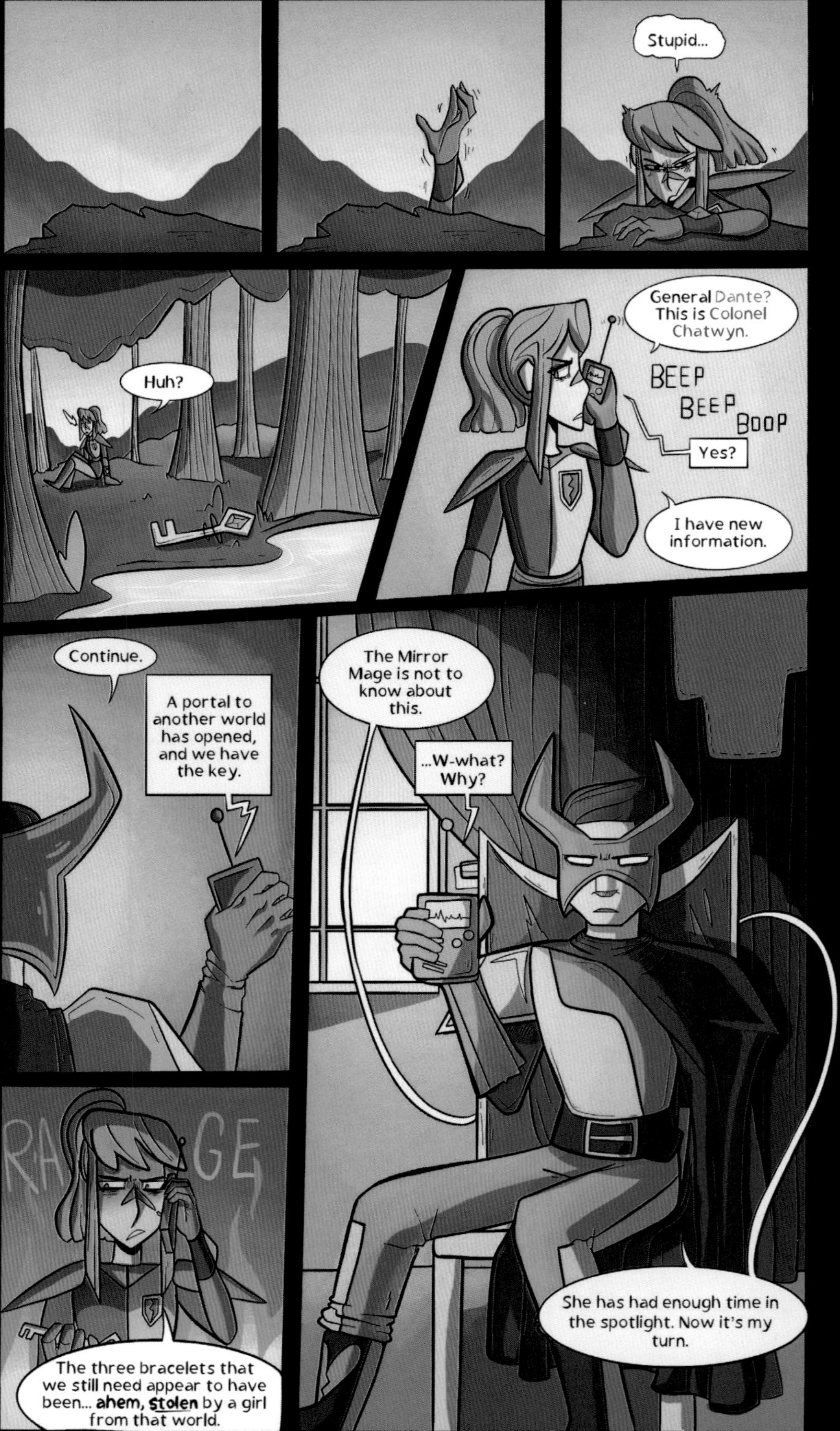
Stupid...
Huh?
General Dante? This is Colonel Chatwyn.
BEEP BEEP BOOP
Yes?
I have new information.
Continue.
A portal to another world has opened, and we have the key.
The Mirror Mage is not to know about this.
...W-what? Why?
RAGE
She has had enough time in the spotlight. Now it's my turn.
The three bracelets that we still need appear to have been... **ahem, stolen** by a girl from that world.

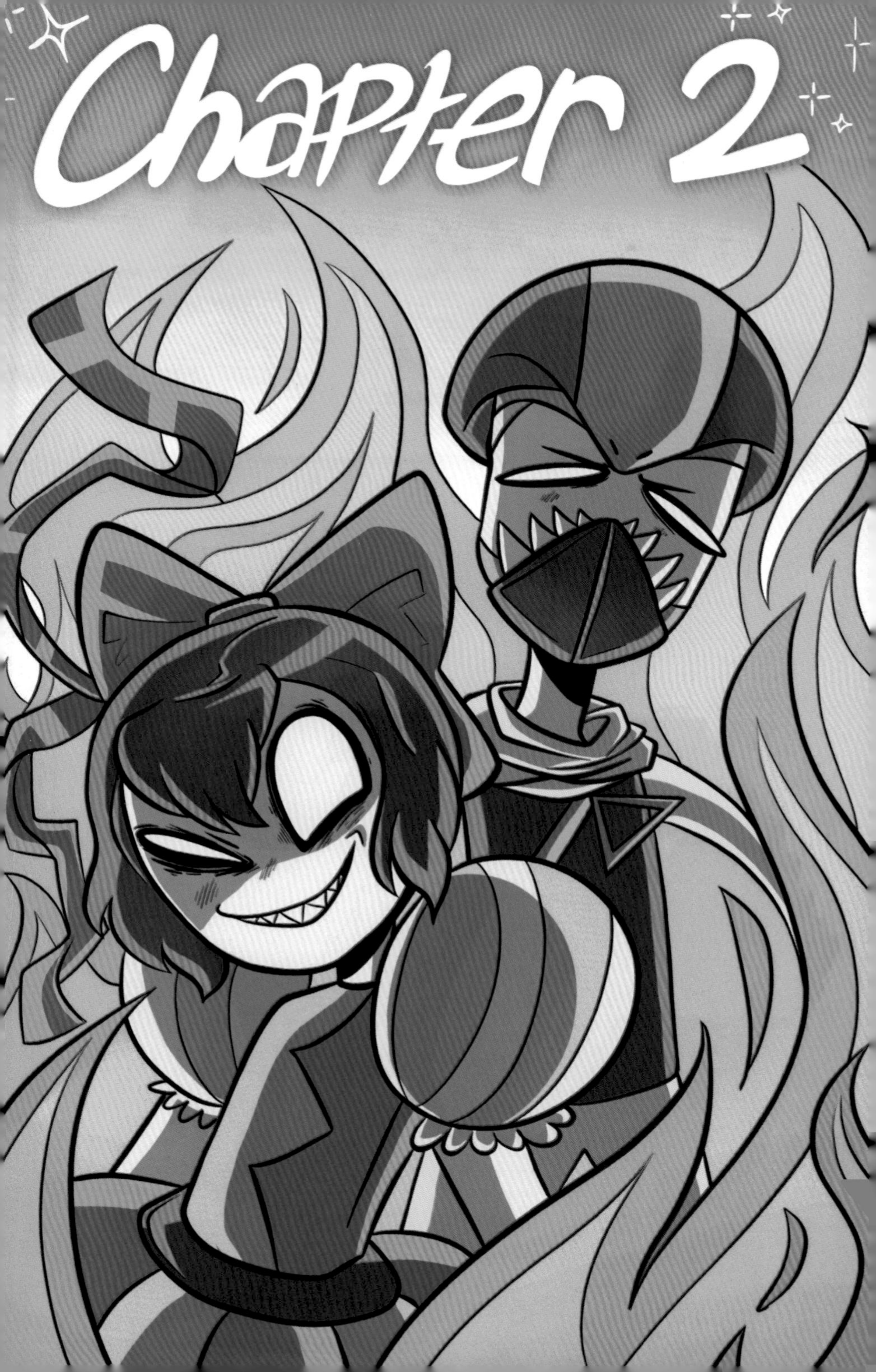
Chapter 2

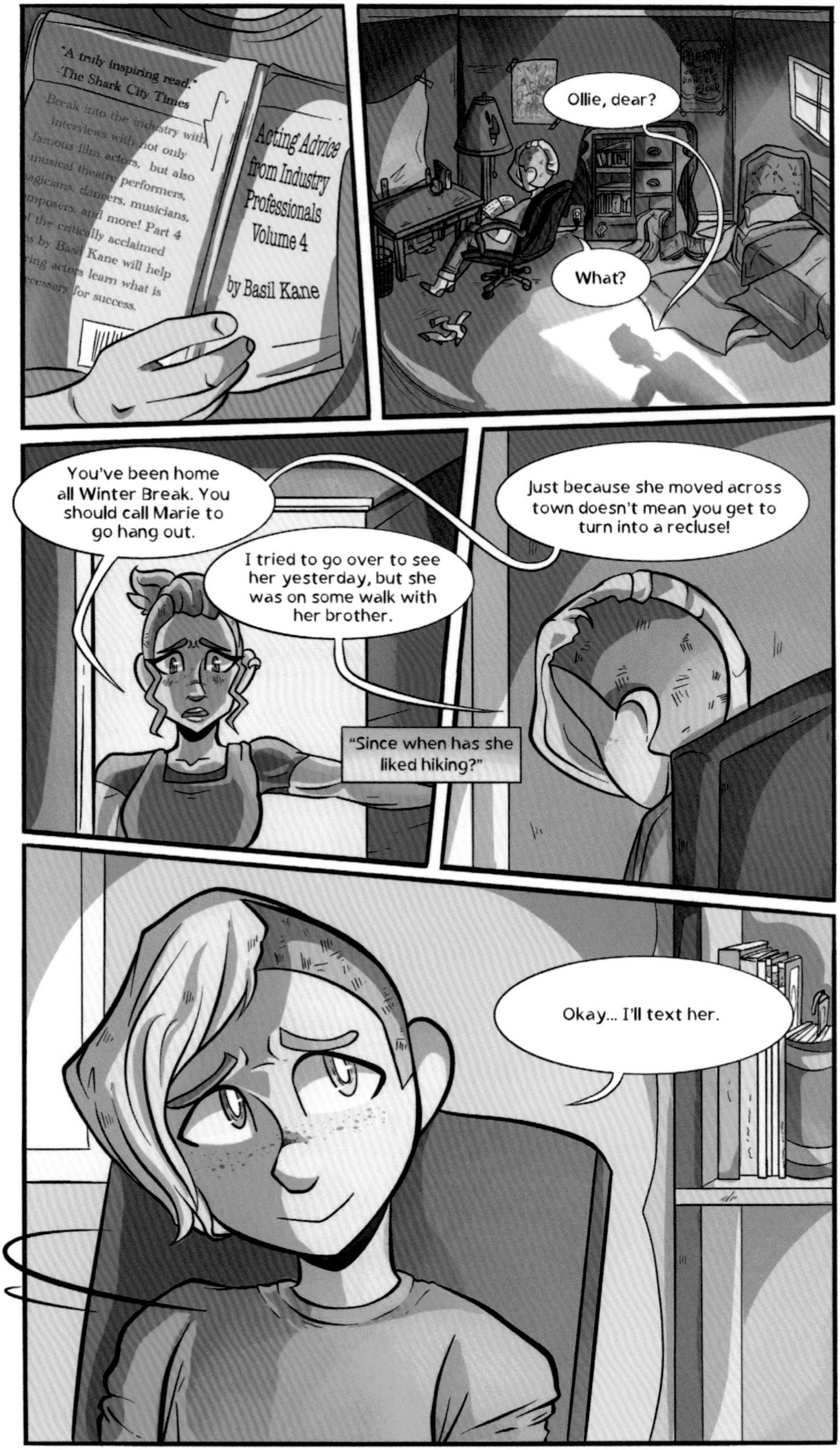
"A truly inspiring read."
-The Shark City Times
Acting Advice from Industry Professionals Volume 4
by Basil Kane
Ollie, dear?
What?
You've been home all Winter Break. You should call Marie to go hang out.
I tried to go over to see her yesterday, but she was on some walk with her brother.
Just because she moved across town doesn't mean you get to turn into a recluse!
"Since when has she liked hiking?"
Okay... I'll text her.

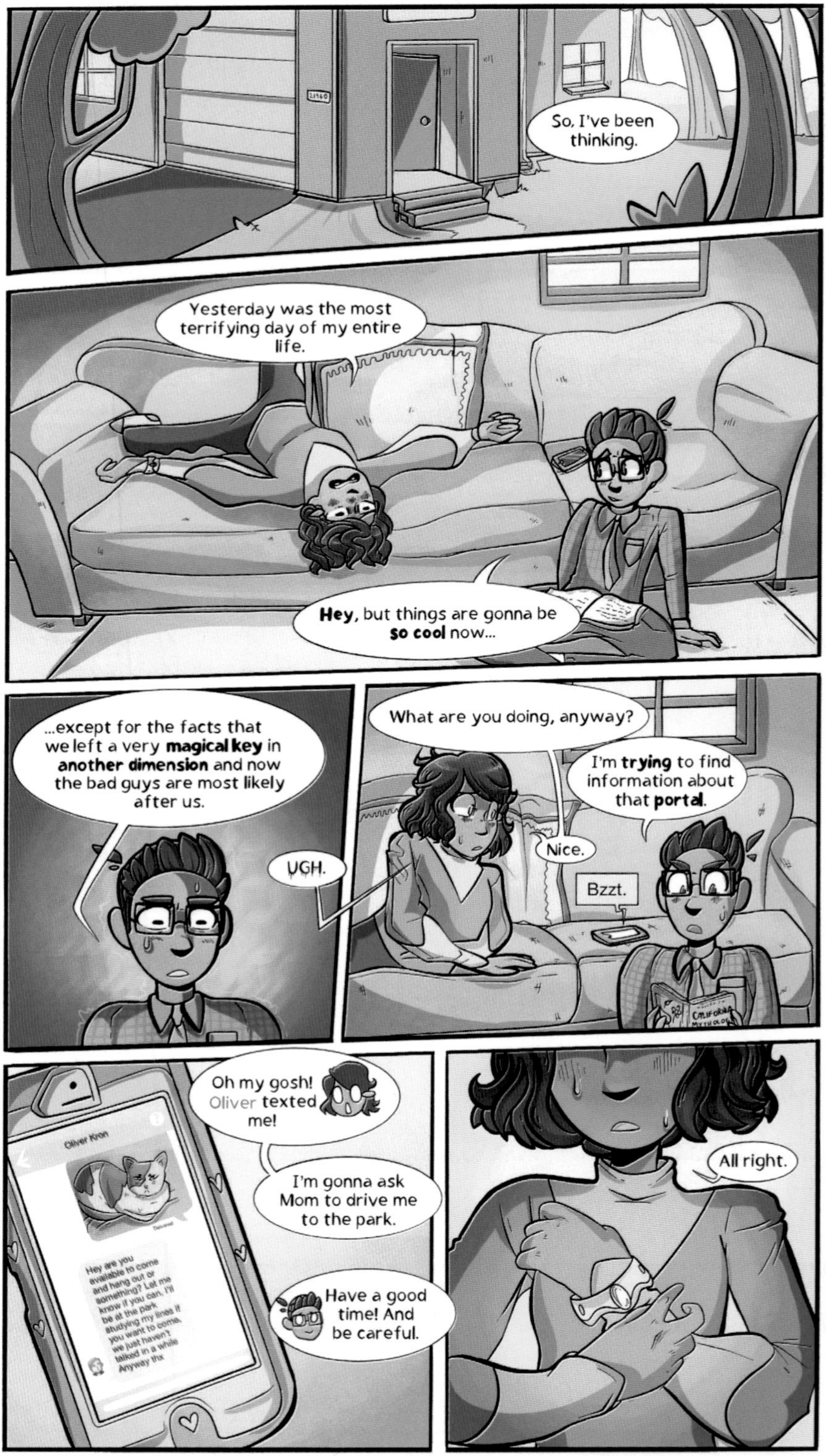

21960
So, I've been thinking.
Yesterday was the most terrifying day of my entire life.
Hey, but things are gonna be so cool now...
...except for the facts that we left a very magical key in another dimension and now the bad guys are most likely after us.
UGH.
What are you doing, anyway?
I'm trying to find information about that portal.
Nice.
Bzzt.
CALIFORNIA MYTHOLOGY
Oh my gosh! Oliver texted me!
I'm gonna ask Mom to drive me to the park.
Oliver Kron
Hey are you available to come and hang out or something? Let me know if you can. I'll be at the park studying my lines if you want to come. we just haven't talked in a while Anyway thx
Have a good time! And be careful.
All right.

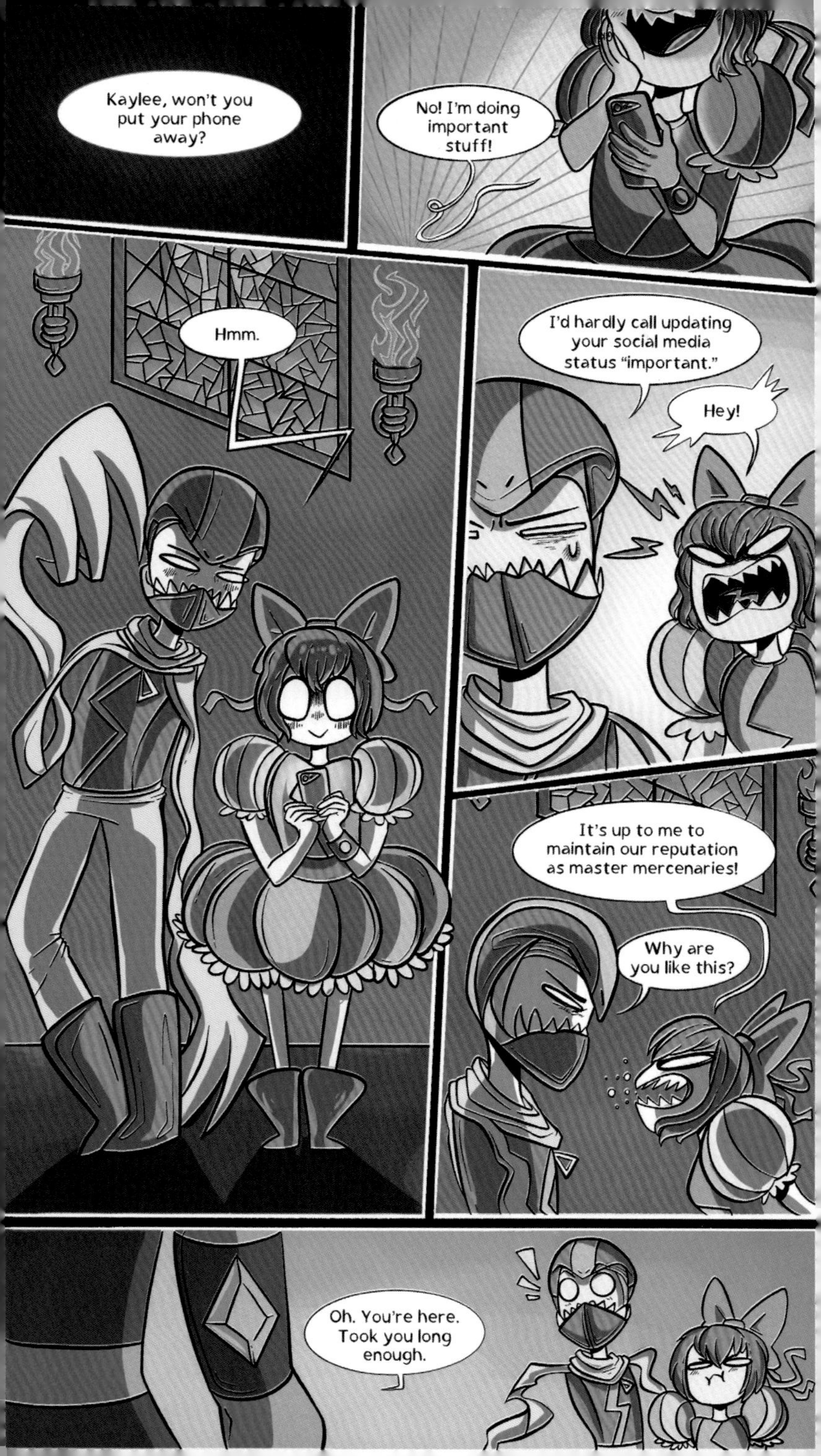

Kaylee, won't you put your phone away?
No! I'm doing important stuff!
Hmm.
I'd hardly call updating your social media status "important."
Hey!
It's up to me to maintain our reputation as master mercenaries!
Why are you like this?
Oh. You're here. Took you long enough.

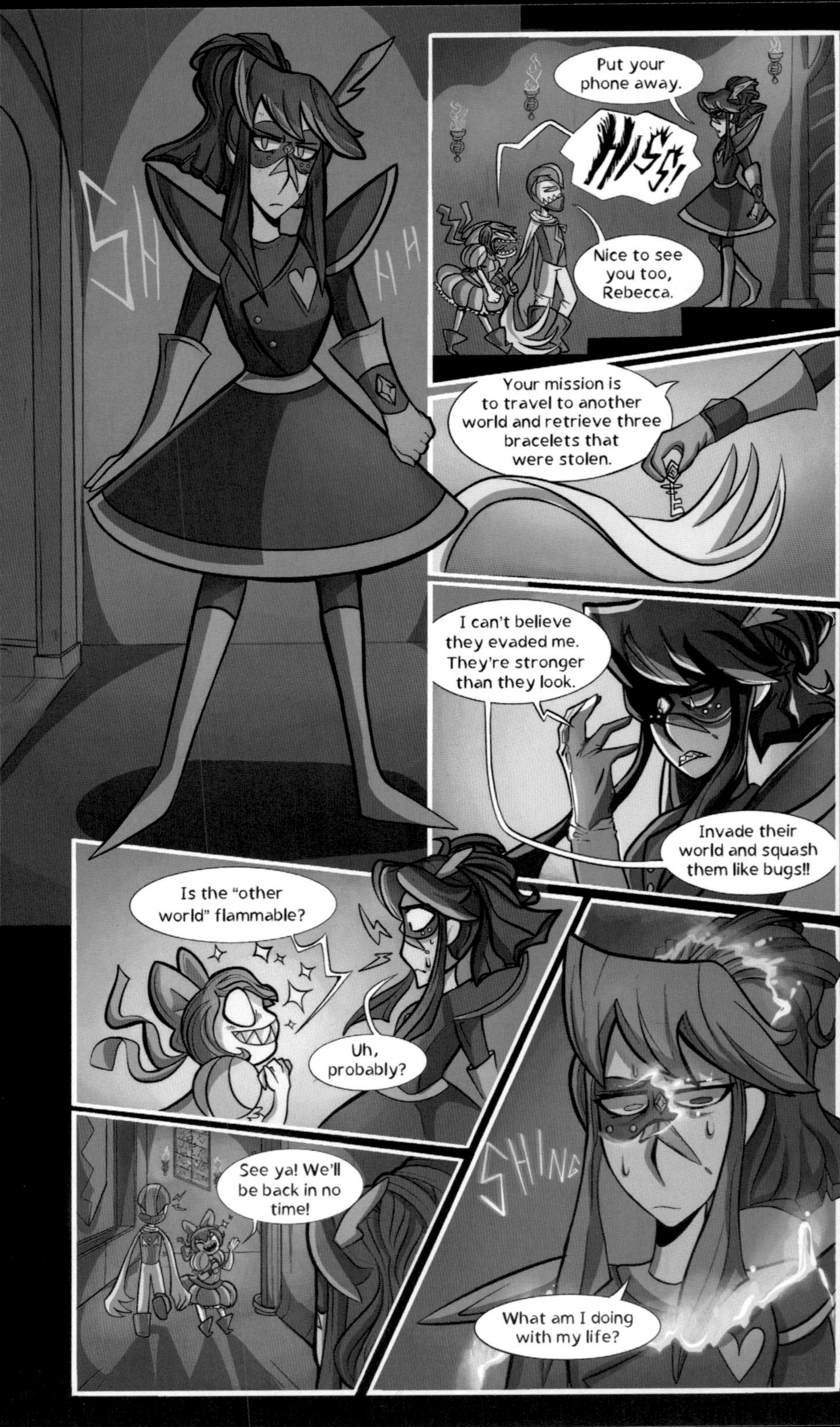
SHHH
Put your phone away.
HISS!
Nice to see you too, Rebecca.
Your mission is to travel to another world and retrieve three bracelets that were stolen.
I can't believe they evaded me. They're stronger than they look.
Invade their world and squash them like bugs!!
Is the "other world" flammable?
Uh, probably?
See ya! We'll be back in no time!
SHING
What am I doing with my life?

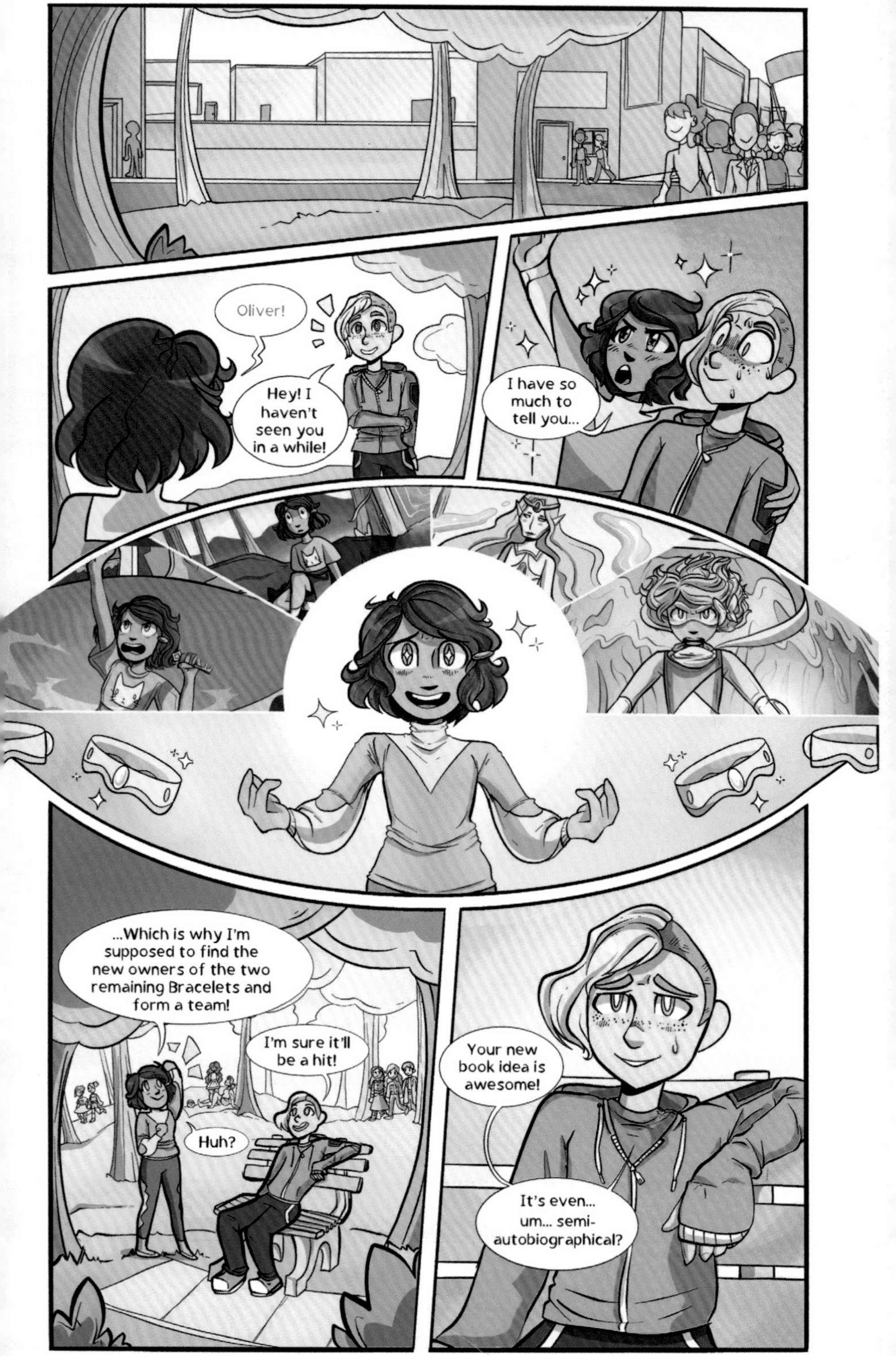
Oliver!
Hey! I haven't seen you in a while!
I have so much to tell you...
...Which is why I'm supposed to find the new owners of the two remaining Bracelets and form a team!
I'm sure it'll be a hit!
Huh?
Your new book idea is awesome!
It's even... um... semi-autobiographical?

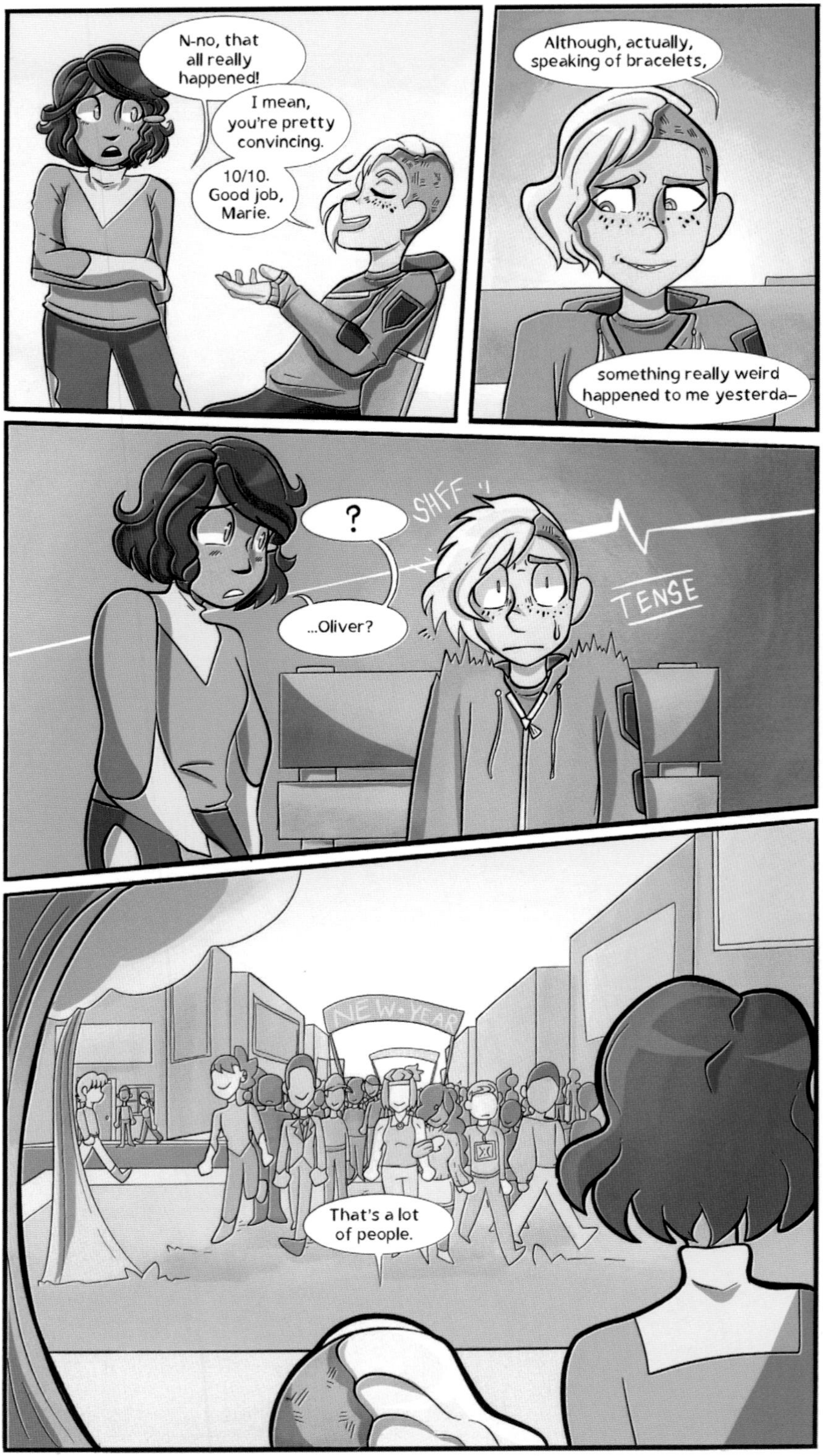

N-no, that all really happened!
I mean, you're pretty convincing.
10/10. Good job, Marie.
Although, actually, speaking of bracelets,
something really weird happened to me yesterda–
?
SHFF
TENSE
...Oliver?
NEW • YEAR
That's a lot of people.

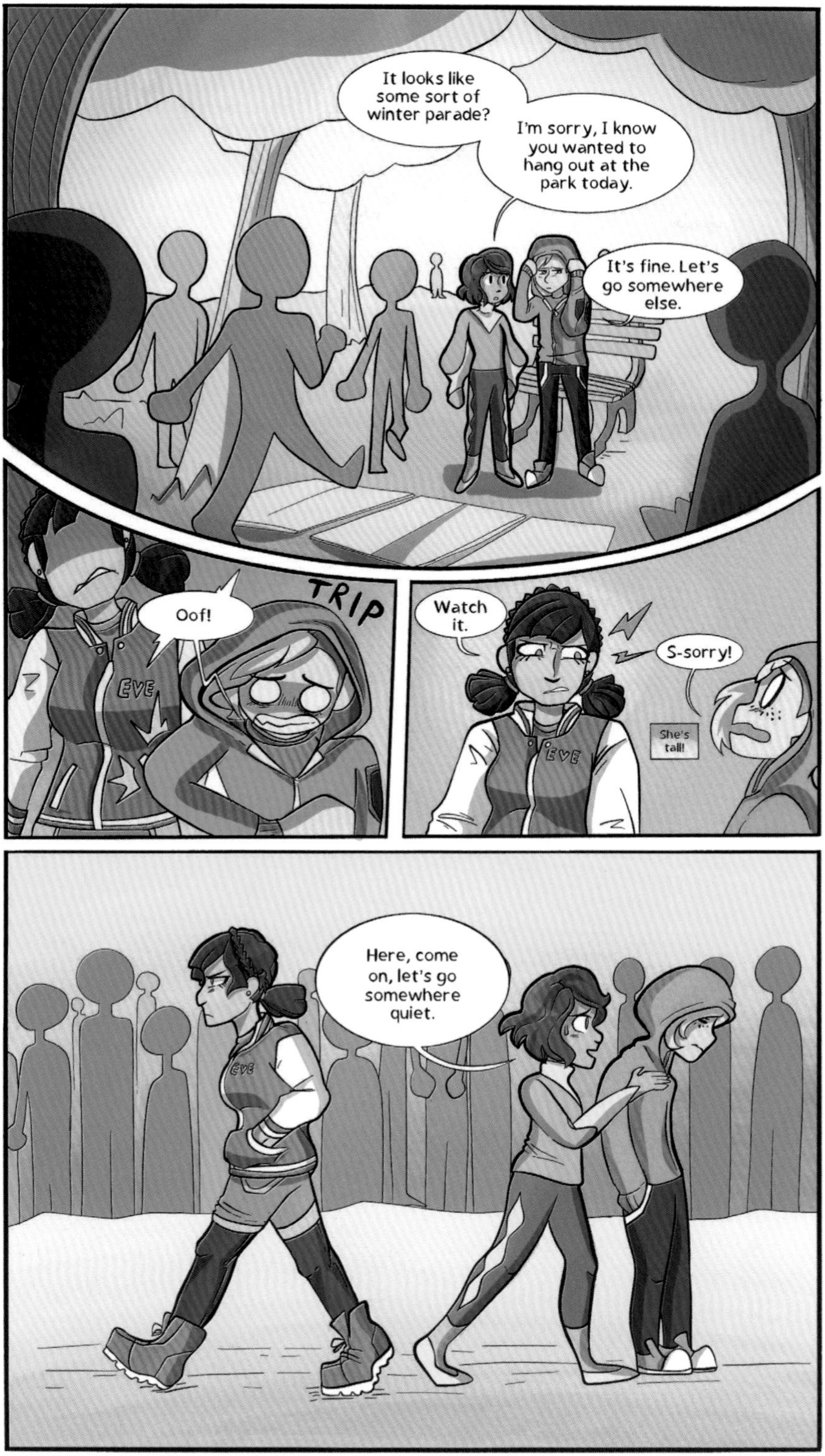
It looks like some sort of winter parade?
I'm sorry, I know you wanted to hang out at the park today.
It's fine. Let's go somewhere else.
Oof!
TRIP
Watch it.
S-sorry!
She's tall!
Here, come on, let's go somewhere quiet.

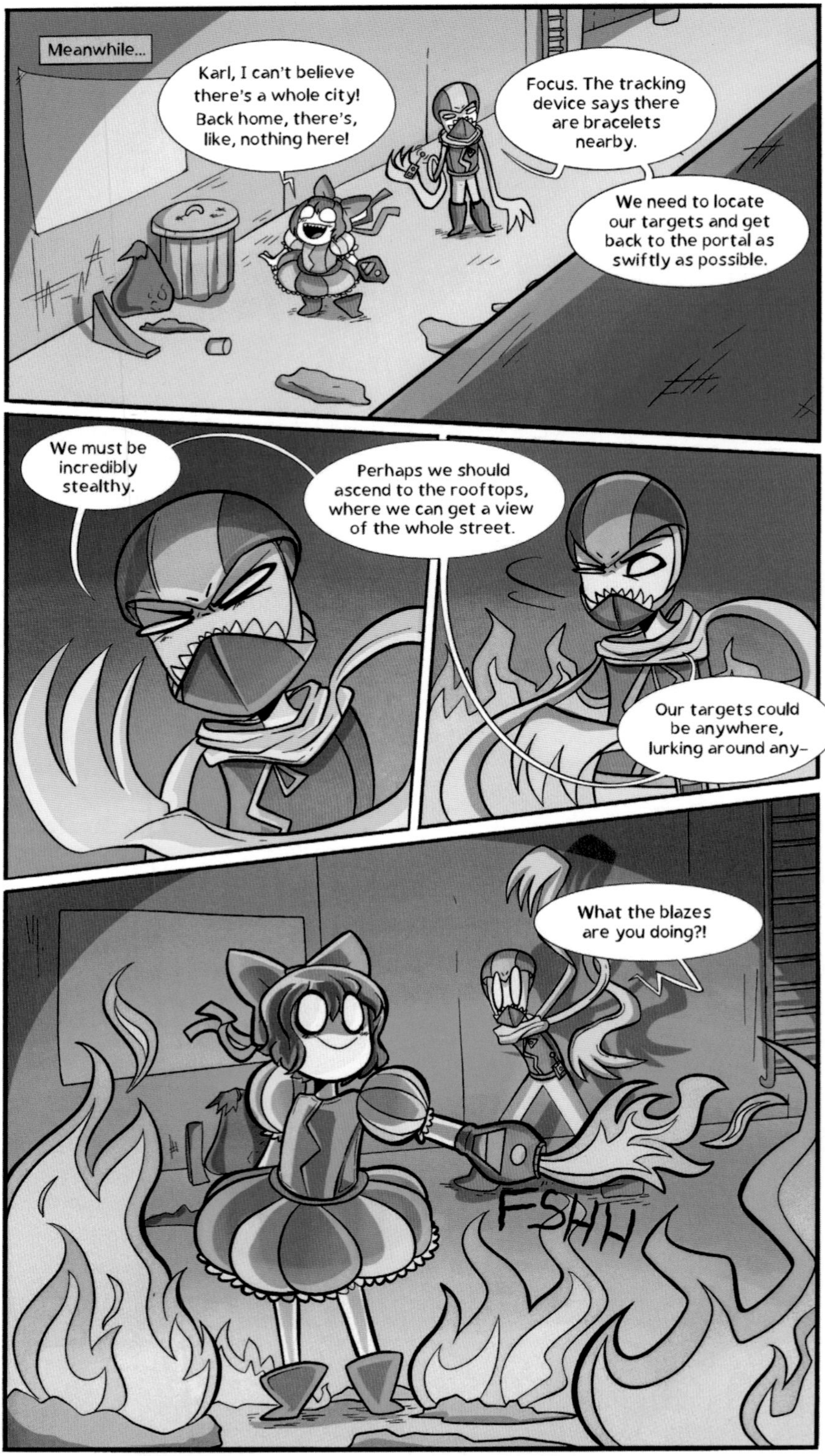
Meanwhile...
Karl, I can't believe there's a whole city! Back home, there's, like, nothing here!
Focus. The tracking device says there are bracelets nearby.
We need to locate our targets and get back to the portal as swiftly as possible.
We must be incredibly stealthy.
Perhaps we should ascend to the rooftops, where we can get a view of the whole street.
Our targets could be anywhere, lurking around any–
What the blazes are you doing?!
FSHH

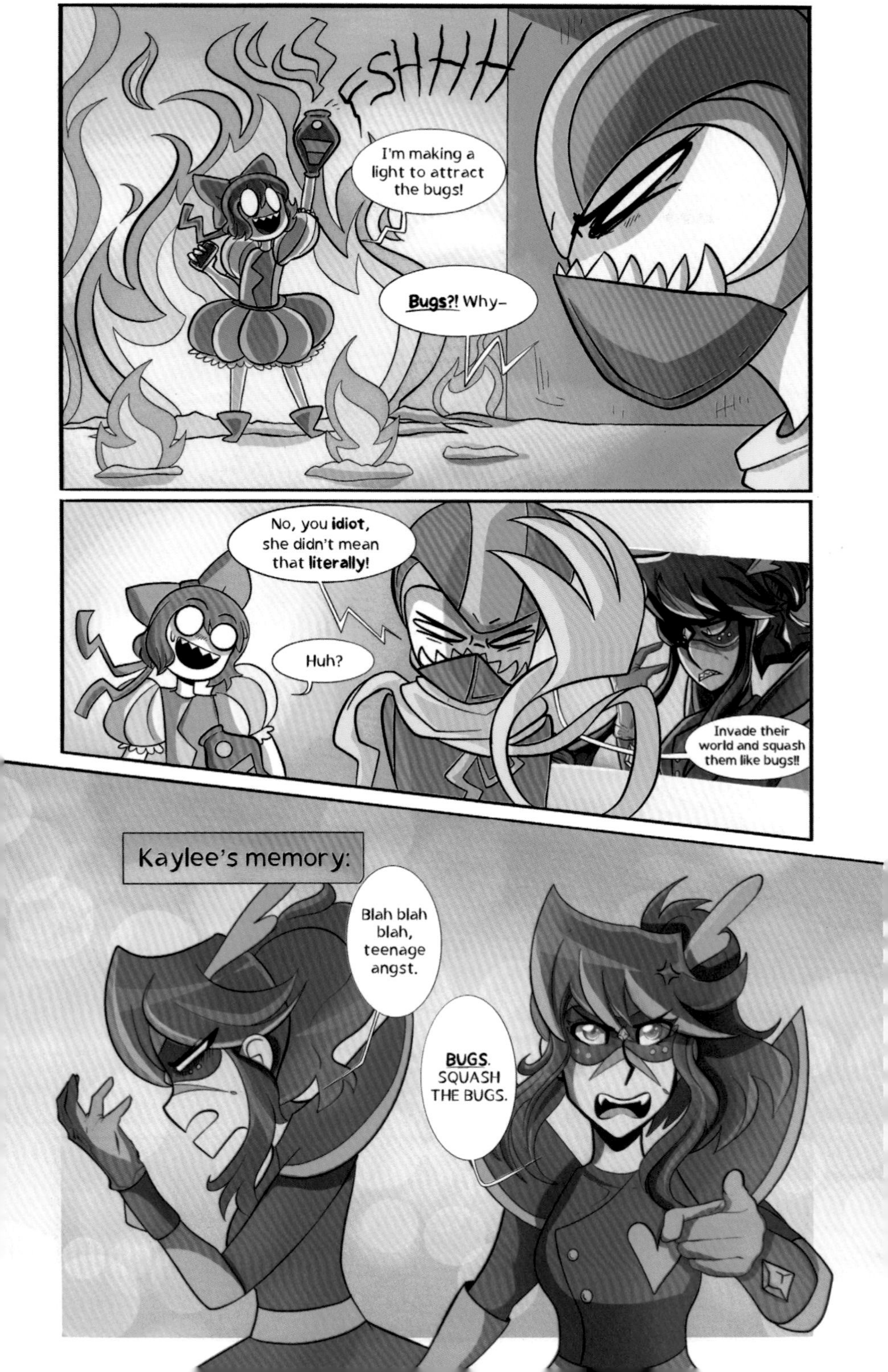
FSHHH
I'm making a light to attract the bugs!
Bugs?! Why-
No, you idiot, she didn't mean that literally!
Huh?
Invade their world and squash them like bugs!!
Kaylee's memory:
Blah blah blah, teenage angst.
BUGS. SQUASH THE BUGS.

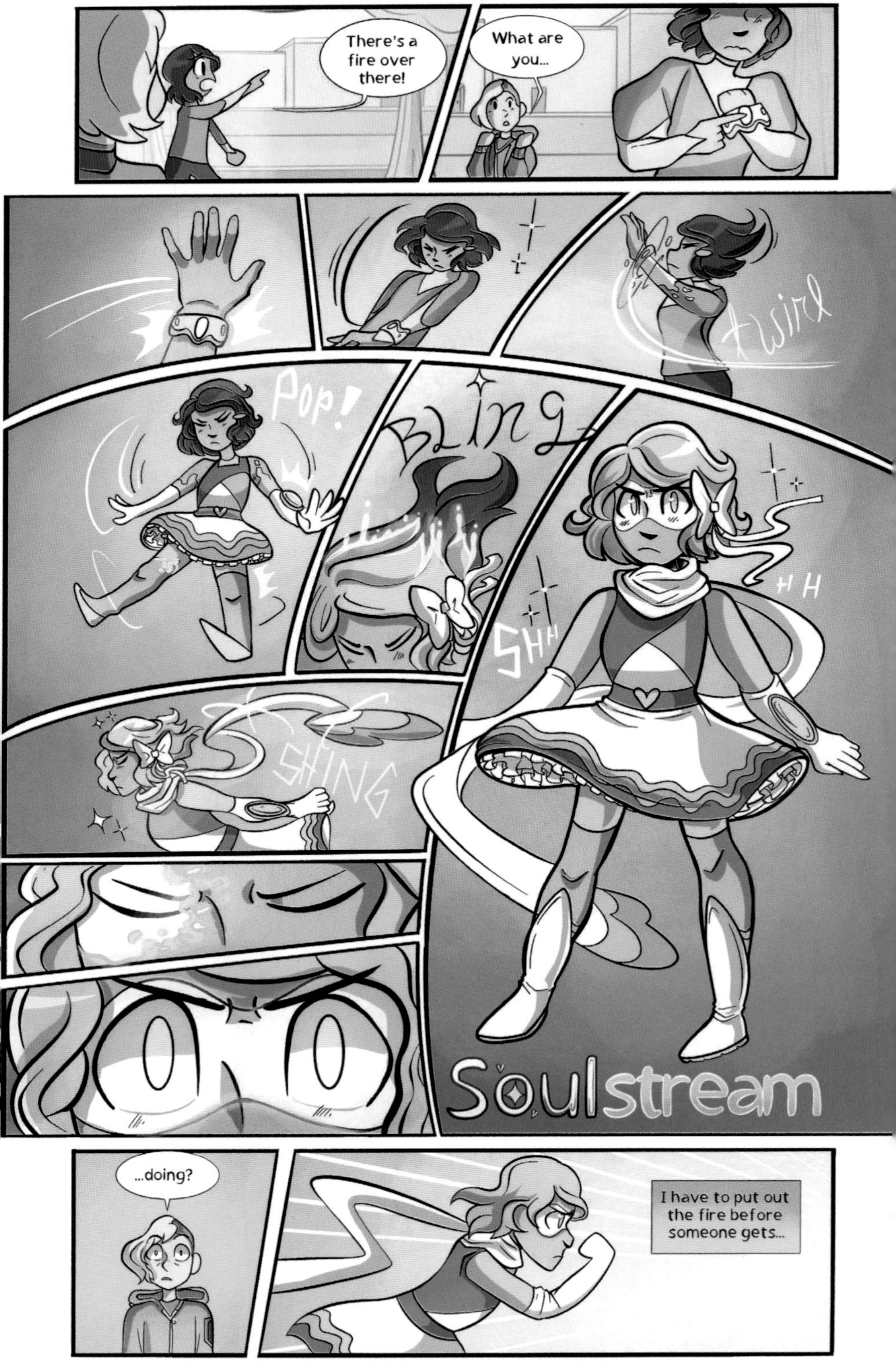

There's a fire over there!
What are you...
twirl
POP!
BLING
SHING
SHH
Soulstream
...doing?
I have to put out the fire before someone gets...

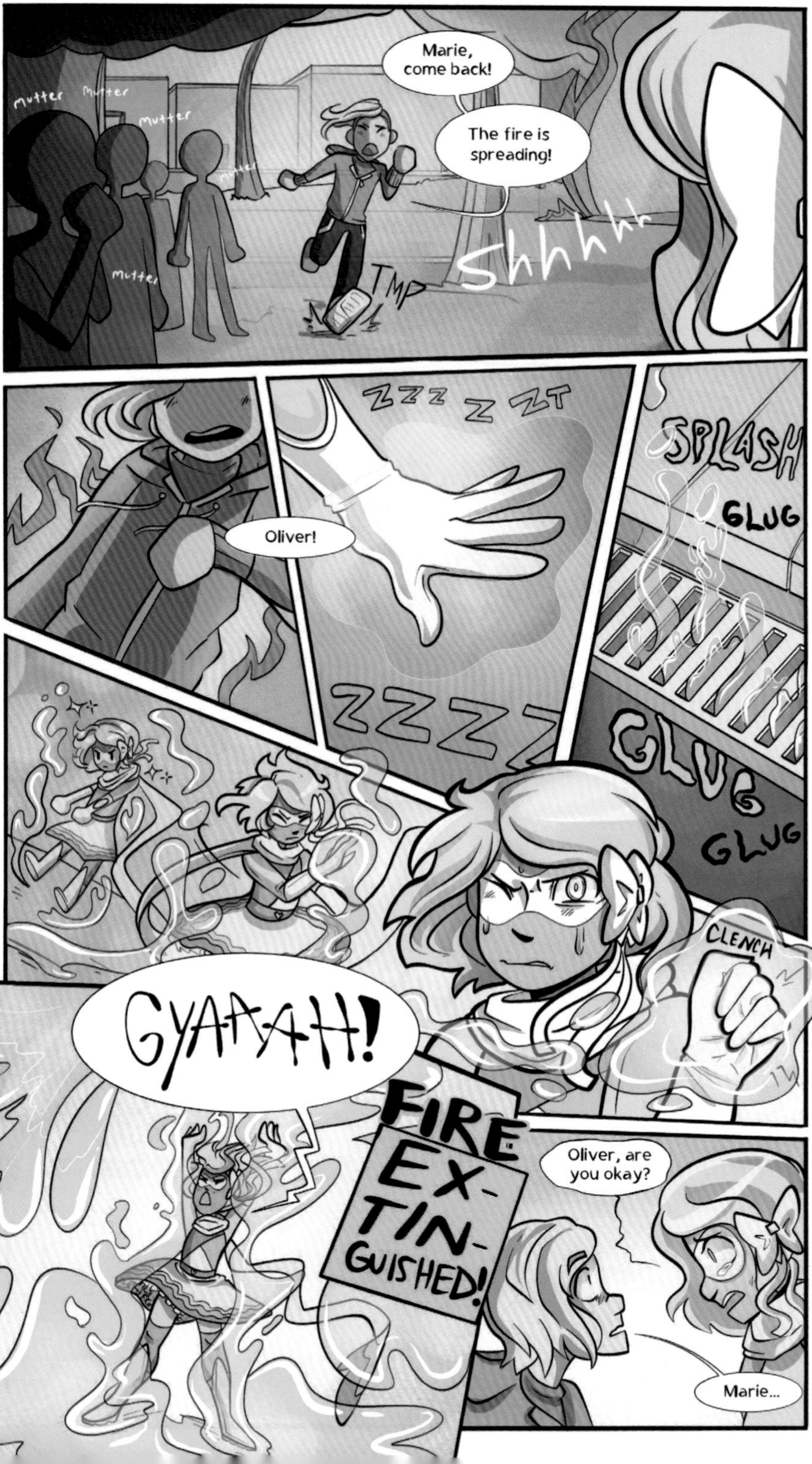

mutter mutter mutter mutter mutter
Marie, come back!
The fire is spreading!
TMP
Shhhhh
Oliver!
ZZZ Z ZT
ZZZZ
SPLASH
GLUG
GLUG
GLUG
CLENCH
GYAAAH!
FIRE EX-TIN-GUISHED!
Oliver, are you okay?
Marie...

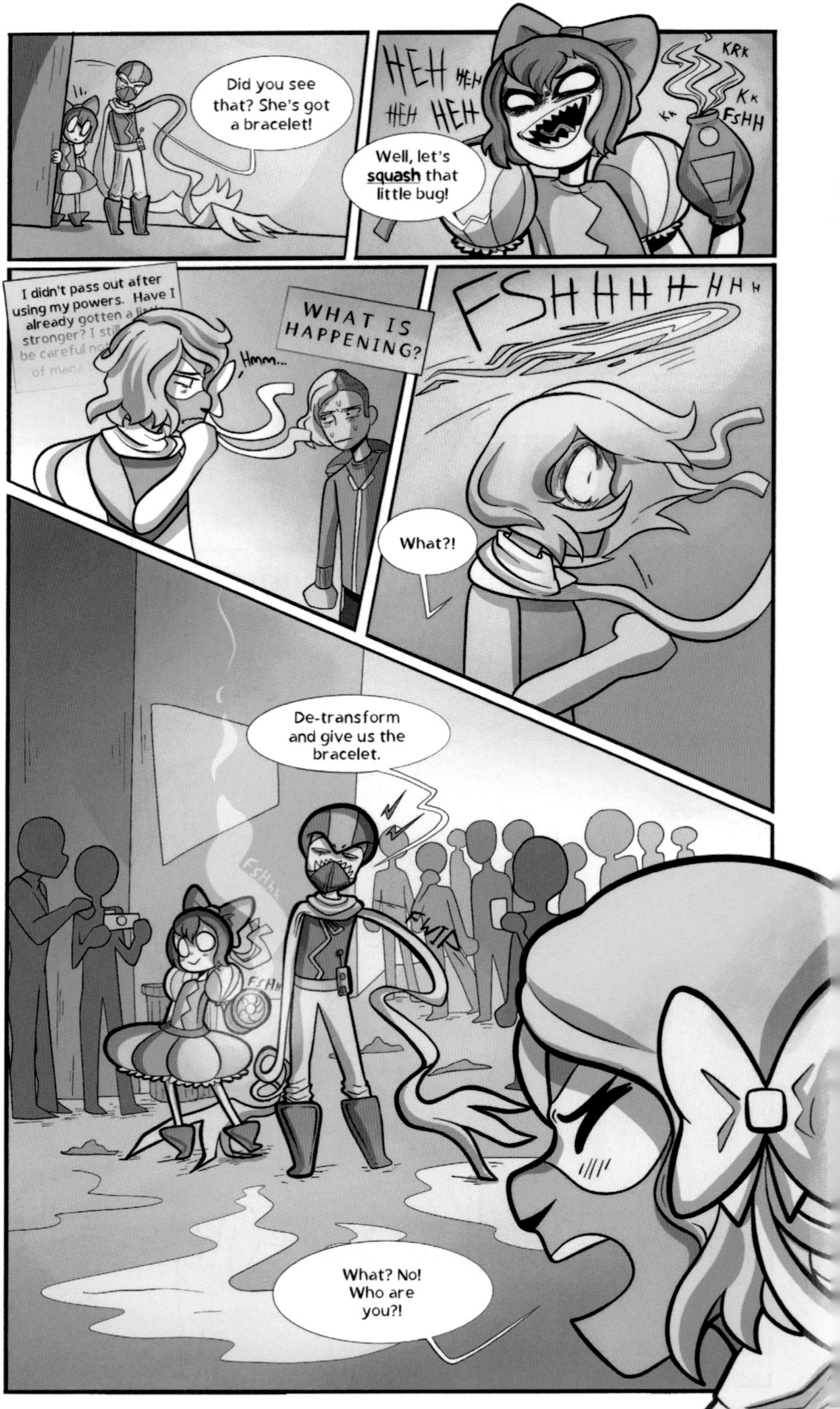
Did you see that? She's got a bracelet!
HEH HEH HEH HEH
Well, let's **squash** that little bug!
KRK K Kk FSHH
I didn't pass out after using my powers. Have I already gotten a
stronger? I still
be careful
Hmm...
WHAT IS HAPPENING?
FSHHHHHHH
What?!
De-transform and give us the bracelet.
FSHhh
FSHH
FWIP
What? No! Who are you?!

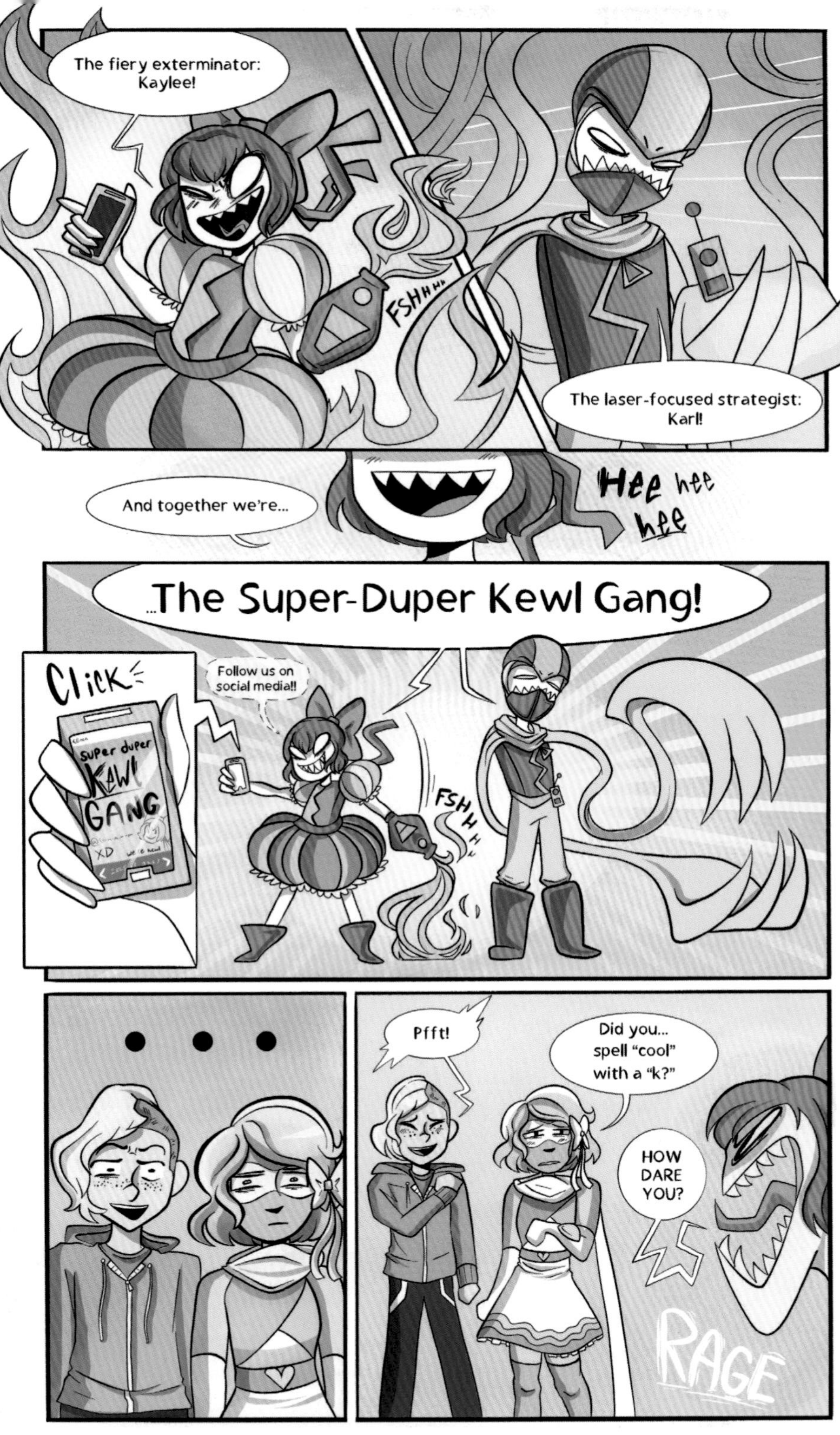
The fiery exterminator: Kaylee!
FSHHHH
The laser-focused strategist: Karl!
And together we're...
Hee hee hee
...The Super-Duper Kewl Gang!
Click
Super duper Kewl Gang
XD
Follow us on social media!!
FSHHHH
Pfft!
Did you... spell "cool" with a "k?"
HOW DARE YOU?
RAGE

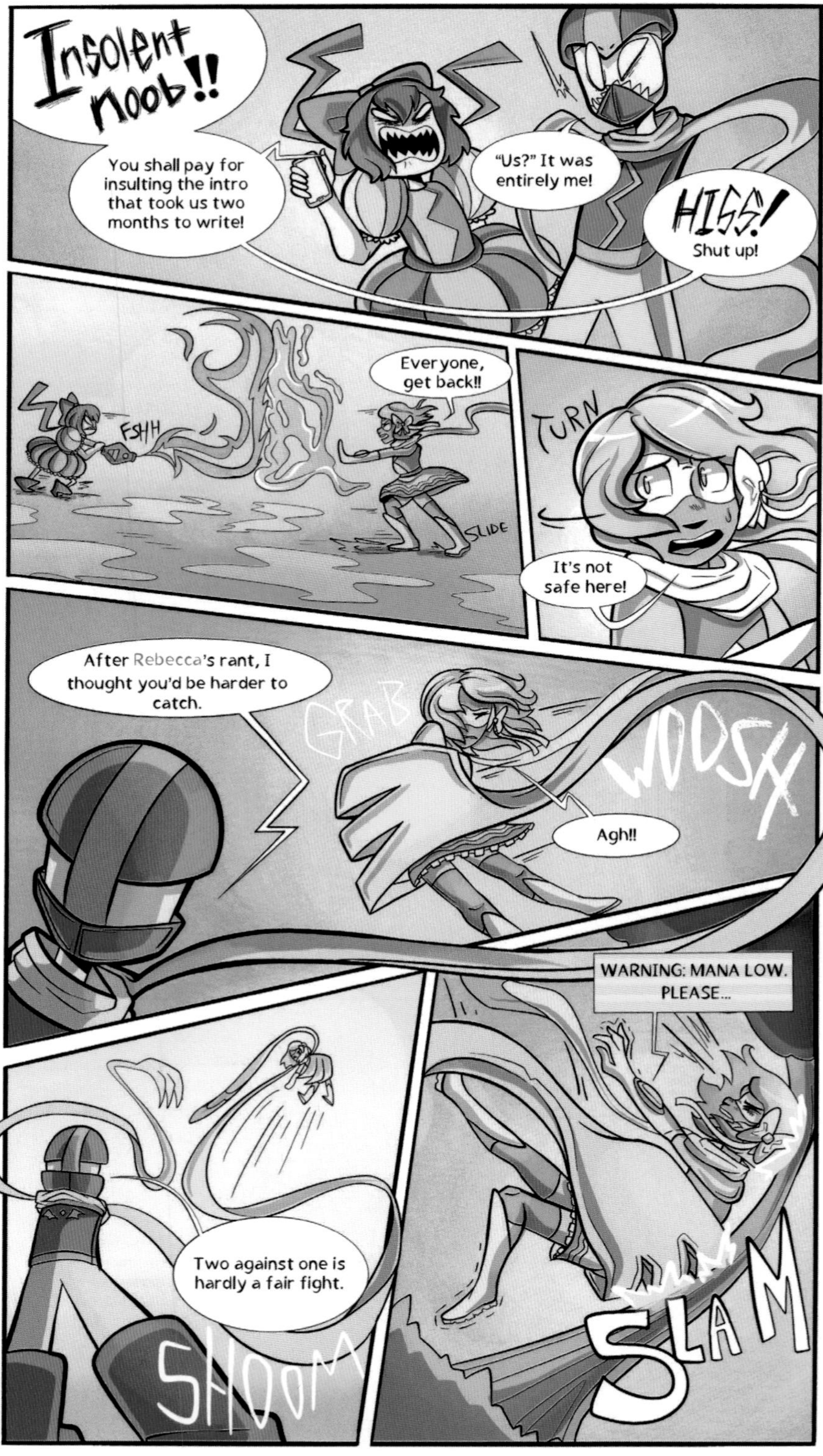
Insolent noob!!
You shall pay for insulting the intro that took us two months to write!
"Us?" It was entirely me!
HISS!
Shut up!
FSHH
Everyone, get back!!
SLIDE
TURN
It's not safe here!
After Rebecca's rant, I thought you'd be harder to catch.
GRAB
WOOSH
Agh!!
WARNING: MANA LOW. PLEASE...
Two against one is hardly a fair fight.
SHOOM
SLAM

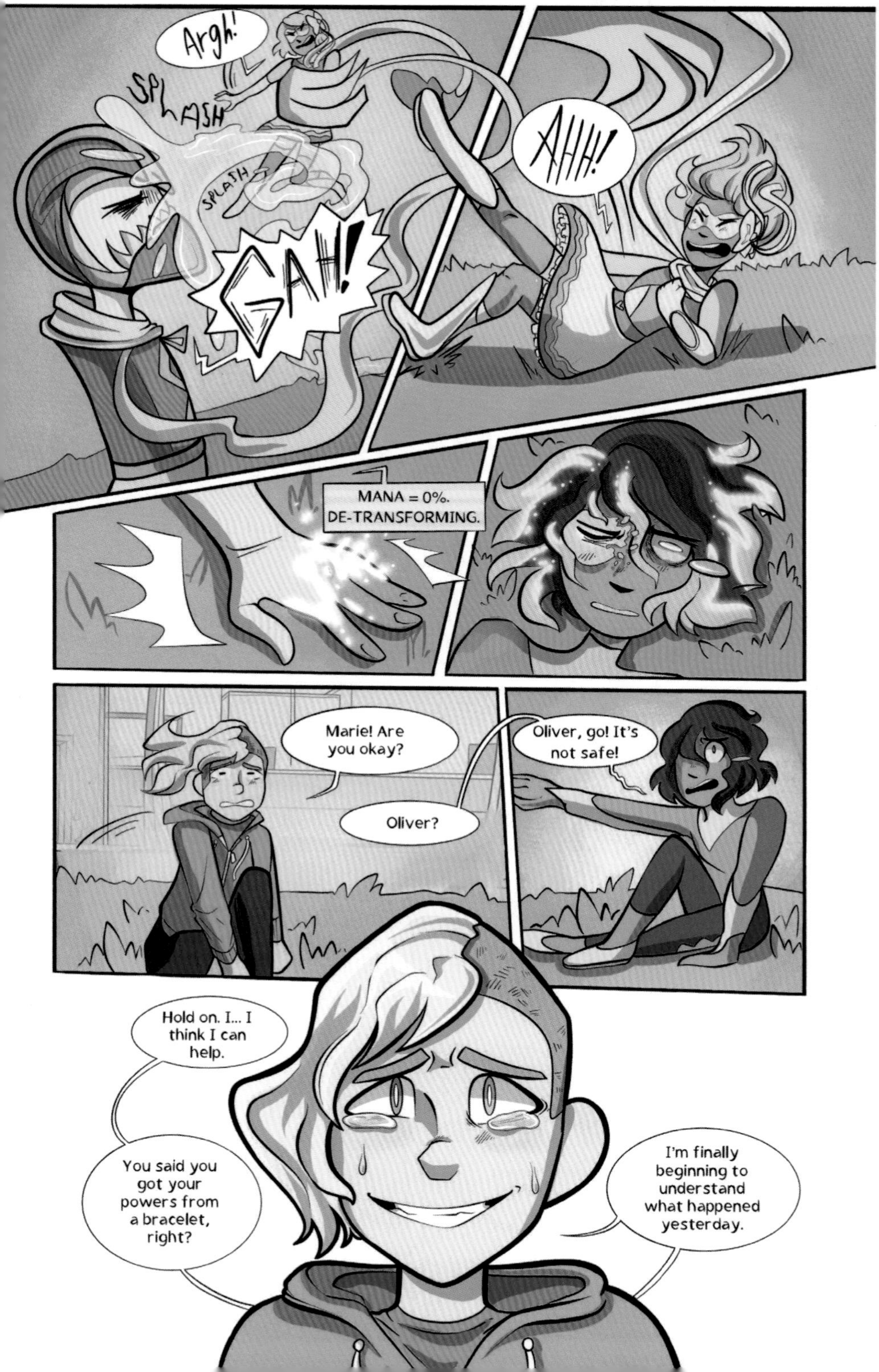
Argh!
SPLASH
SPLASH
GAH!
AHH!
MANA = 0%.
DE-TRANSFORMING.
Marie! Are you okay?
Oliver?
Oliver, go! It's not safe!
Hold on. I... I think I can help.
You said you got your powers from a bracelet, right?
I'm finally beginning to understand what happened yesterday.

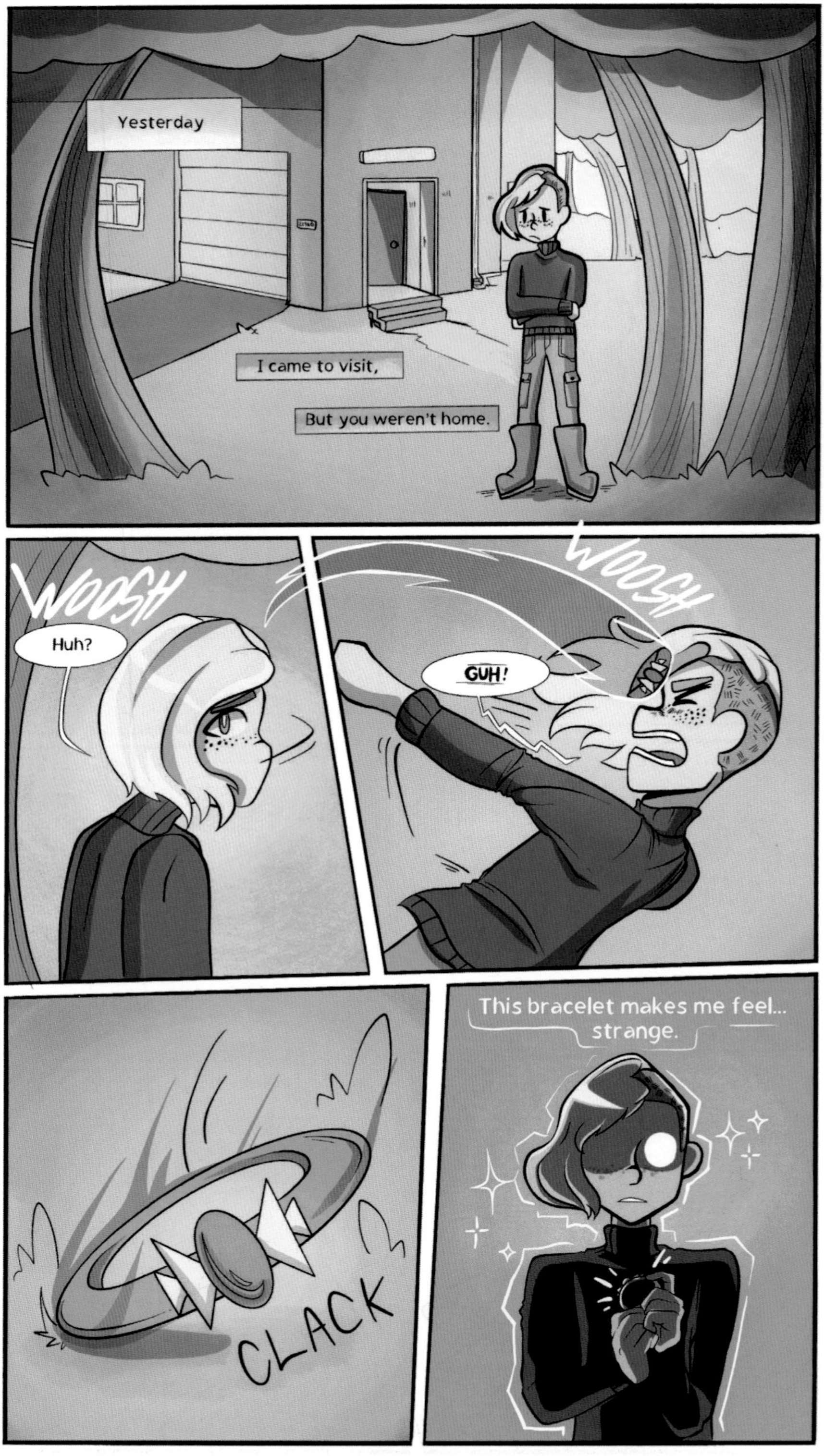
Yesterday
I came to visit,
But you weren't home.
WOOSH
Huh?
WOOSH
GUH!
CLACK
This bracelet makes me feel... strange.

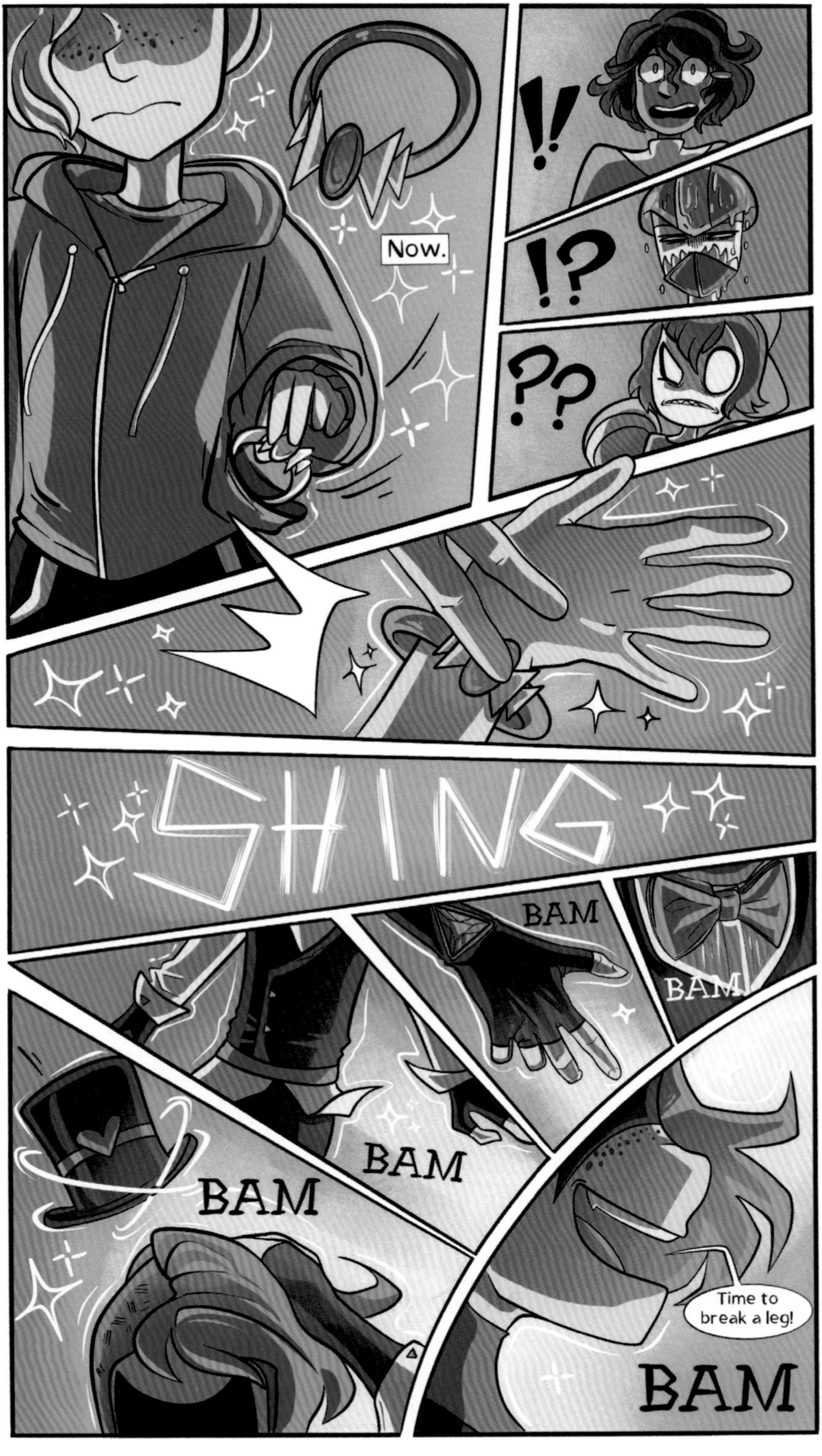
Now.
!!
!?
??
SHING
BAM
BAM
BAM
BAM
Time to break a leg!
BAM

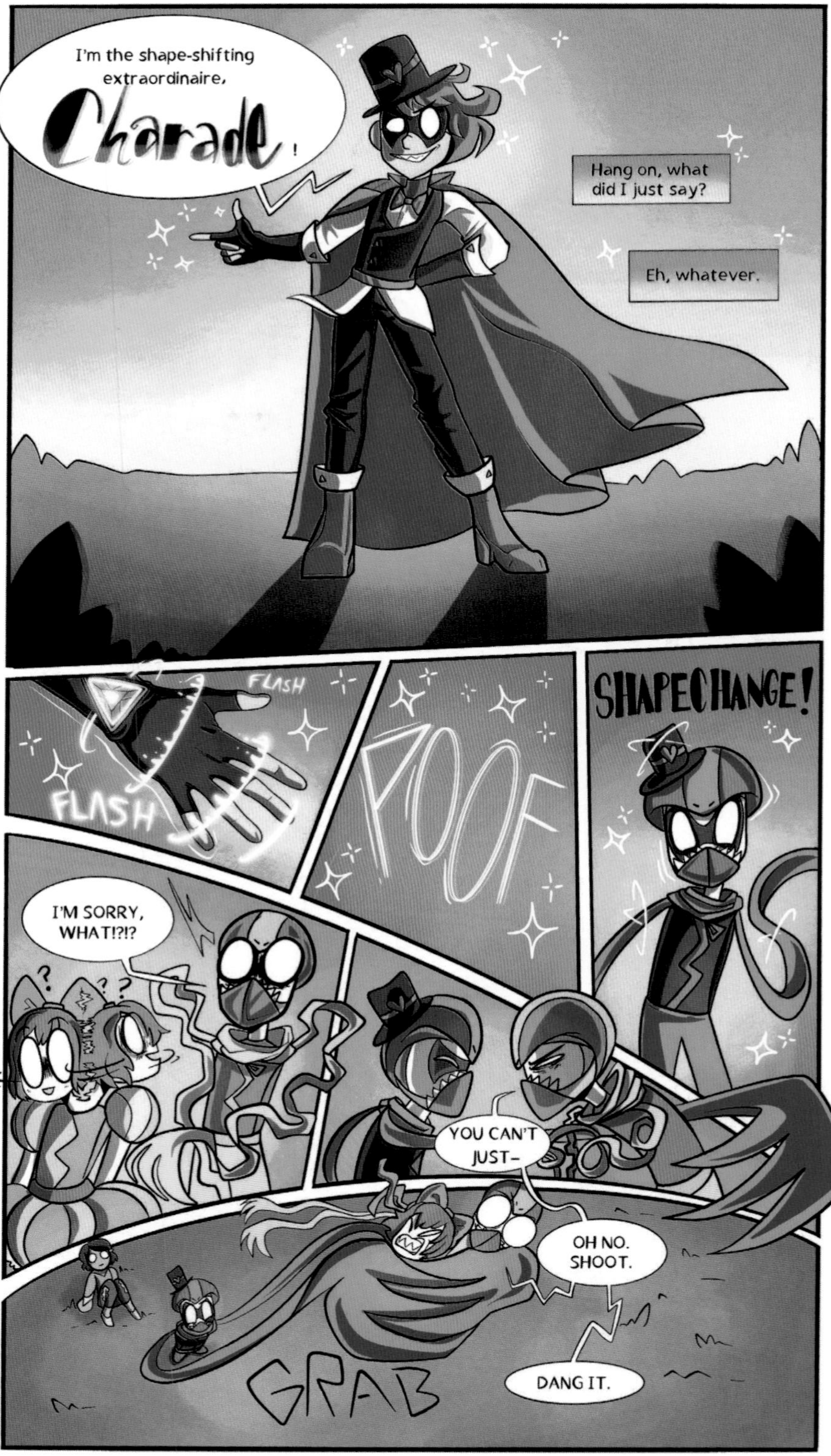

I'm the shape-shifting extraordinaire,
Charade!
Hang on, what did I just say?
Eh, whatever.
FLASH
FLASH
POOF
SHAPECHANGE!
I'M SORRY, WHAT!?!?
YOU CAN'T JUST-
OH NO. SHOOT.
DANG IT.
GRAB

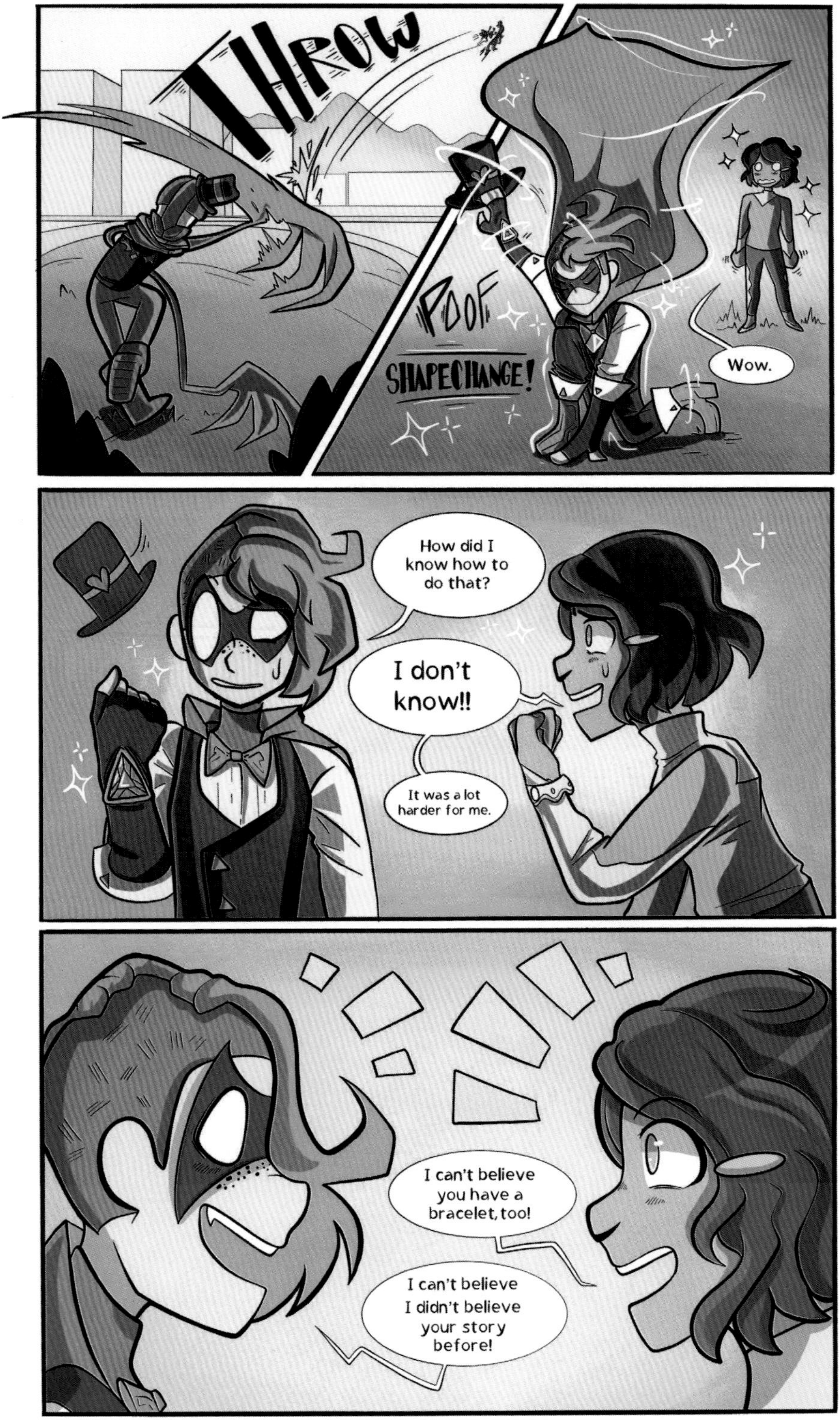
THROW
POOF
SHAPECHANGE!
Wow.
How did I know how to do that?
I don't know!!
It was a lot harder for me.
I can't believe you have a bracelet, too!
I can't believe I didn't believe your story before!

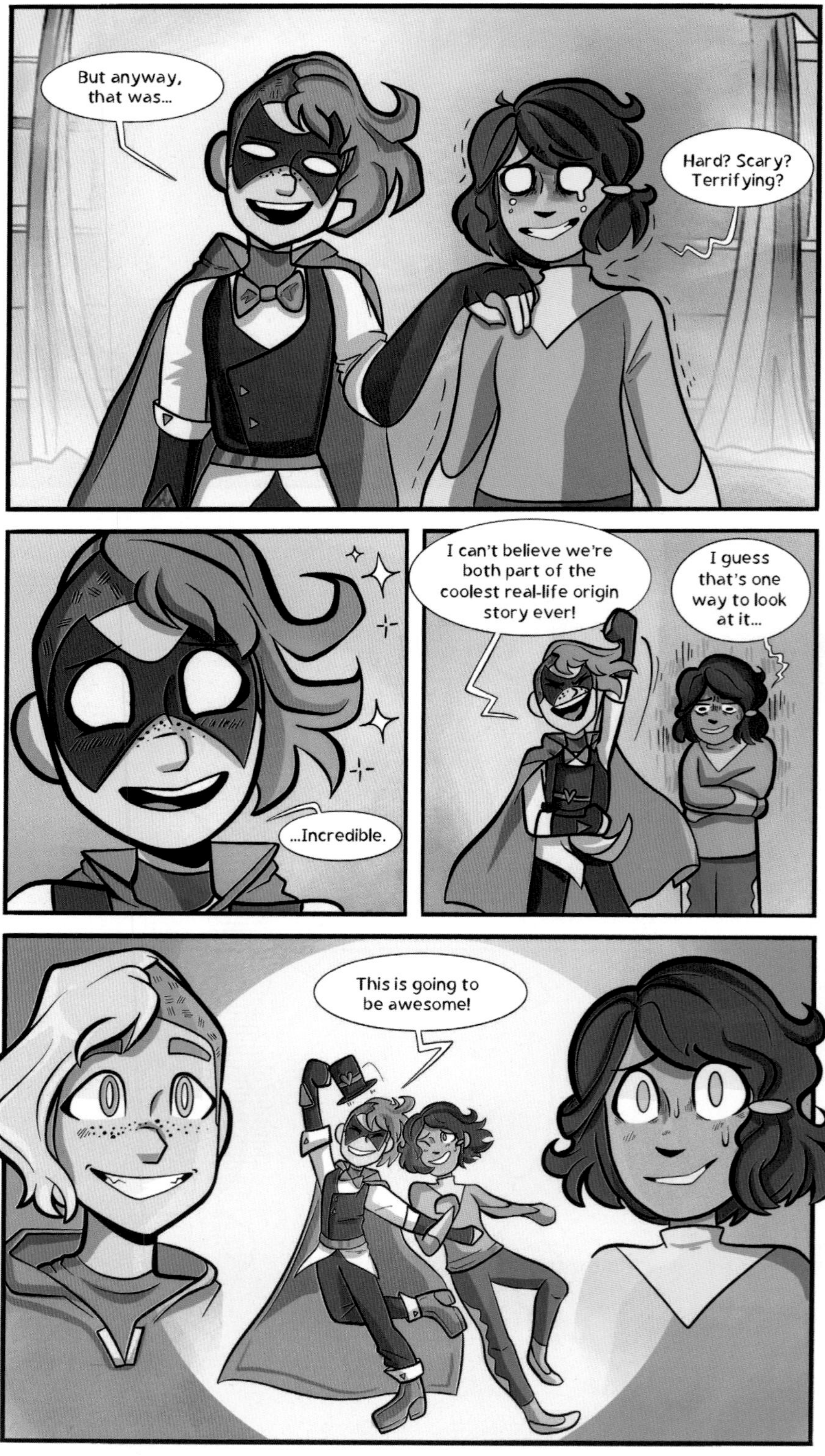
But anyway, that was...
Hard? Scary? Terrifying?
...Incredible.
I can't believe we're both part of the coolest real-life origin story ever!
I guess that's one way to look at it...
This is going to be awesome!

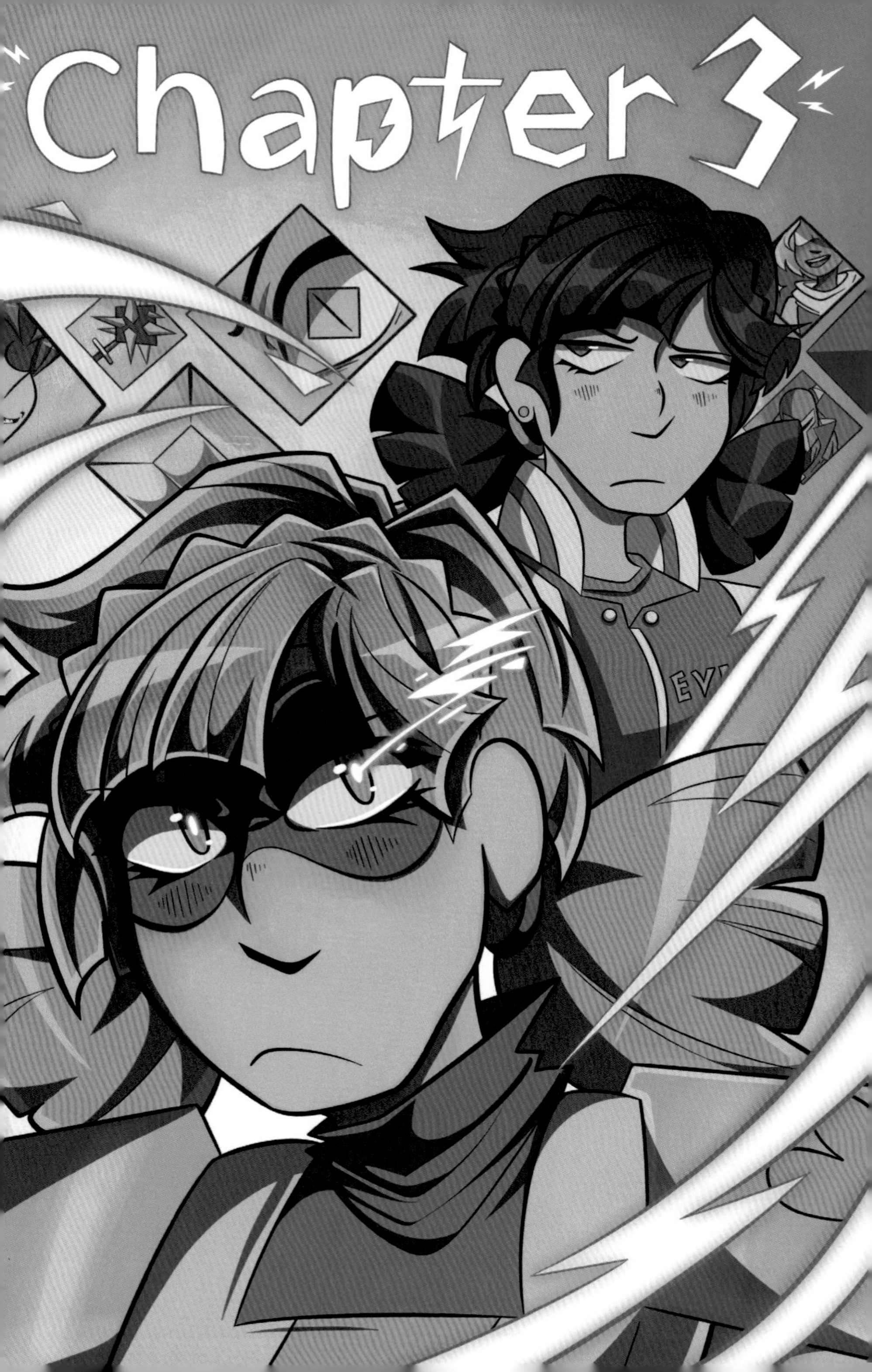
Chapter 3

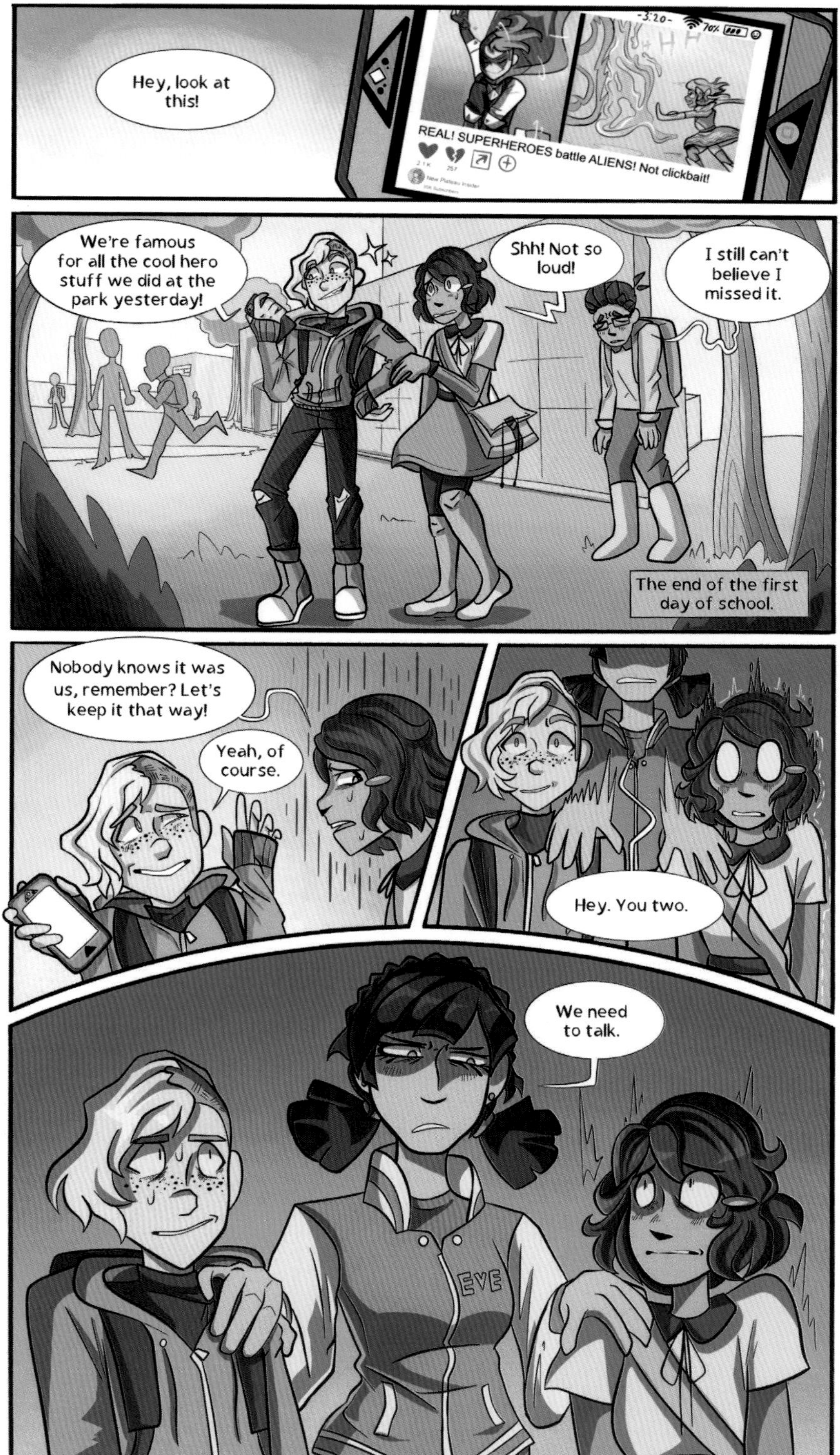
Hey, look at this!
REAL! SUPERHEROES battle ALIENS! Not clickbait!
We're famous for all the cool hero stuff we did at the park yesterday!
Shh! Not so loud!
I still can't believe I missed it.
The end of the first day of school.
Nobody knows it was us, remember? Let's keep it that way!
Yeah, of course.
Hey. You two.
We need to talk.
EVE

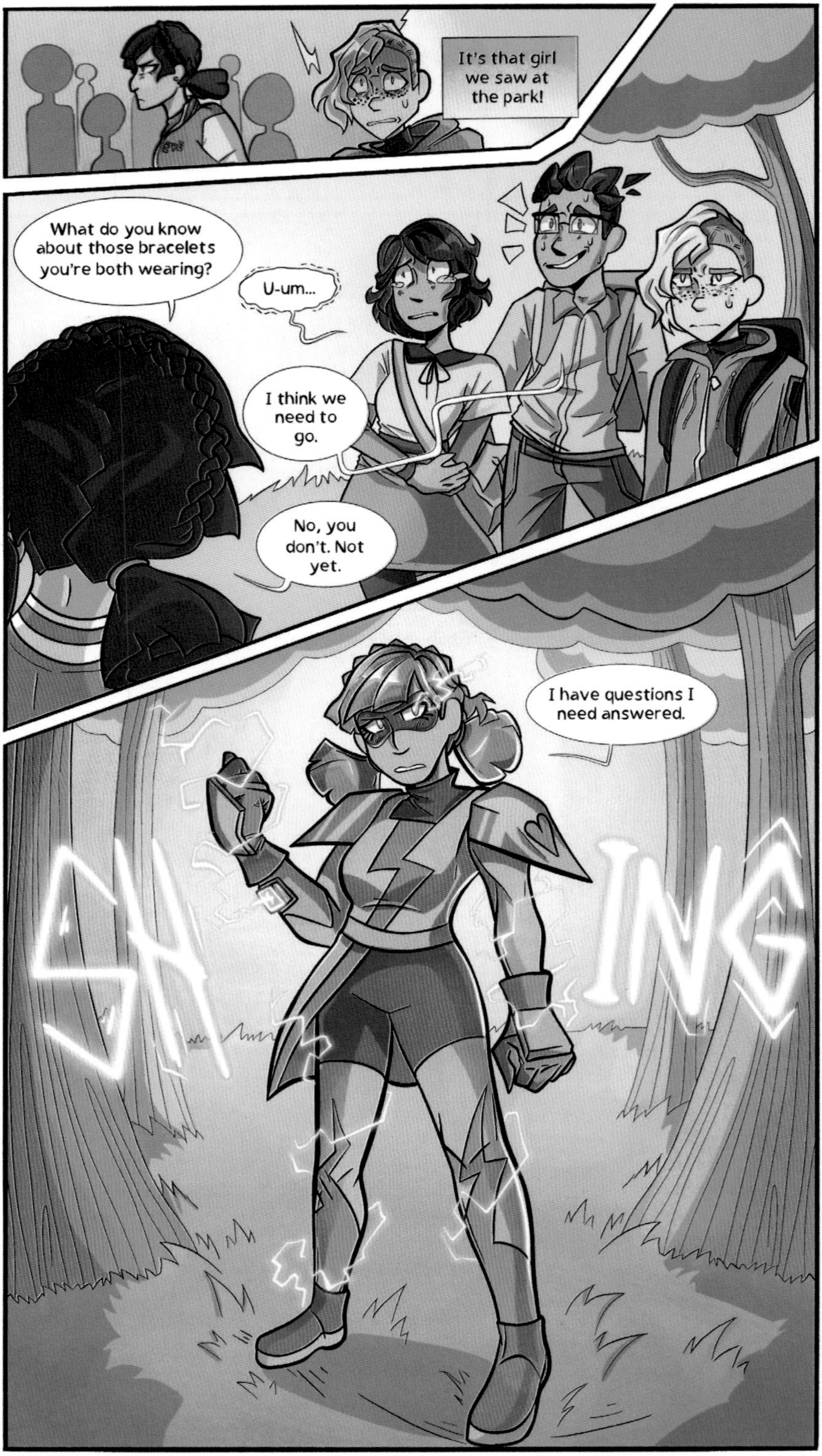
It's that girl we saw at the park!
What do you know about those bracelets you're both wearing?
U-um...
I think we need to go.
No, you don't. Not yet.
I have questions I need answered.
SHING

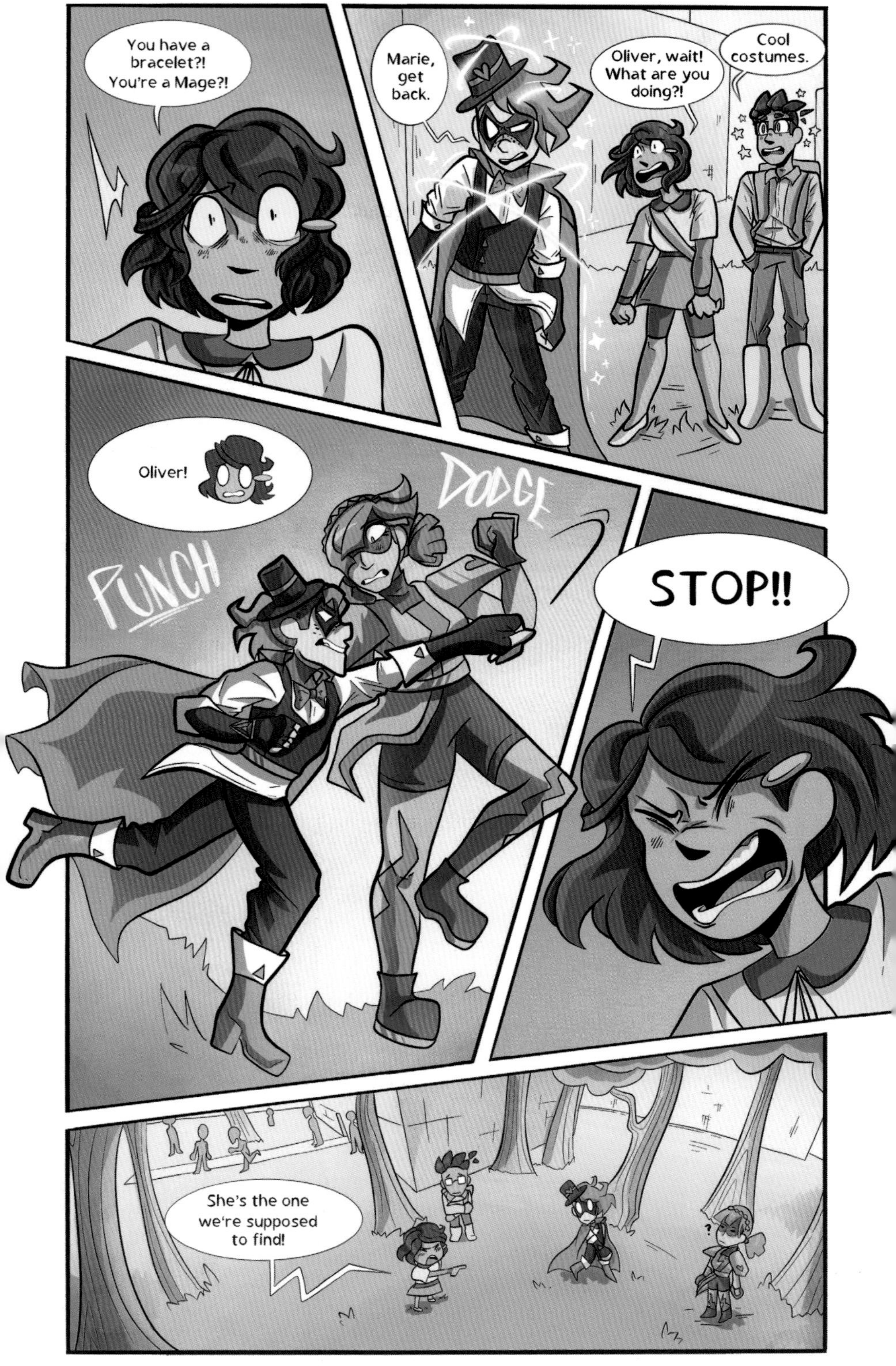
You have a bracelet?! You're a Mage?!
Marie, get back.
Oliver, wait! What are you doing?!
Cool costumes.
Oliver!
DODGE
PUNCH
STOP!!
She's the one we're supposed to find!

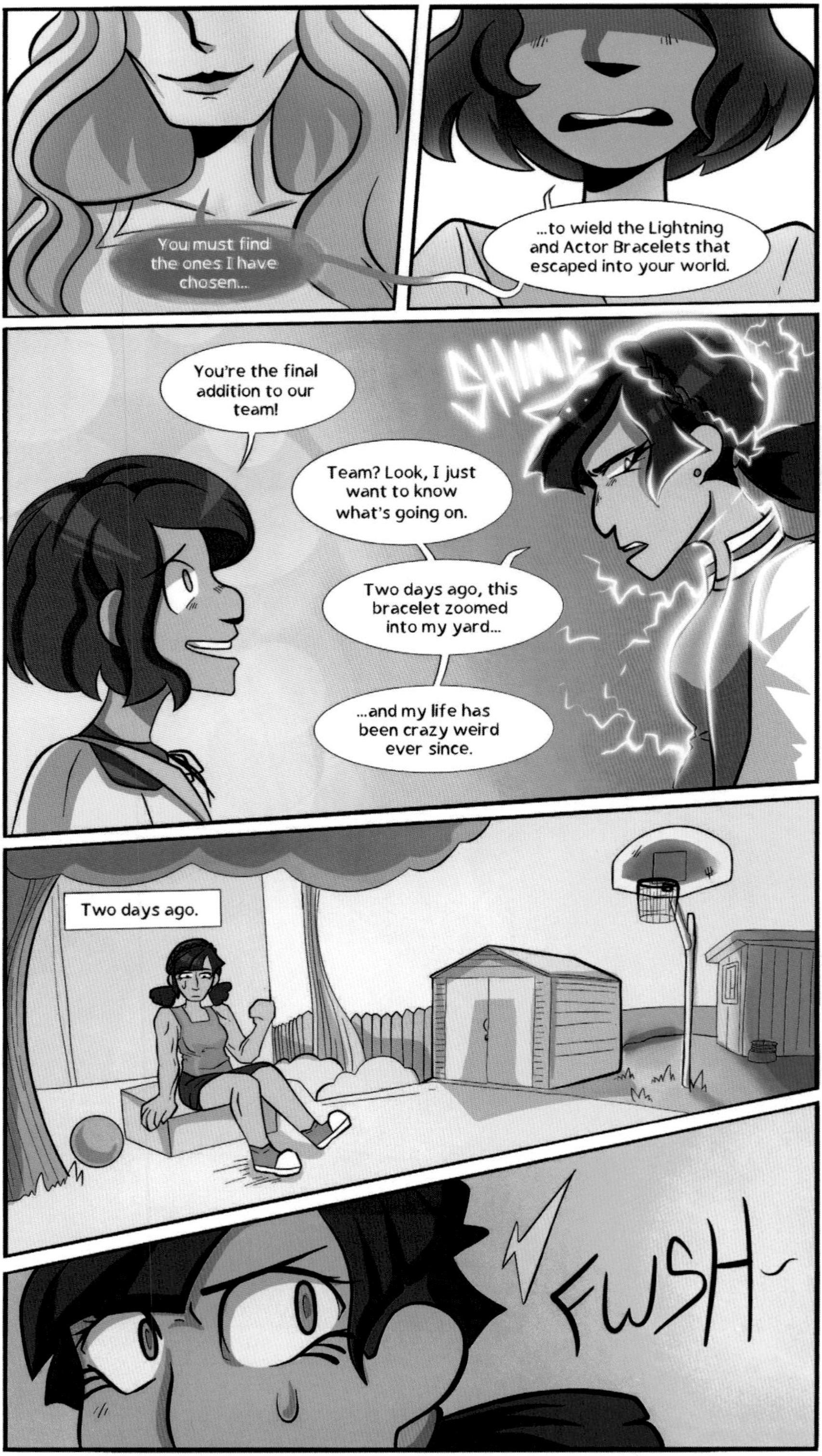

You must find the ones I have chosen...
...to wield the Lightning and Actor Bracelets that escaped into your world.
SHINE
You're the final addition to our team!
Team? Look, I just want to know what's going on.
Two days ago, this bracelet zoomed into my yard...
...and my life has been crazy weird ever since.
Two days ago.
FWSH

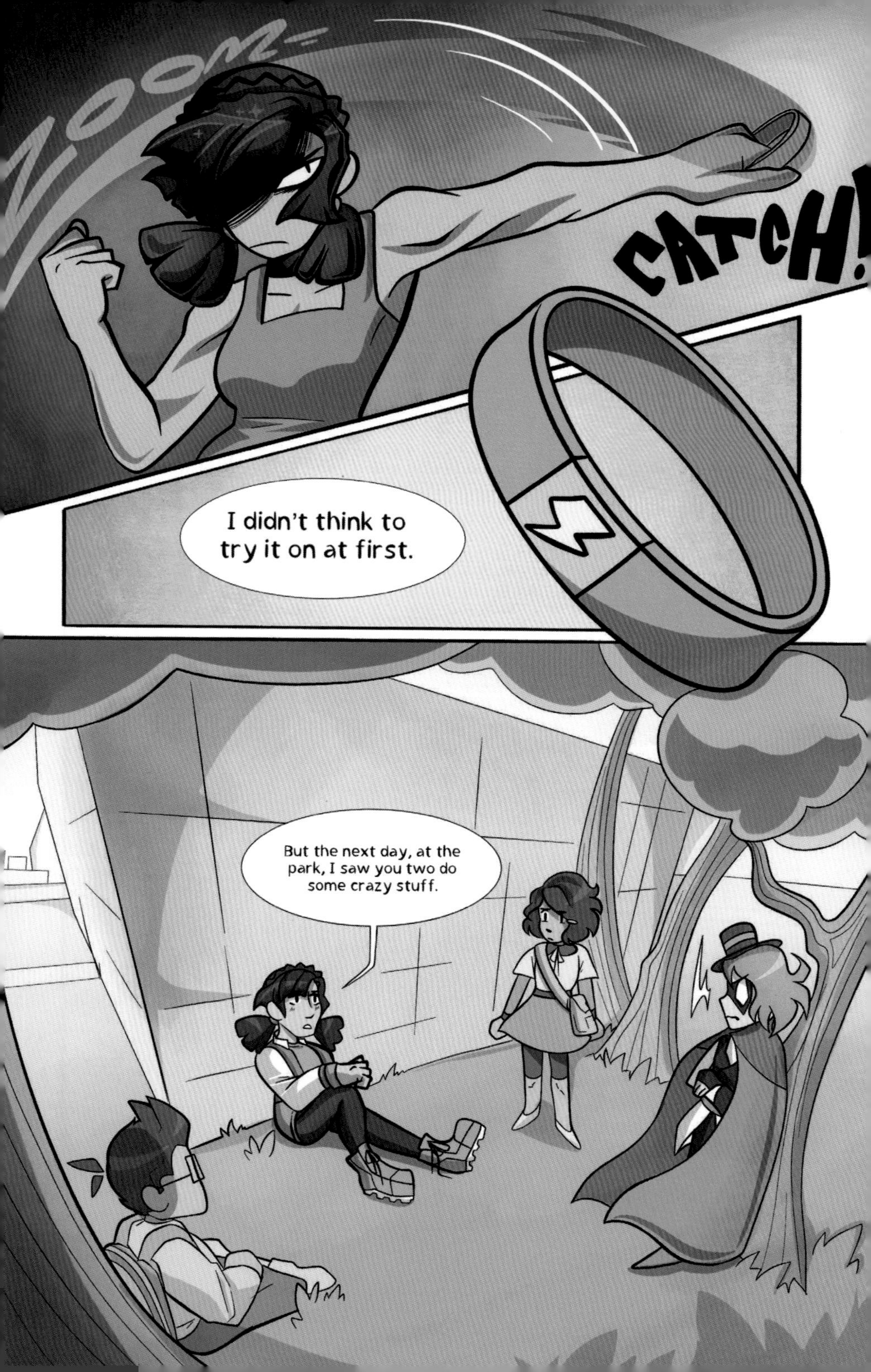
ZOOM
CATCH!
I didn't think to try it on at first.
But the next day, at the park, I saw you two do some crazy stuff.

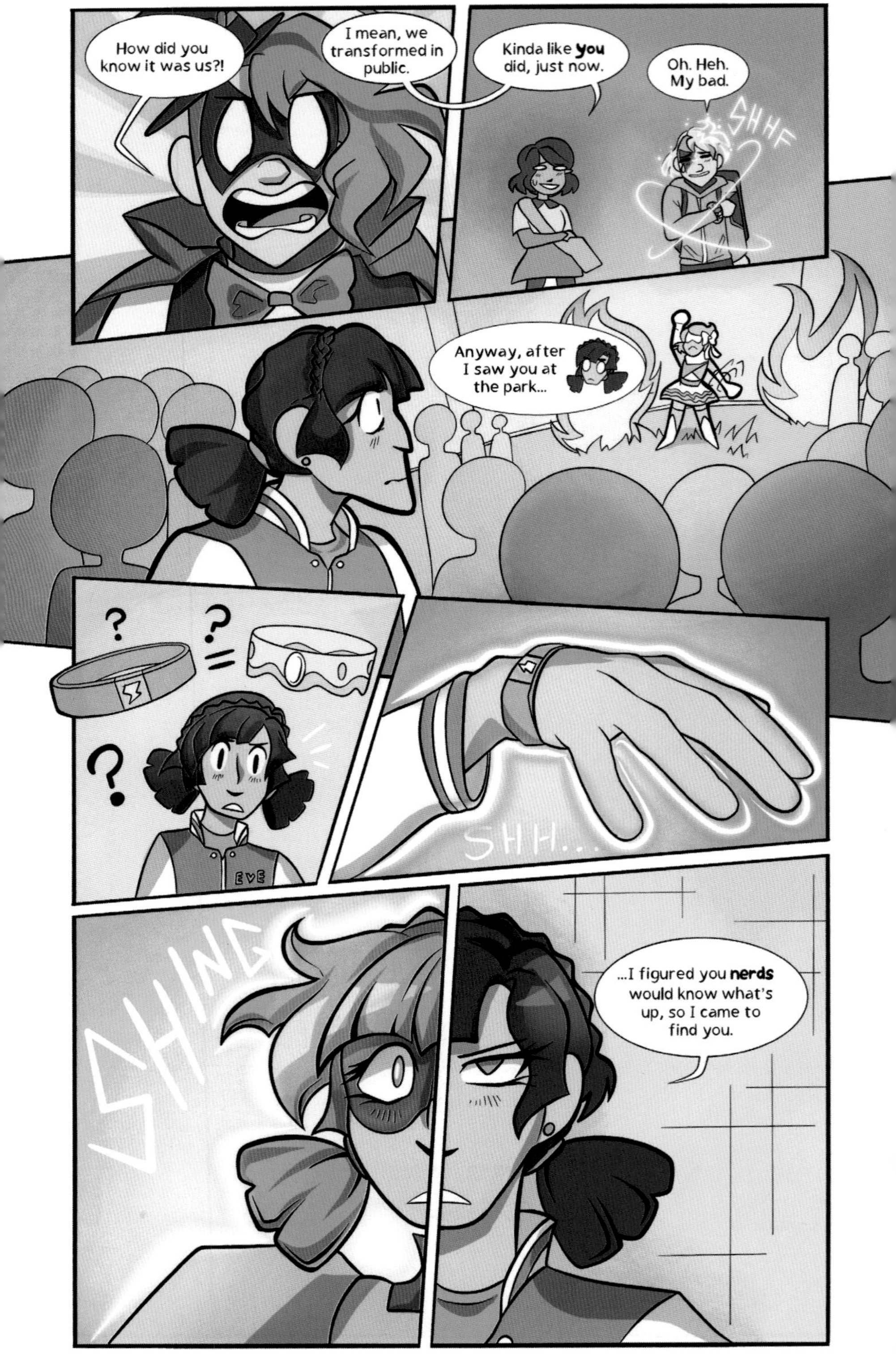
How did you know it was us?!
I mean, we transformed in public.
Kinda like **you** did, just now.
Oh. Heh. My bad.
SHHF
Anyway, after I saw you at the park...
SHH...
EVE
SHING
...I figured you **nerds** would know what's up, so I came to find you.

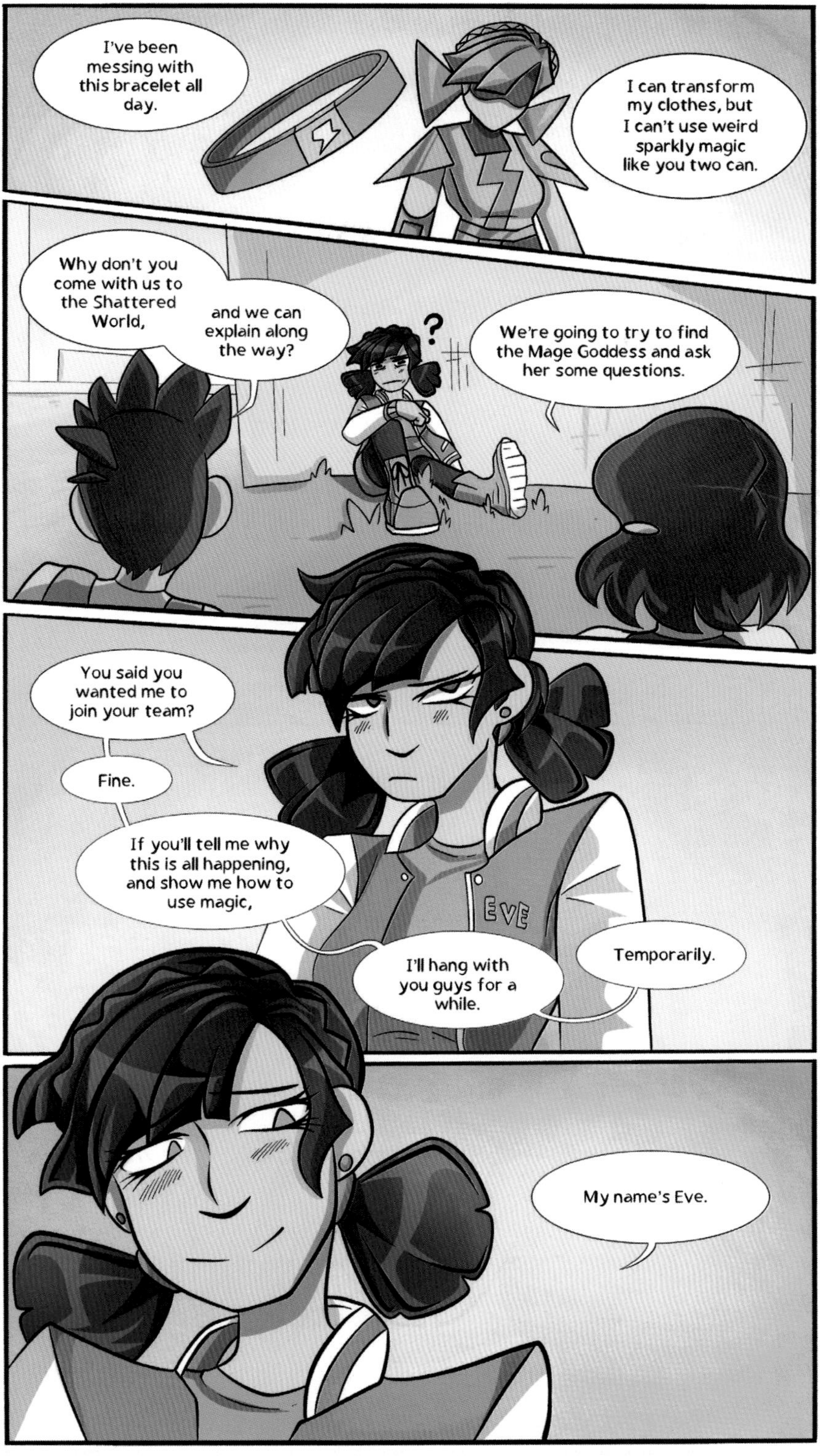
I've been messing with this bracelet all day.
I can transform my clothes, but I can't use weird sparkly magic like you two can.
Why don't you come with us to the Shattered World,
and we can explain along the way?
We're going to try to find the Mage Goddess and ask her some questions.
?
You said you wanted me to join your team?
Fine.
If you'll tell me why this is all happening, and show me how to use magic,
I'll hang with you guys for a while.
Temporarily.
EVE
My name's Eve.

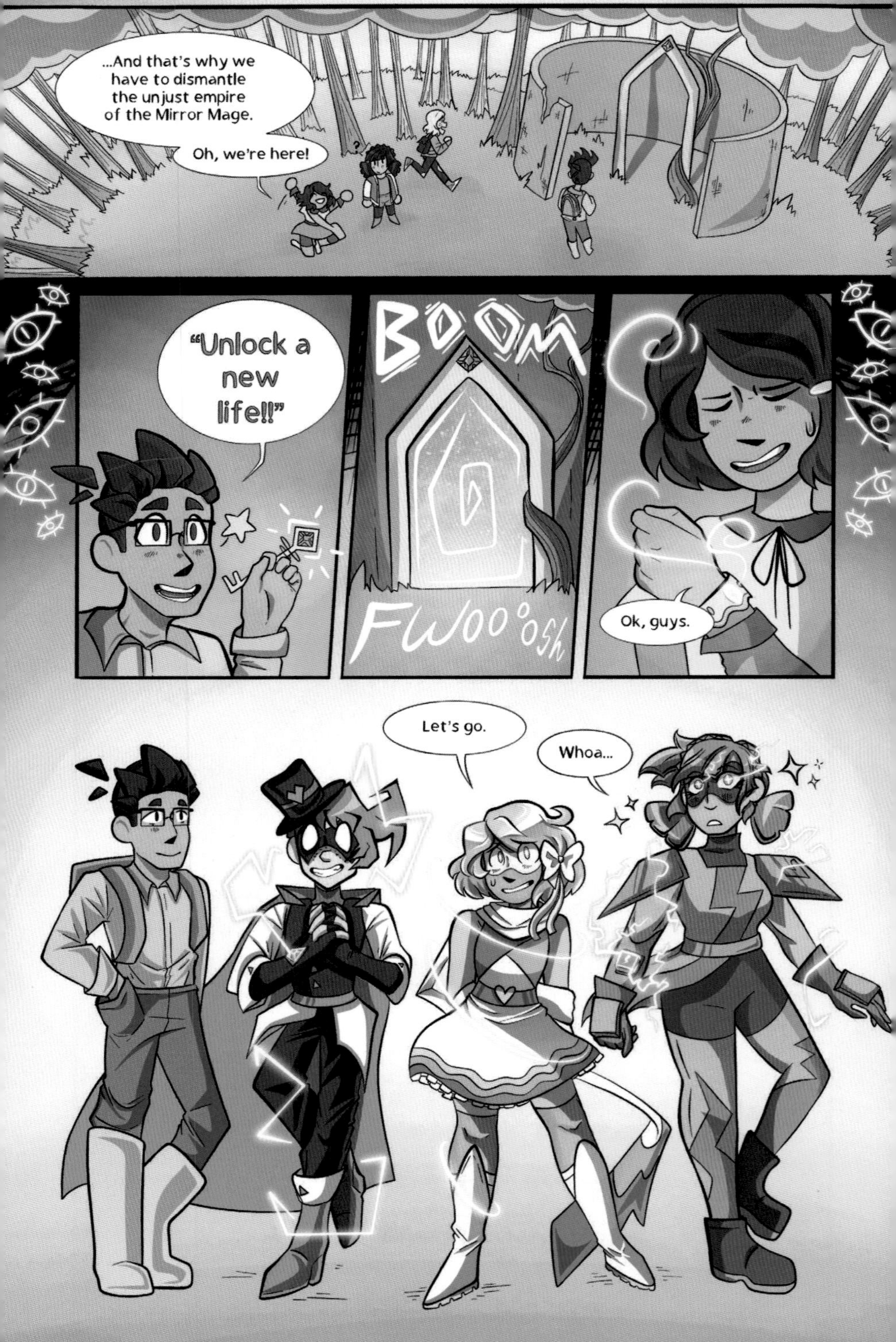
...And that's why we have to dismantle the unjust empire of the Mirror Mage.
Oh, we're here!
"Unlock a new life!!"
BOOM
FWOOoOSh
Ok, guys.
Let's go.
Whoa...

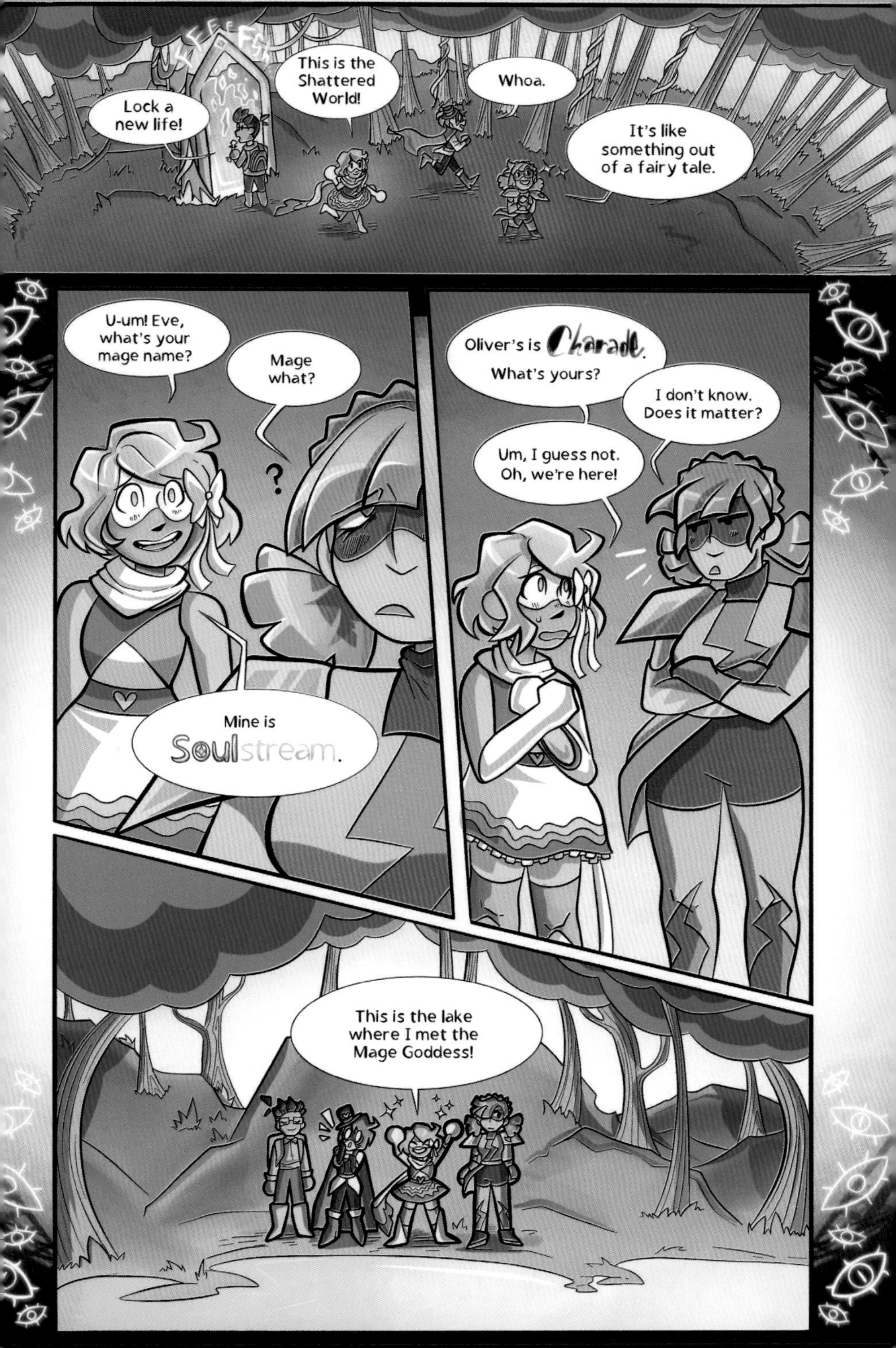

FFFFFSH
Lock a new life!
This is the Shattered World!
Whoa.
It's like something out of a fairy tale.
U-um! Eve, what's your mage name?
Mage what?
?
Mine is Soulstream.
Oliver's is Charade. What's yours?
I don't know. Does it matter?
Um, I guess not. Oh, we're here!
This is the lake where I met the Mage Goddess!

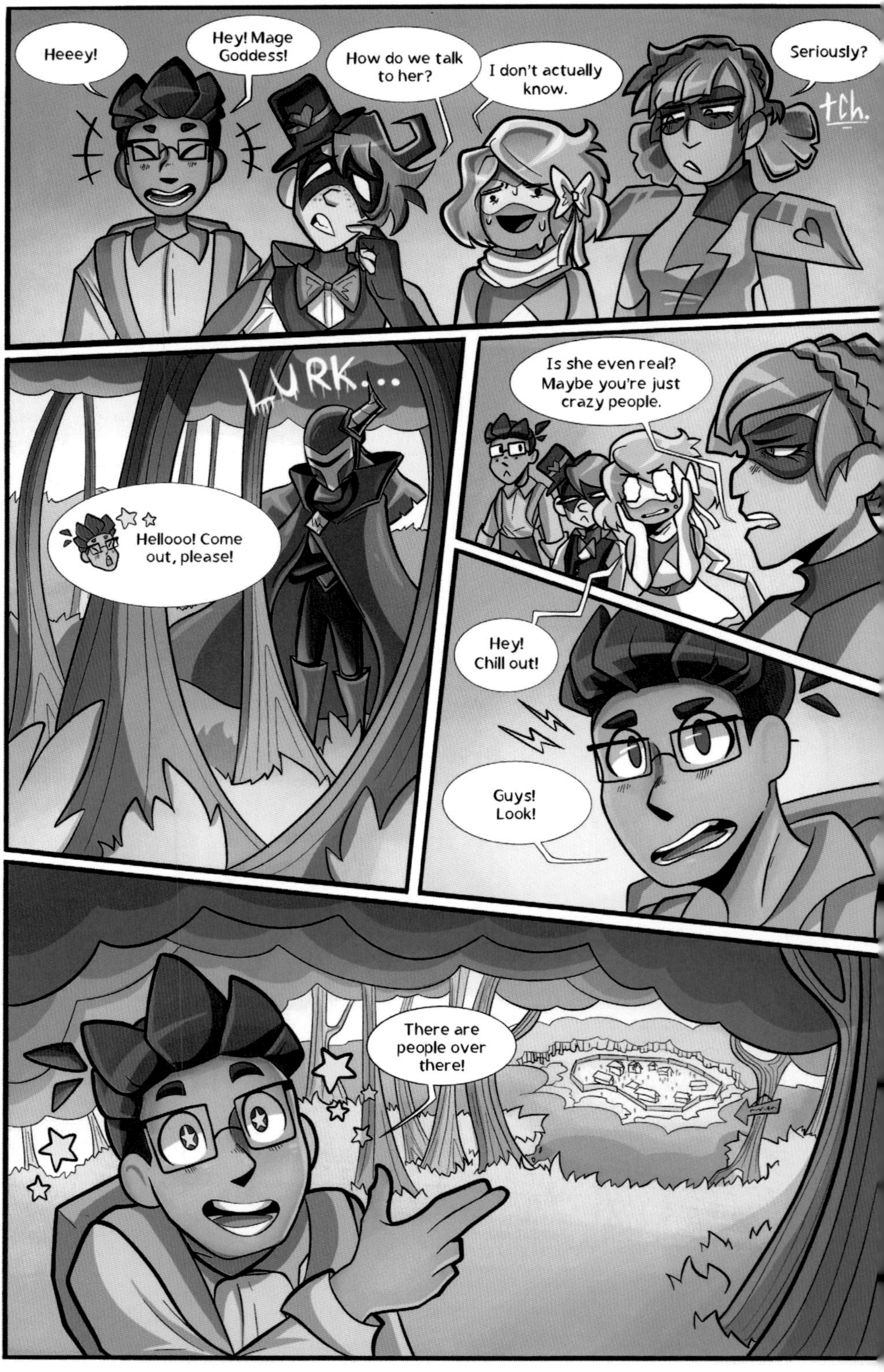
Heeey!
Hey! Mage Goddess!
How do we talk to her?
I don't actually know.
Seriously?
tch.
LURK...
Hellooo! Come out, please!
Is she even real? Maybe you're just crazy people.
Hey! Chill out!
Guys! Look!
There are people over there!

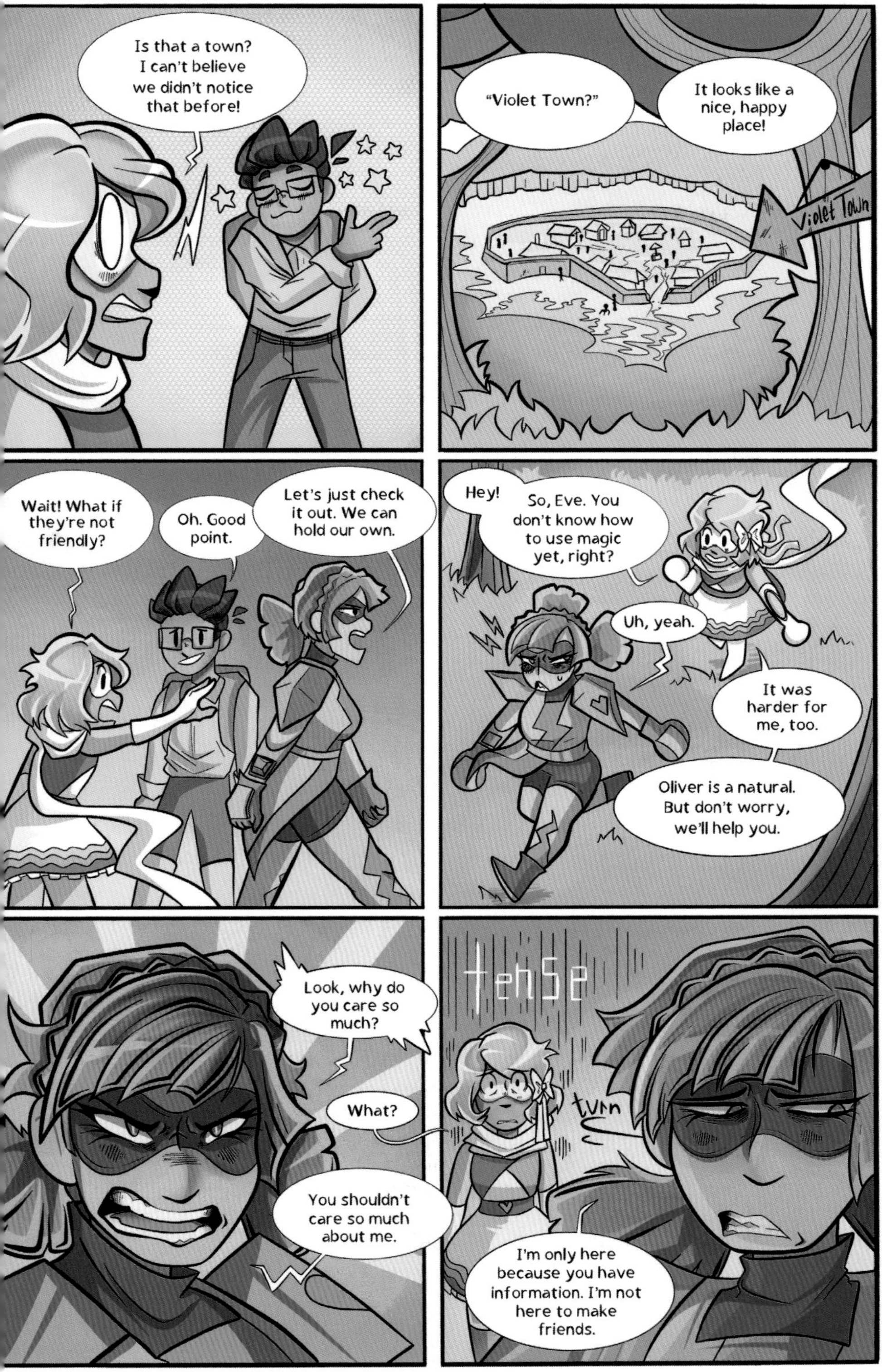
Is that a town? I can't believe we didn't notice that before!
"Violet Town?"
It looks like a nice, happy place!
Violet Town
Wait! What if they're not friendly?
Oh. Good point.
Let's just check it out. We can hold our own.
Hey!
So, Eve. You don't know how to use magic yet, right?
Uh, yeah.
It was harder for me, too.
Oliver is a natural. But don't worry, we'll help you.
Look, why do you care so much?
What?
You shouldn't care so much about me.
tense
turn
I'm only here because you have information. I'm not here to make friends.

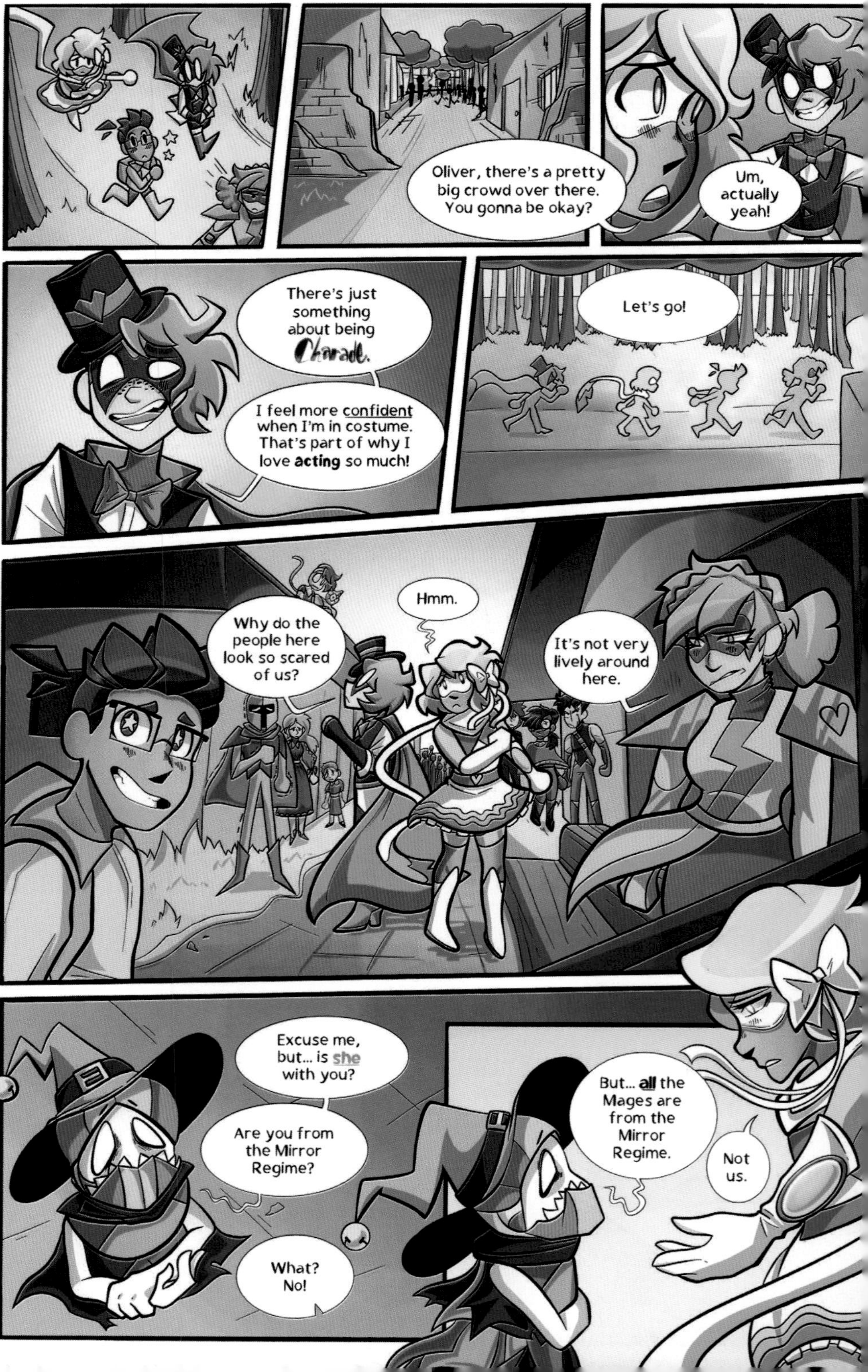

Oliver, there's a pretty big crowd over there. You gonna be okay?
Um, actually yeah!
There's just something about being Charade.
I feel more confident when I'm in costume. That's part of why I love acting so much!
Let's go!
Why do the people here look so scared of us?
Hmm.
It's not very lively around here.
Excuse me, but... is she with you?
Are you from the Mirror Regime?
What? No!
But... all the Mages are from the Mirror Regime.
Not us.

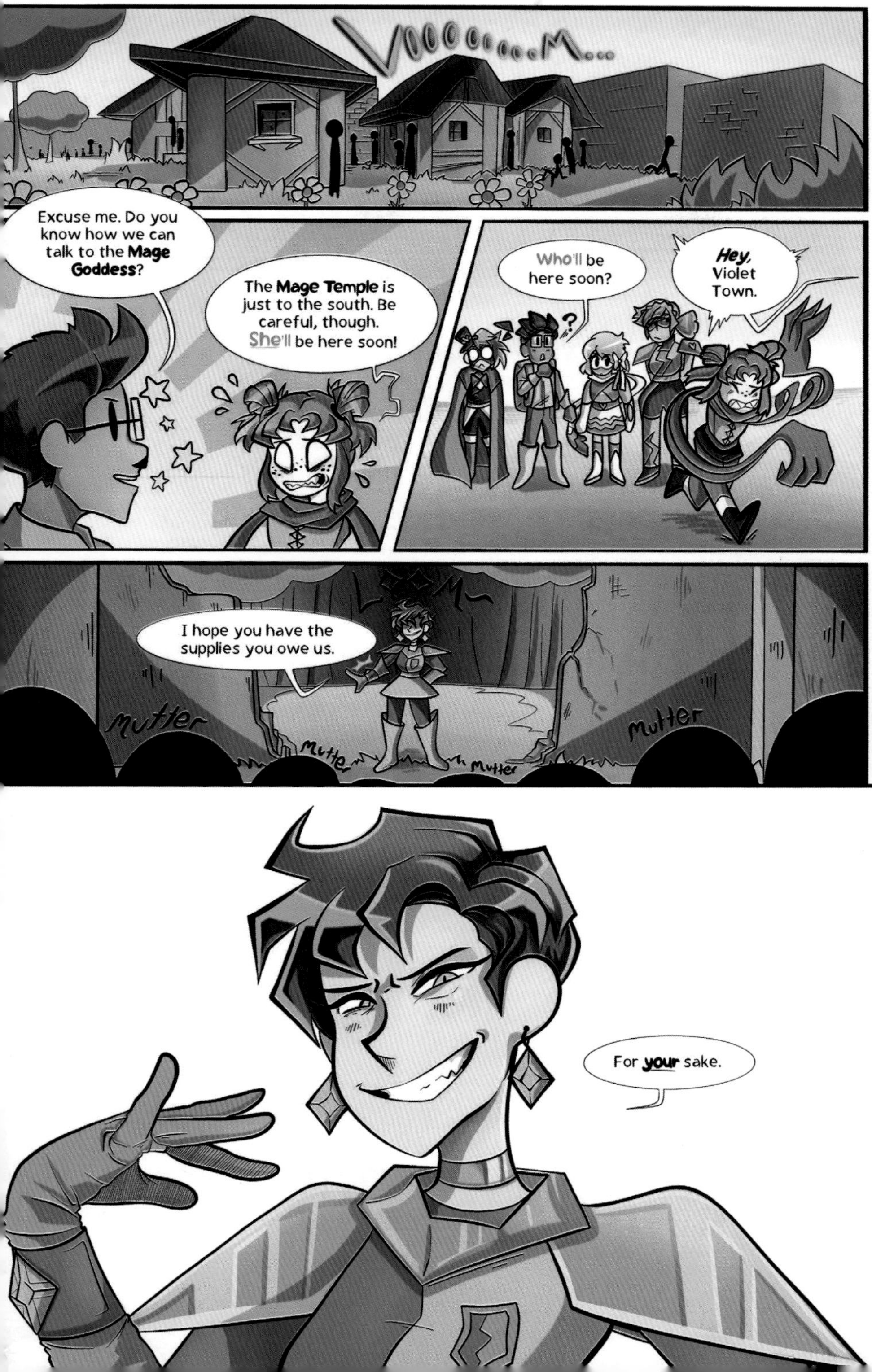
VOOOooo...M...
Excuse me. Do you know how we can talk to the **Mage Goddess**?
The **Mage Temple** is just to the south. Be careful, though. She'll be here soon!
Who'll be here soon?
?
Hey, Violet Town.
I hope you have the supplies you owe us.
mutter
mutter
mutter
mutter
For **your** sake.

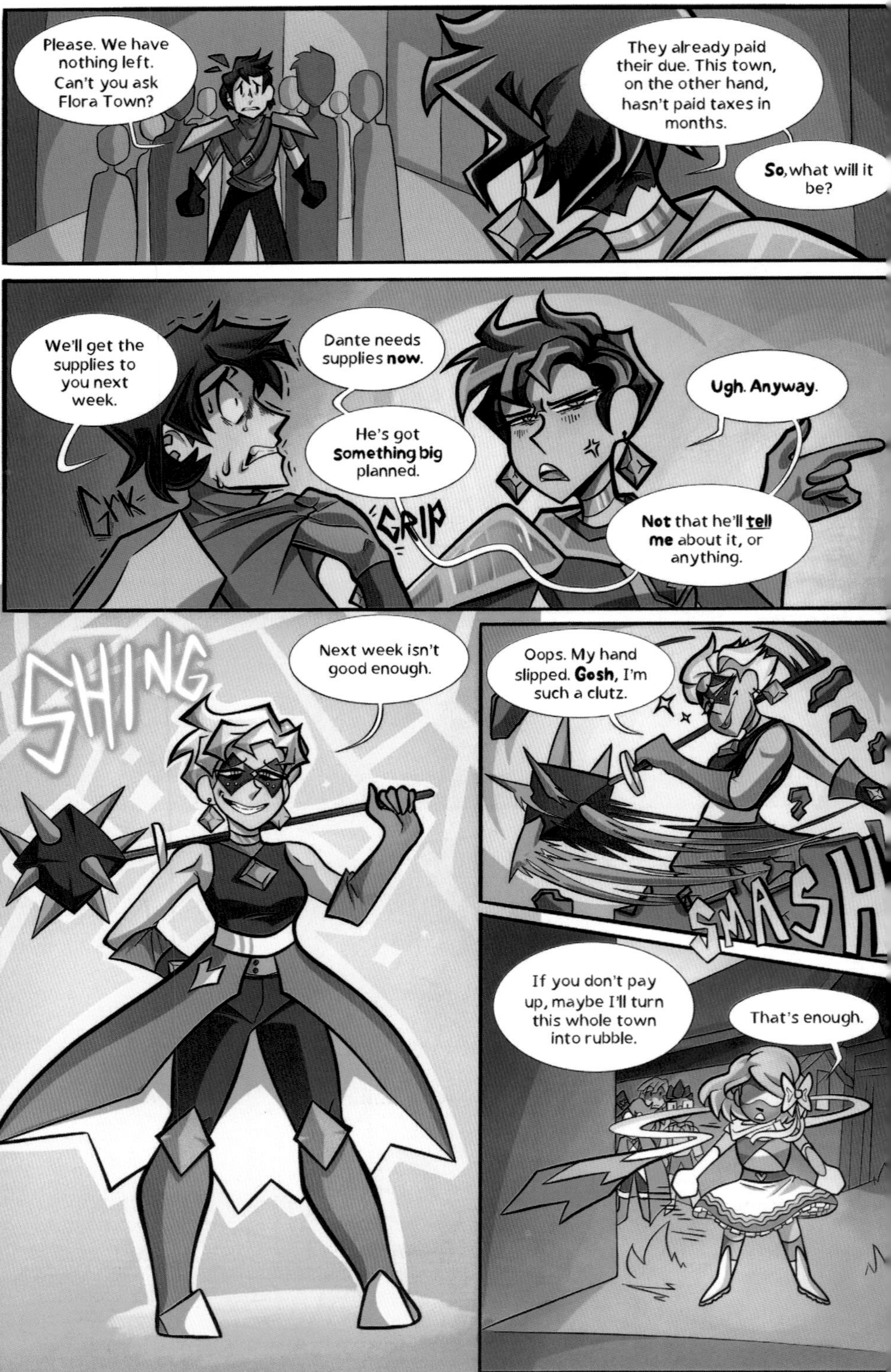
Please. We have nothing left. Can't you ask Flora Town?
They already paid their due. This town, on the other hand, hasn't paid taxes in months.
So, what will it be?
GRK
We'll get the supplies to you next week.
Dante needs supplies now.
He's got something big planned.
GRIP
Ugh. Anyway.
Not that he'll tell me about it, or anything.
SHING
Next week isn't good enough.
Oops. My hand slipped. Gosh, I'm such a clutz.
SMASH
If you don't pay up, maybe I'll turn this whole town into rubble.
That's enough.

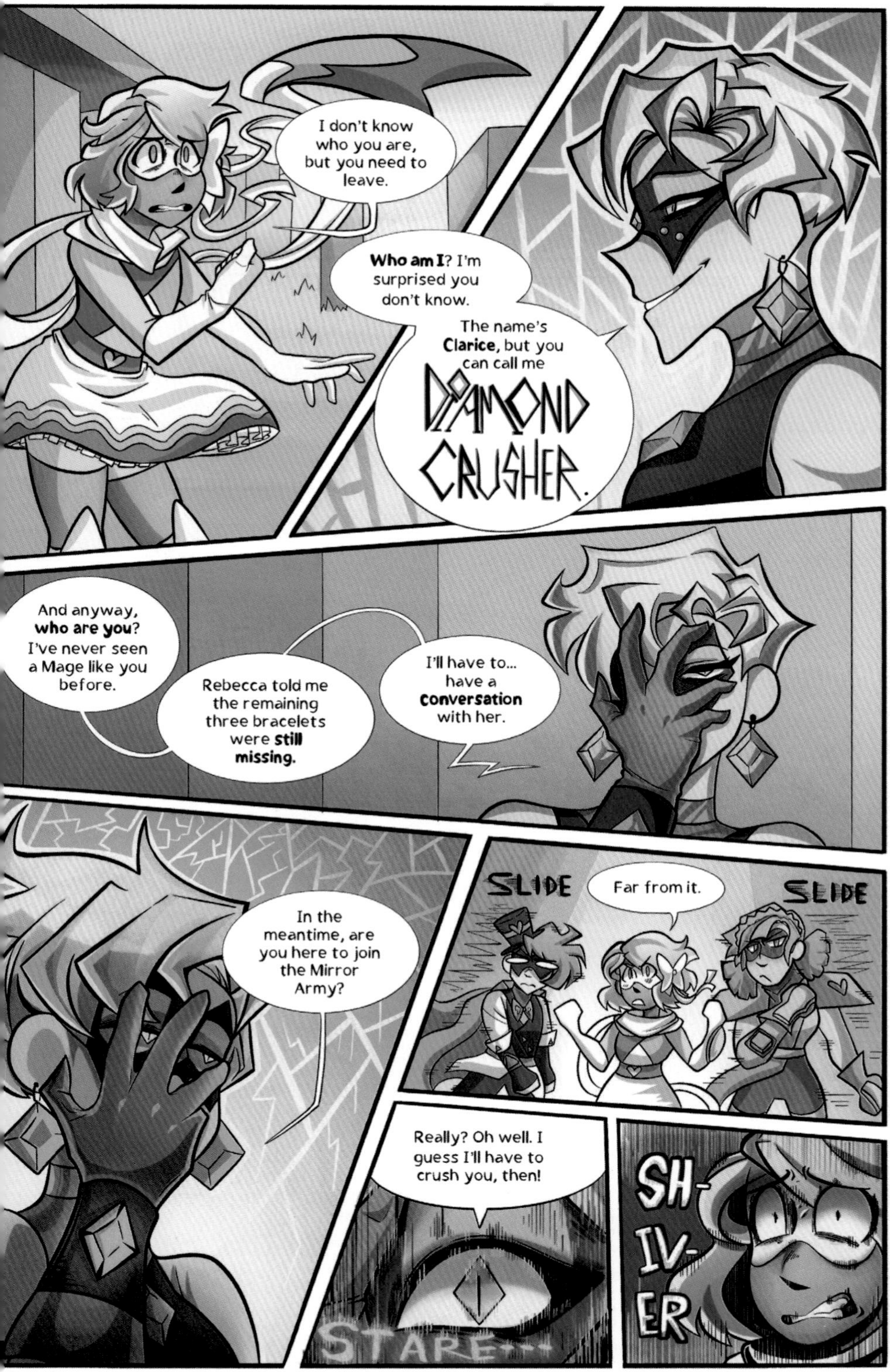
I don't know who you are, but you need to leave.
Who am I? I'm surprised you don't know.
The name's Clarice, but you can call me DIAMOND CRUSHER.
And anyway, who are you? I've never seen a Mage like you before.
Rebecca told me the remaining three bracelets were still missing.
I'll have to... have a conversation with her.
In the meantime, are you here to join the Mirror Army?
SLIDE
Far from it.
SLIDE
Really? Oh well. I guess I'll have to crush you, then!
STARE...
SH-IV-ER

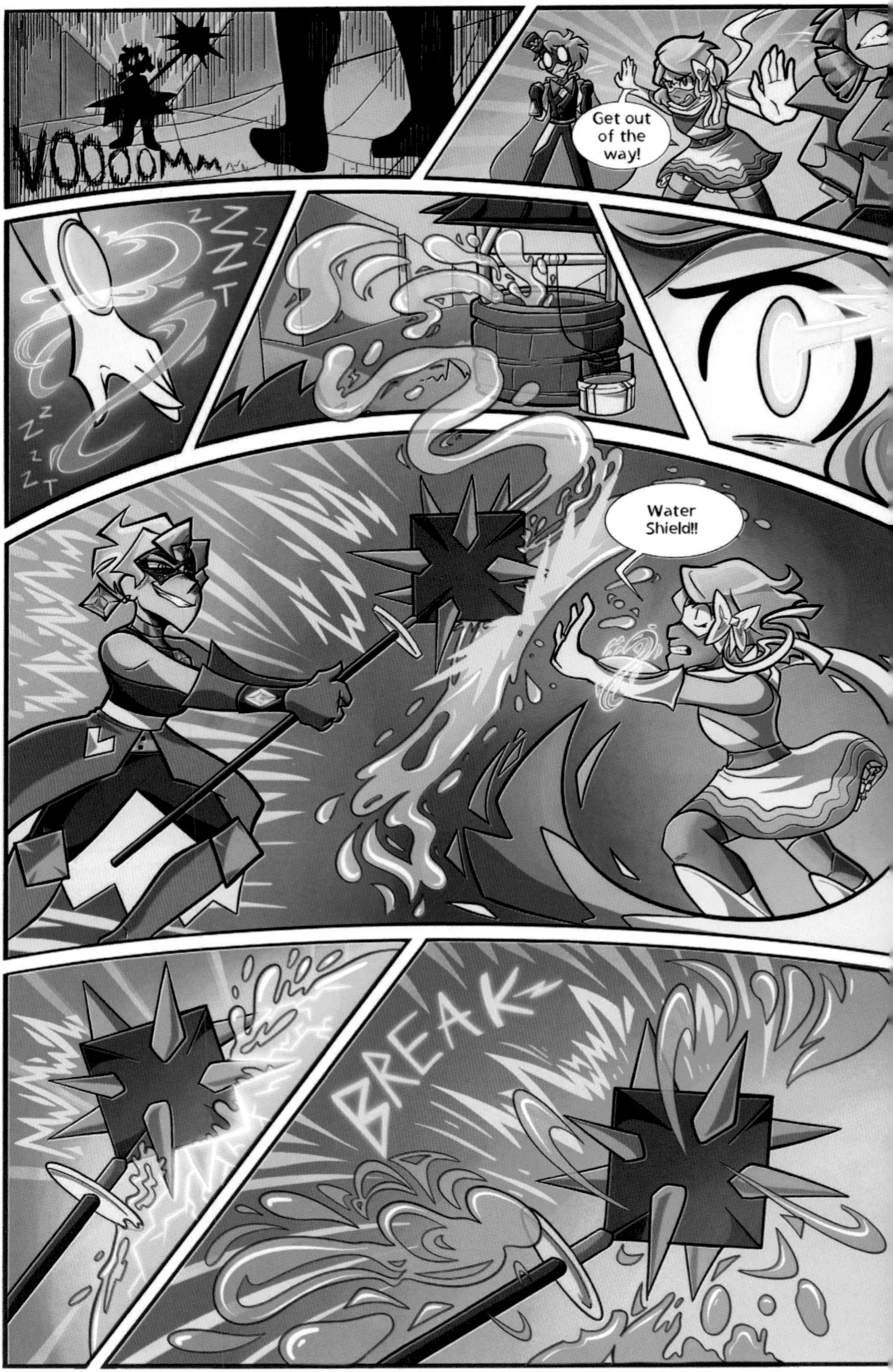
VOOOOMM
Get out of the way!
ZZZT
ZZZT
Water Shield!!
BREAK

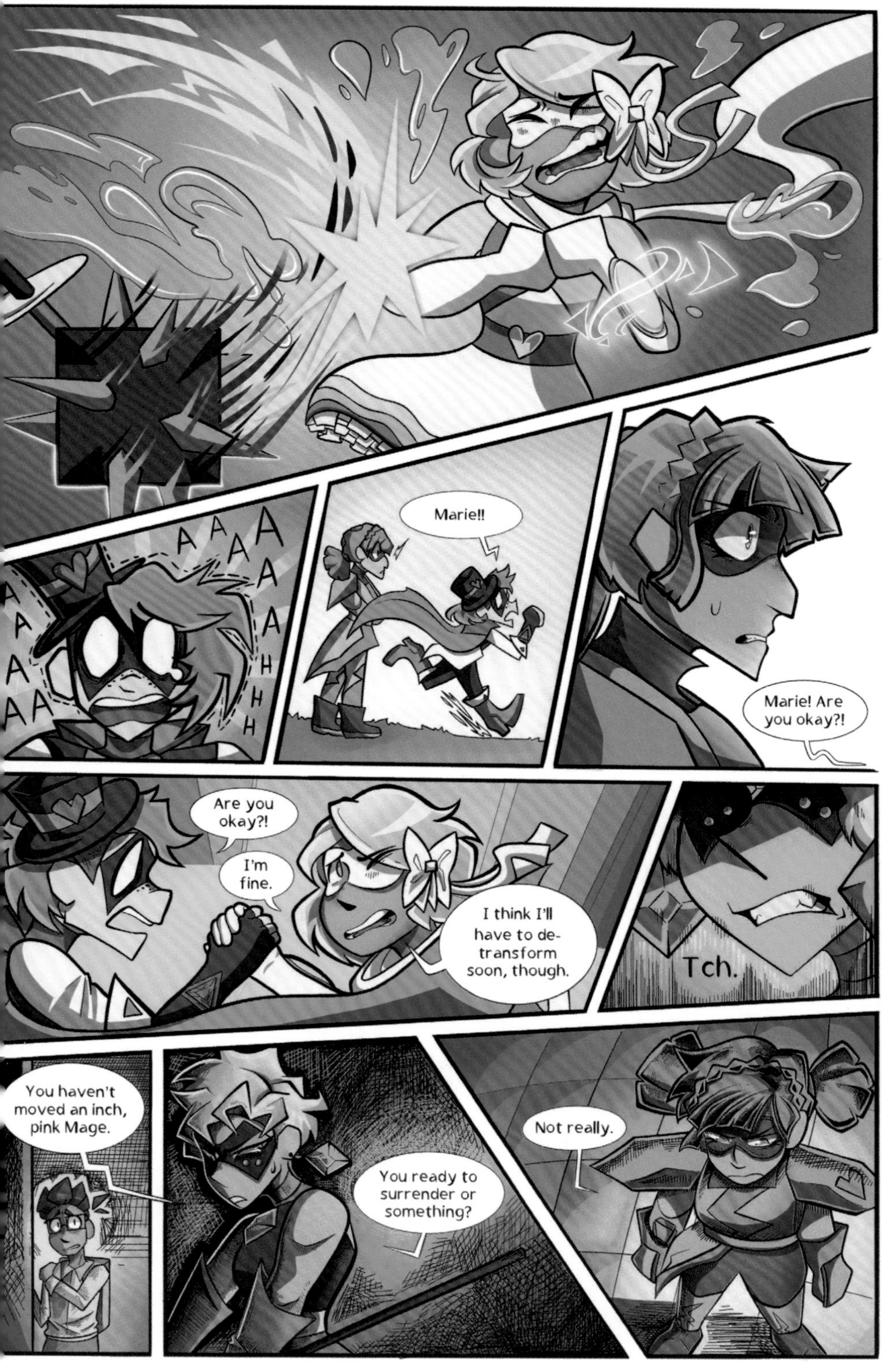
AAAAAAAAAAAHHHH
Marie!!
Marie! Are you okay?!
Are you okay?!
I'm fine.
I think I'll have to de-transform soon, though.
Tch.
You haven't moved an inch, pink Mage.
You ready to surrender or something?
Not really.

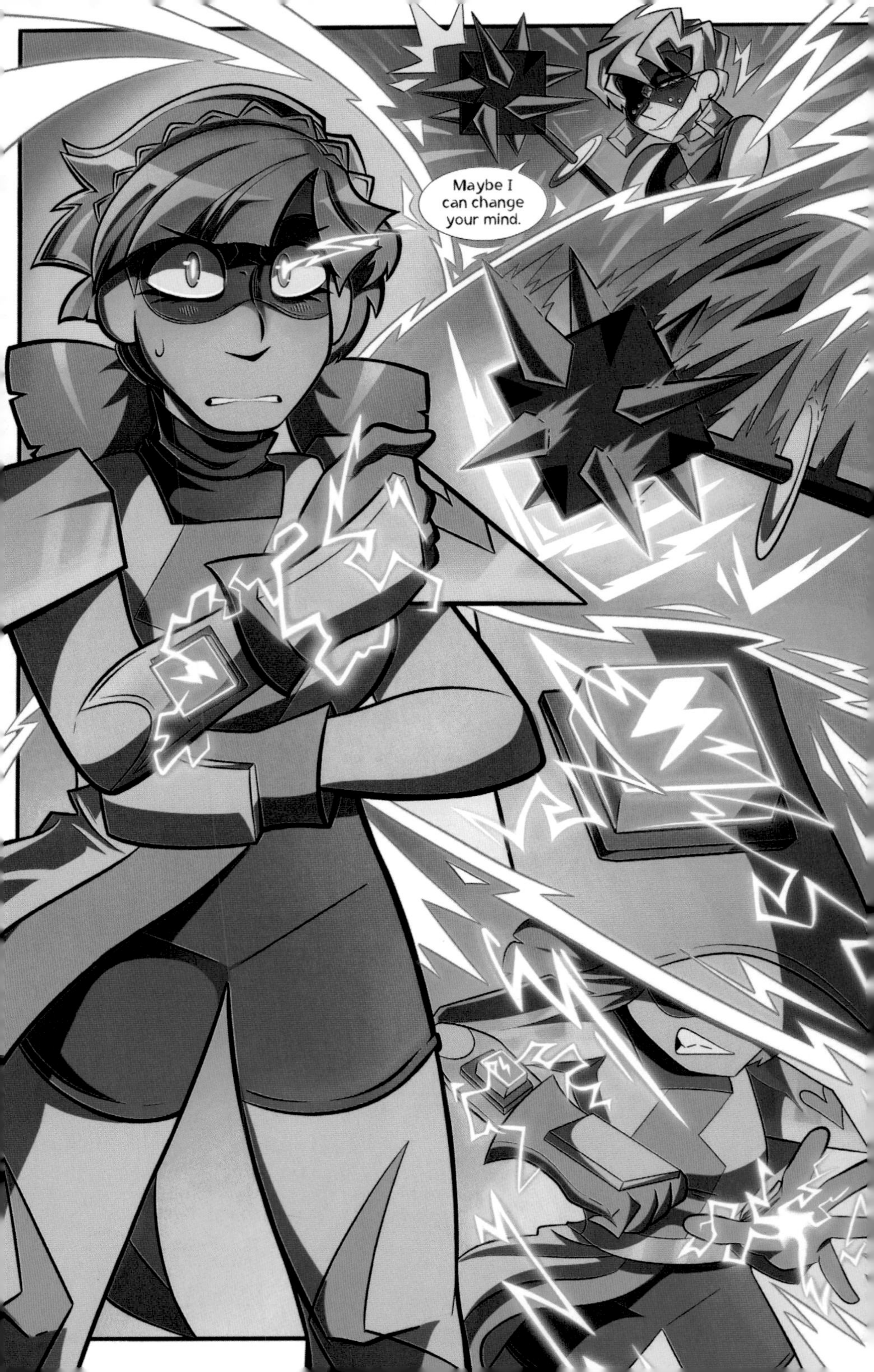
Maybe I can change your mind.

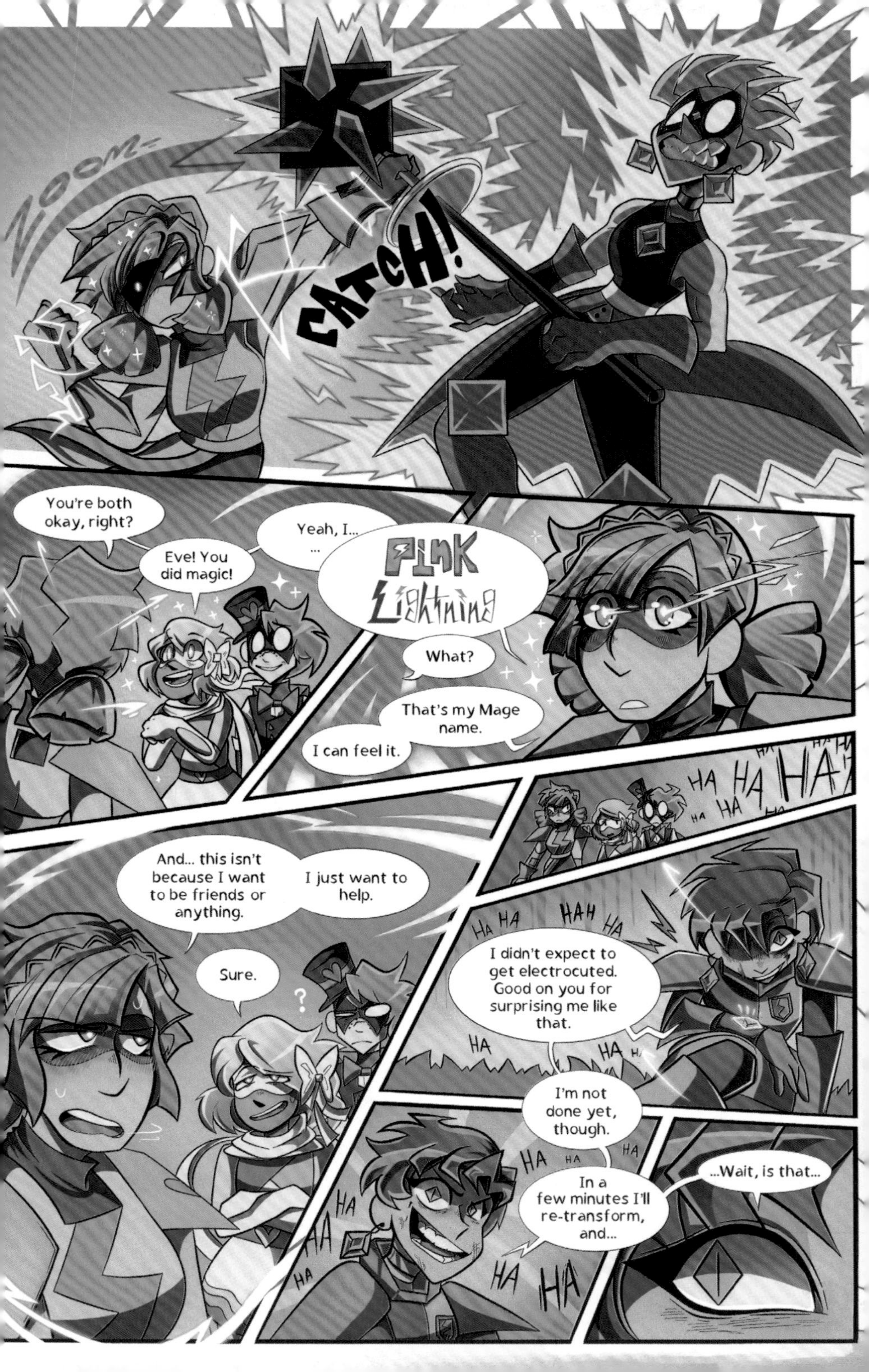
ZOOM
CATCH!
You're both okay, right?
Eve! You did magic!
Yeah, I... ...
Pink Lightning
What?
That's my Mage name.
I can feel it.
HA HA HA HA HA HA
And... this isn't because I want to be friends or anything.
I just want to help.
Sure.
?
HA HA HAH HA
I didn't expect to get electrocuted. Good on you for surprising me like that.
HA HA HA
I'm not done yet, though.
HA HA HA HA HA HA
In a few minutes I'll re-transform, and...
HA HA HA HA
...Wait, is that...

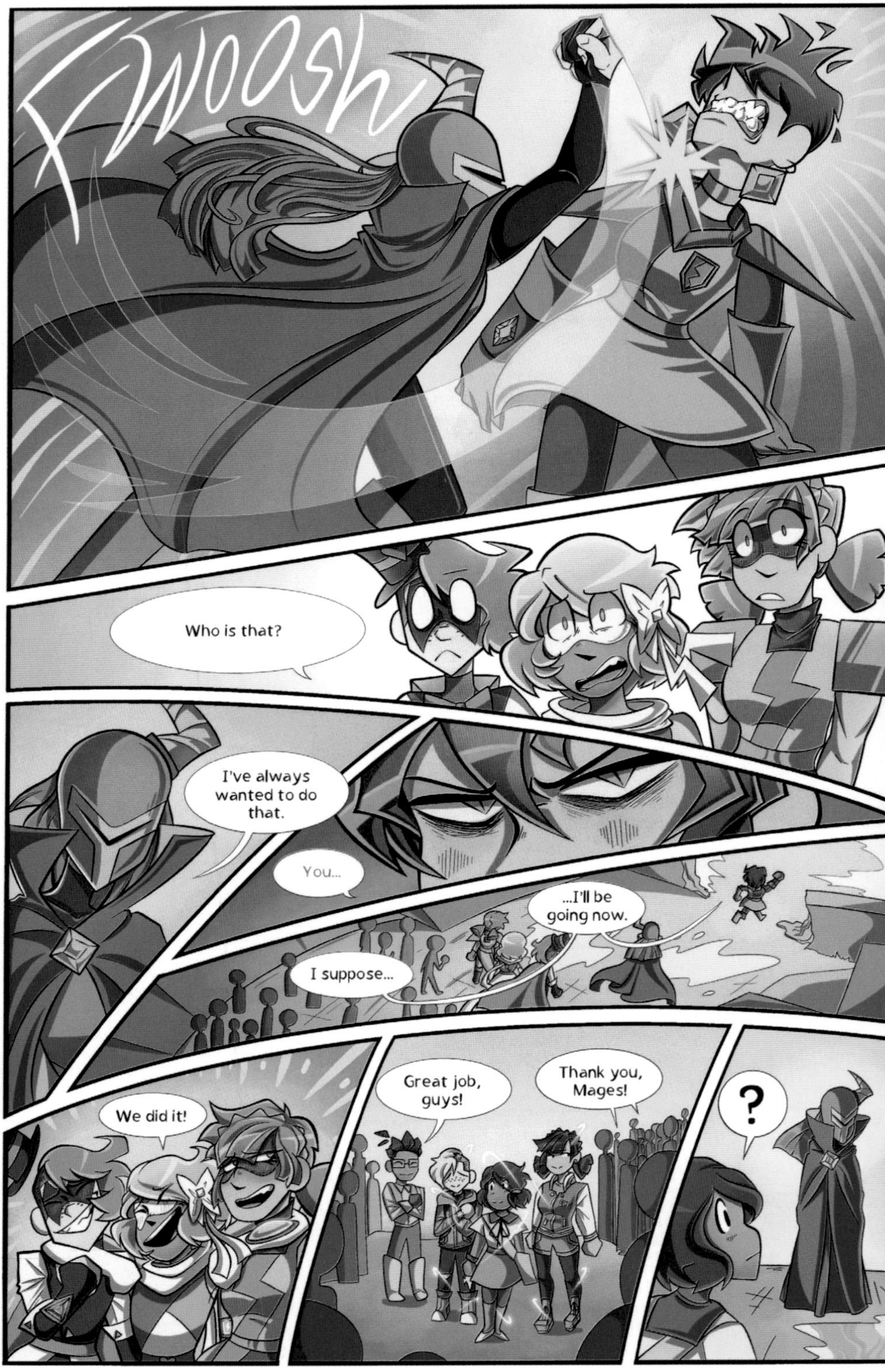
FWOOSH
Who is that?
I've always wanted to do that.
You...
...I'll be going now.
I suppose...
We did it!
Great job, guys!
Thank you, Mages!
?

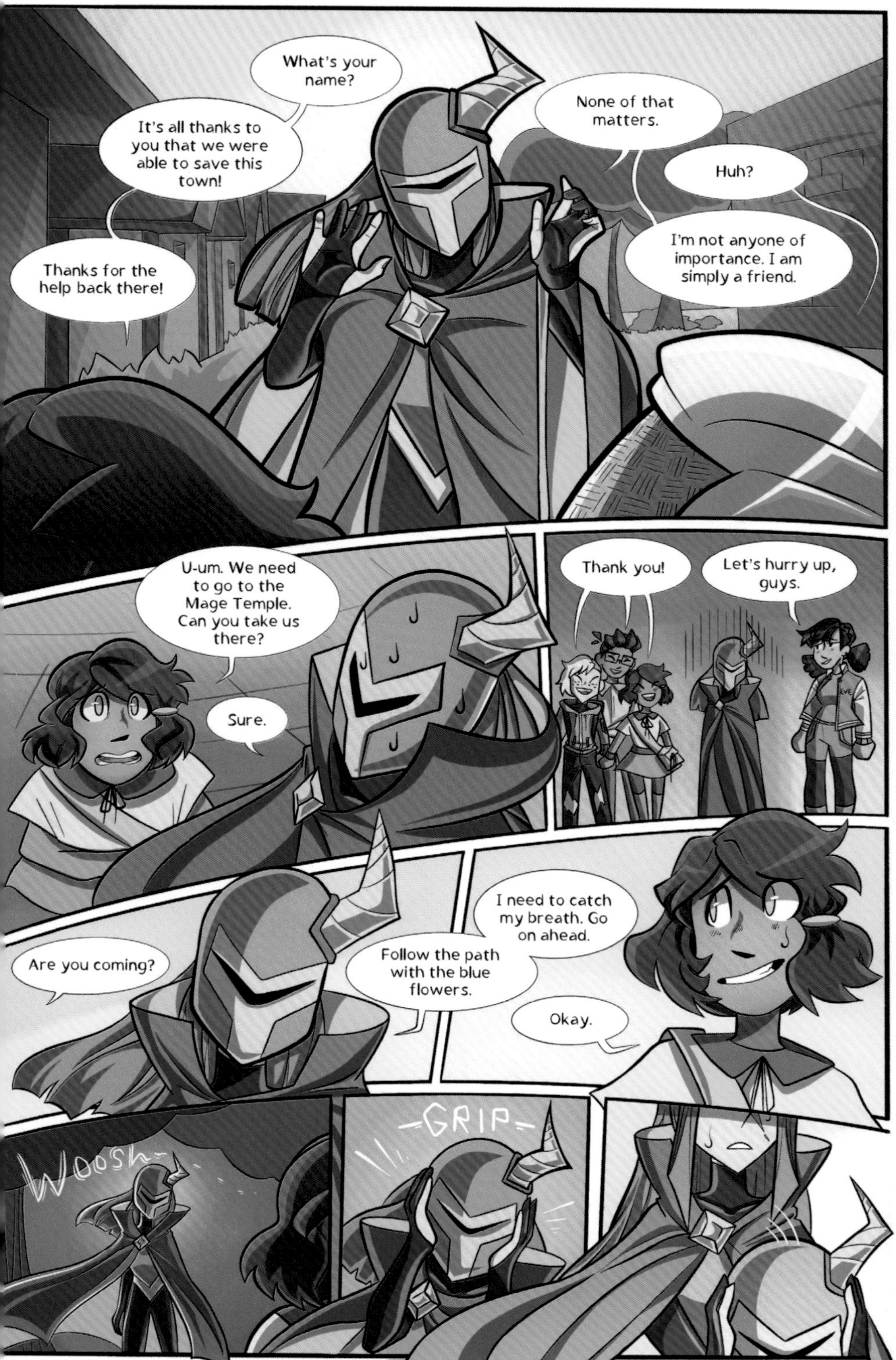
Thanks for the help back there!
It's all thanks to you that we were able to save this town!
What's your name?
None of that matters.
Huh?
I'm not anyone of importance. I am simply a friend.
U-um. We need to go to the Mage Temple. Can you take us there?
Sure.
Thank you!
Let's hurry up, guys.
Are you coming?
I need to catch my breath. Go on ahead.
Follow the path with the blue flowers.
Okay.
Woosh
GRIP

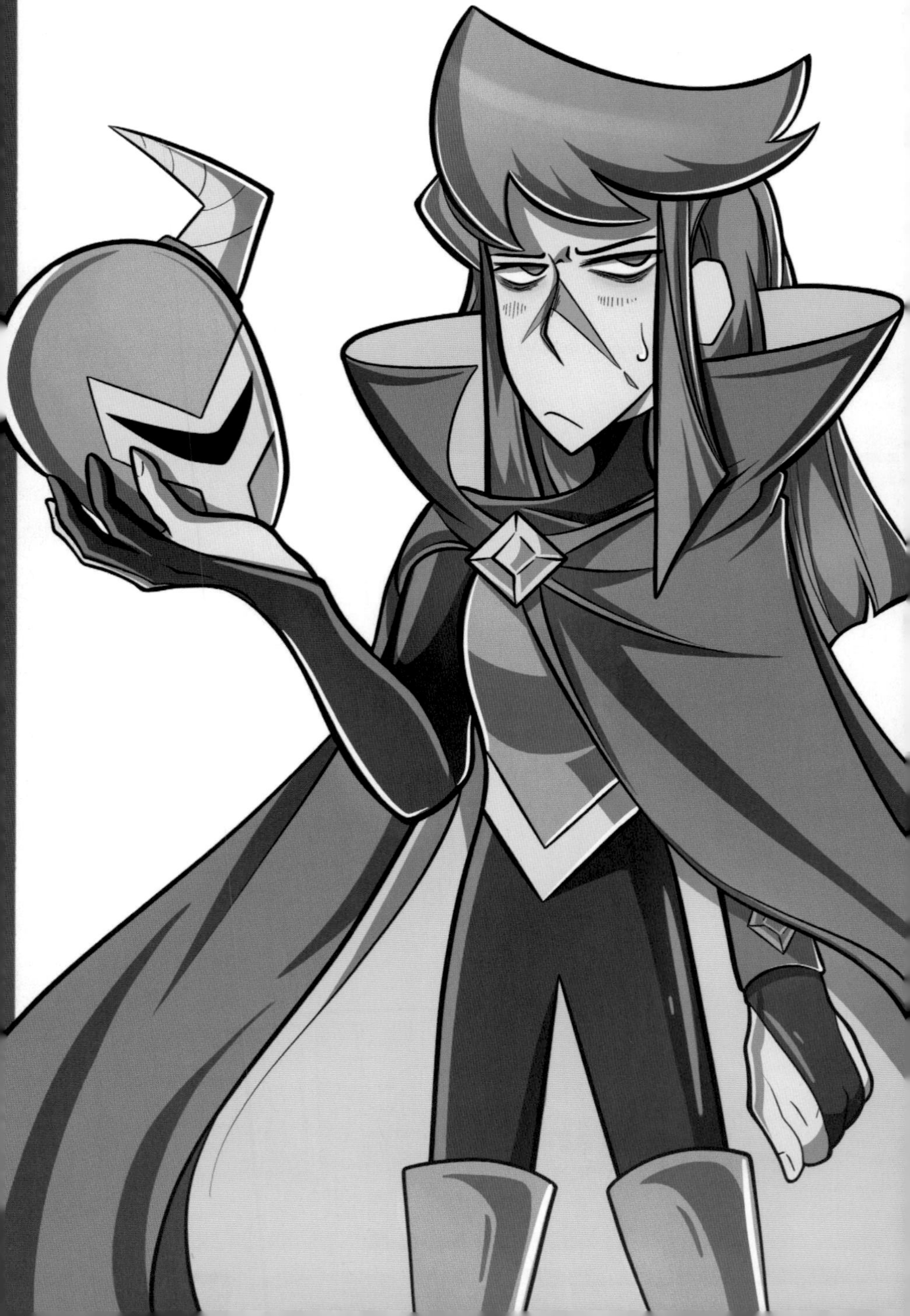

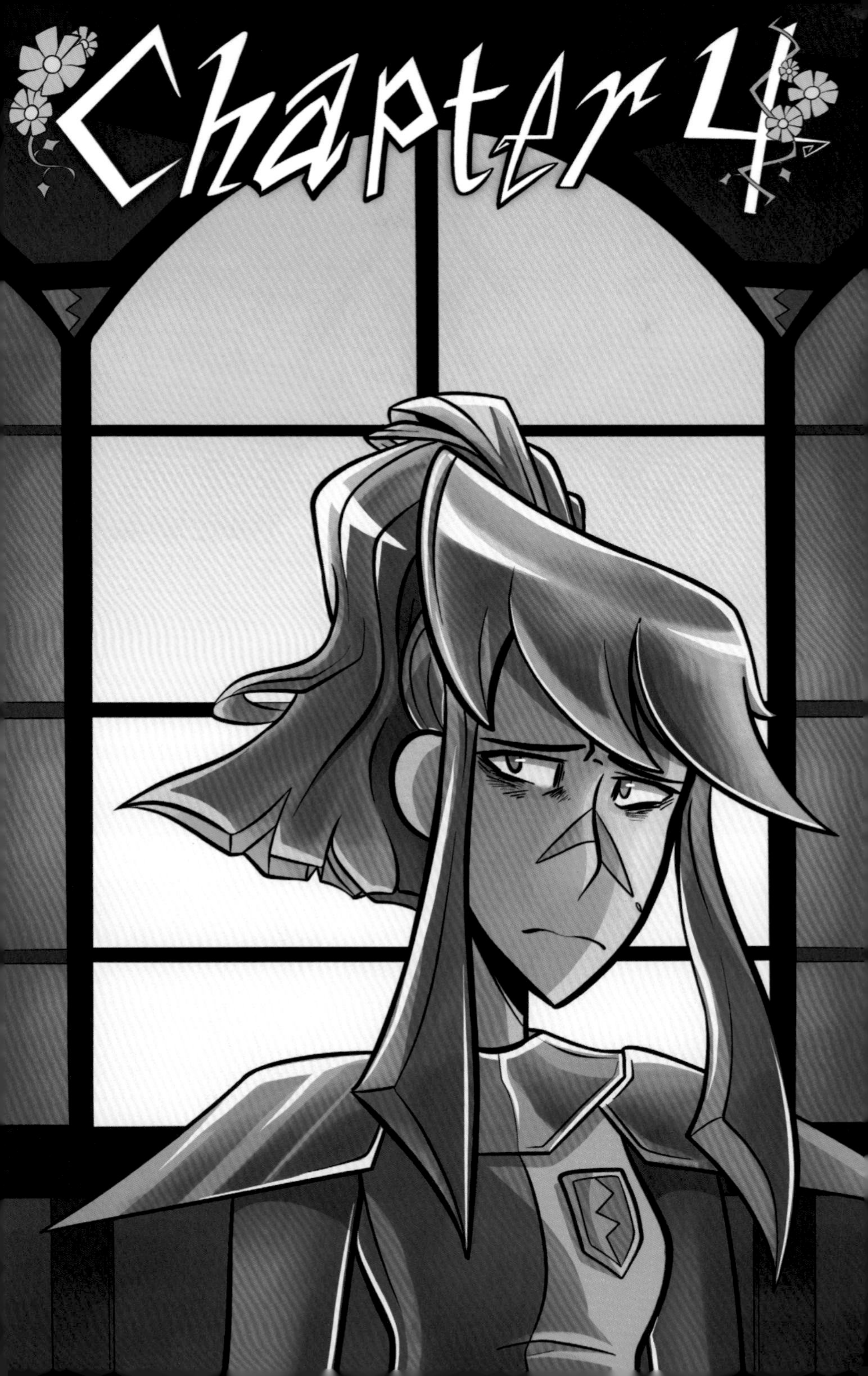
Chapter 4

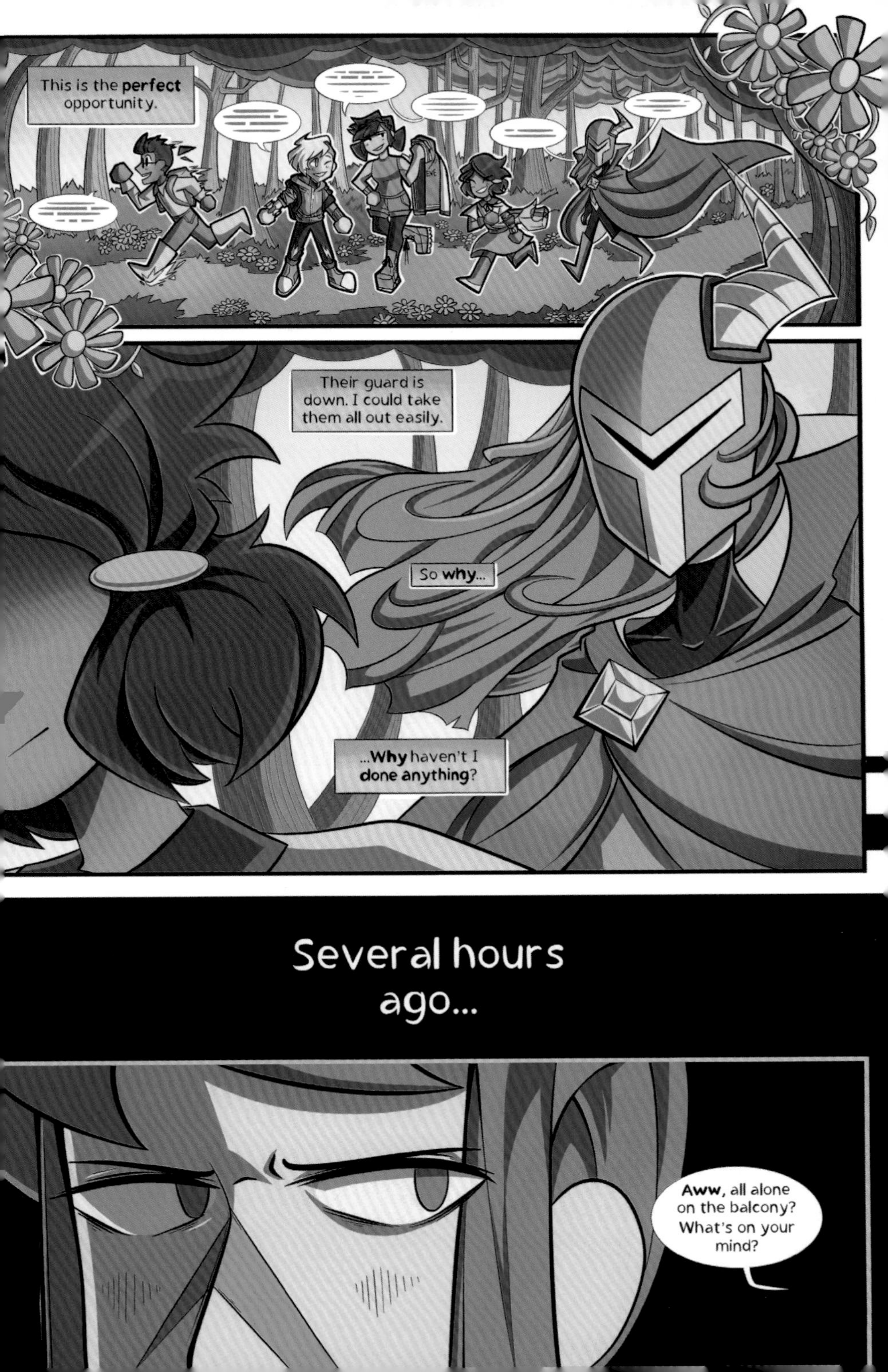
This is the **perfect** opportunity.
Their guard is down. I could take them all out easily.
So **why**...
...**Why** haven't I **done anything**?
Several hours ago...
Aww, all alone on the balcony? What's on your mind?

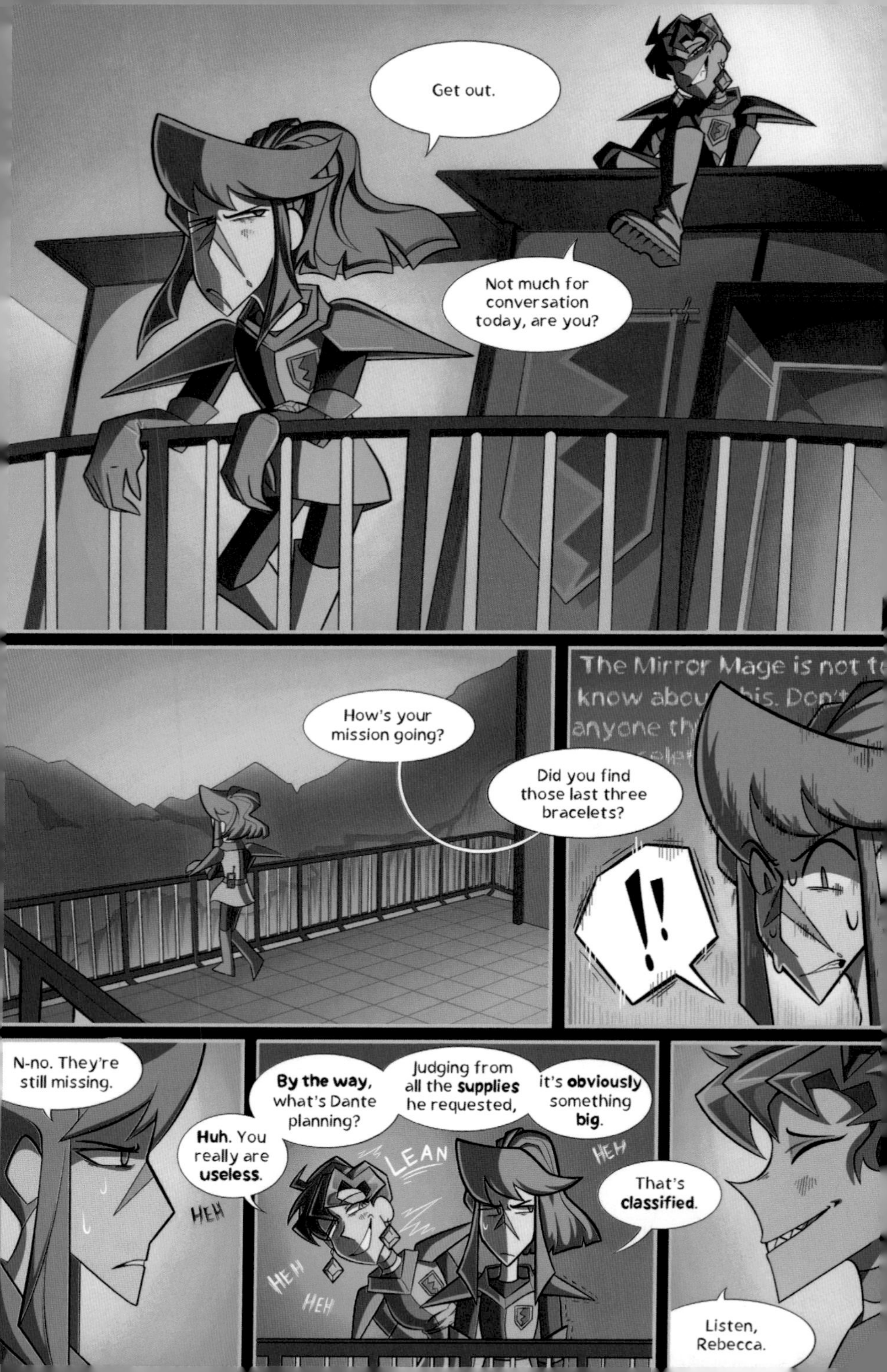
Get out.
Not much for conversation today, are you?
How's your mission going?
Did you find those last three bracelets?
The Mirror Mage is not
!!
N-no. They're still missing.
HEH
Huh. You really are **useless**.
By the way, what's Dante planning?
Judging from all the **supplies** he requested,
it's **obviously** something **big**.
LEAN
HEH
HEH
HEH
That's **classified**.
Listen, Rebecca.

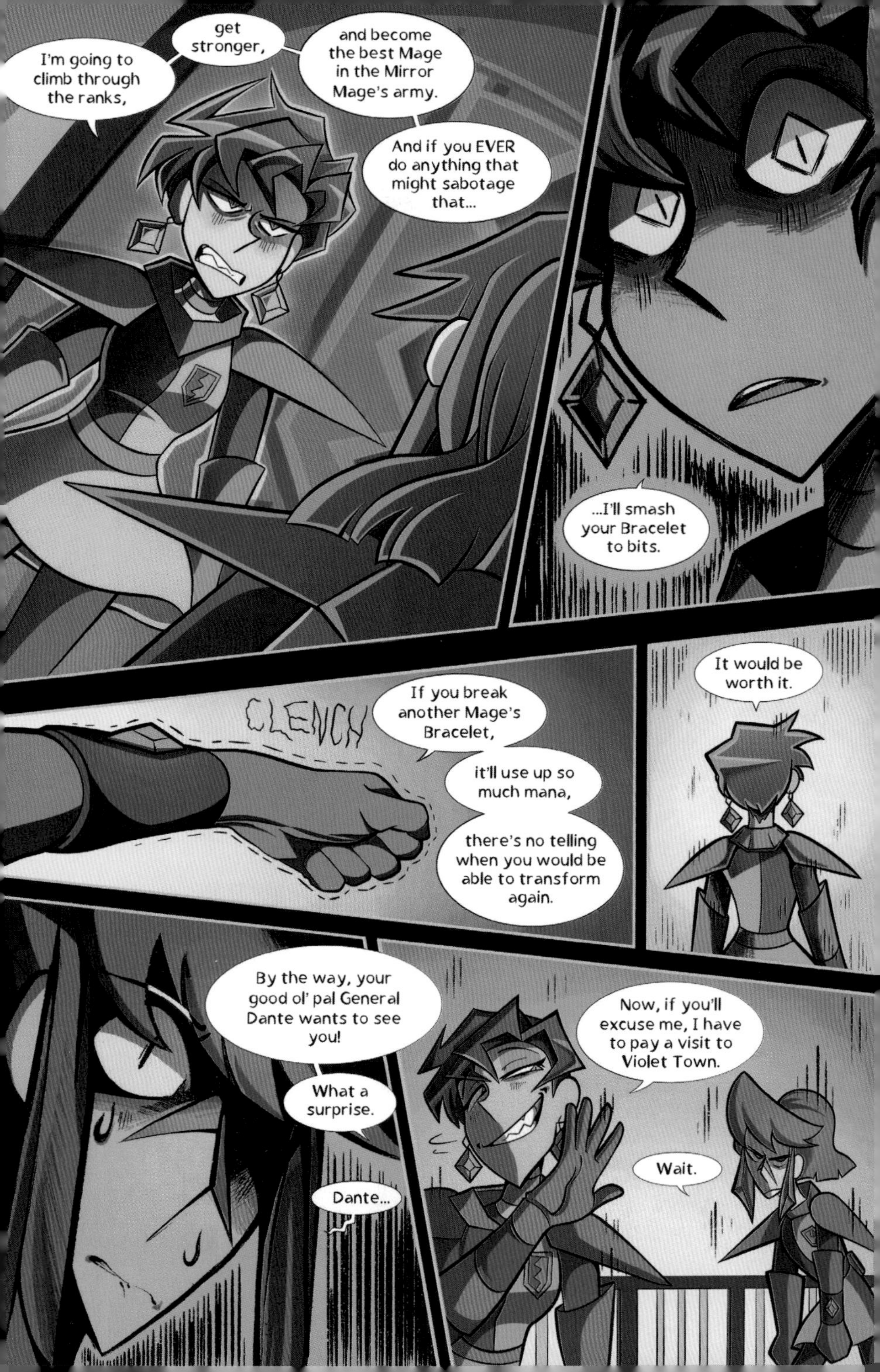

I'm going to climb through the ranks,
get stronger,
and become the best Mage in the Mirror Mage's army.
And if you EVER do anything that might sabotage that...
...I'll smash your Bracelet to bits.
CLENCH
If you break another Mage's Bracelet,
it'll use up so much mana,
there's no telling when you would be able to transform again.
It would be worth it.
By the way, your good ol' pal General Dante wants to see you!
What a surprise.
Dante...
Now, if you'll excuse me, I have to pay a visit to Violet Town.
Wait.

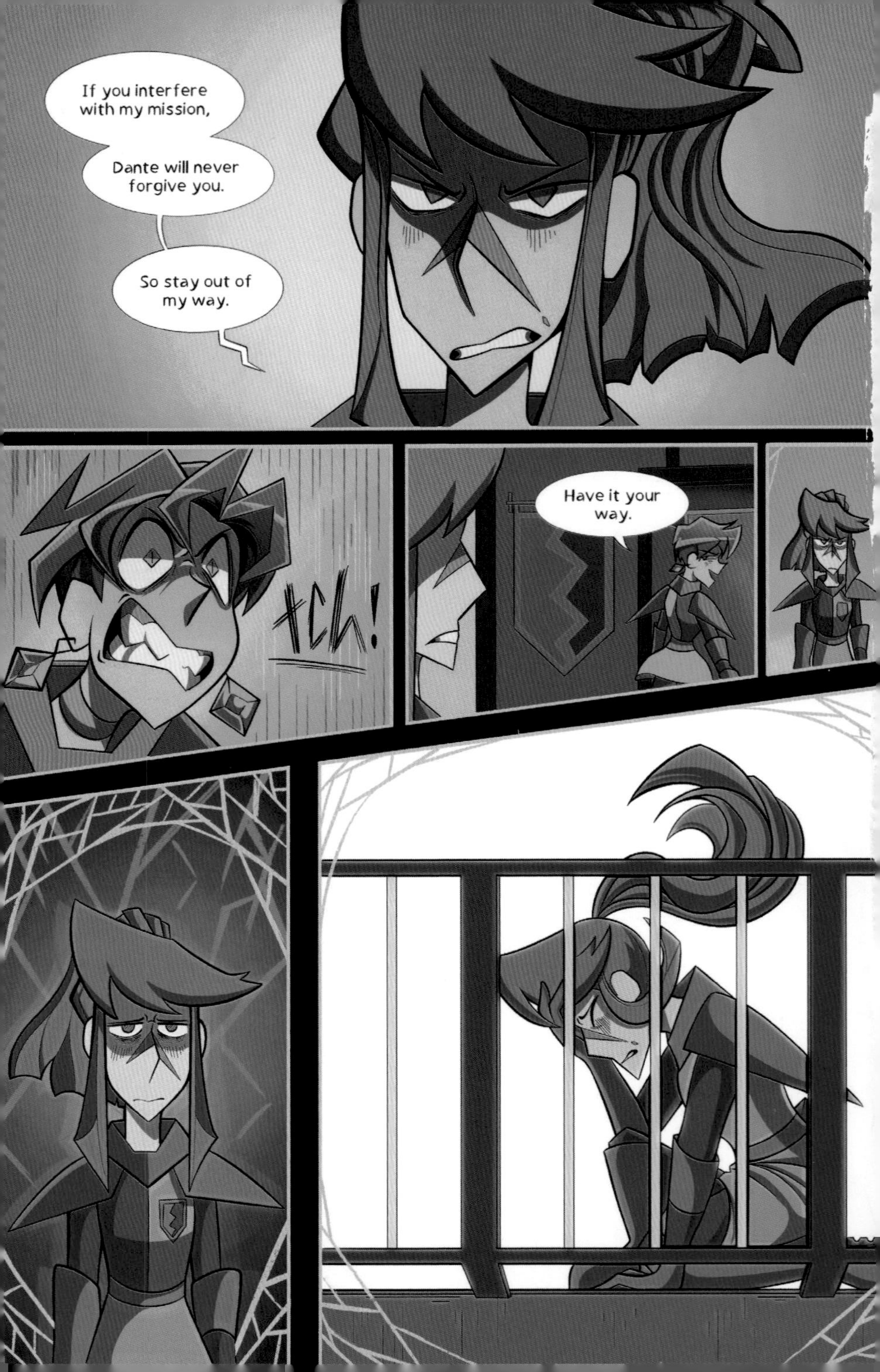
If you interfere with my mission,
Dante will never forgive you.
So stay out of my way.
TCH!
Have it your way.

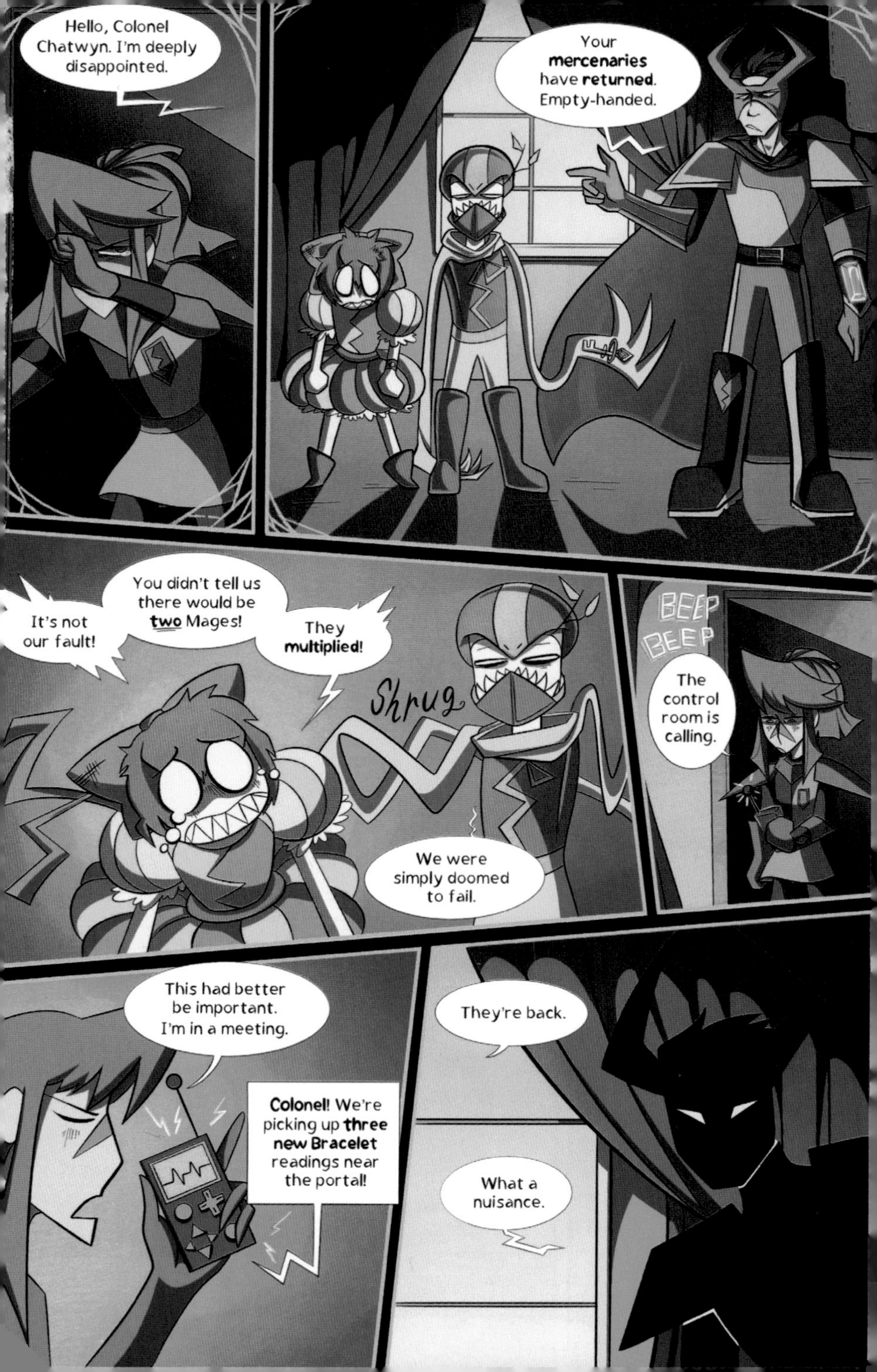

Hello, Colonel Chatwyn. I'm deeply disappointed.
Your mercenaries have returned. Empty-handed.
It's not our fault!
You didn't tell us there would be two Mages!
They multiplied!
Shrug
We were simply doomed to fail.
BEEP BEEP
The control room is calling.
This had better be important. I'm in a meeting.
Colonel! We're picking up three new Bracelet readings near the portal!
They're back.
What a nuisance.

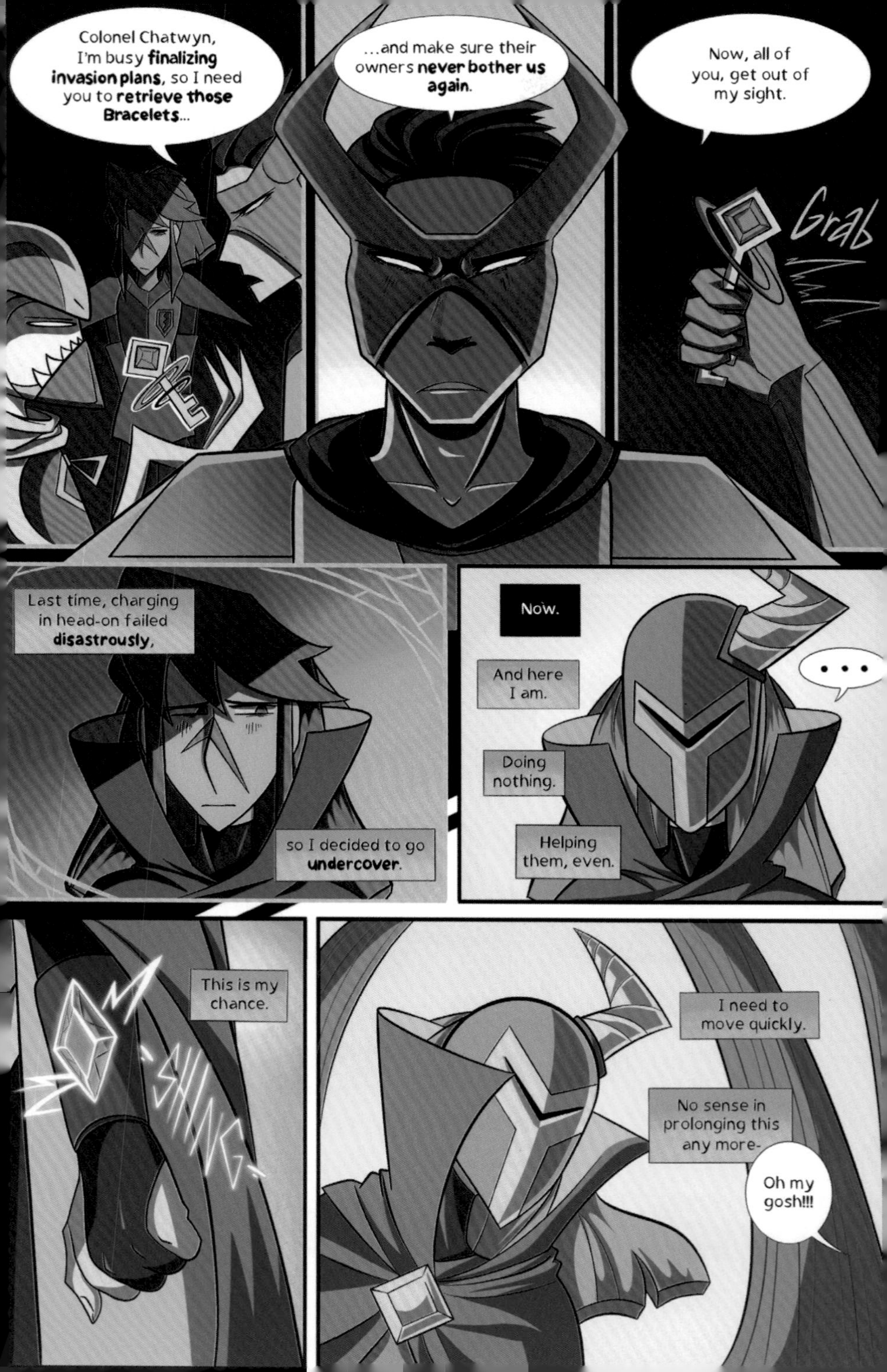
Colonel Chatwyn, I'm busy finalizing invasion plans, so I need you to retrieve those Bracelets...
...and make sure their owners never bother us again.
Now, all of you, get out of my sight.
Grab
Last time, charging in head-on failed disastrously,
so I decided to go undercover.
Now.
And here I am.
Doing nothing.
Helping them, even.
...
This is my chance.
SHING
I need to move quickly.
No sense in prolonging this any more-
Oh my gosh!!!

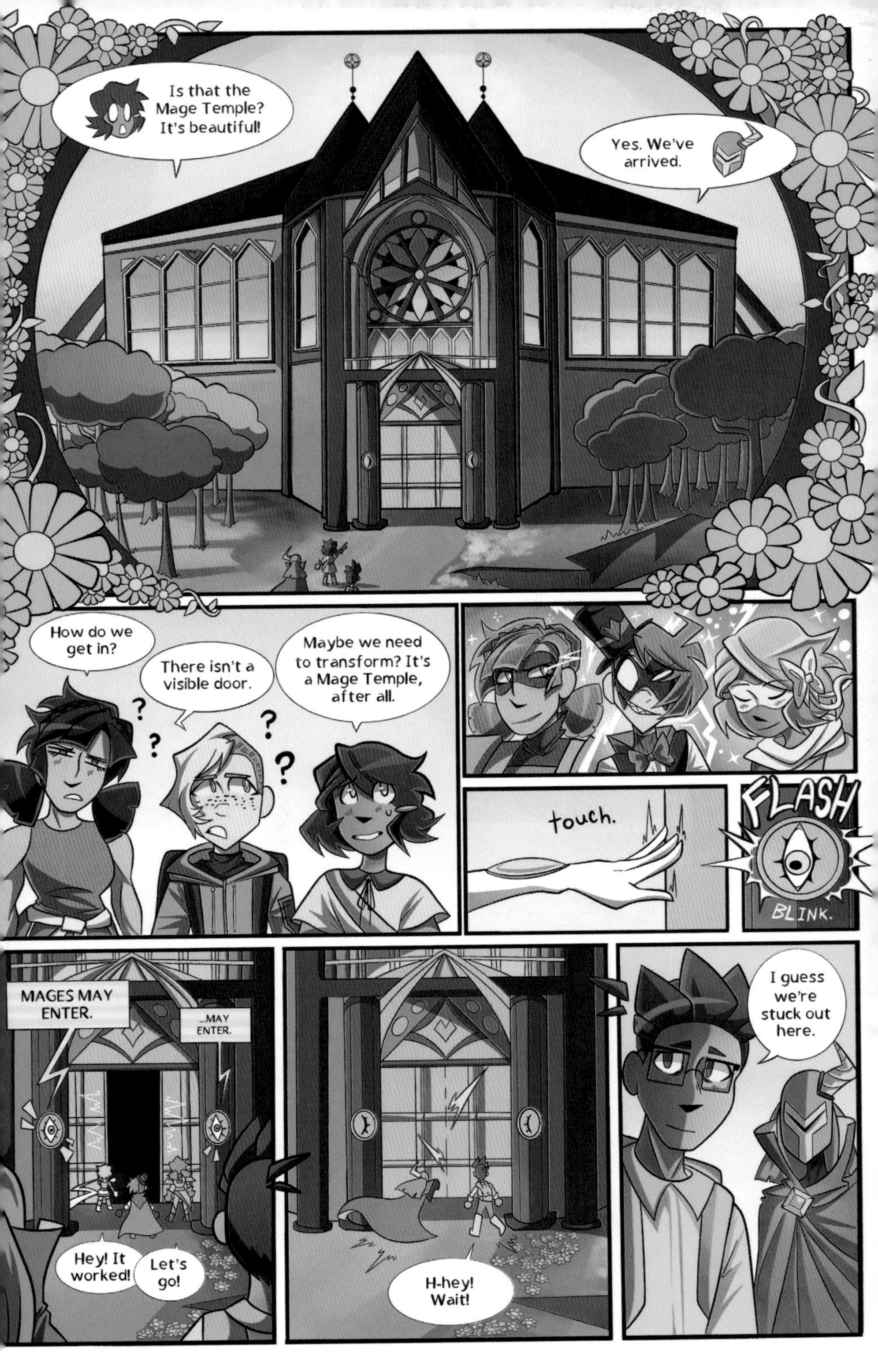
Is that the Mage Temple? It's beautiful!
Yes. We've arrived.
How do we get in?
There isn't a visible door.
Maybe we need to transform? It's a Mage Temple, after all.
touch.
FLASH
BLINK.
MAGES MAY ENTER.
...MAY ENTER.
Hey! It worked!
Let's go!
H-hey! Wait!
I guess we're stuck out here.

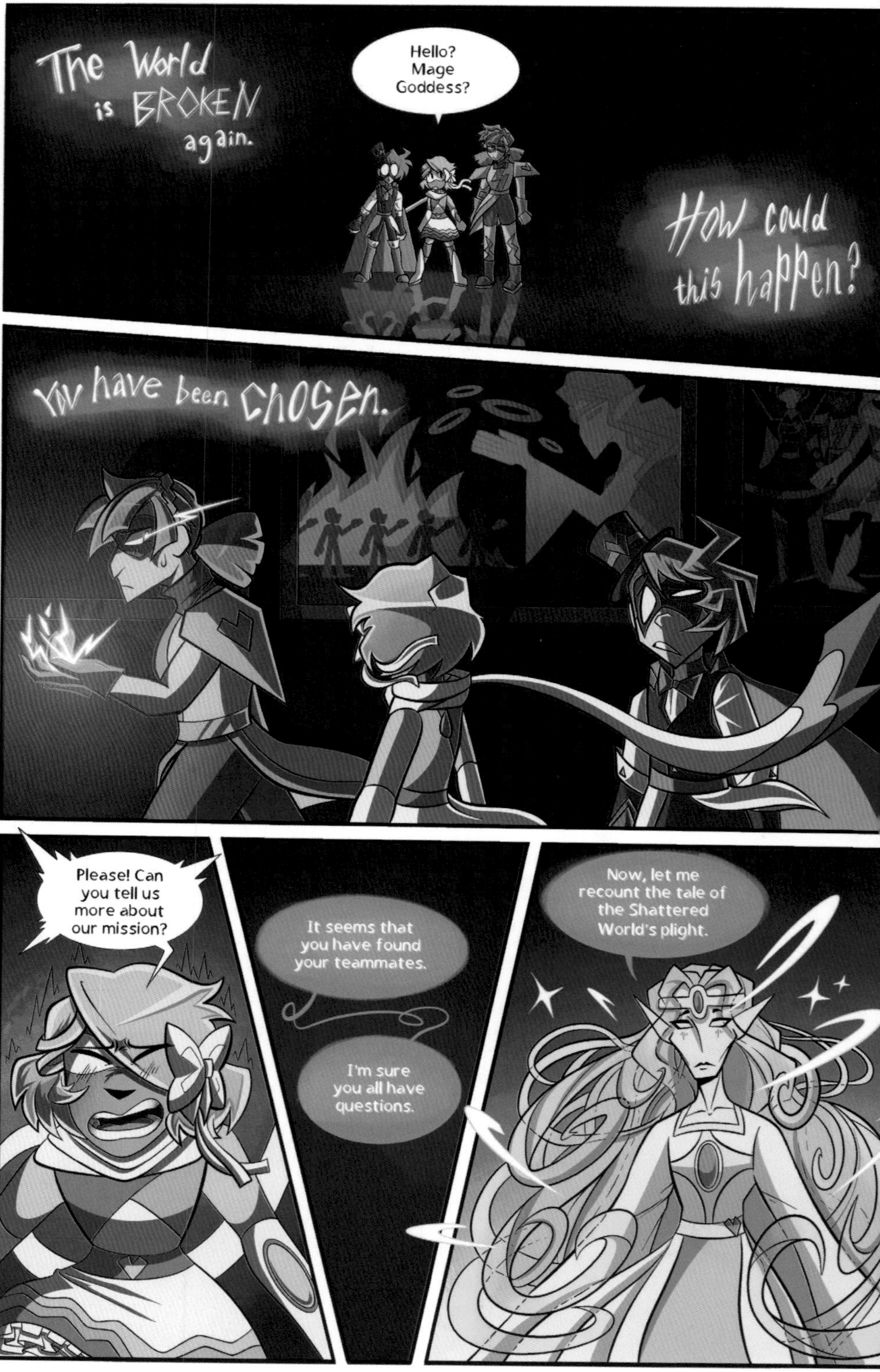
The World is BROKEN again.
Hello? Mage Goddess?
How could this happen?
You have been chosen.
Please! Can you tell us more about our mission?
It seems that you have found your teammates.
I'm sure you all have questions.
Now, let me recount the tale of the Shattered World's plight.

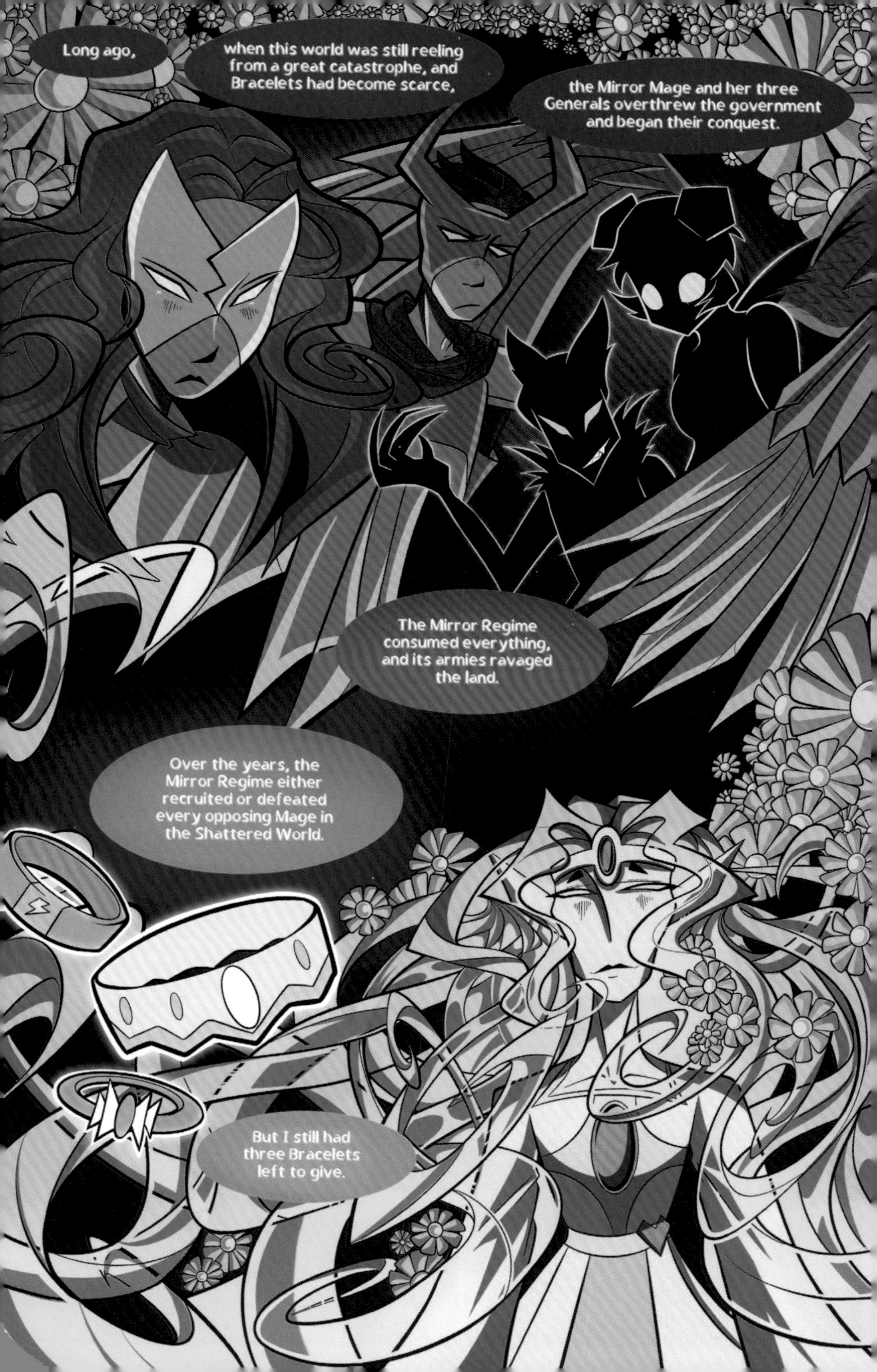

Long ago,
when this world was still reeling from a great catastrophe, and Bracelets had become scarce,
the Mirror Mage and her three Generals overthrew the government and began their conquest.
The Mirror Regime consumed everything, and its armies ravaged the land.
Over the years, the Mirror Regime either recruited or defeated every opposing Mage in the Shattered World.
But I still had three Bracelets left to give.

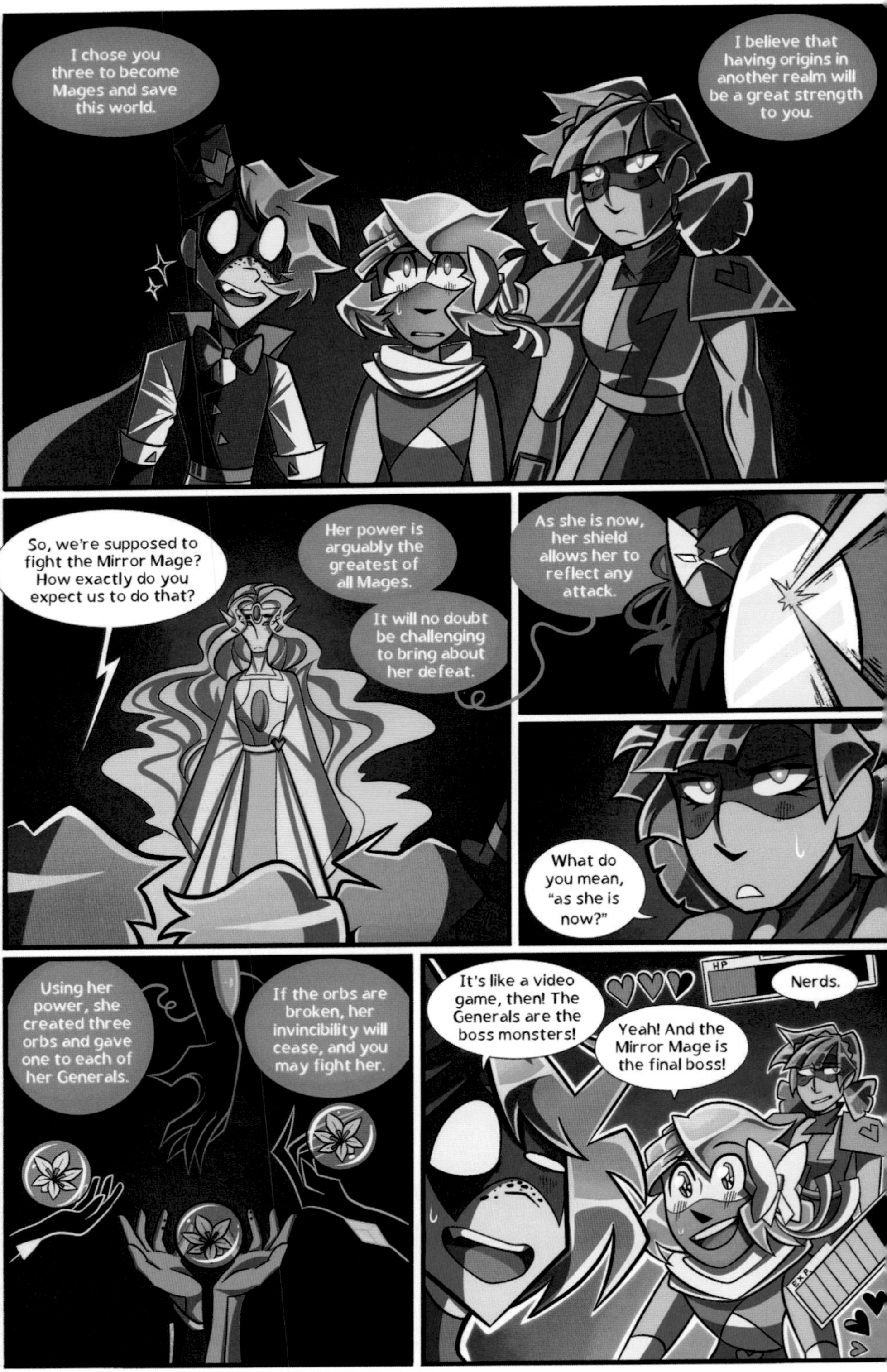
I chose you three to become Mages and save this world.
I believe that having origins in another realm will be a great strength to you.
So, we're supposed to fight the Mirror Mage? How exactly do you expect us to do that?
Her power is arguably the greatest of all Mages.
It will no doubt be challenging to bring about her defeat.
As she is now, her shield allows her to reflect any attack.
What do you mean, "as she is now?"
Using her power, she created three orbs and gave one to each of her Generals.
If the orbs are broken, her invincibility will cease, and you may fight her.
It's like a video game, then! The Generals are the boss monsters!
HP
Nerds.
Yeah! And the Mirror Mage is the final boss!
EXP

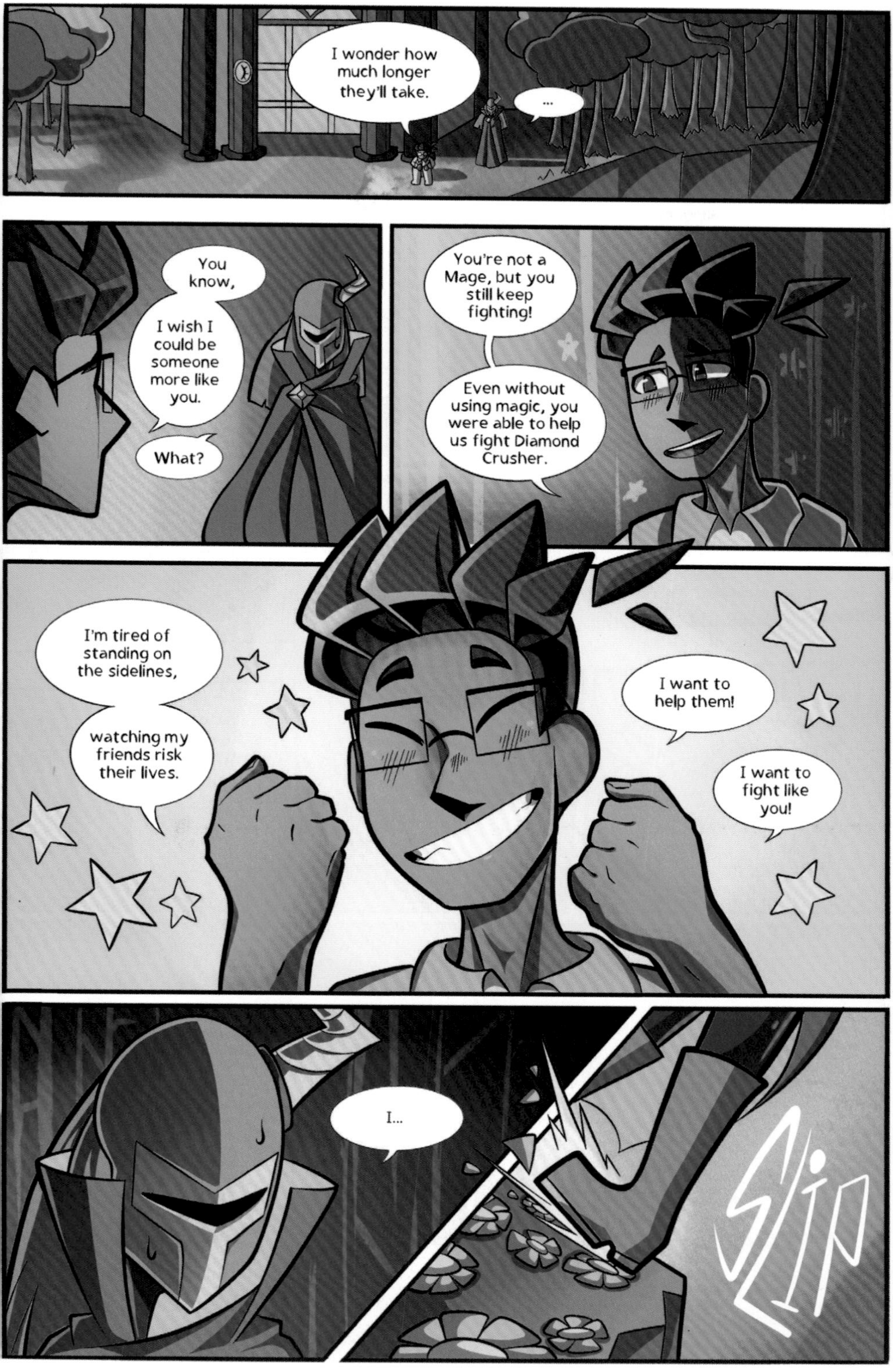

I wonder how much longer they'll take.
...
You know,
I wish I could be someone more like you.
What?
You're not a Mage, but you still keep fighting!
Even without using magic, you were able to help us fight Diamond Crusher.
I'm tired of standing on the sidelines,
watching my friends risk their lives.
I want to help them!
I want to fight like you!
I...
Slip

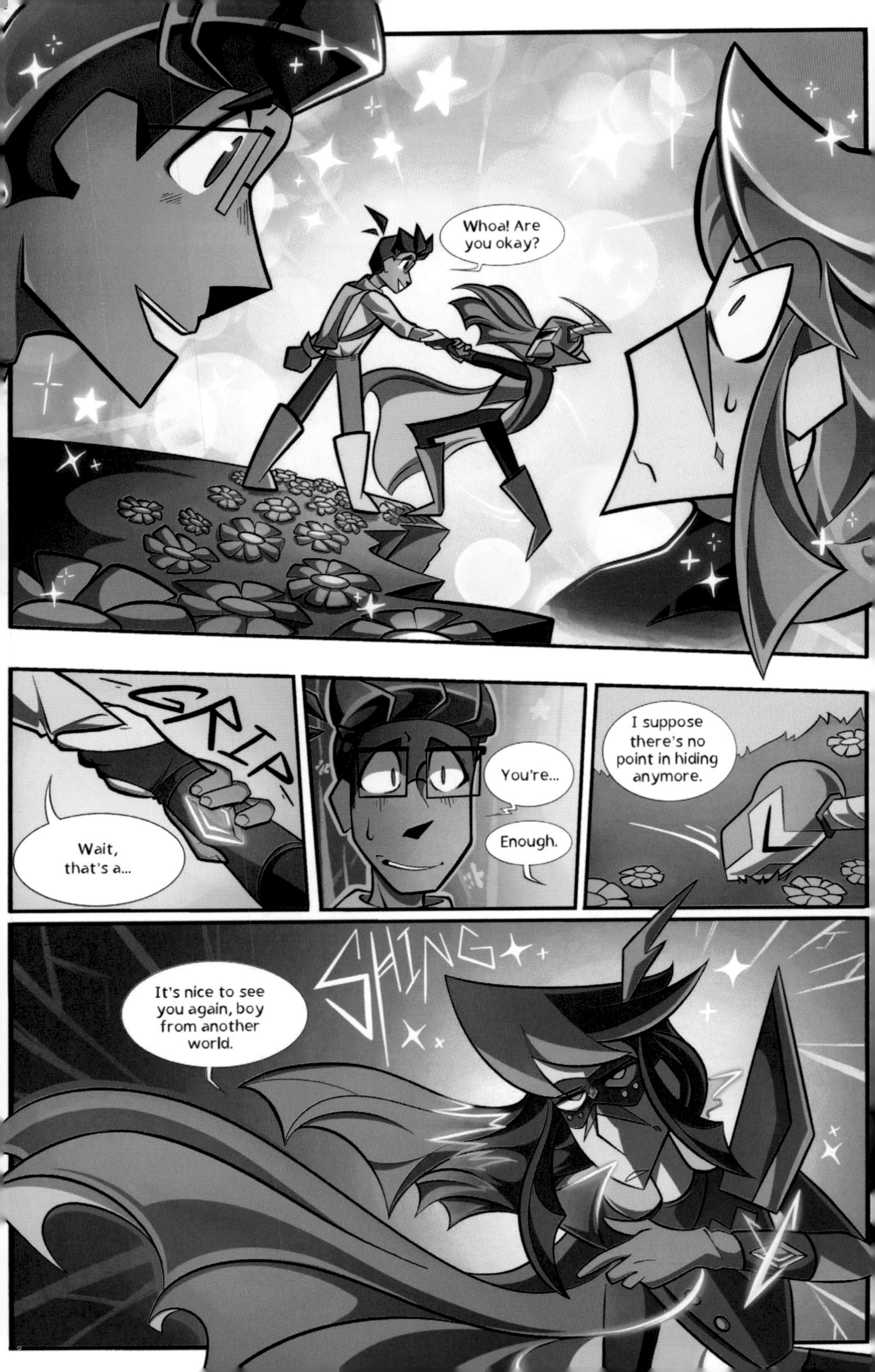

Whoa! Are you okay?
GRIP
Wait, that's a...
You're...
Enough.
I suppose there's no point in hiding anymore.
SHING
It's nice to see you again, boy from another world.

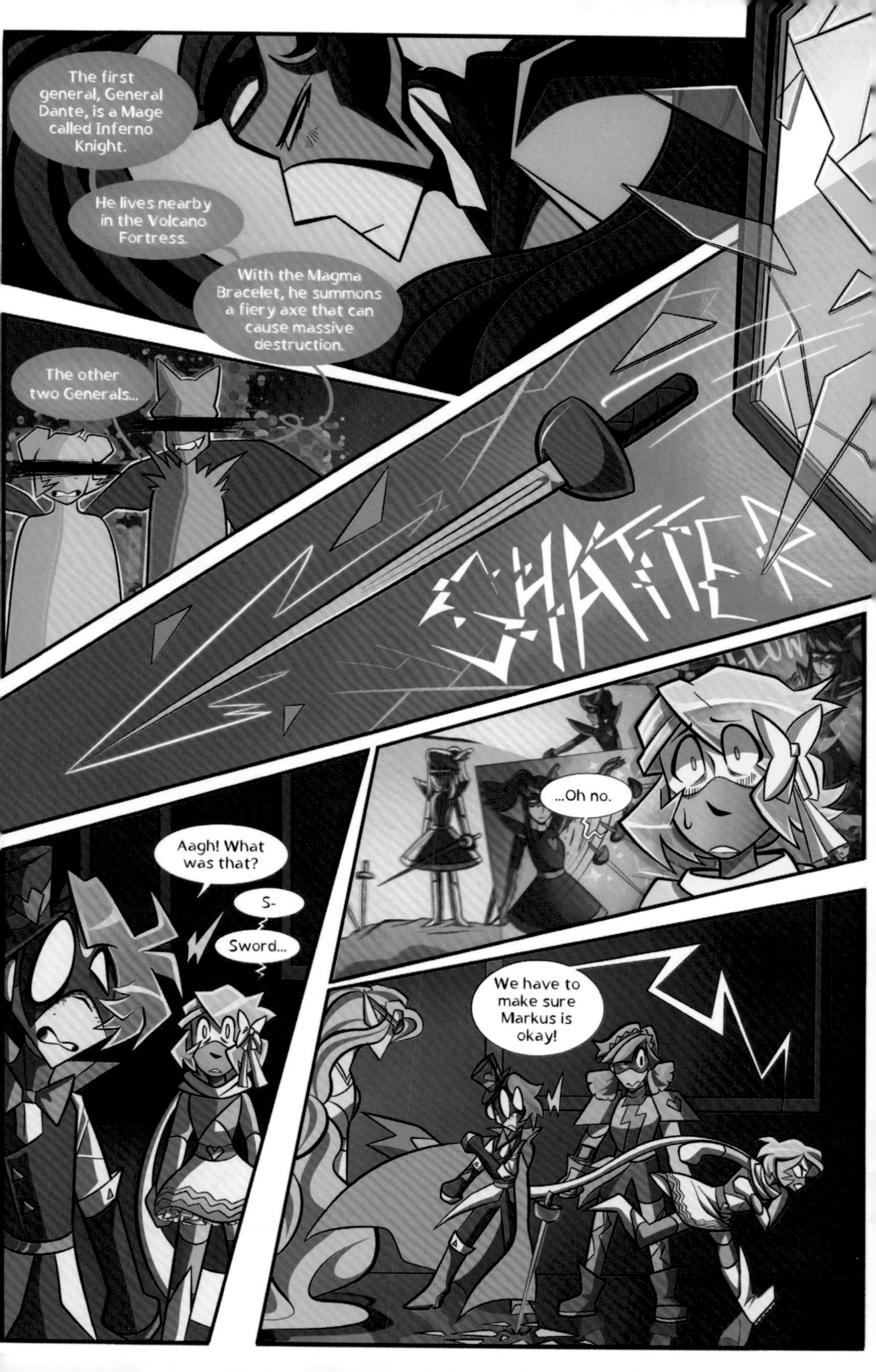
The first general, General Dante, is a Mage called Inferno Knight.
He lives nearby in the Volcano Fortress.
With the Magma Bracelet, he summons a fiery axe that can cause massive destruction.
The other two Generals...
SHATTER
...Oh no.
Aagh! What was that?
S-
Sword...
We have to make sure Markus is okay!

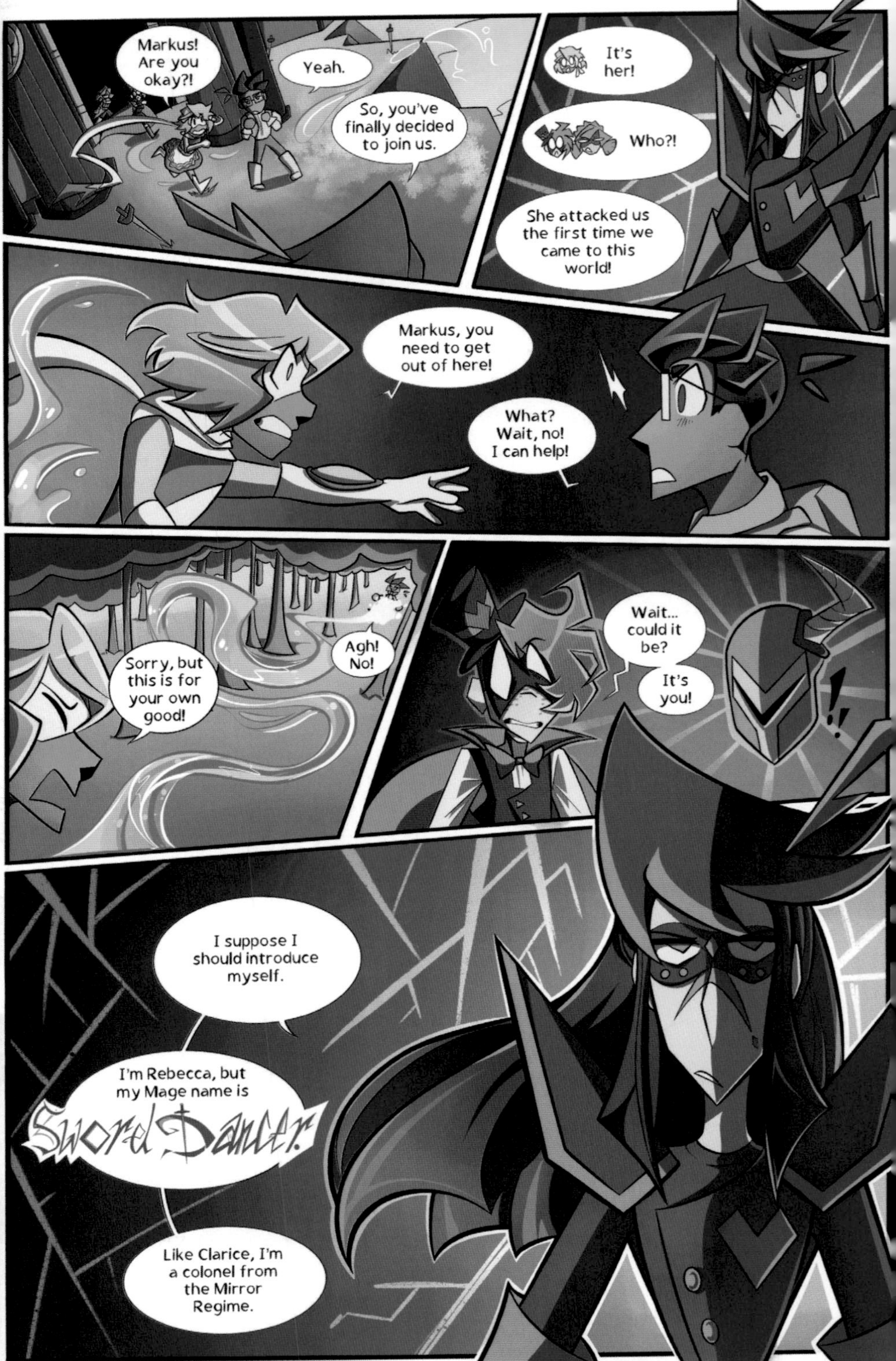
Markus! Are you okay?!
Yeah.
So, you've finally decided to join us.
It's her!
Who?!
She attacked us the first time we came to this world!
Markus, you need to get out of here!
What? Wait, no! I can help!
Sorry, but this is for your own good!
Agh! No!
Wait... could it be?
It's you!
I suppose I should introduce myself.
I'm Rebecca, but my Mage name is
Sword Dancer.
Like Clarice, I'm a colonel from the Mirror Regime.

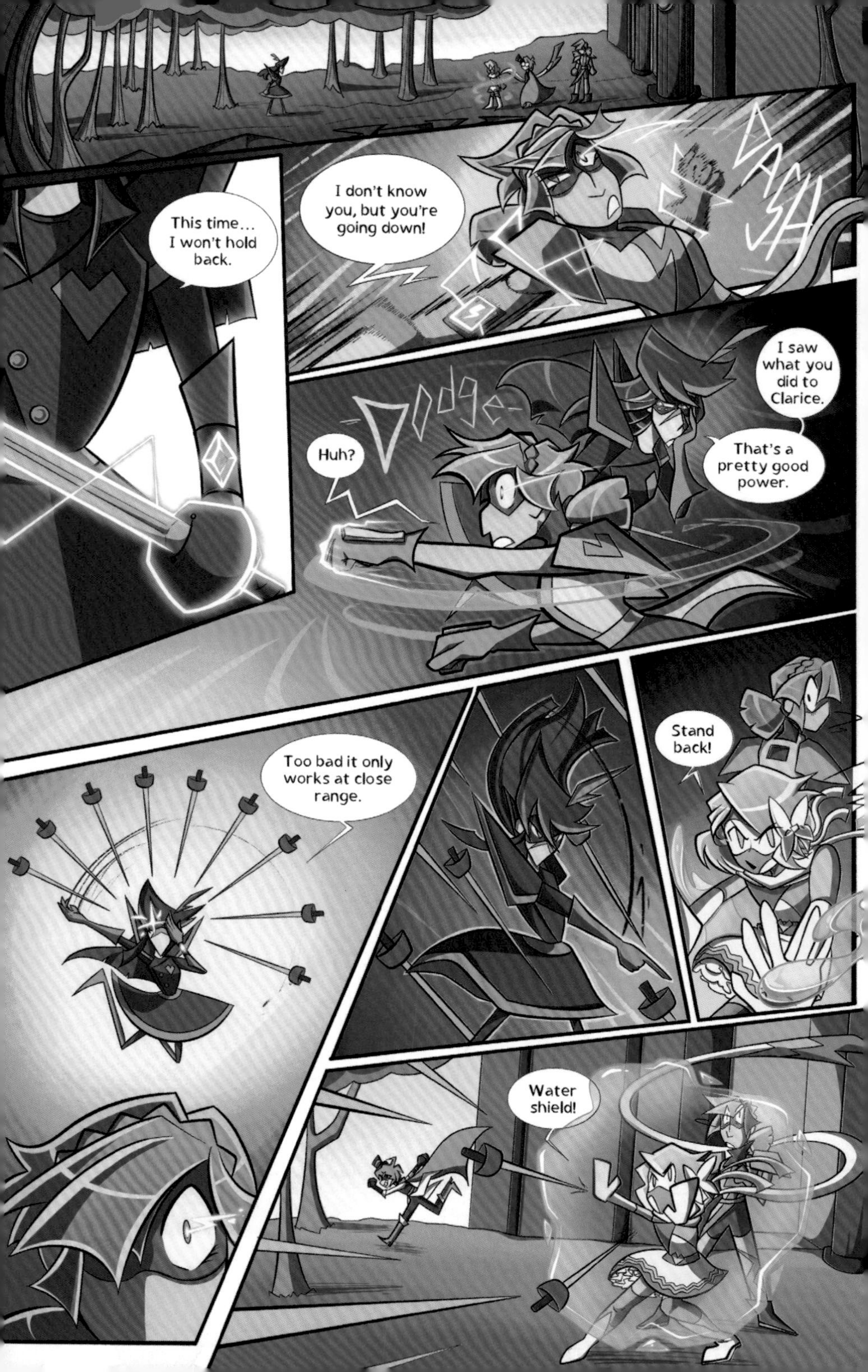
This time… I won't hold back.
I don't know you, but you're going down!
DASH
Dodge
Huh?
I saw what you did to Clarice.
That's a pretty good power.
Too bad it only works at close range.
Stand back!
Water shield!

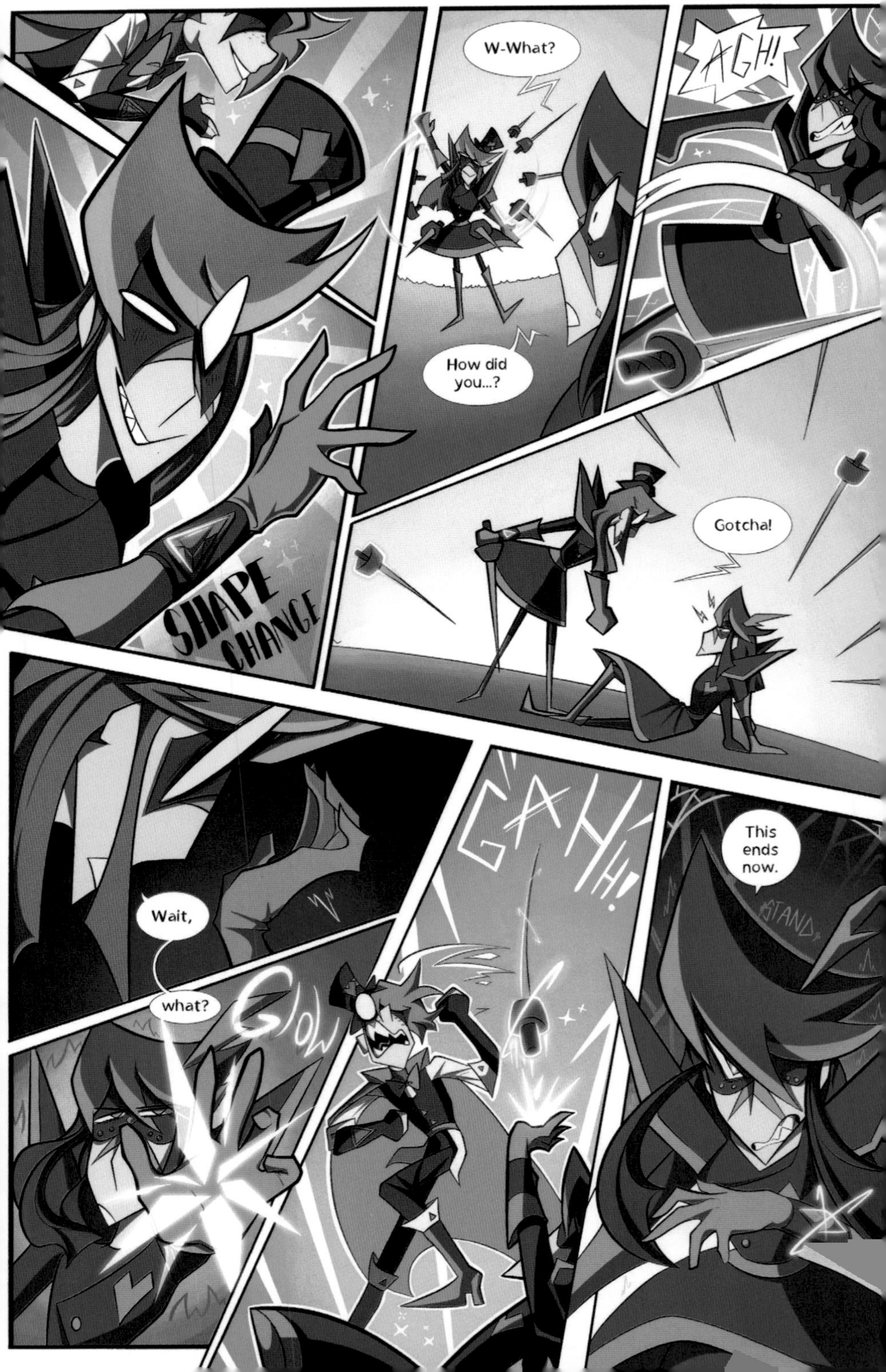
SHAPE CHANGE
W-What?
How did you...?
AGH!
Gotcha!
Wait,
what?
GLOW
GAHH!
This ends now.
STAND

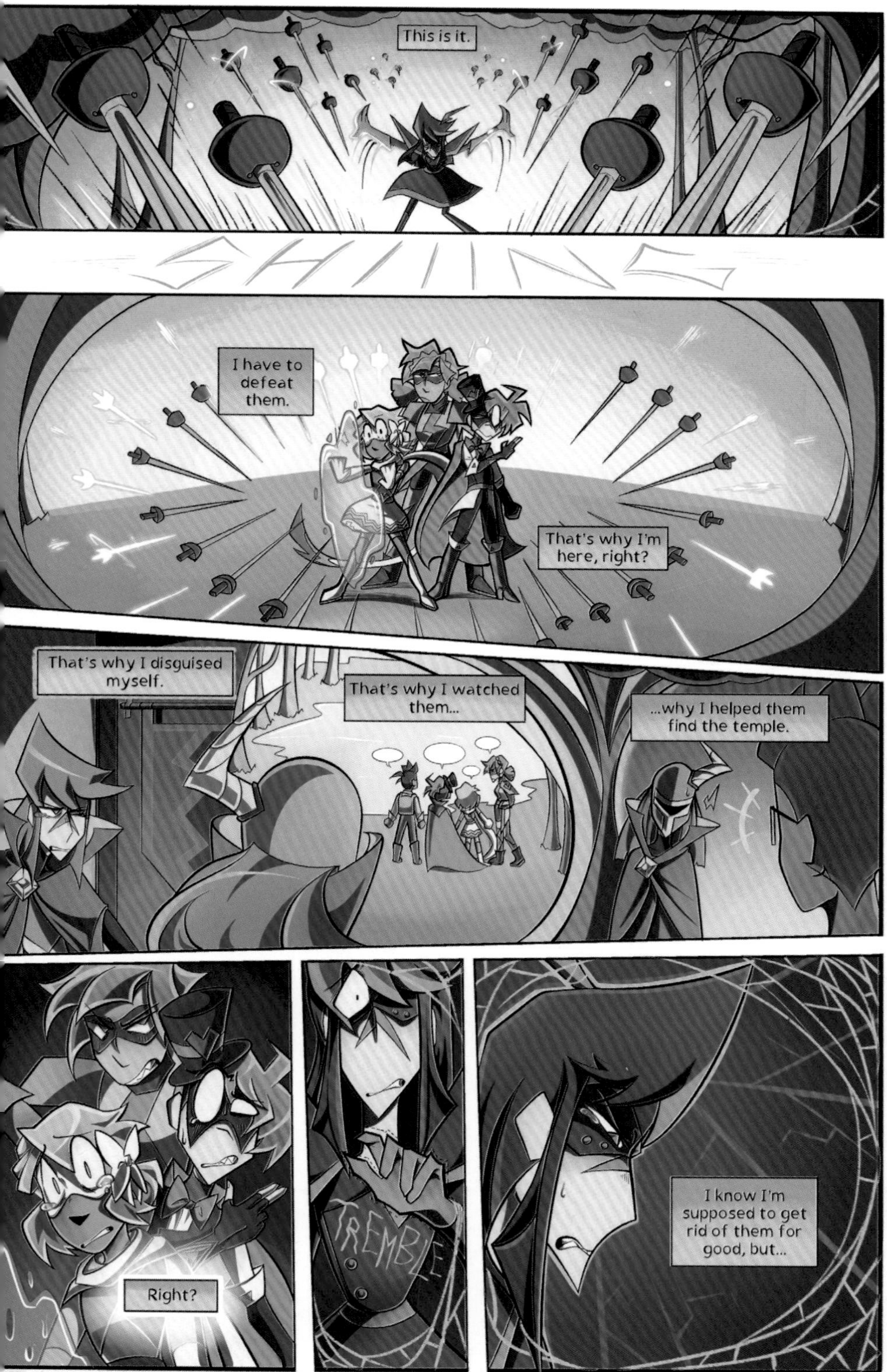

This is it.
SHIING
I have to defeat them.
That's why I'm here, right?
That's why I disguised myself.
That's why I watched them...
...why I helped them find the temple.
Right?
TREMBLE
I know I'm supposed to get rid of them for good, but...

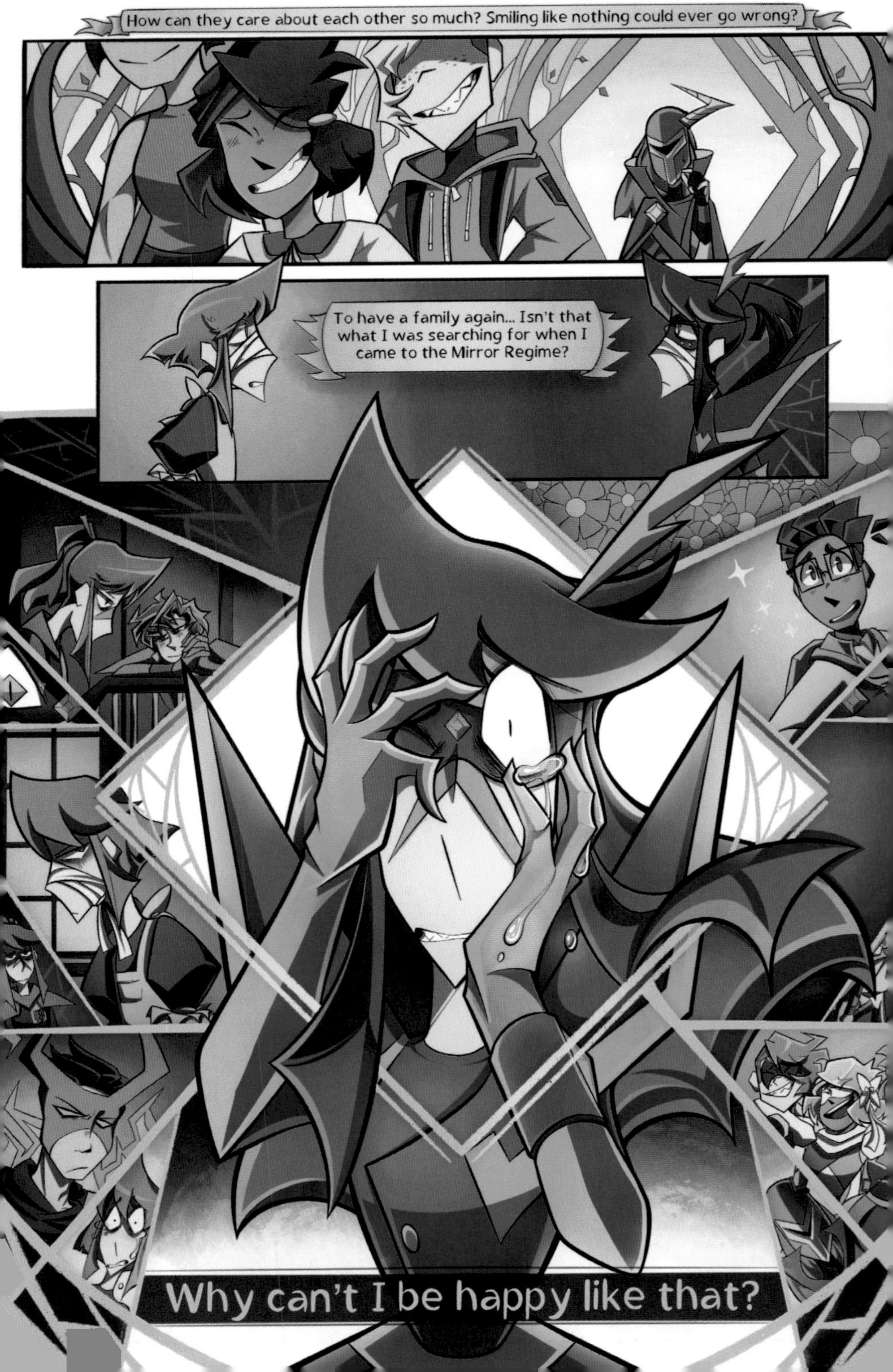
How can they care about each other so much? Smiling like nothing could ever go wrong?
To have a family again... Isn't that what I was searching for when I came to the Mirror Regime?
Why can't I be happy like that?

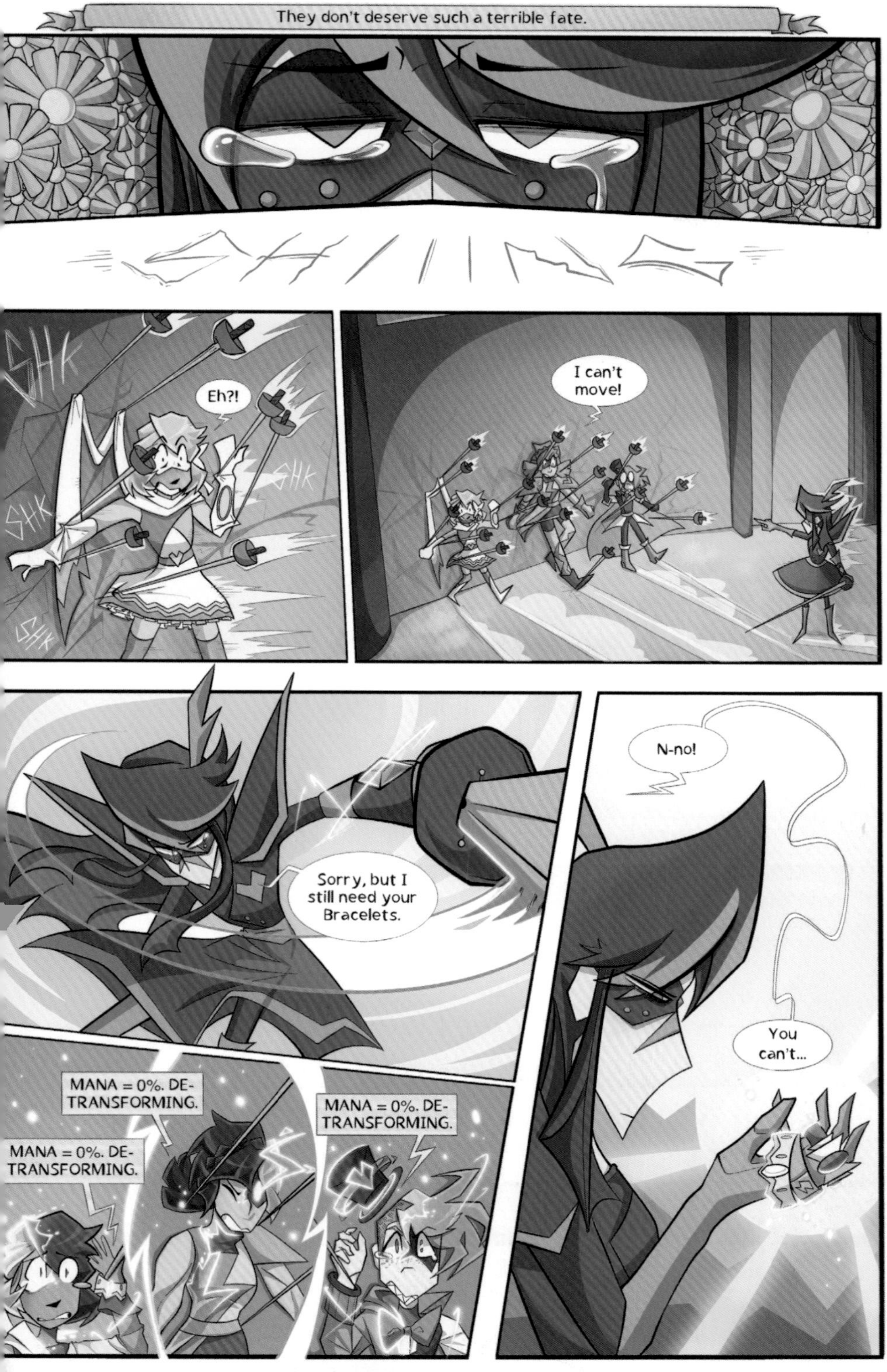
They don't deserve such a terrible fate.
SHIIING
SHK
Eh?!
SHK
SHK
SHK
I can't move!
Sorry, but I still need your Bracelets.
N-no!
You can't...
MANA = 0%. DE-TRANSFORMING.
MANA = 0%. DE-TRANSFORMING.
MANA = 0%. DE-TRANSFORMING.

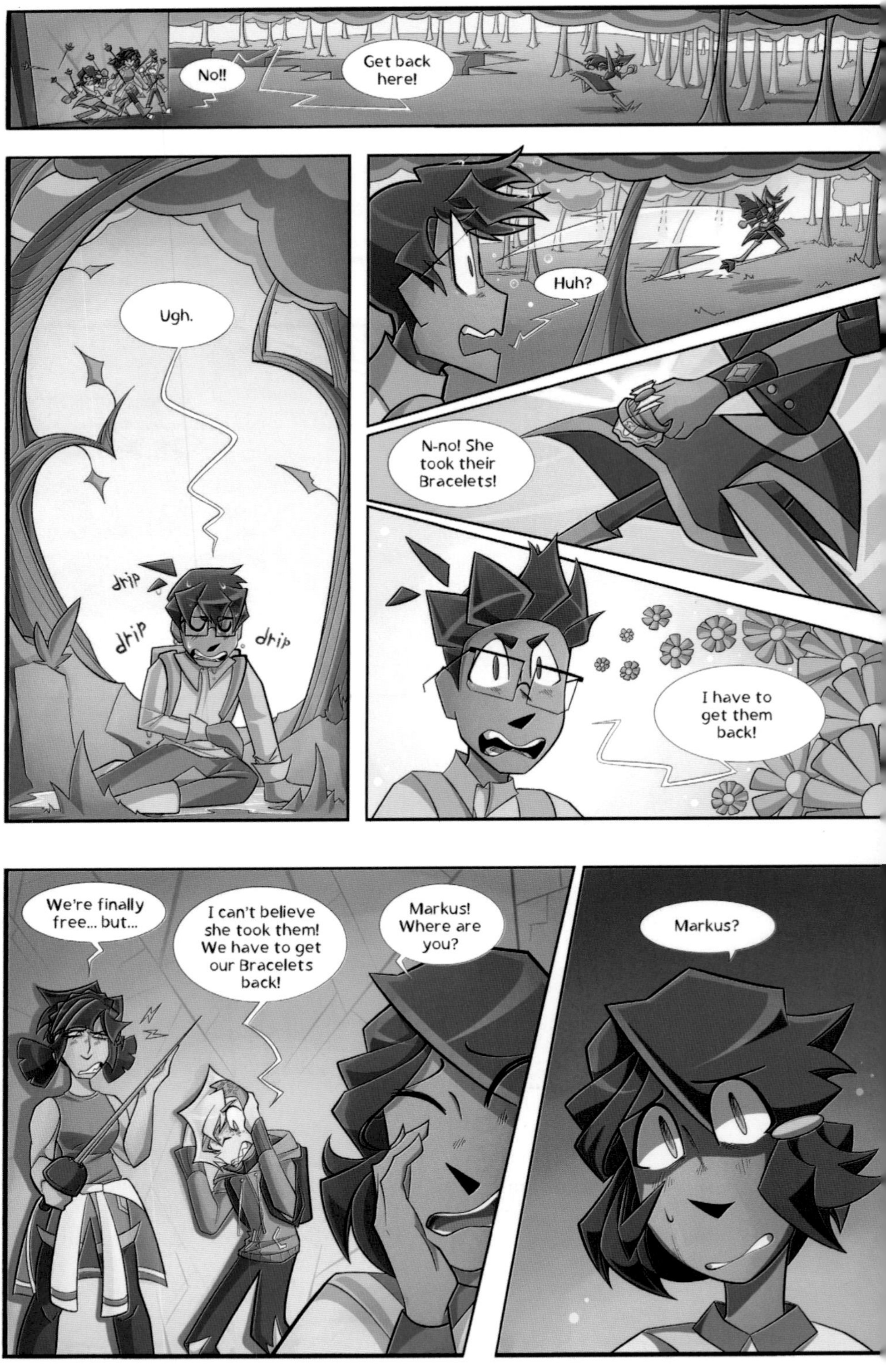
No!!
Get back here!
Ugh.
drip
drip
drip
Huh?
N-no! She took their Bracelets!
I have to get them back!
We're finally free... but...
I can't believe she took them! We have to get our Bracelets back!
Markus! Where are you?
Markus?

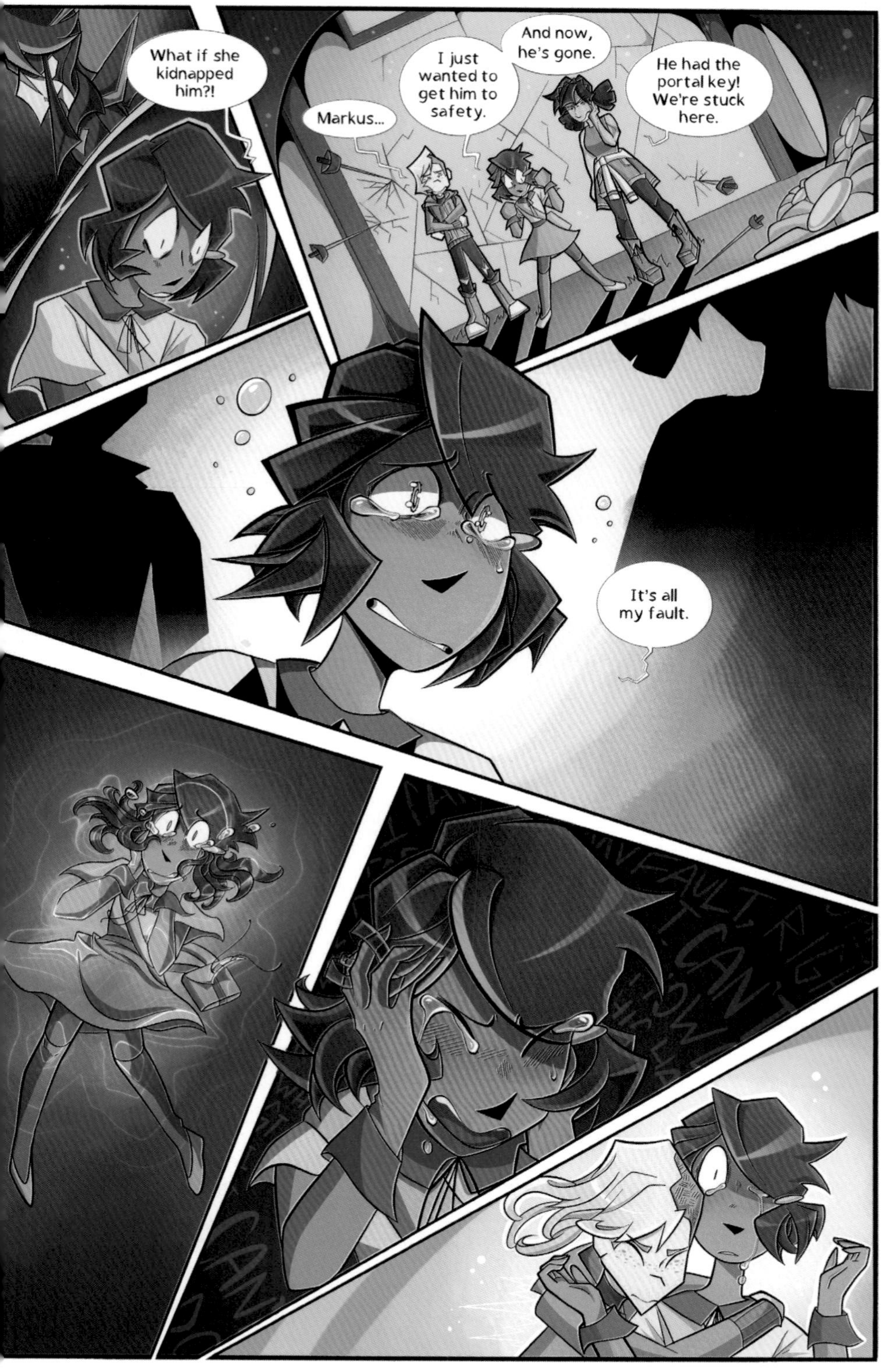
What if she kidnapped him?!
Markus...
I just wanted to get him to safety.
And now, he's gone.
He had the portal key! We're stuck here.
It's all my fault.

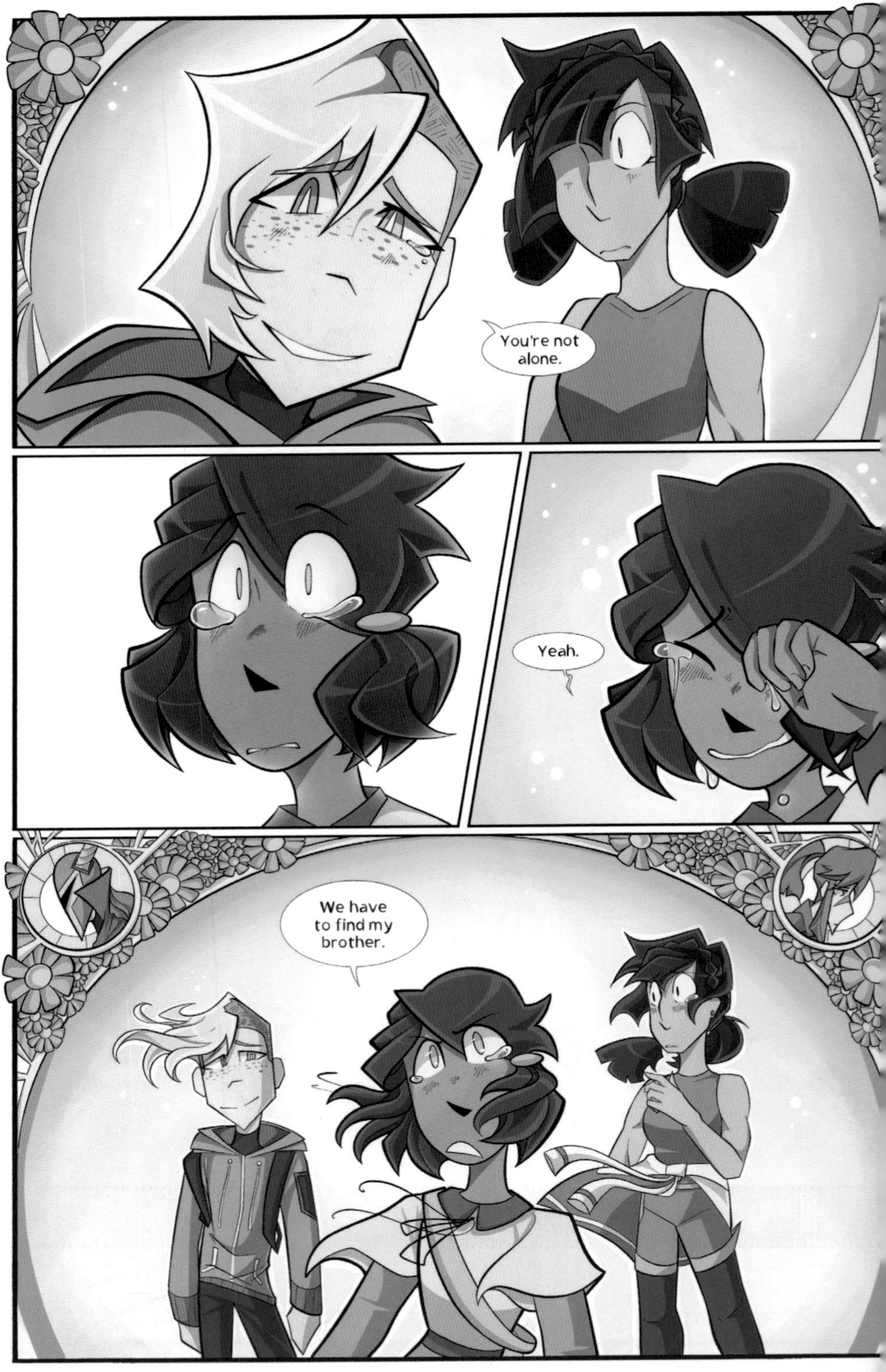
You're not alone.
Yeah.
We have to find my brother.

Chapter 5

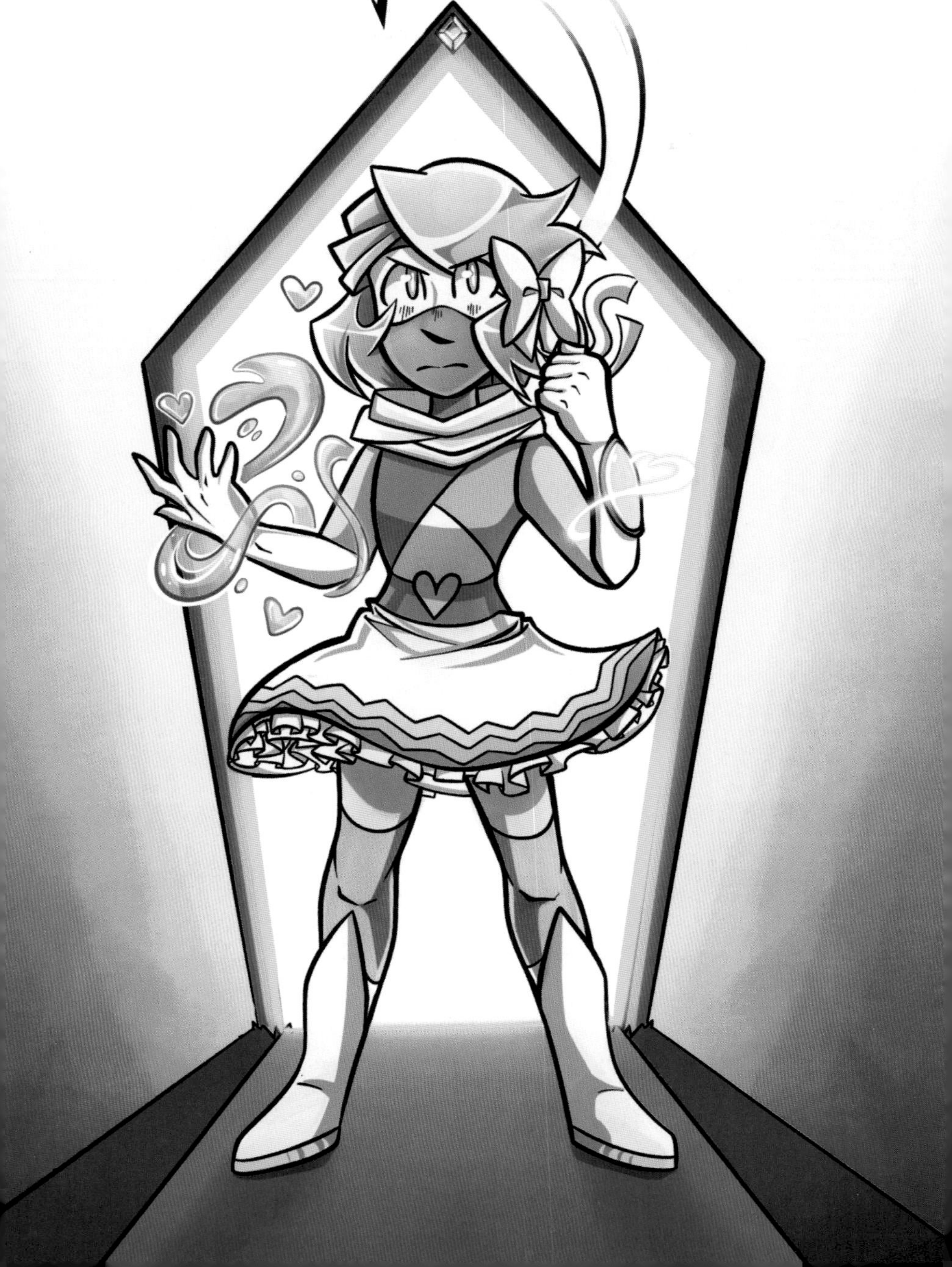

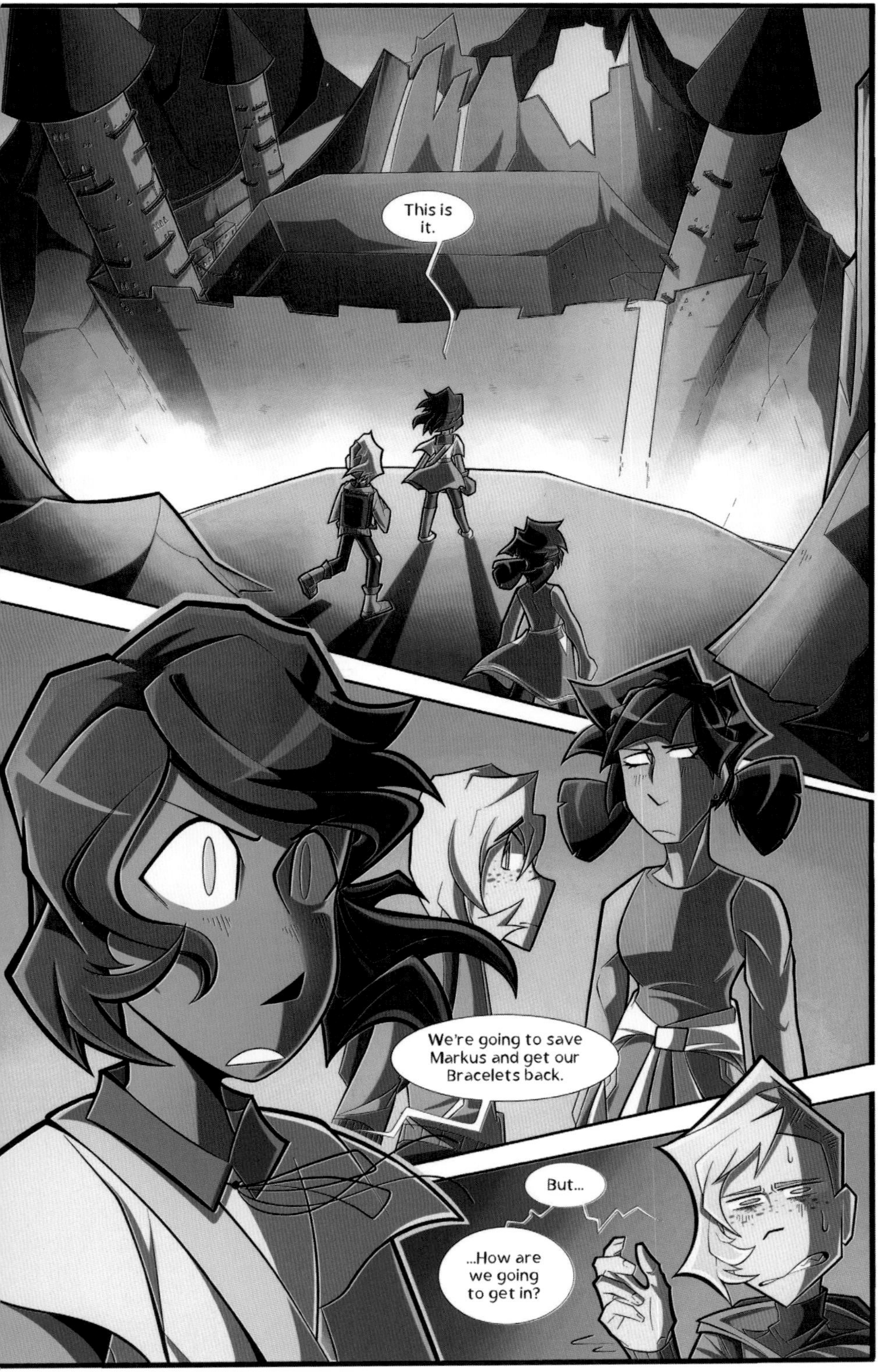
This is it.
We're going to save Markus and get our Bracelets back.
But...
...How are we going to get in?

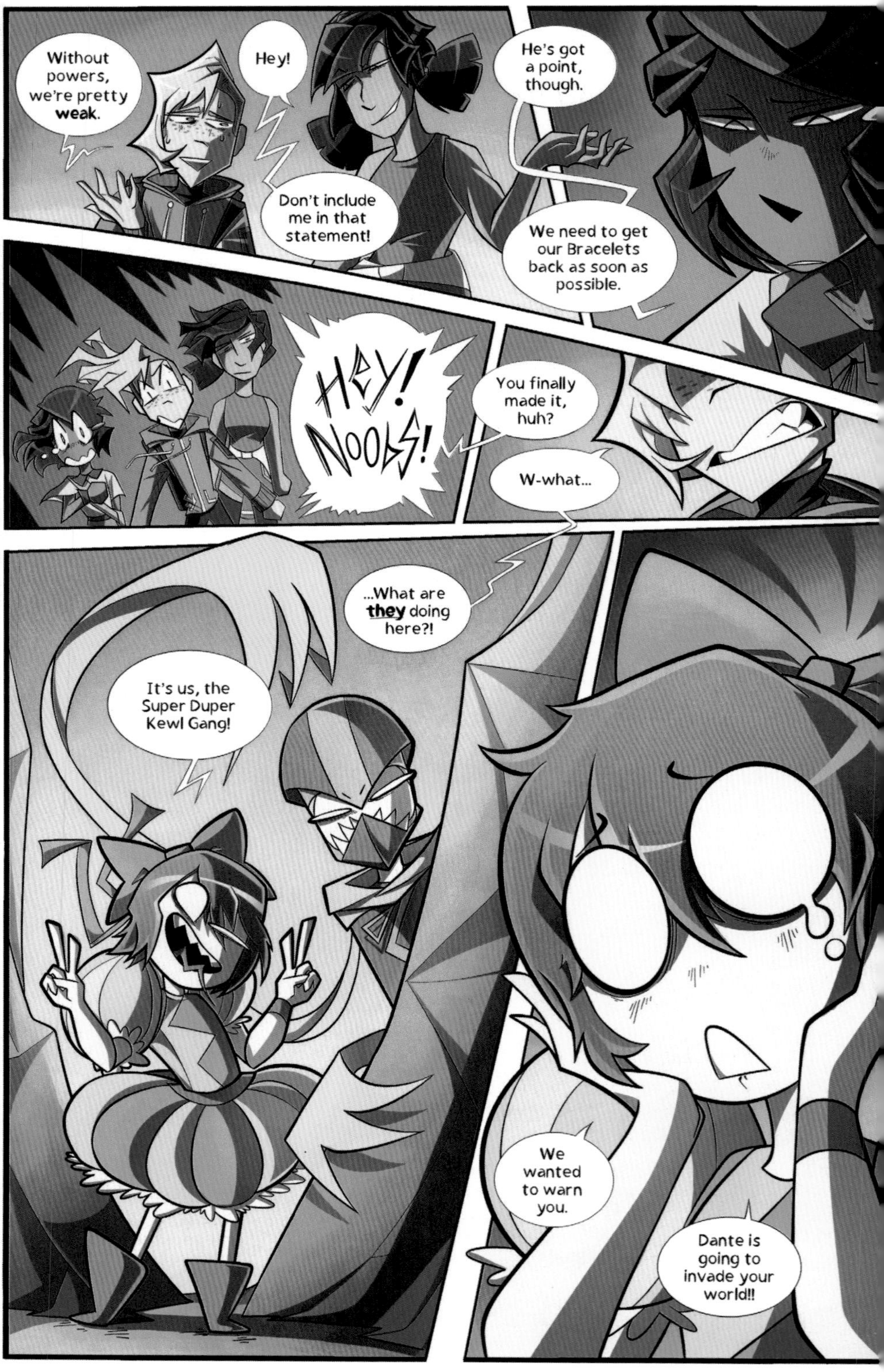
Without powers, we're pretty **weak**.
Hey!
Don't include me in that statement!
He's got a point, though.
We need to get our Bracelets back as soon as possible.
HEY! NOOBS!
You finally made it, huh?
W-what...
...What are **they** doing here?!
It's us, the Super Duper Kewl Gang!
We wanted to warn you.
Dante is going to invade your world!!

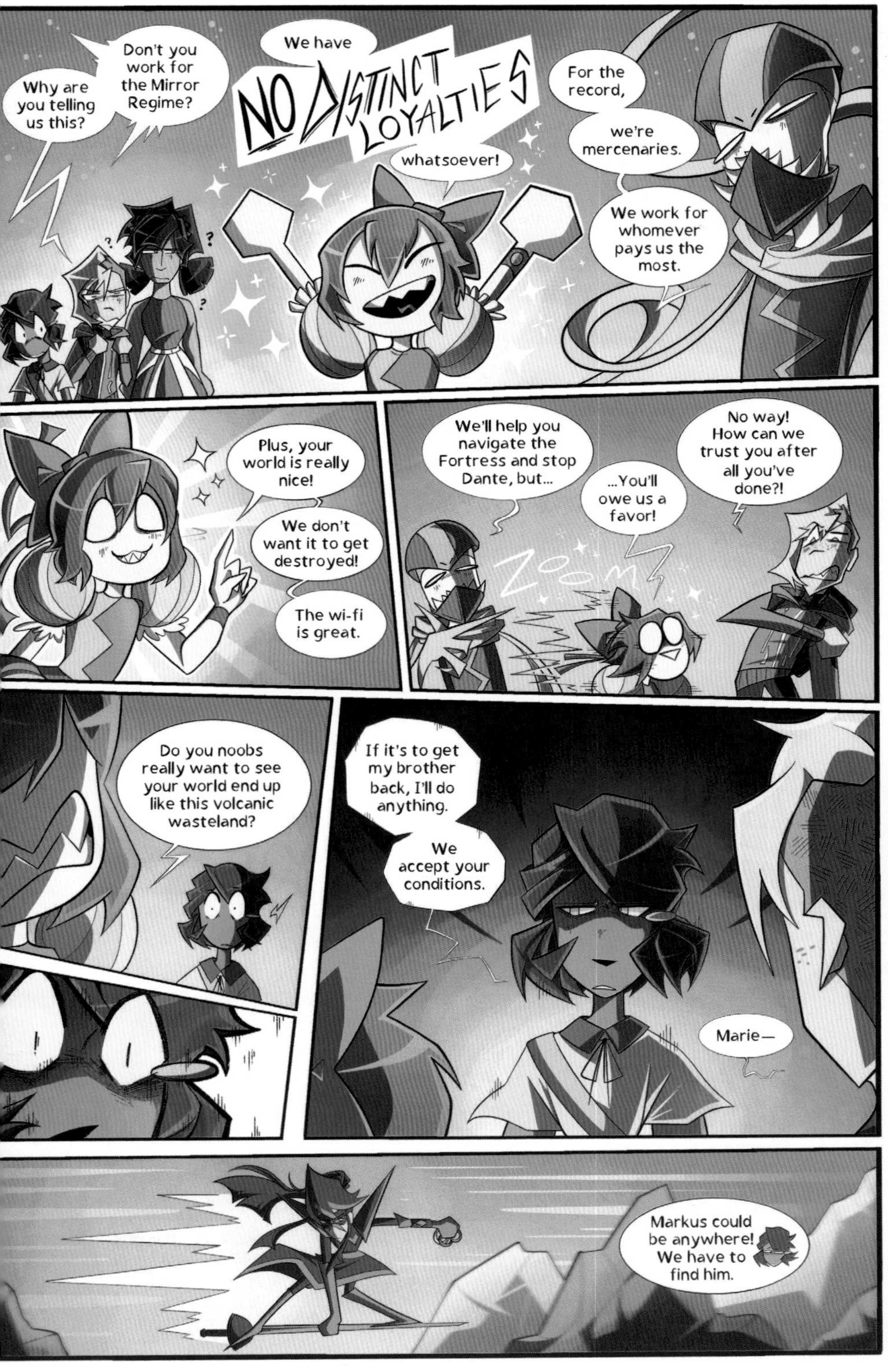
Why are you telling us this?
Don't you work for the Mirror Regime?
We have
NO DISTINCT LOYALTIES
whatsoever!
For the record,
we're mercenaries.
We work for whomever pays us the most.
Plus, your world is really nice!
We don't want it to get destroyed!
The wi-fi is great.
We'll help you navigate the Fortress and stop Dante, but...
...You'll owe us a favor!
ZOOM
No way! How can we trust you after all you've done?!
Do you noobs really want to see your world end up like this volcanic wasteland?
If it's to get my brother back, I'll do anything.
We accept your conditions.
Marie—
Markus could be anywhere! We have to find him.

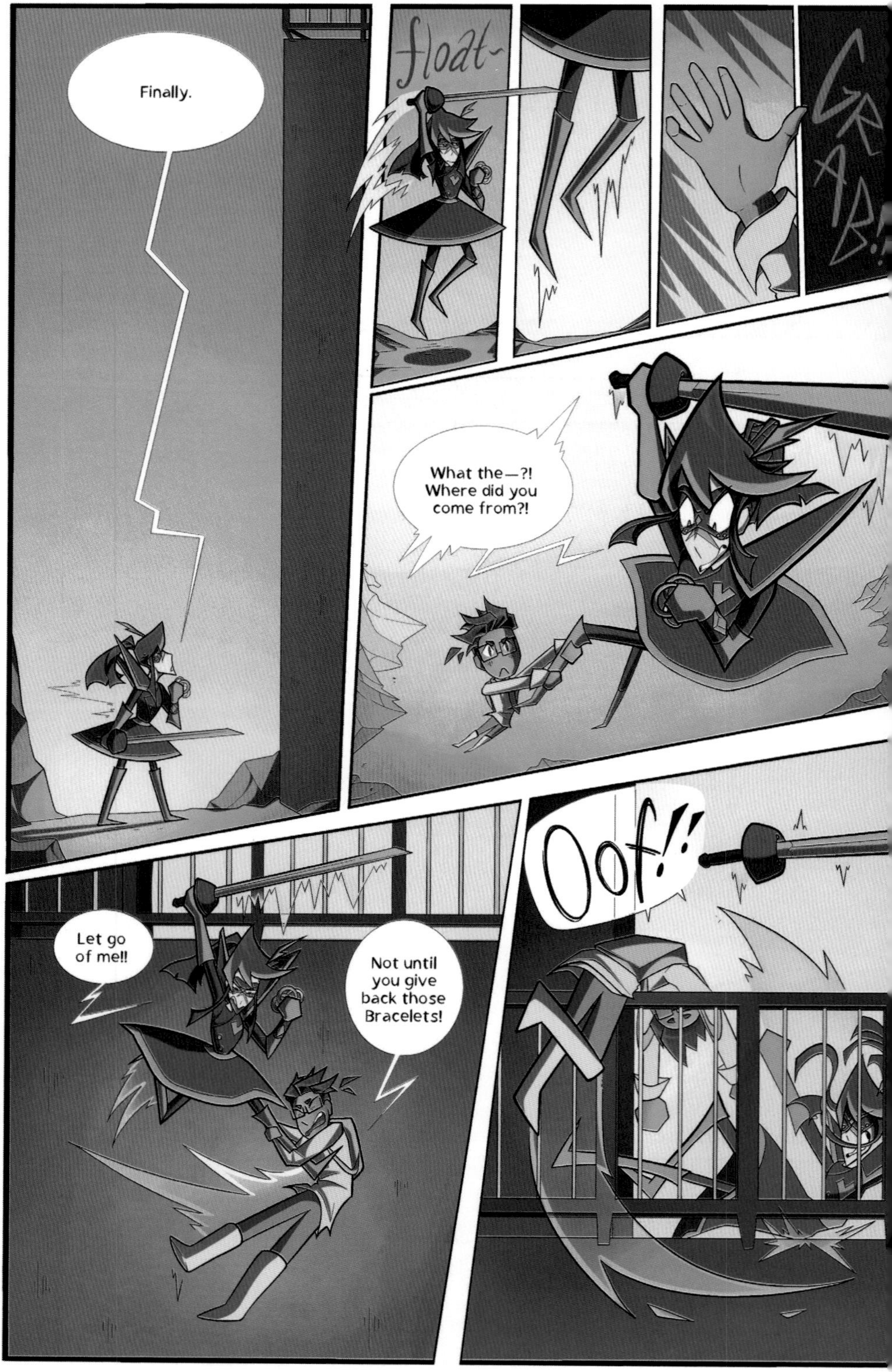
Finally.
float~
GRAB!!
What the—?! Where did you come from?!
Let go of me!!
Not until you give back those Bracelets!
Oof!!

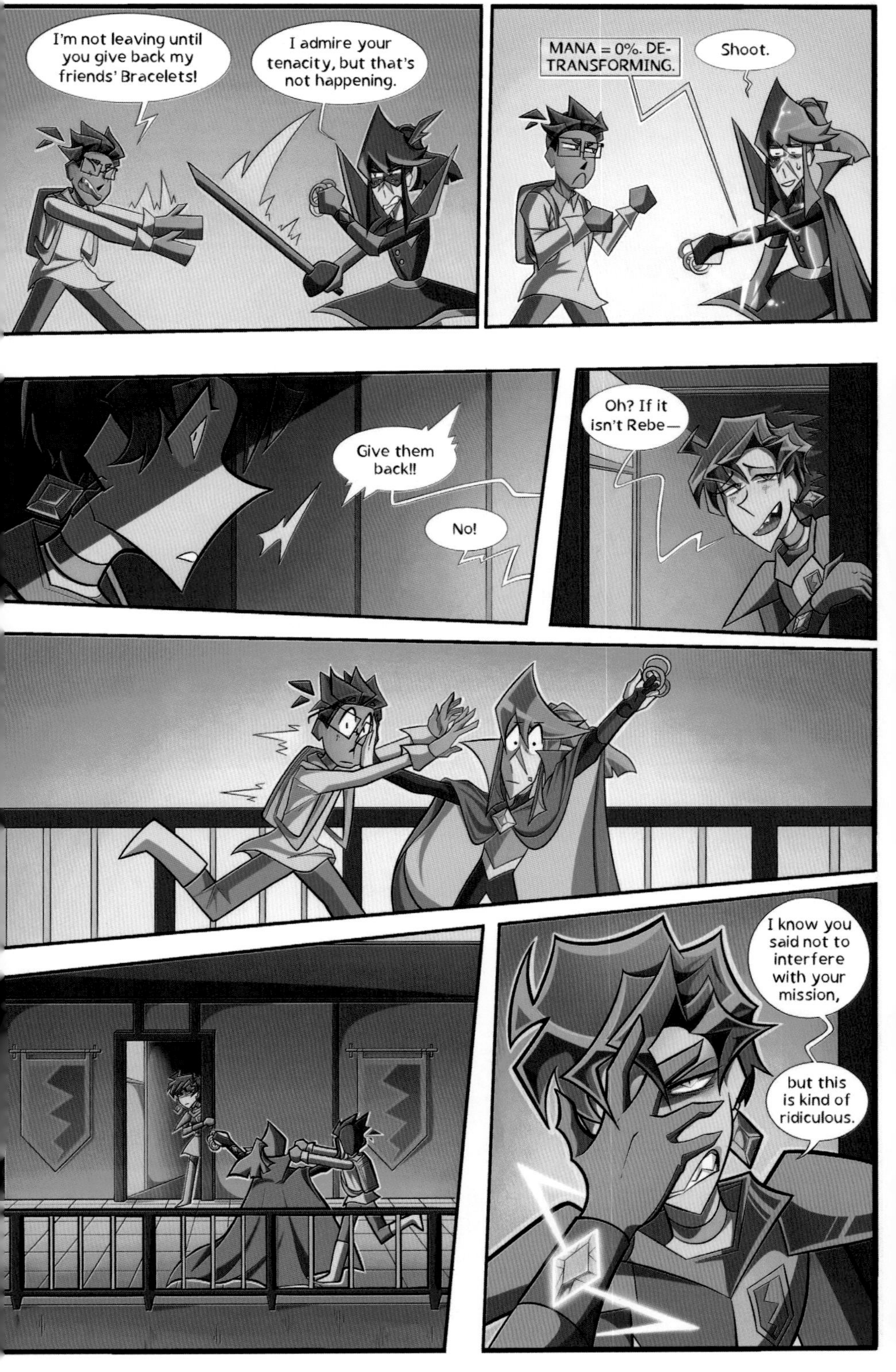
I'm not leaving until you give back my friends' Bracelets!
I admire your tenacity, but that's not happening.
MANA = 0%. DE-TRANSFORMING.
Shoot.
Give them back!!
No!
Oh? If it isn't Rebe—
I know you said not to interfere with your mission,
but this is kind of ridiculous.

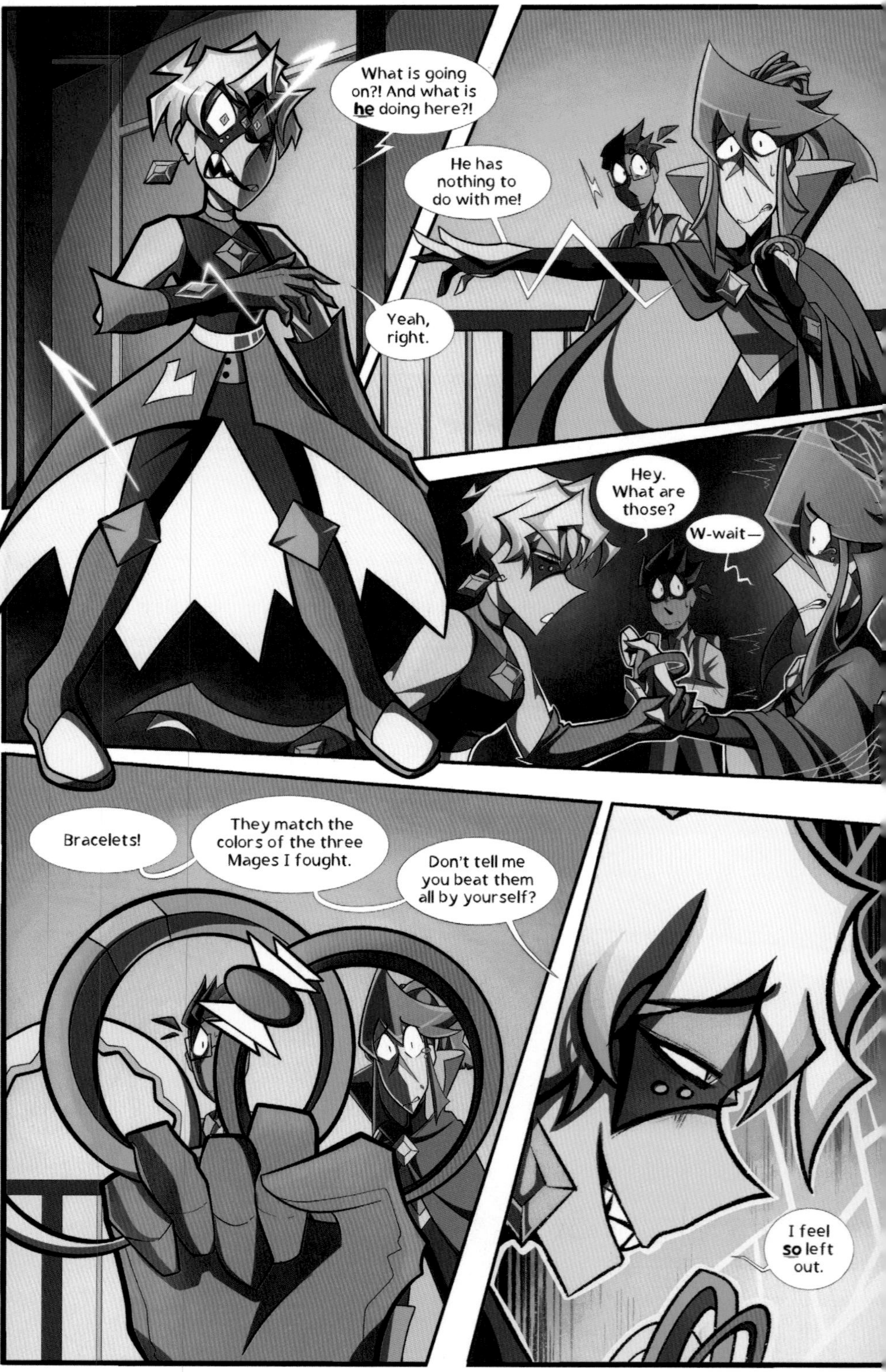
What is going on?! And what is **he** doing here?!
He has nothing to do with me!
Yeah, right.
Hey. What are those?
W-wait—
Bracelets!
They match the colors of the three Mages I fought.
Don't tell me you beat them all by yourself?
I feel **so** left out.

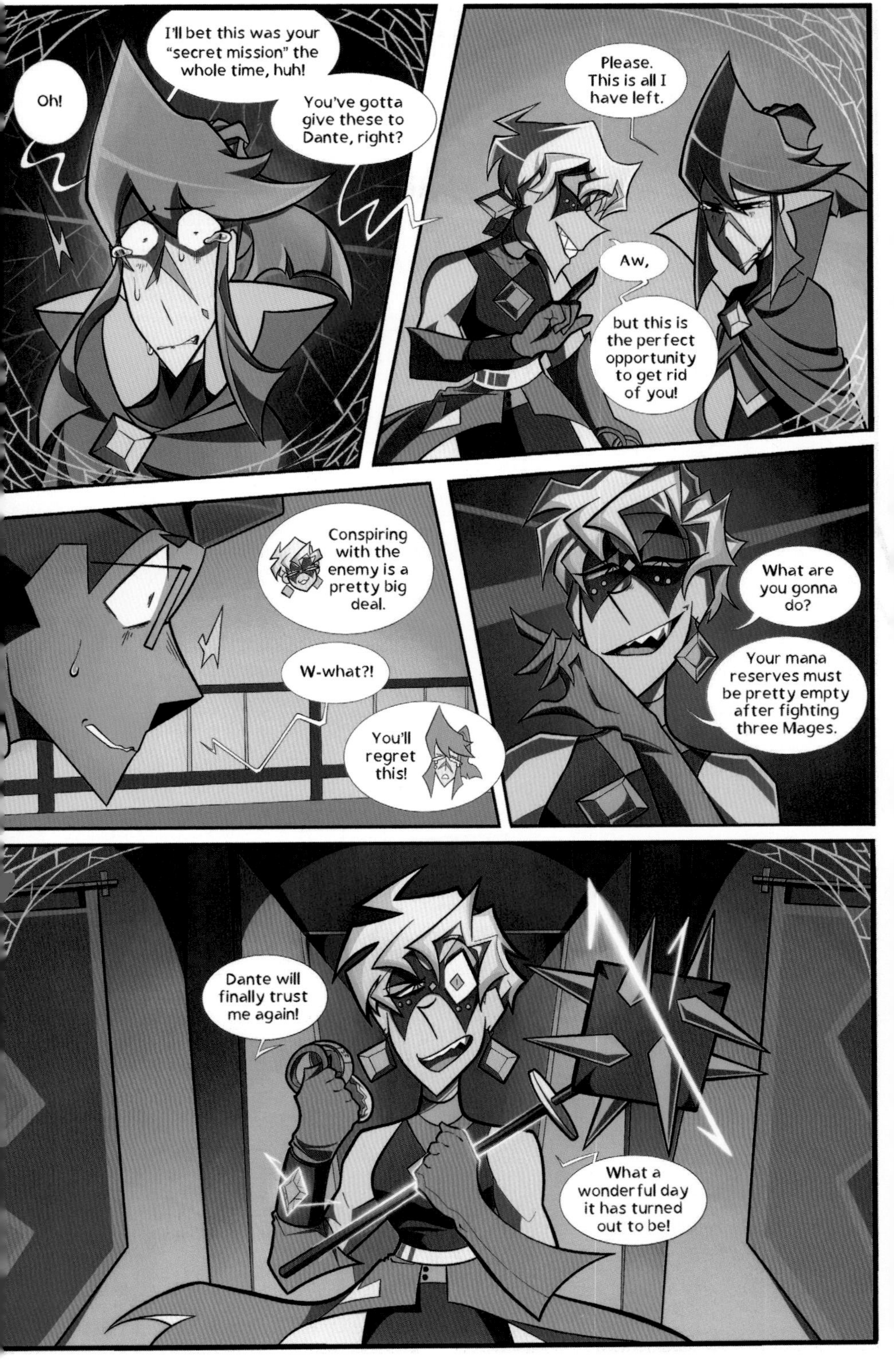
Oh!
I'll bet this was your "secret mission" the whole time, huh!
You've gotta give these to Dante, right?
Please. This is all I have left.
Aw,
but this is the perfect opportunity to get rid of you!
Conspiring with the enemy is a pretty big deal.
W-what?!
You'll regret this!
What are you gonna do?
Your mana reserves must be pretty empty after fighting three Mages.
Dante will finally trust me again!
What a wonderful day it has turned out to be!

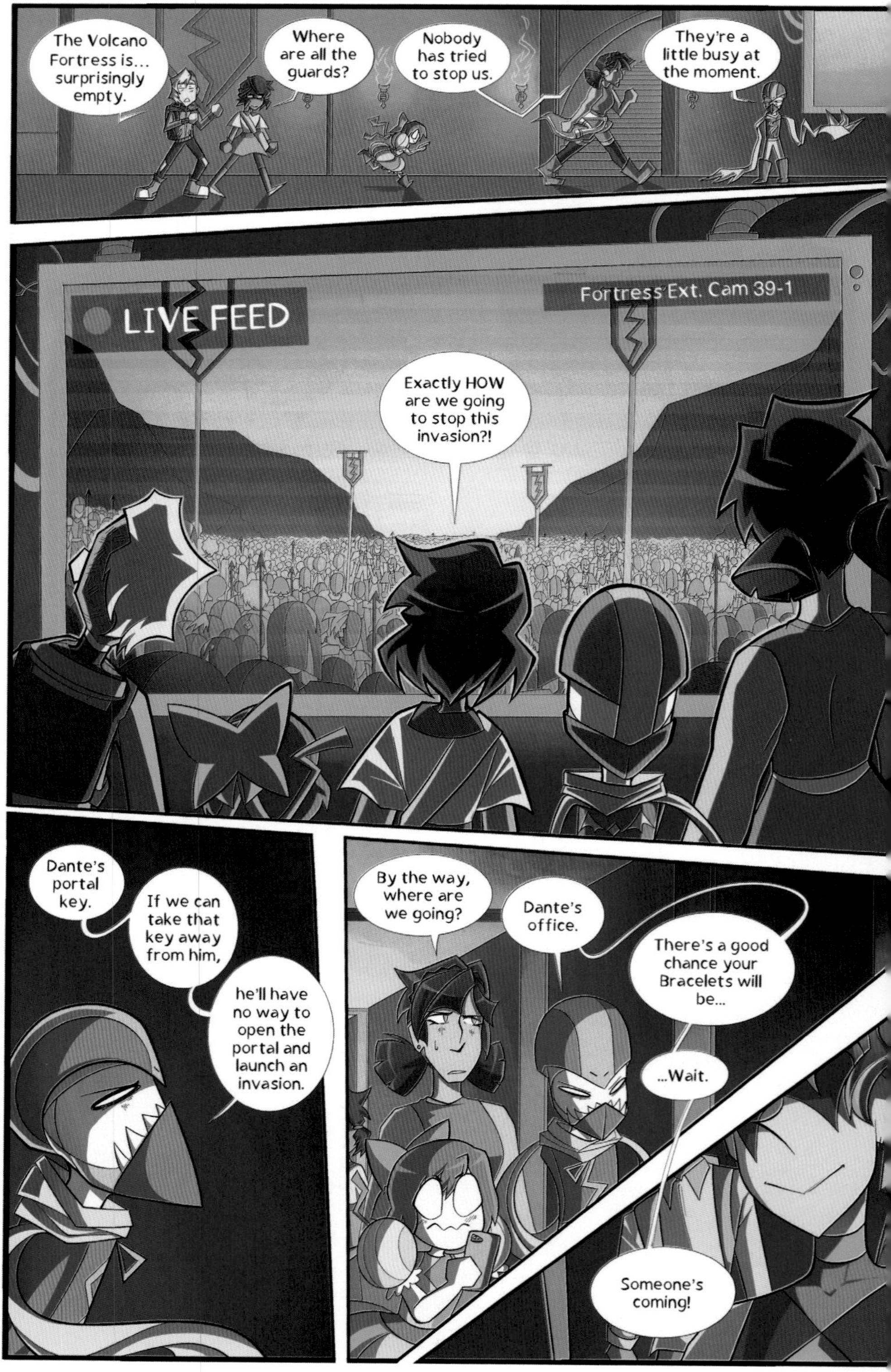
The Volcano Fortress is... surprisingly empty.
Where are all the guards?
Nobody has tried to stop us.
They're a little busy at the moment.
LIVE FEED
Fortress Ext. Cam 39-1
Exactly HOW are we going to stop this invasion?!
Dante's portal key.
If we can take that key away from him,
he'll have no way to open the portal and launch an invasion.
By the way, where are we going?
Dante's office.
There's a good chance your Bracelets will be...
...Wait.
Someone's coming!

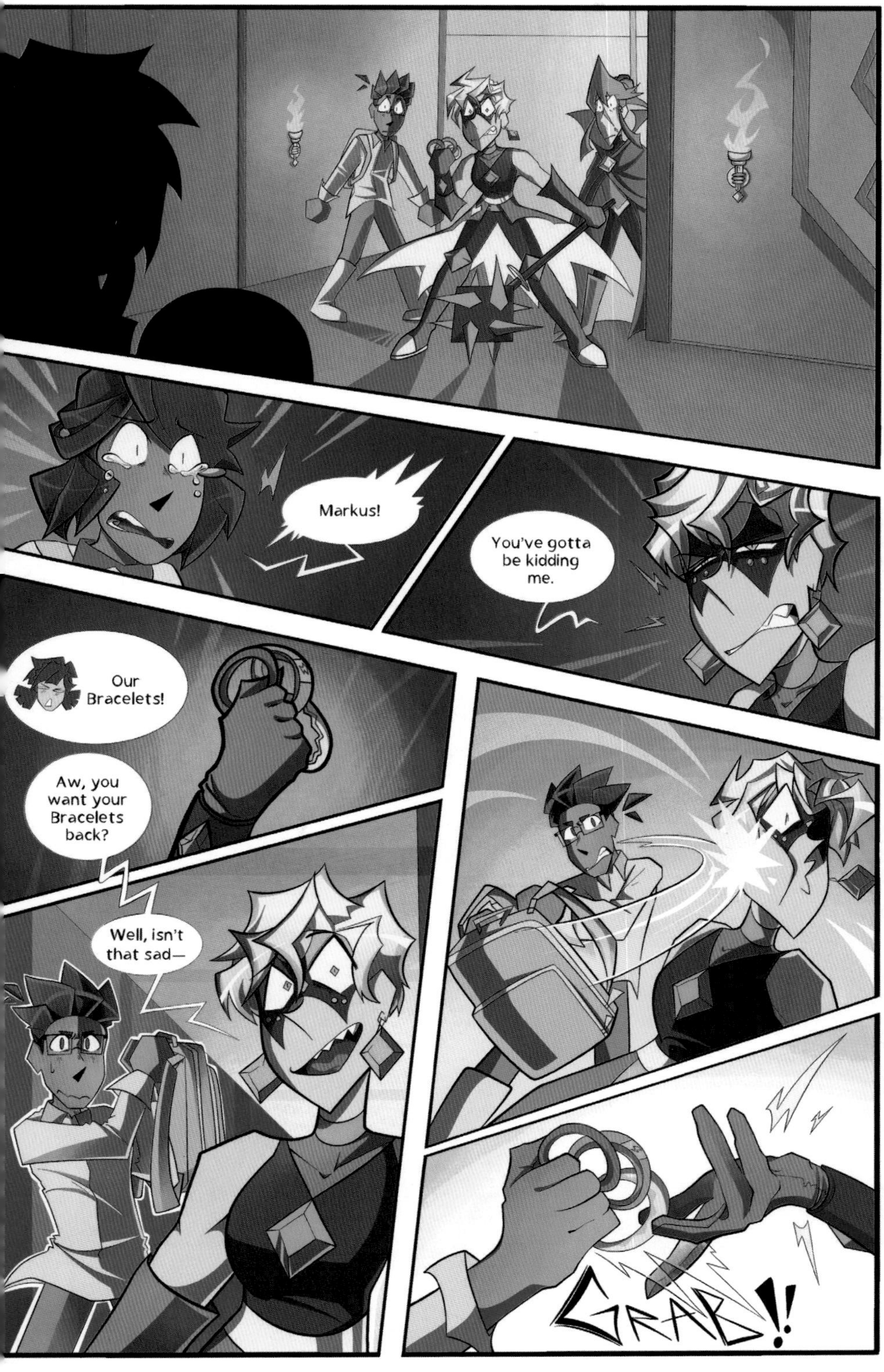
Markus!
You've gotta be kidding me.
Our Bracelets!
Aw, you want your Bracelets back?
Well, isn't that sad—
GRAB!!

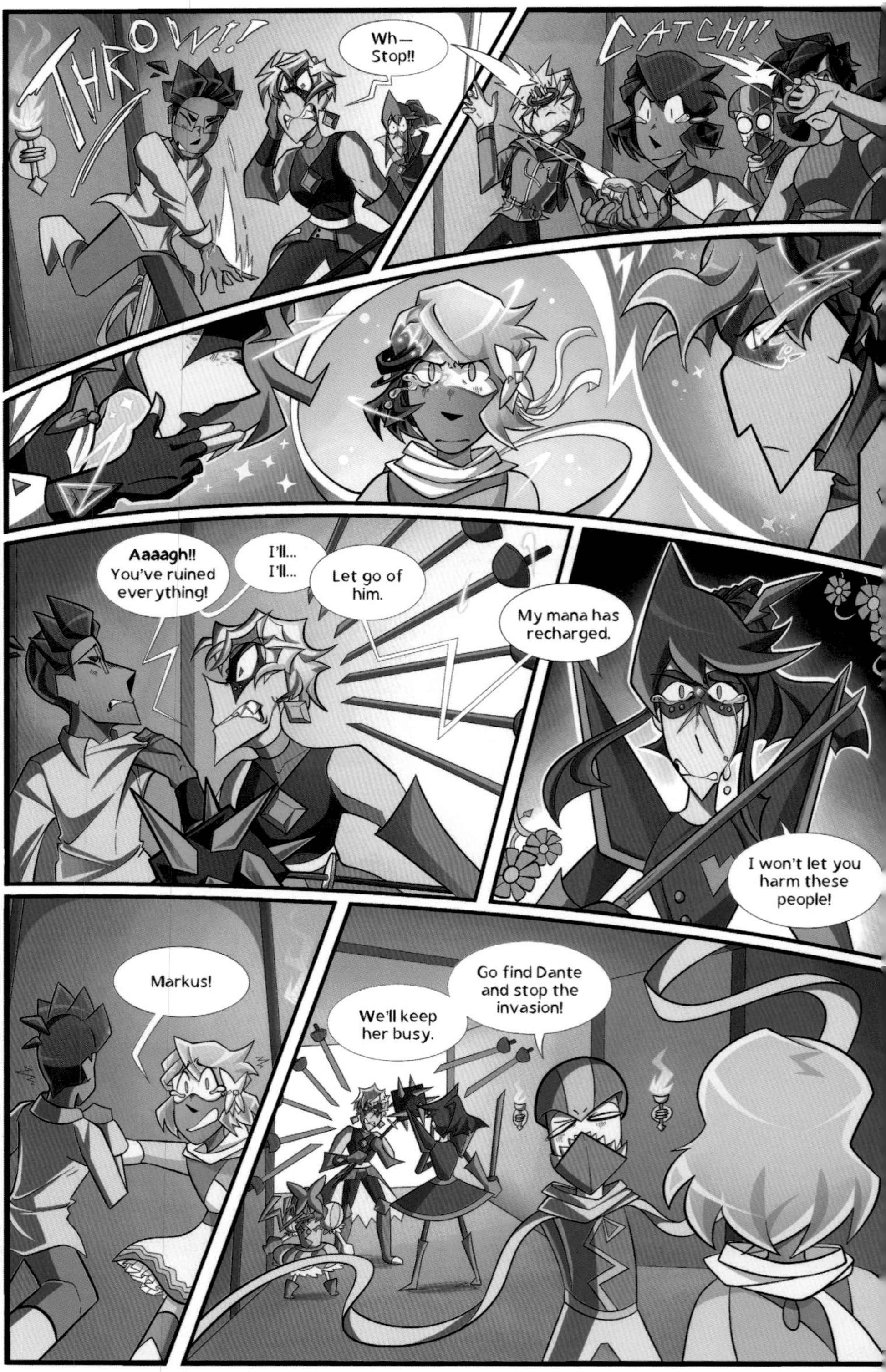
THROW!!
Wh— Stop!!
CATCH!!
Aaaagh!! You've ruined everything!
I'll... I'll...
Let go of him.
My mana has recharged.
I won't let you harm these people!
Markus!
Go find Dante and stop the invasion!
We'll keep her busy.

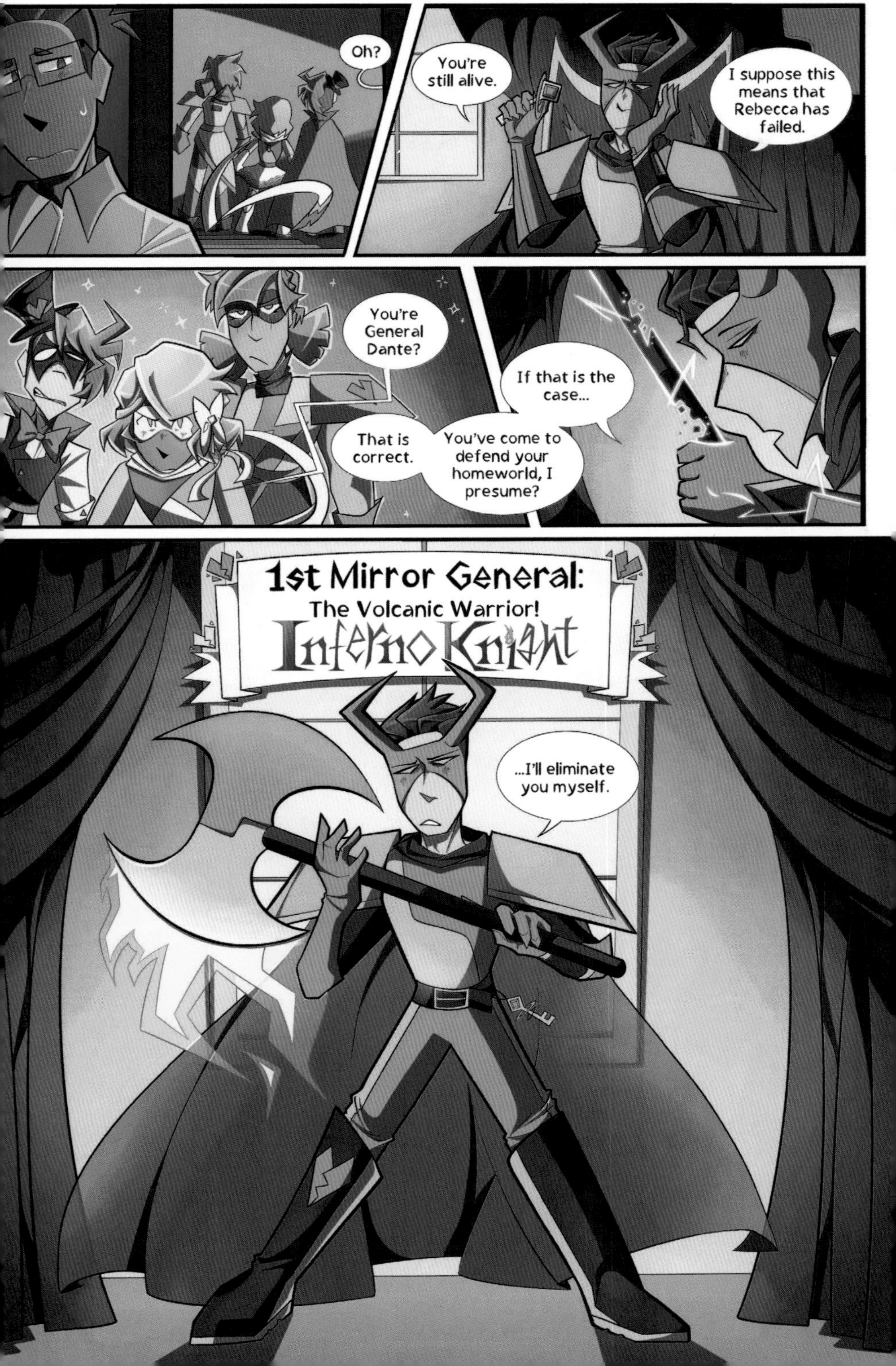
Oh?
You're still alive.
I suppose this means that Rebecca has failed.
You're General Dante?
That is correct.
If that is the case...
You've come to defend your homeworld, I presume?
1st Mirror General:
The Volcanic Warrior!
Inferno Knight
...I'll eliminate you myself.

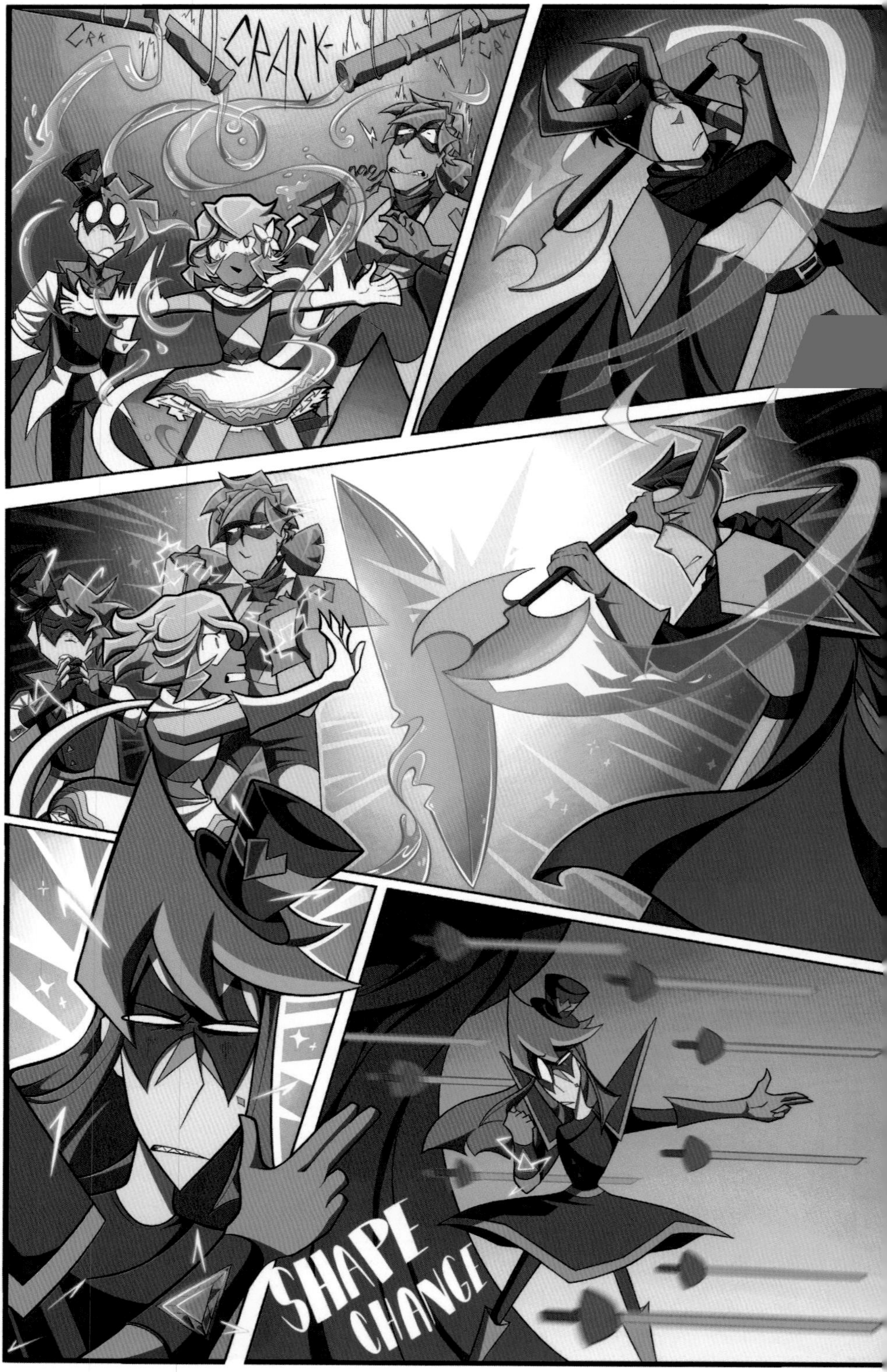

CRK
CRACK
CRK
SHAPE CHANGE

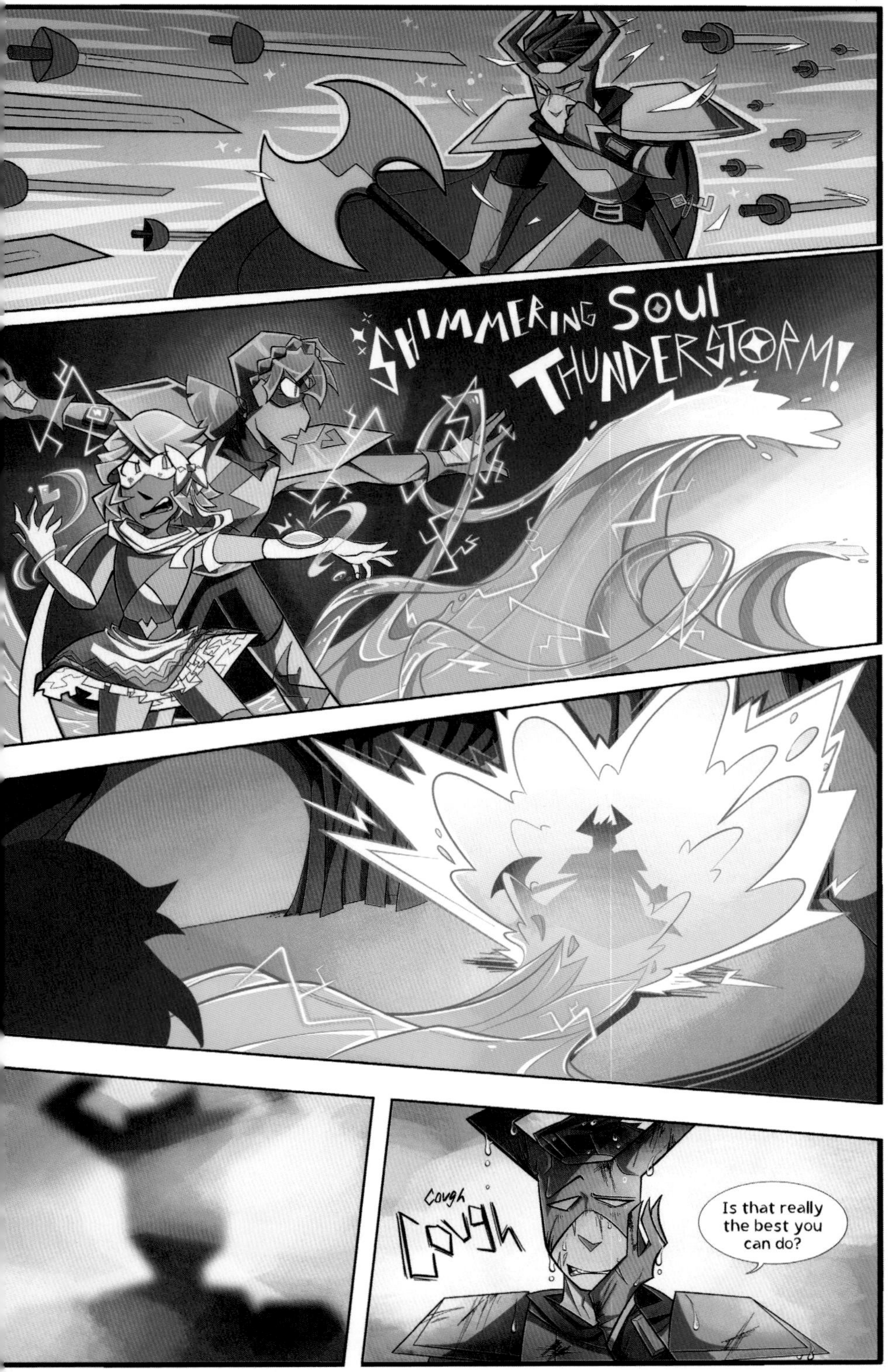
SHIMMERING SOUL THUNDERSTORM!
Cough
Cough
Is that really the best you can do?

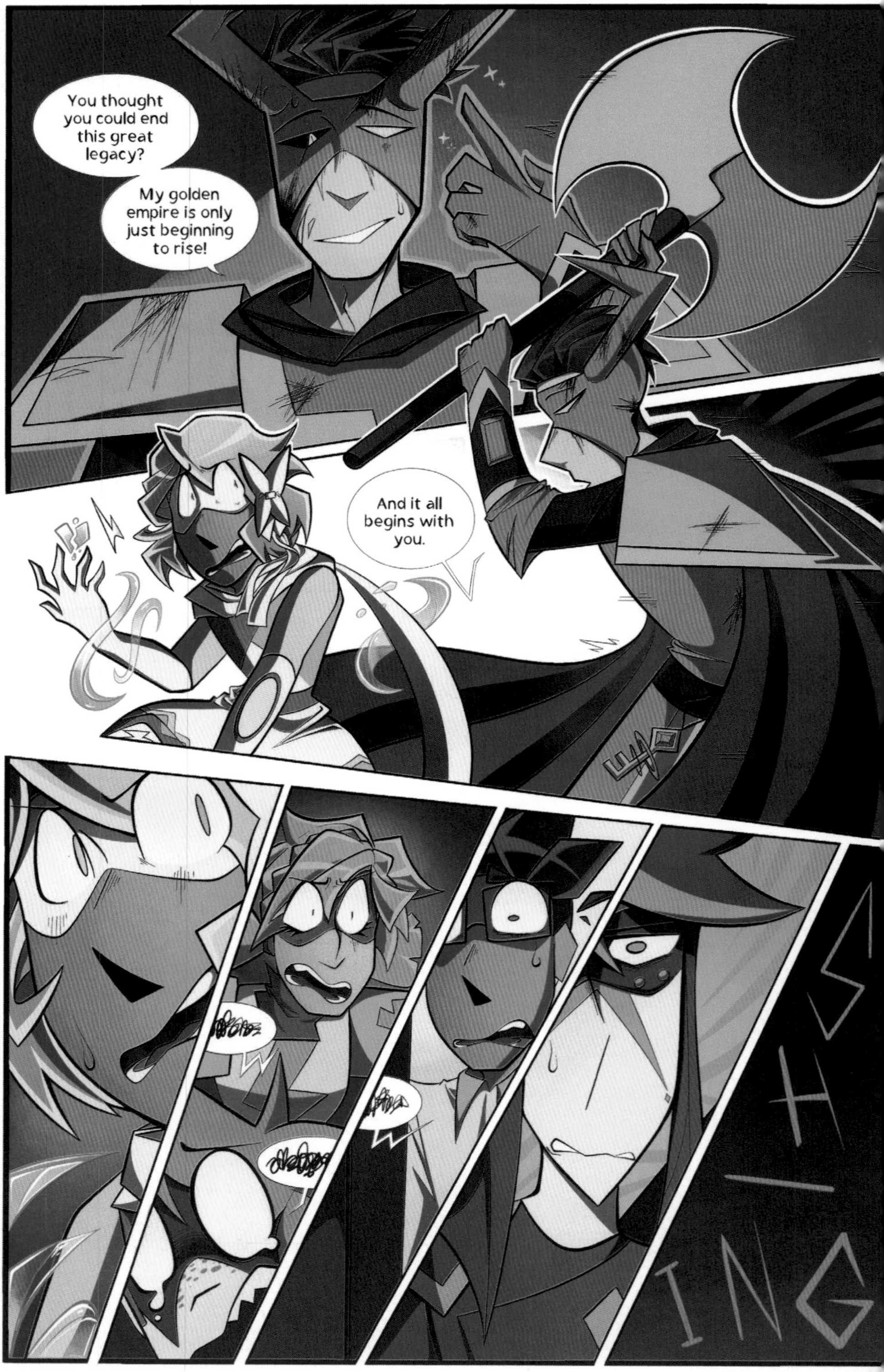
You thought you could end this great legacy?
My golden empire is only just beginning to rise!
And it all begins with you.
SHHHING

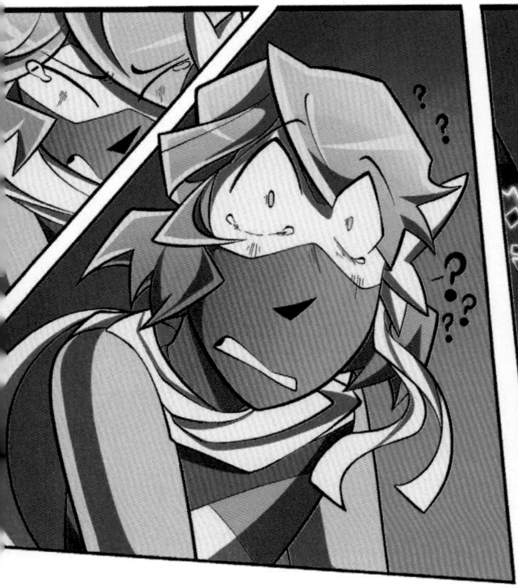

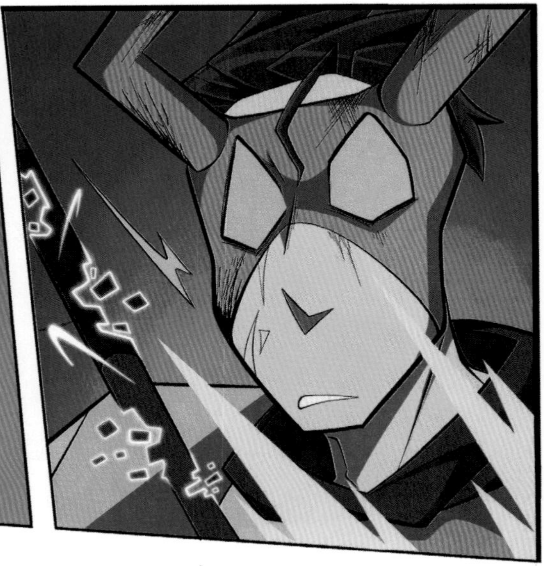

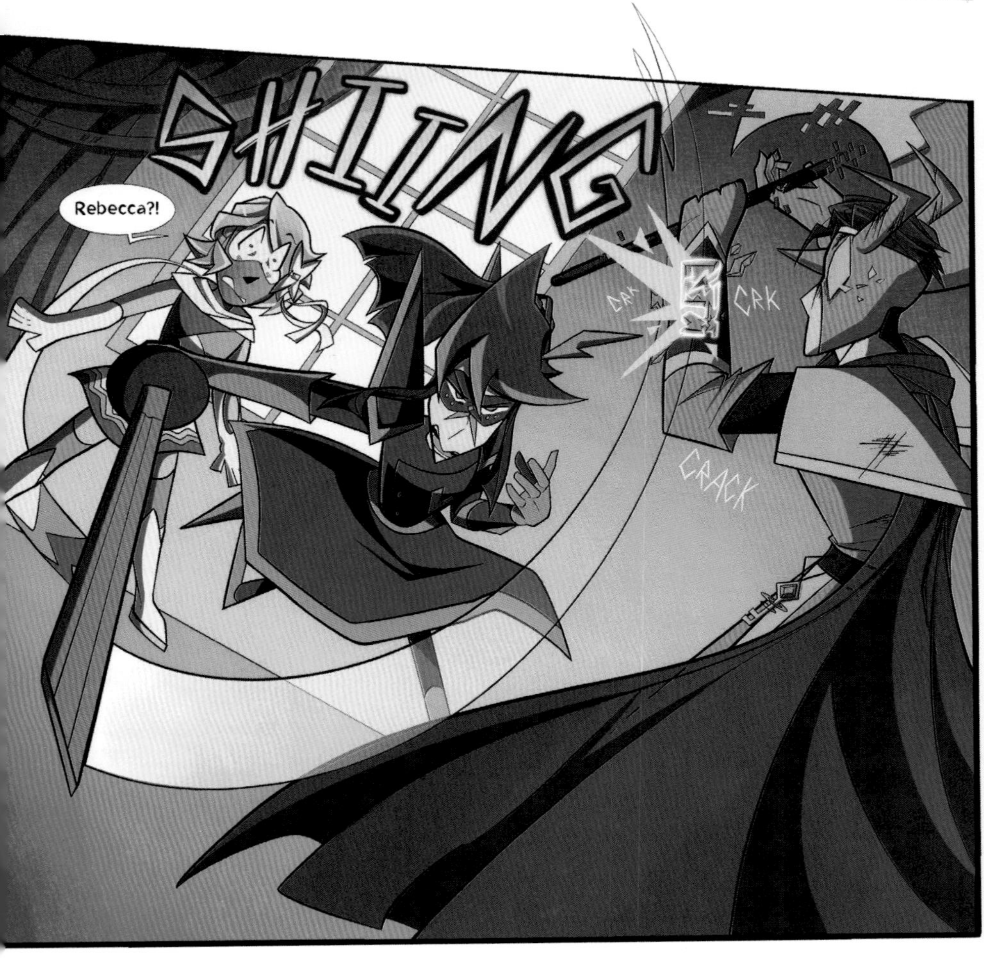
SHIING
Rebecca?!
CRK
CRK
CRACK

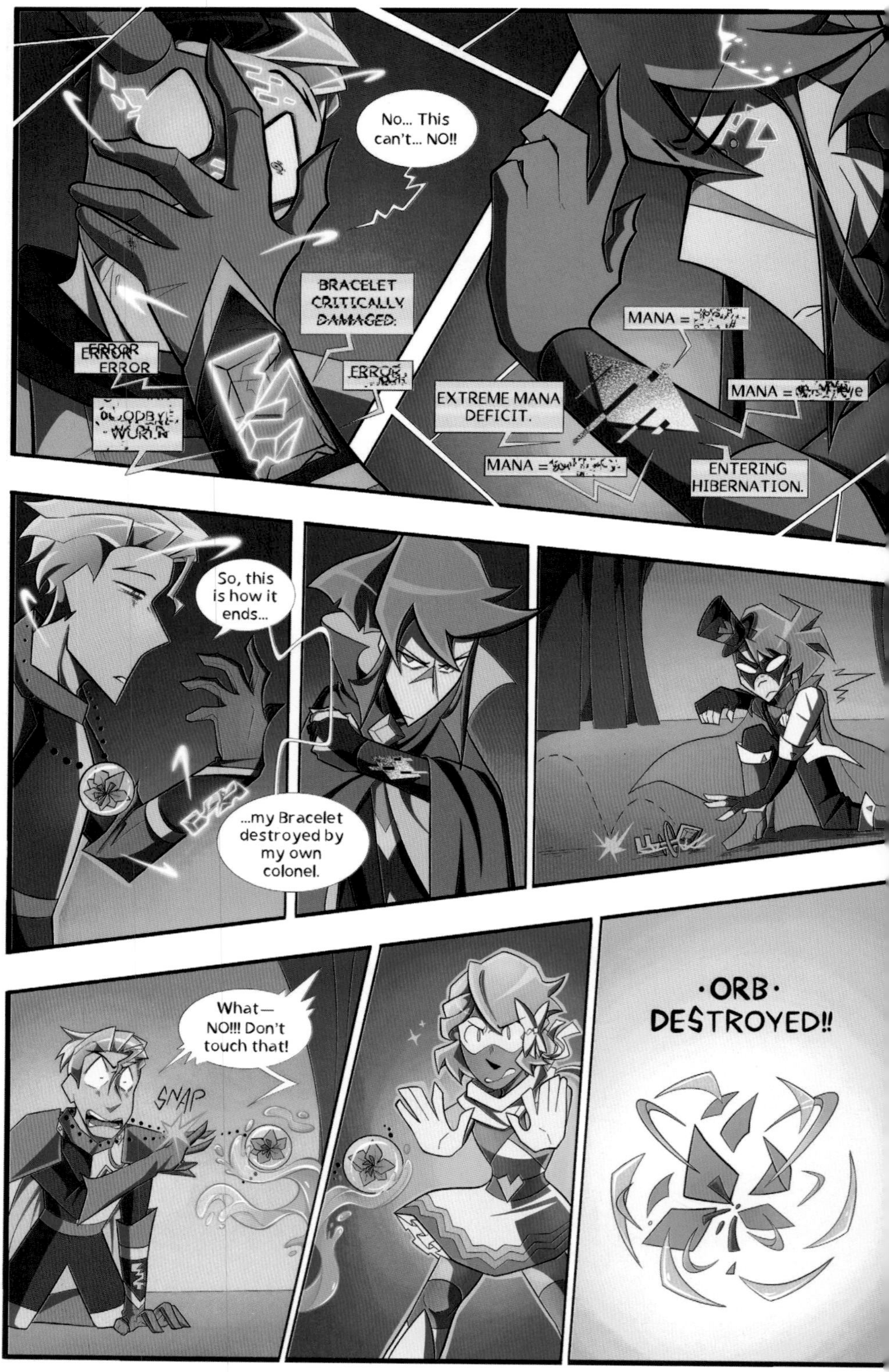
No... This can't... NO!!
BRACELET CRITICALLY DAMAGED.
ERROR ERROR ERROR
ERROR
EXTREME MANA DEFICIT.
MANA =
MANA =
MANA =
ENTERING HIBERNATION.
So, this is how it ends...
...my Bracelet destroyed by my own colonel.
What— NO!!! Don't touch that!
SNAP
·ORB· DESTROYED!!

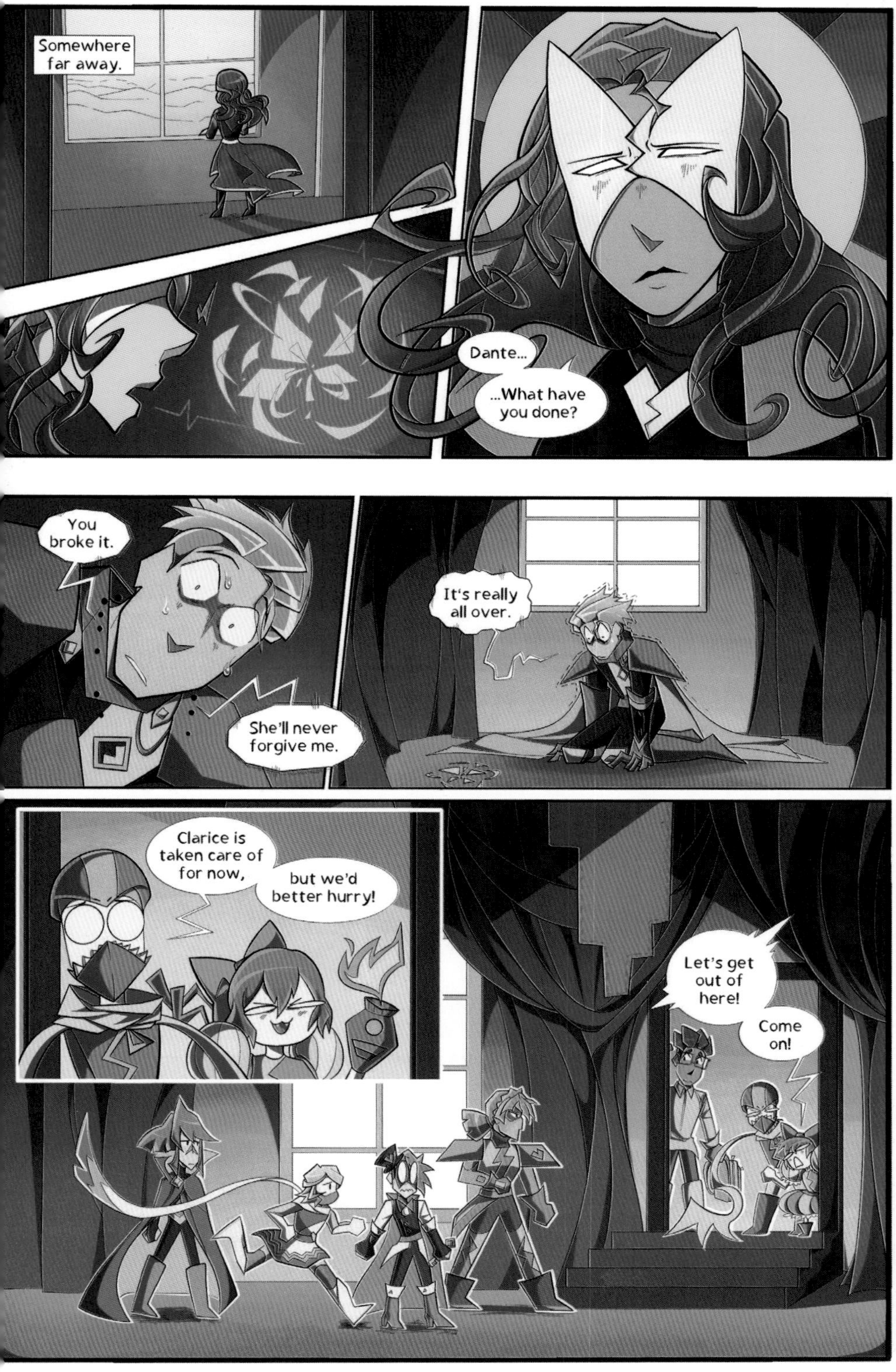
Somewhere far away.
Dante...
...What have you done?
You broke it.
She'll never forgive me.
It's really all over.
Clarice is taken care of for now,
but we'd better hurry!
Let's get out of here!
Come on!

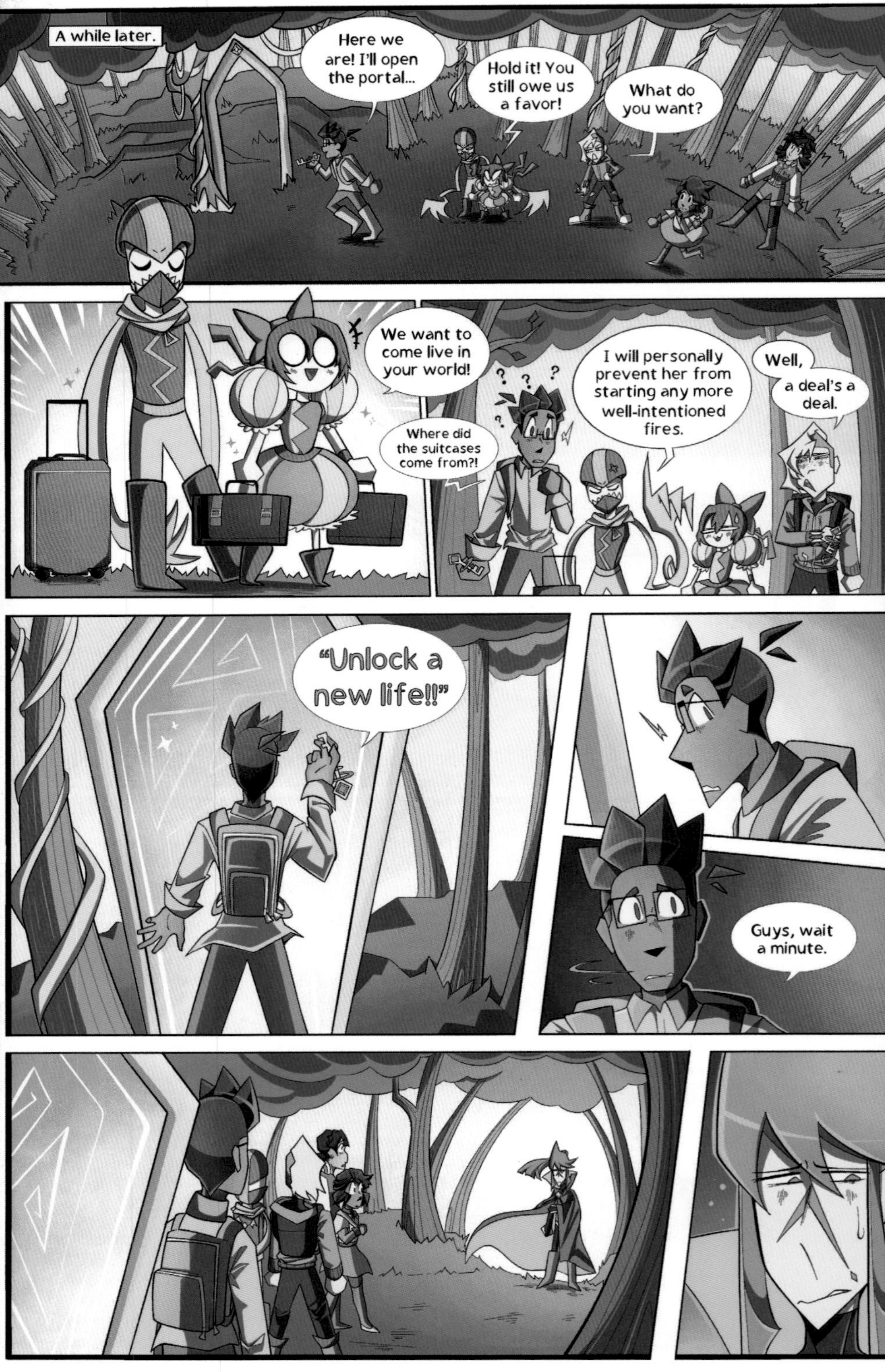
A while later.
Here we are! I'll open the portal...
Hold it! You still owe us a favor!
What do you want?
We want to come live in your world!
Where did the suitcases come from?!
I will personally prevent her from starting any more well-intentioned fires.
Well, a deal's a deal.
"Unlock a new life!!"
Guys, wait a minute.

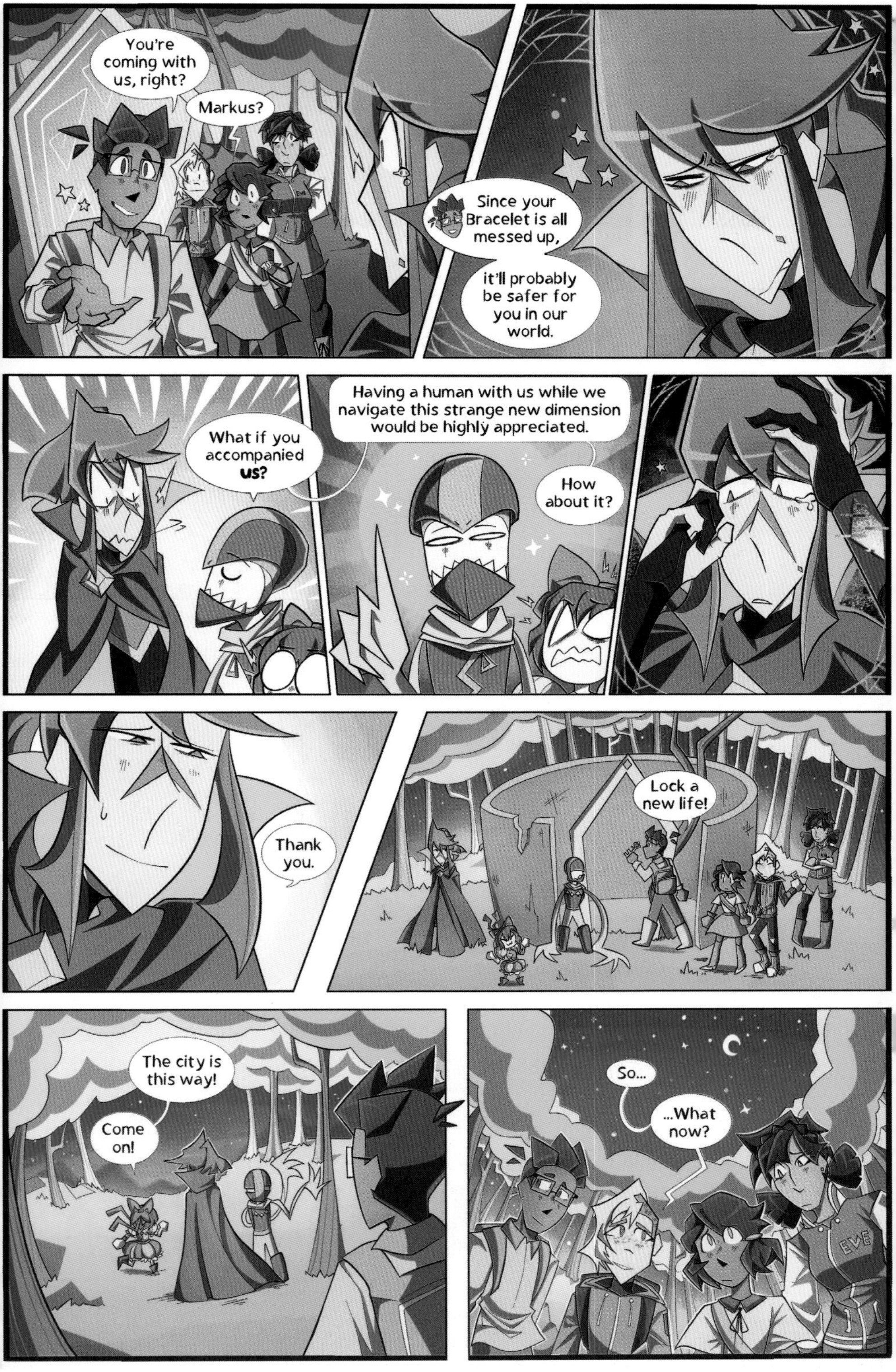
You're coming with us, right?
Markus?
Since your Bracelet is all messed up,
it'll probably be safer for you in our world.
What if you accompanied **us?**
Having a human with us while we navigate this strange new dimension would be highly appreciated.
How about it?
Thank you.
Lock a new life!
The city is this way!
Come on!
So...
...What now?

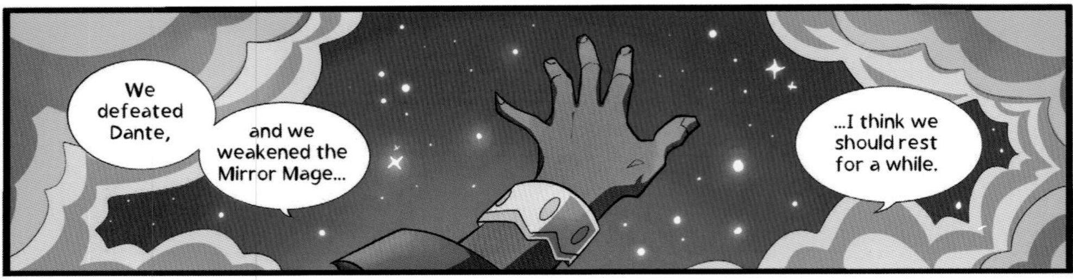
We defeated Dante,
and we weakened the Mirror Mage...
...I think we should rest for a while.

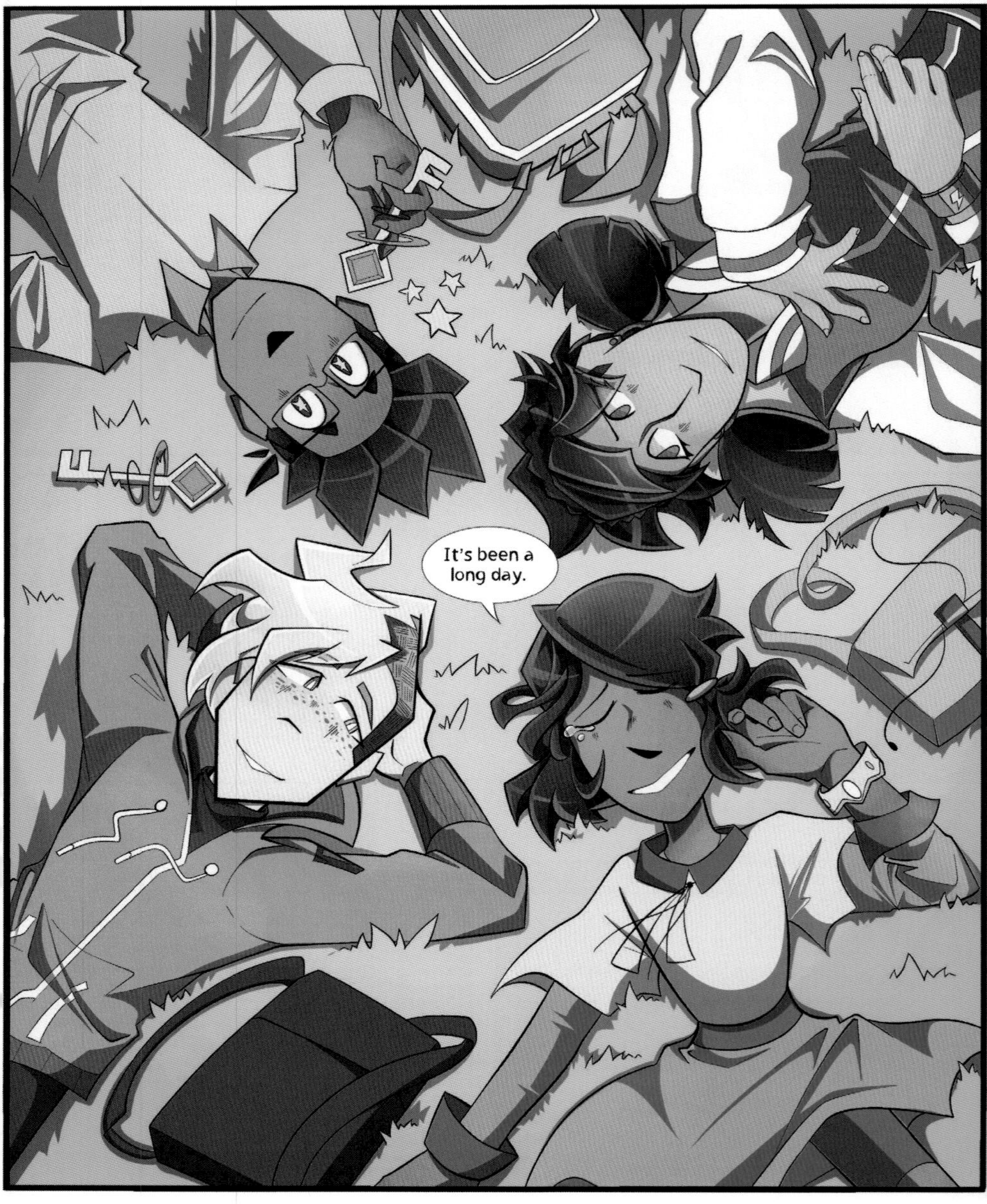
It's been a long day.

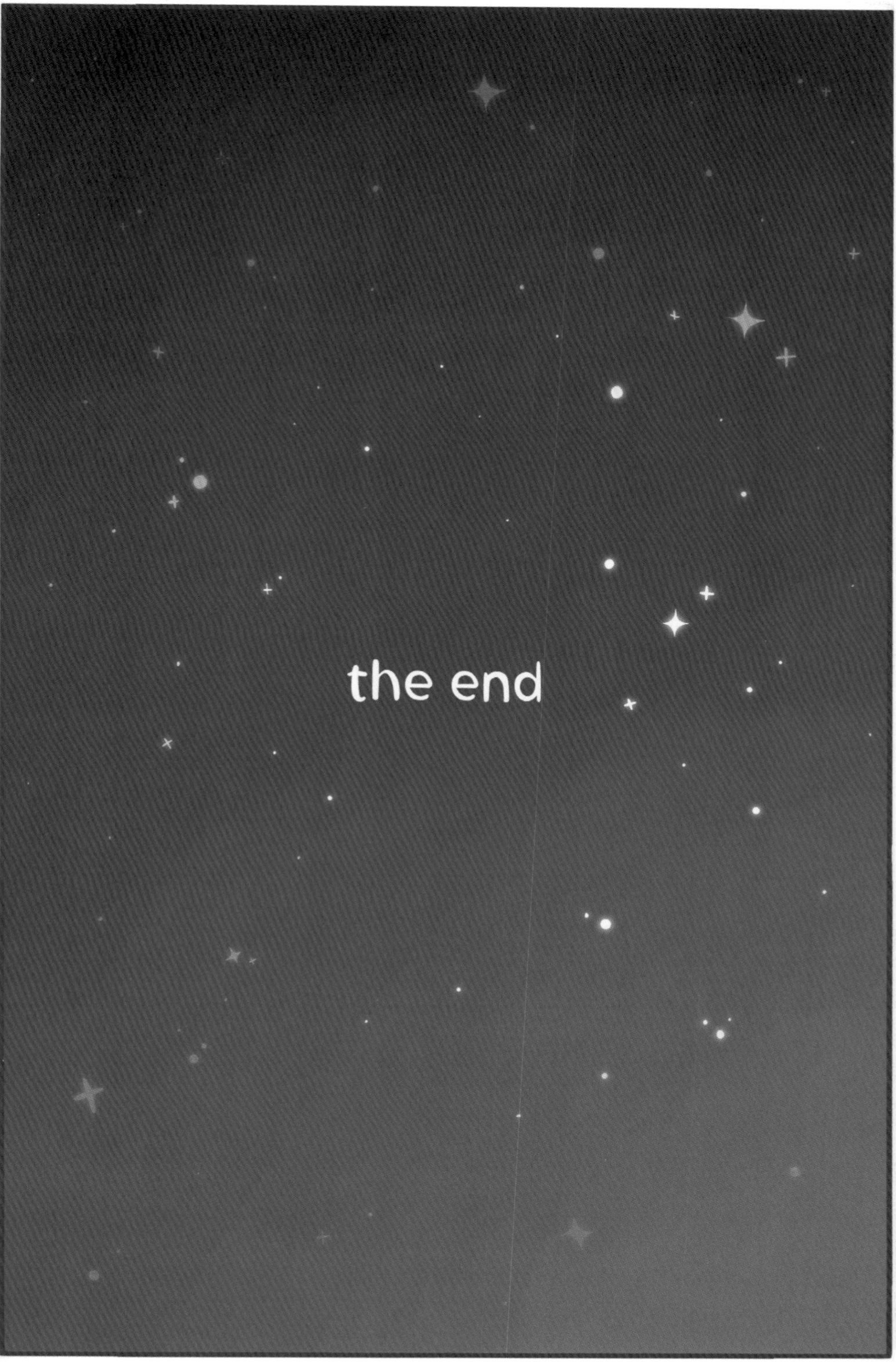
the end

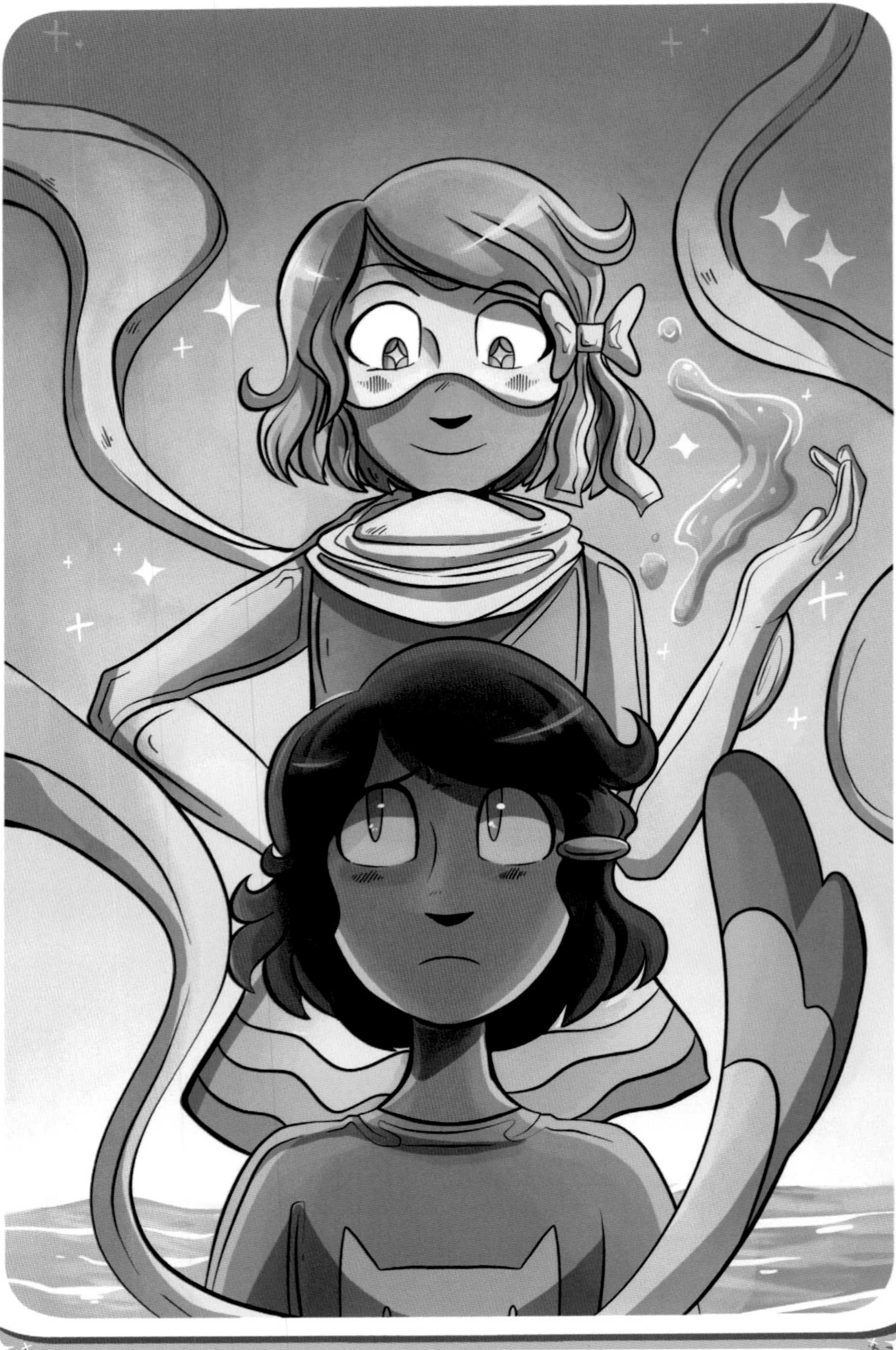

— Cover Gallery —

SOULSTREAM Ashcan Exclusive Cover
By Saida Woolf

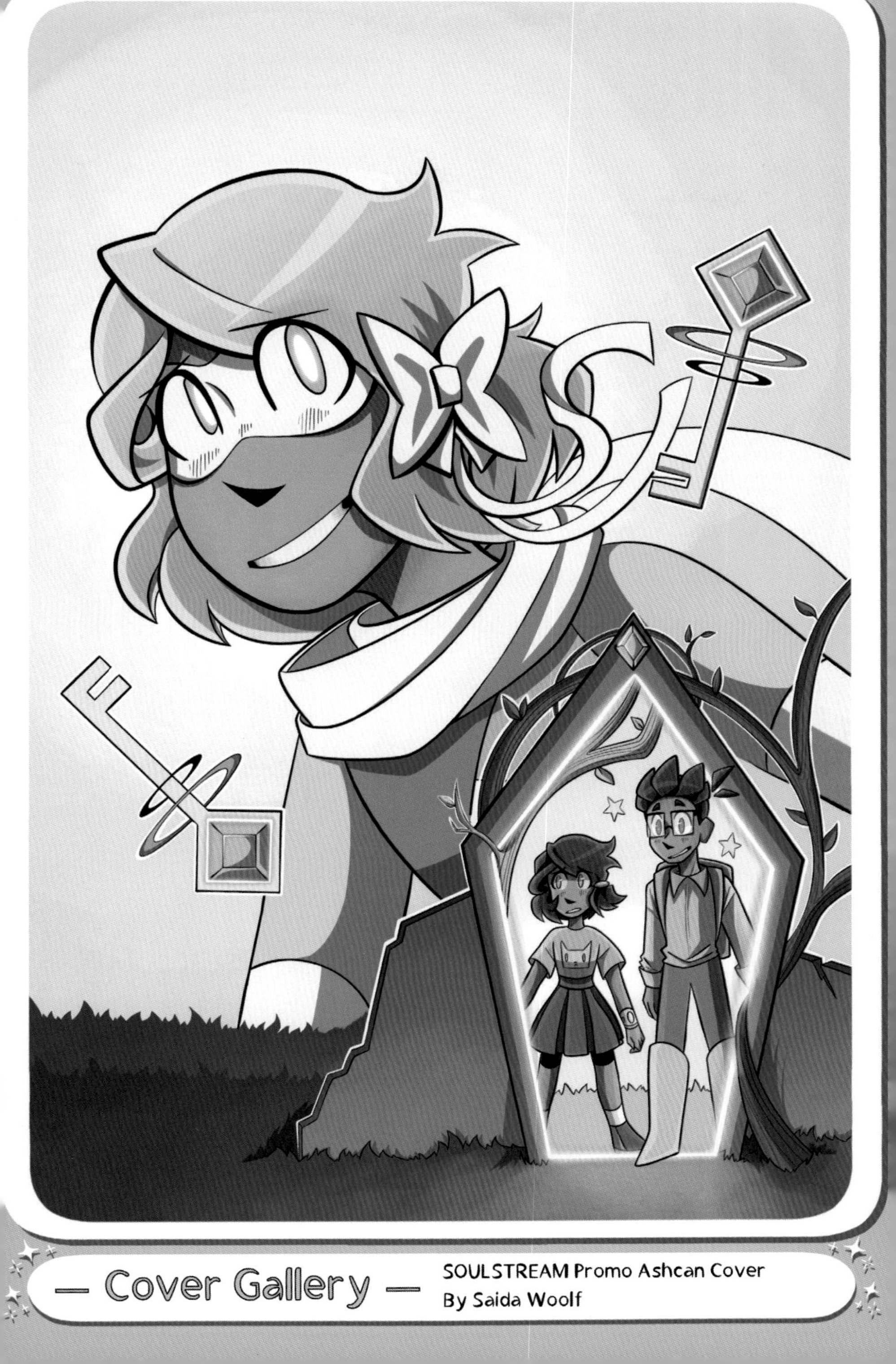

— Cover Gallery —

SOULSTREAM Promo Ashcan Cover
By Saida Woolf

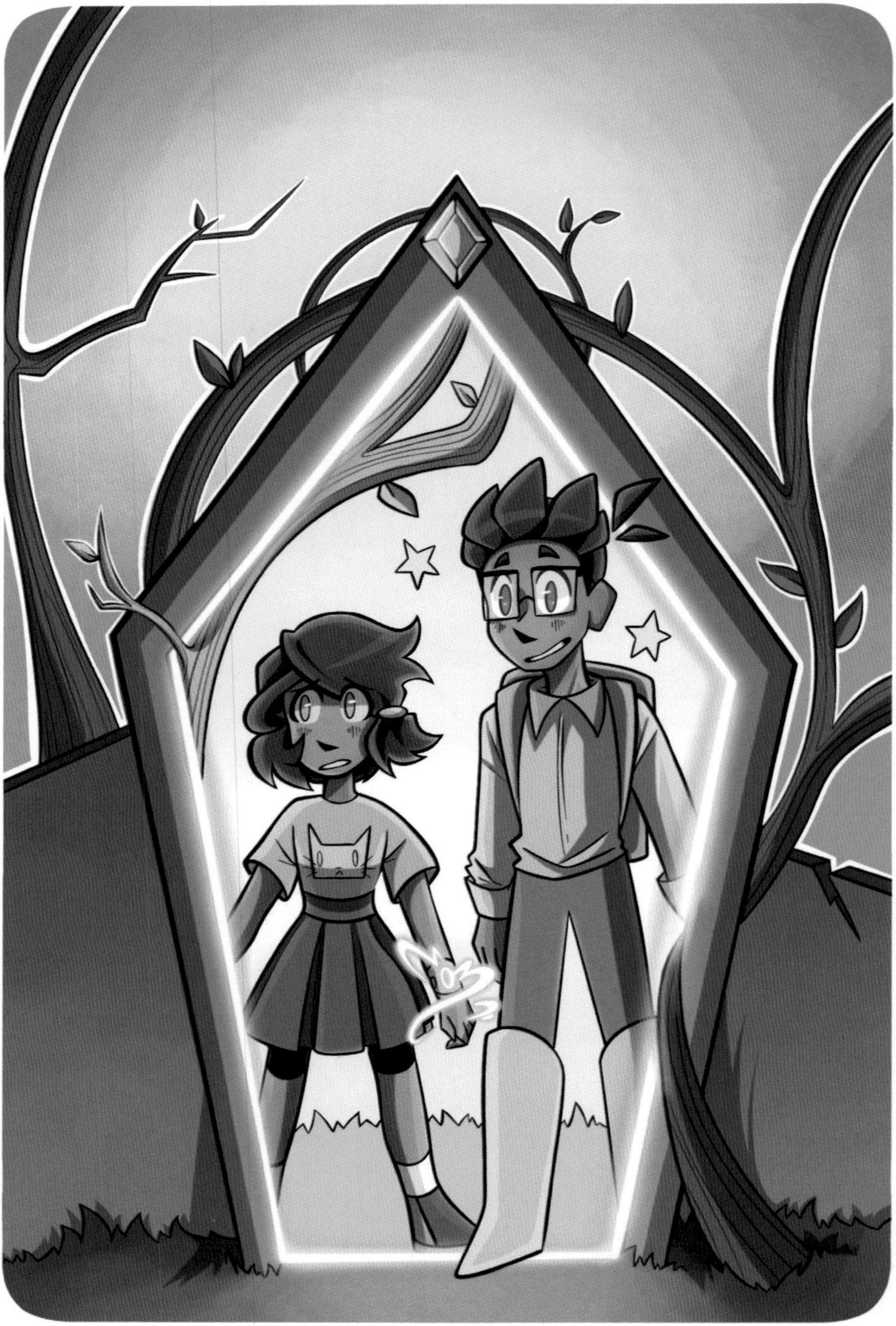

— Cover Gallery —

SOULSTREAM Issue #1 Cover
By Saida Woolf

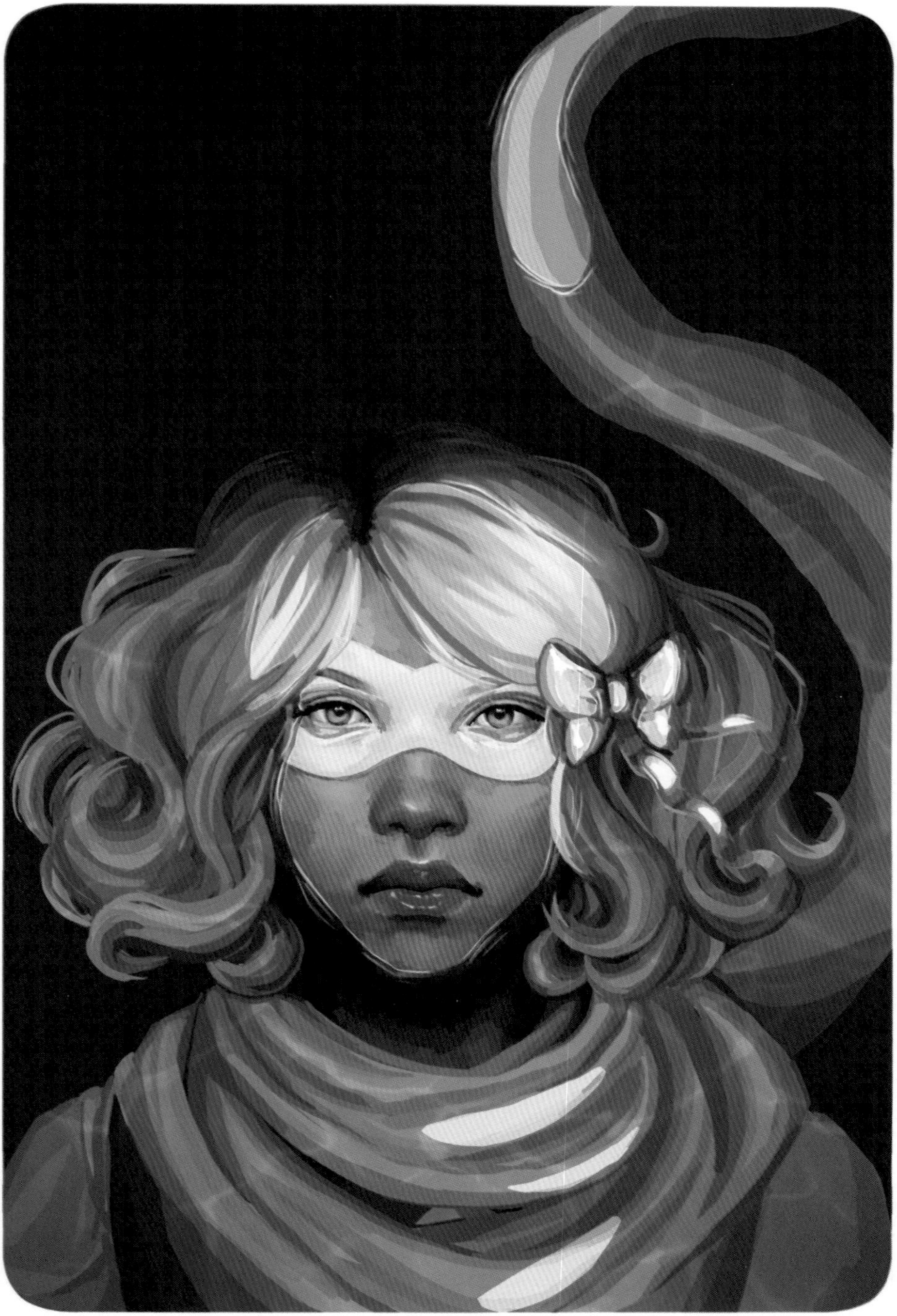

— Cover Gallery —

SOULSTREAM Issue #1 Variant Cover
By Cora Sweeney

Concept Art

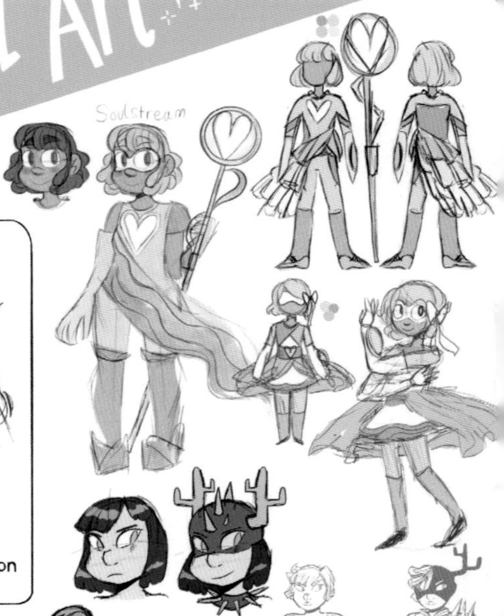
Soulstream

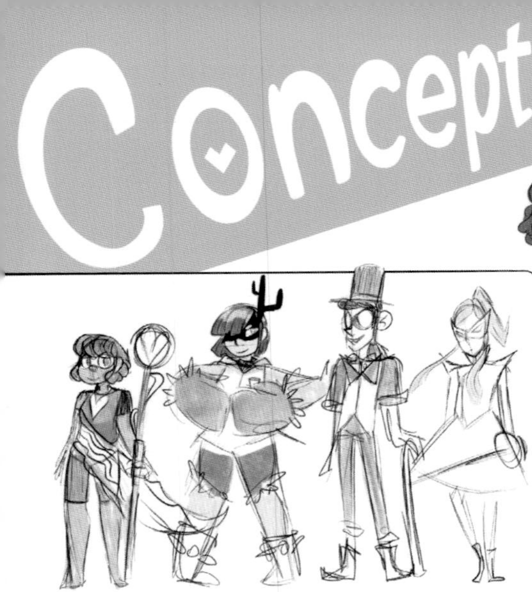

The very first piece of Soulstream concept art. Drawn on January 6th, 2019.

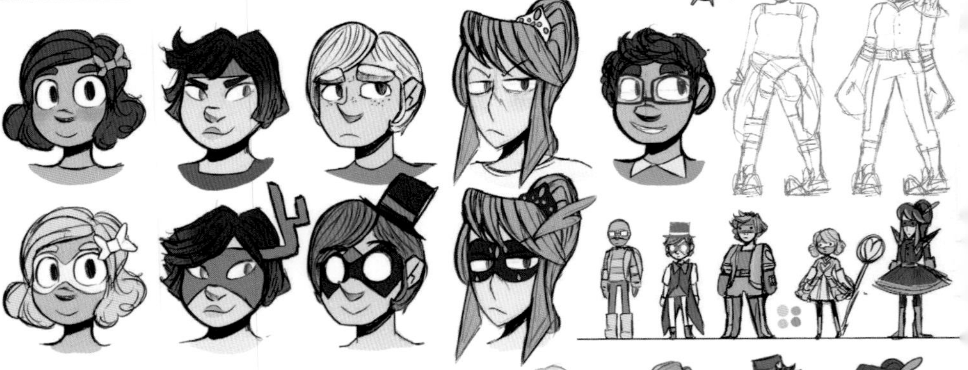

Many of the Soulstream characters went through drastic changes to become who they are today. In an early version of the story, Eve was from Mars and had cactus-themed powers, Rebecca was from the past, and Marie and Oliver were the only characters who had Bracelets.

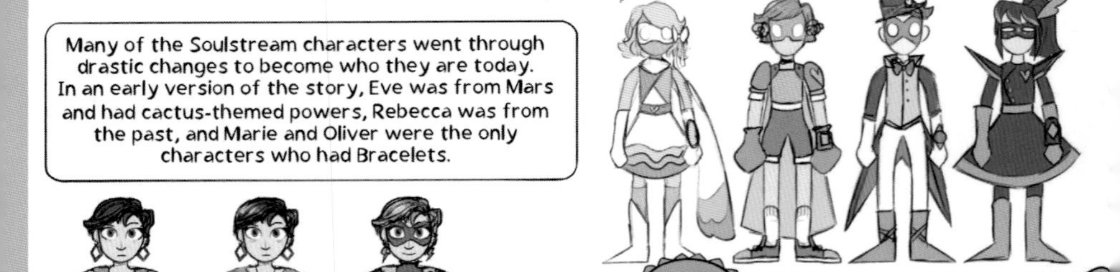

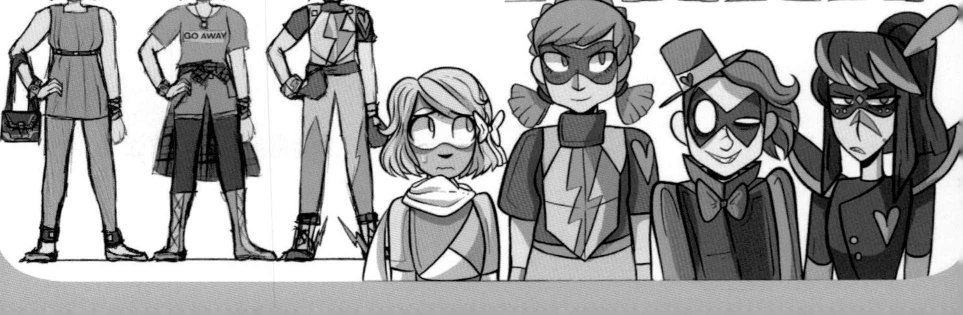
GO AWAY

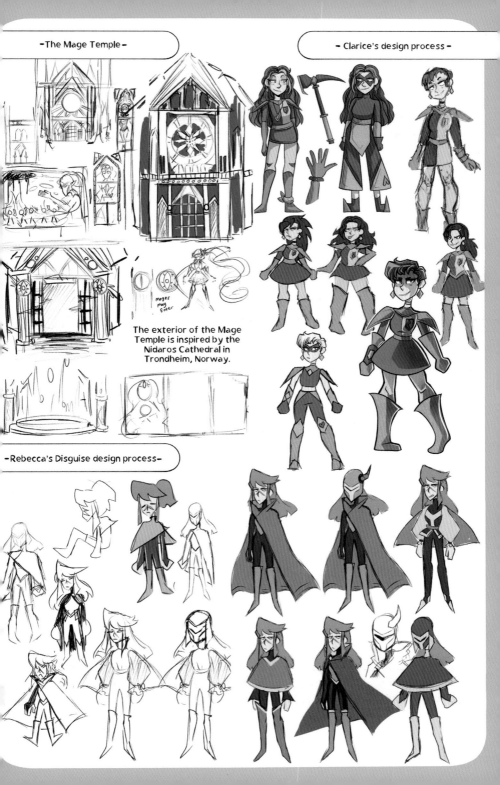

-The Mage Temple-

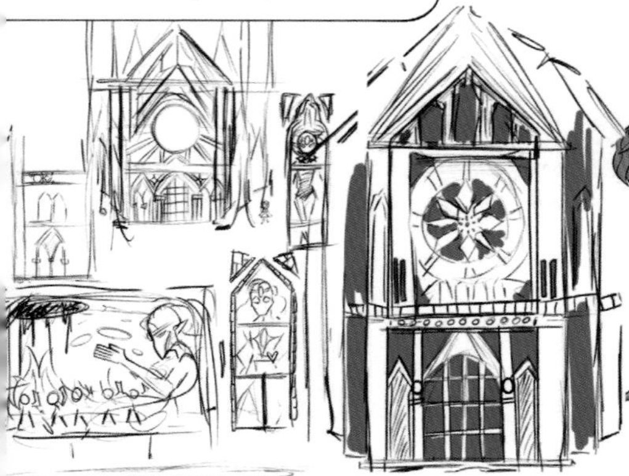

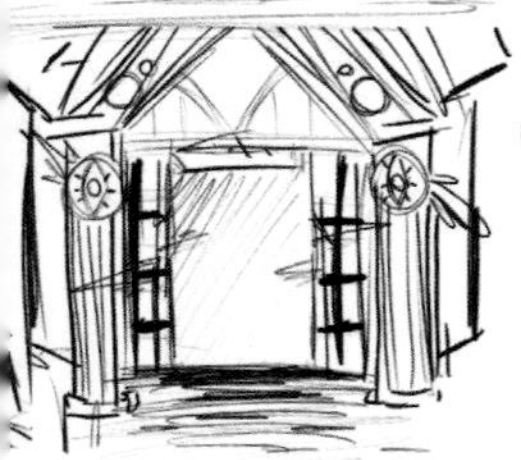

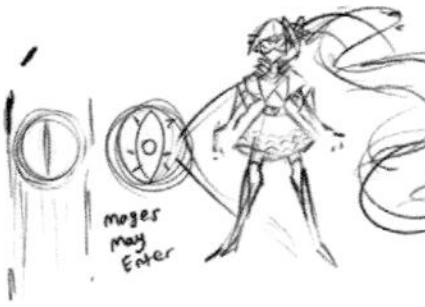
mages may Enter

The exterior of the Mage Temple is inspired by the Nidaros Cathedral in Trondheim, Norway.

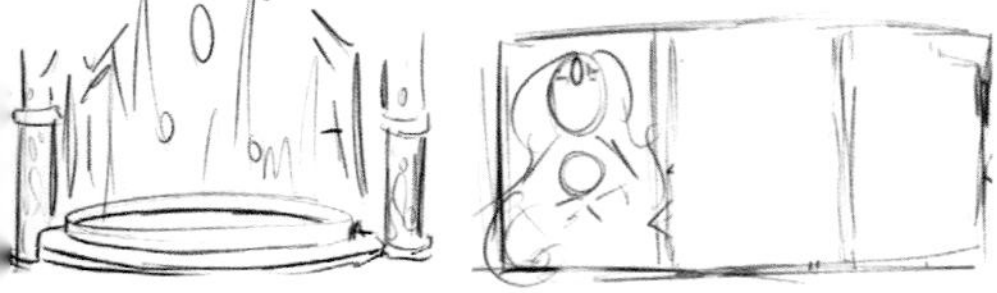

- Clarice's design process -

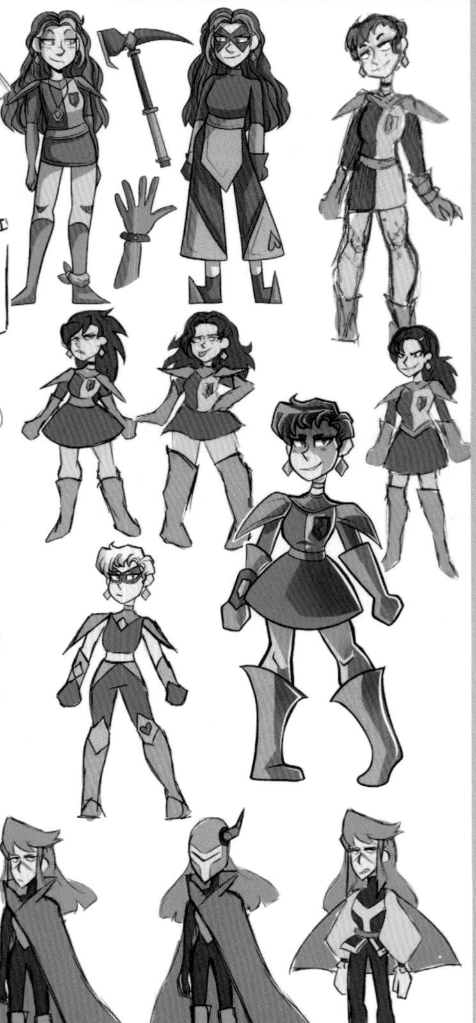

-Rebecca's Disguise design process-

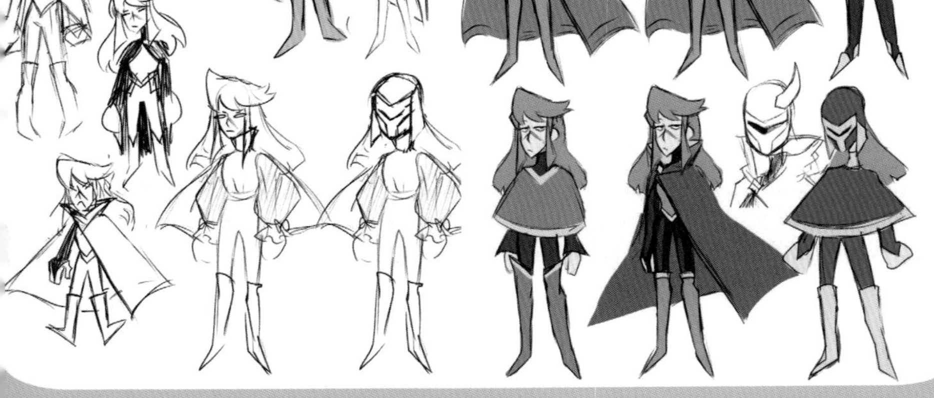

Soulstream Art Gallery

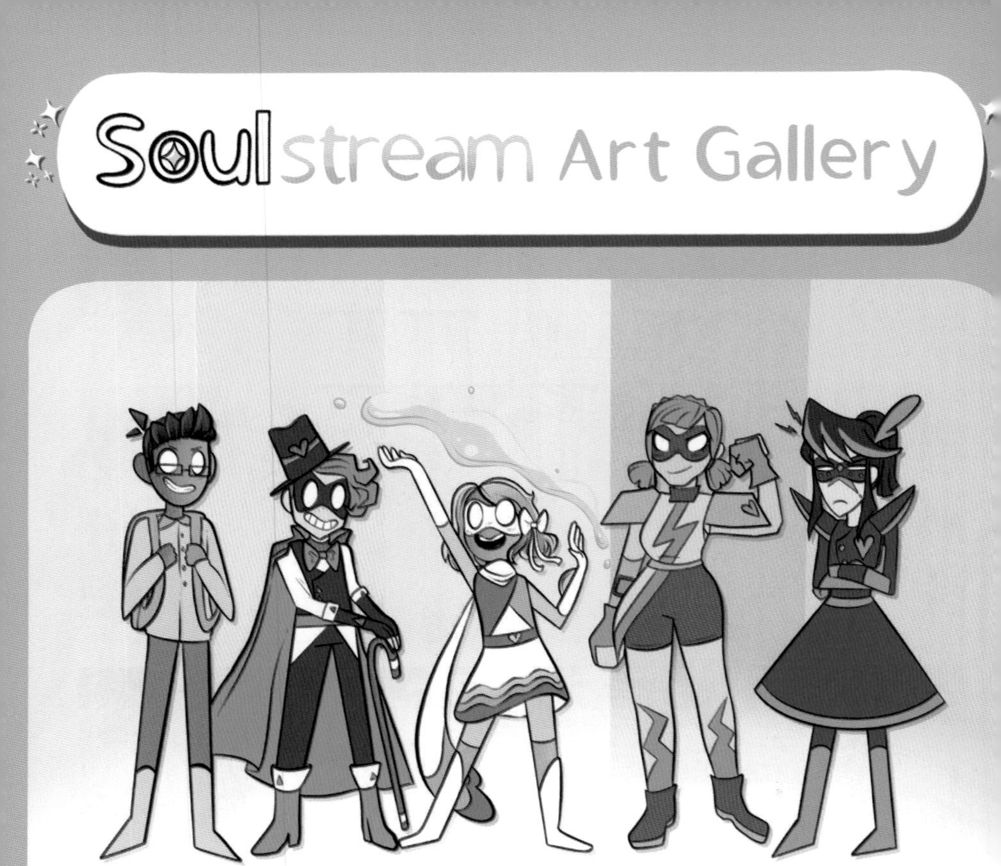

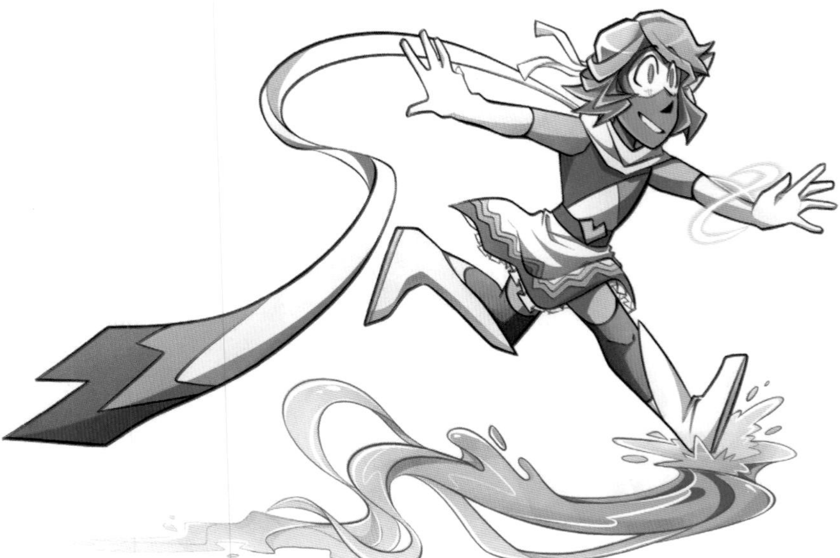

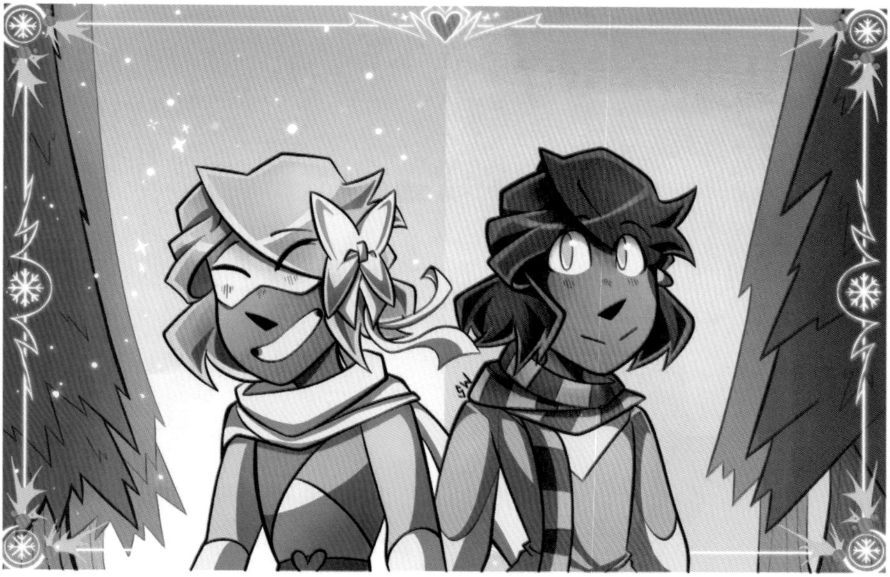

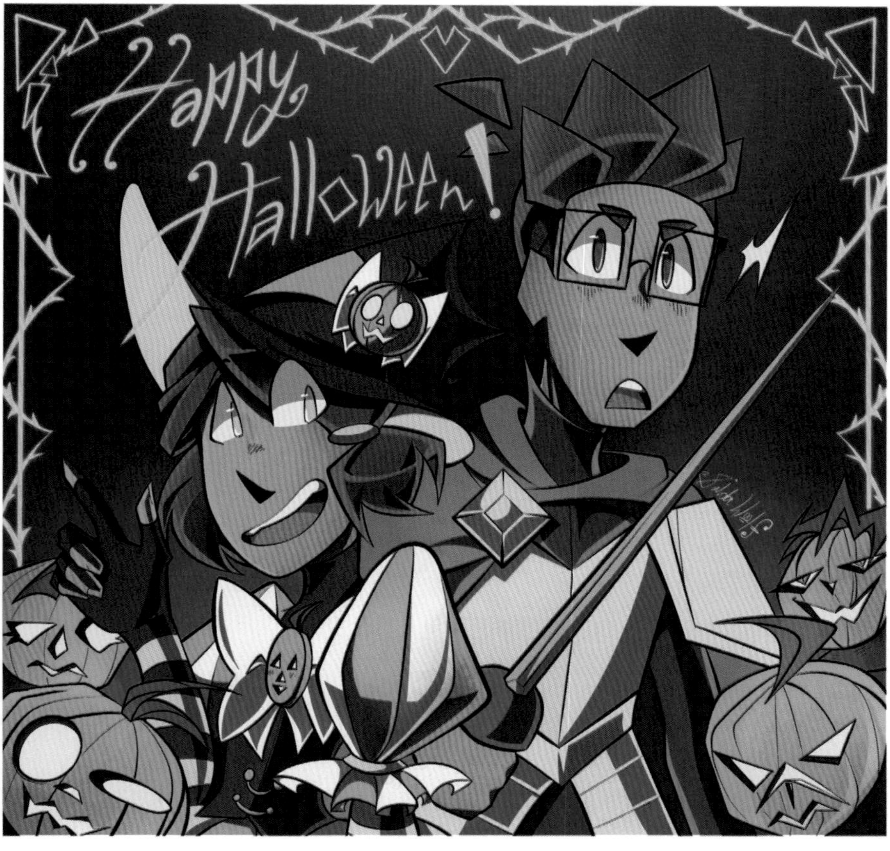
Happy Halloween!

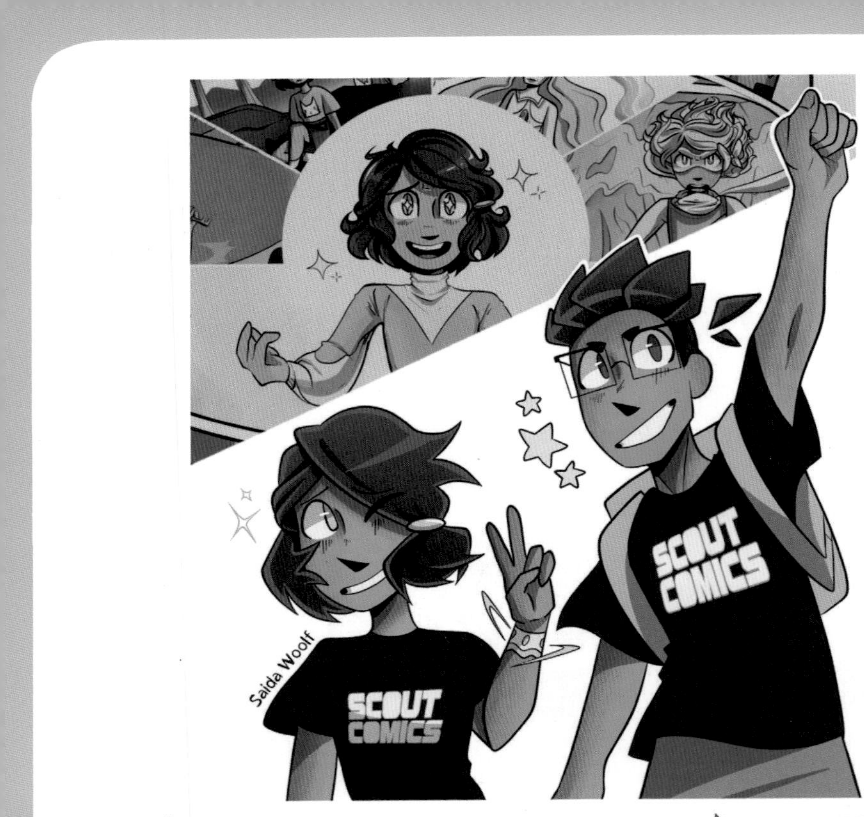
SCOUT COMICS
SCOUT COMICS
Saida Woolf

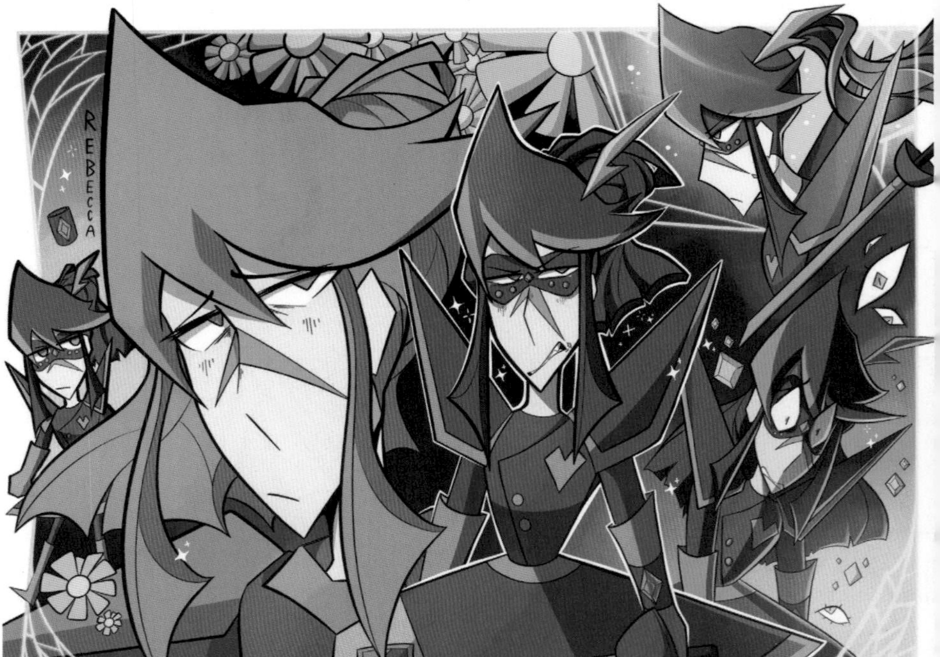
REBECCA

Marie Rosales

Age 14 • Grade 9 • Ocean Bracelet

ATTACK ☆★★★★
DEFENSE ☆☆☆☆★
Magic ☆☆☆☆★

Likes:
RPG games
Writing stories
Reading
Cats

Power: Can control and manipulate nearby water. Unfortunately, she can't create water.

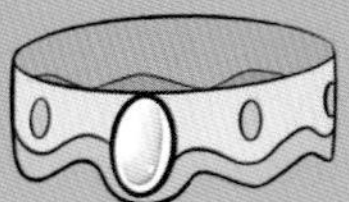

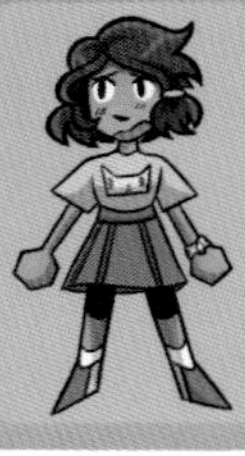

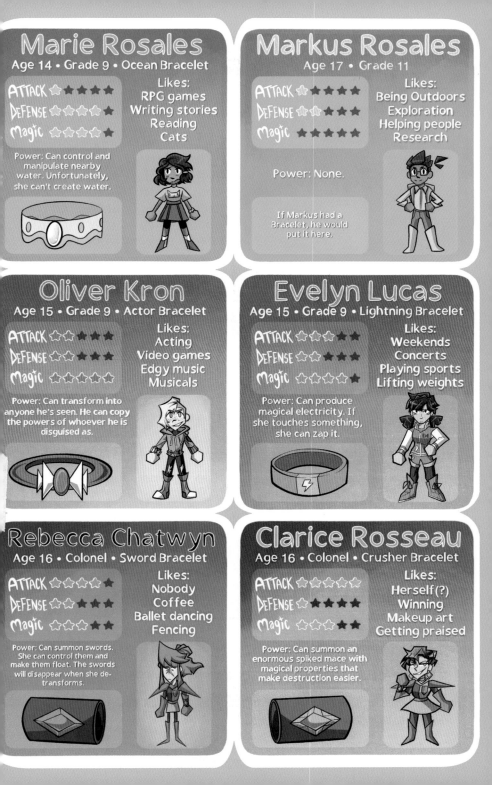

Markus Rosales

Age 17 • Grade 11

ATTACK ☆★★★★
DEFENSE ☆☆★★★
Magic ★★★★★

Likes:
Being Outdoors
Exploration
Helping people
Research

Power: None.

If Markus had a Bracelet, he would put it here.

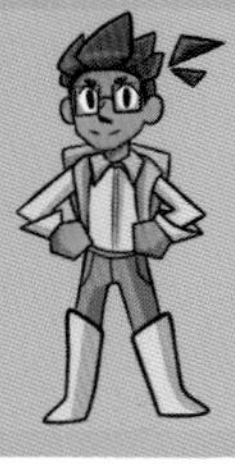

Oliver Kron

Age 15 • Grade 9 • Actor Bracelet

ATTACK ☆☆★★★
DEFENSE ☆☆★★★
Magic ☆☆☆☆☆

Likes:
Acting
Video games
Edgy music
Musicals

Power: Can transform into anyone he's seen. He can copy the powers of whoever he is disguised as.

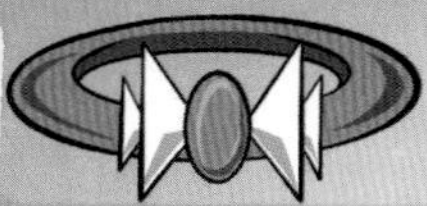

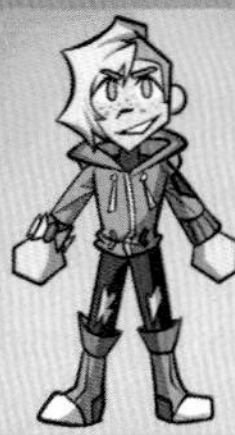

Evelyn Lucas

Age 15 • Grade 9 • Lightning Bracelet

ATTACK ☆☆☆★★
DEFENSE ☆☆★★★
Magic ☆☆☆☆★

Likes:
Weekends
Concerts
Playing sports
Lifting weights

Power: Can produce magical electricity. If she touches something, she can zap it.

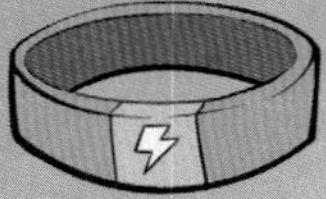

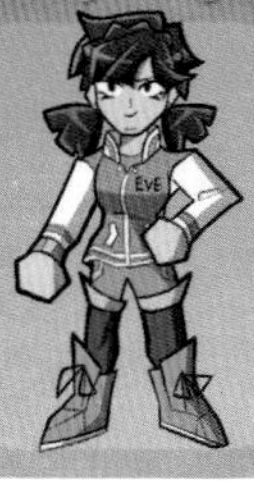
EVE

Rebecca Chatwyn

Age 16 • Colonel • Sword Bracelet

ATTACK ☆☆☆☆★
DEFENSE ☆☆★★★
Magic ☆☆☆★★

Likes:
Nobody
Coffee
Ballet dancing
Fencing

Power: Can summon swords. She can control them and make them float. The swords will disappear when she de-transforms.

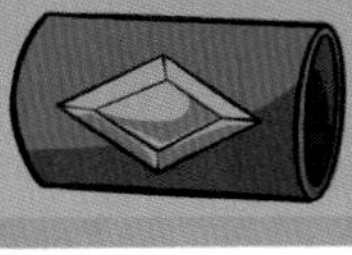

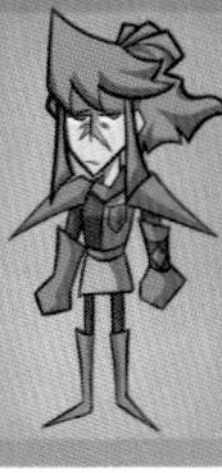

Clarice Rosseau

Age 16 • Colonel • Crusher Bracelet

ATTACK ☆☆☆☆☆
DEFENSE ☆★★★★
Magic ☆☆☆★★

Likes:
Herself(?)
Winning
Makeup art
Getting praised

Power: Can summon an enormous spiked mace with magical properties that make destruction easier.

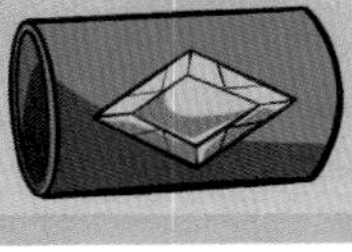

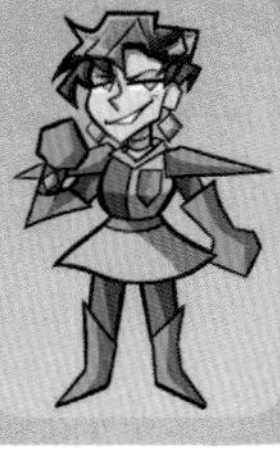

About the Author

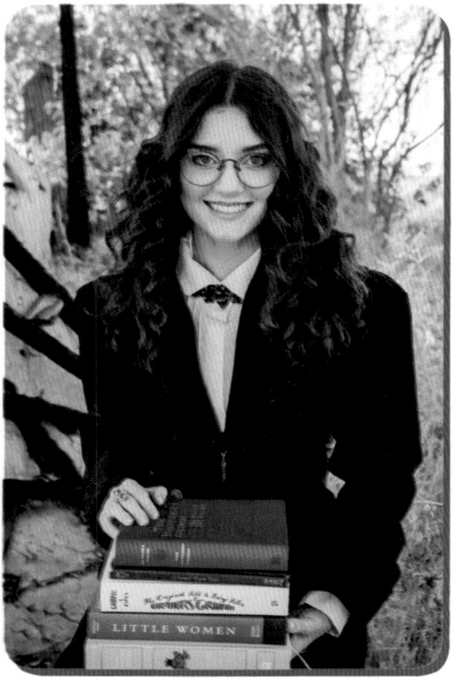
LITTLE WOMEN

Photo by Irina Piertz

Saida Woolf began working on Soulstream as a sophomore in high school. Two years later, she is still just as passionate about the characters of her story and is grateful for the opportunity to share it with readers everywhere as part of the Scout Comics team.

Homeschooled in the Sierra Nevadas, she not only developed a love of art and reading from an early age, but also excelled in science fairs and the performing arts. She spends all her time developing and promoting Soulstream—to the detriment of her social life.

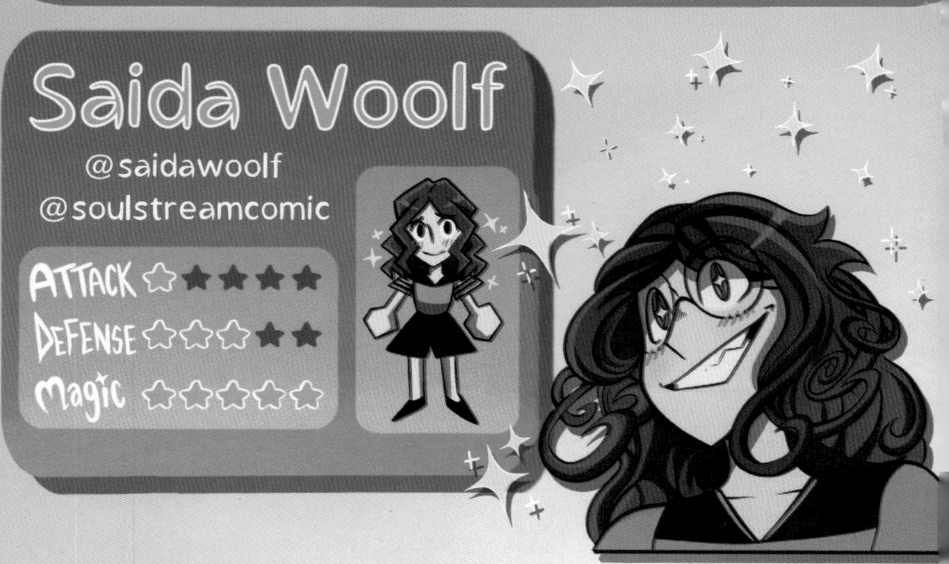
Saida Woolf
@saidawoolf
@soulstreamcomic
ATTACK
DEFENSE
Magic